'We live most intensely when we are falling, a truth that wrings the heart.'

J. M. COETZEE, The Master of Petersburg

'That scene, like the one before it, is perfectly believable and totally made up.'

LAURENT BINET, HHhH

For Ary

≡ Part One ≡

Croydon Aerodrome

23 APRIL 1937

'*Florence.*' The pilot turns in his seat and winks, as if the flight is a secret, or a first. Esmond repeats the word in his mind and releases a shiver. He is the only passenger – the biplane belongs to Grandi, the ambassador, and sits at a steep angle to the ground, forcing him into a tilt. Out of the window is the long body of Croydon Aerodrome and, in front of it, his family. Except for his sister Anna's white organdie they are uniformed in black, as though for a funeral.

The plane pulses towards the main runway. Esmond presses a hand, and then his face, to the throbbing glass, and sees his father raise his good arm. For a moment he thinks it's a wave, then his mother raises hers, a steely thrust up and forward, and he realises they are saluting and sinks back into his seat.

'I apologise for the position in which you find yourself.' The pilot leans over a tasselled shoulder, his smile Italian, his moustache so thin it might be inked on.

'That's all right,' Esmond says. 'I feel like I'm in an H. G. Wells.'

The pilot laughs. 'A ship to the stars.'

At the runway's mouth, the noise from the engines drops. The pilot raises the window beside him, checks the dials on the dashboard and straightens his cap. '*Andiamo*,' he says. Esmond looks between the tapering wings towards his father. Sir Lionel's face is ripe and red above the black tunic, chest barrelled. His empty sleeve is pinned alongside campaign ribbons, the '14–15 Star, the Victory Medal. He catches Esmond's eye and smiles with unconvinced detachment, like a man inspecting the menu in a failing French restaurant.

Lady Ursula is taller than her husband, her own black shirt worn with gabardine slacks. Her hair lifts in a spring gust as she stands there, saluting, hard-set in face powder. She glances down at Rudyard, his brother, crouched with a Jack Russell, and says something sharp, then back at the plane.

'Your sister is a little beautiful,' the pilot says.

Esmond laughs. 'Yes, just a little.'

'A handsome family.' A green light winks on the control tower. 'You are ready?'

The plane gives a breathy roar and bounds down the runway, throwing Esmond into his seat. He has to crane his neck to keep his eyes on Rudyard, who is up and waving, Anna pale beside him, arms lifted. His parents hold their salutes, as if posing for posthumous statues.

A schoolboyish whoop. He is no longer canted back but upright, weightless. He looks down at his family – four faces turned towards him – and feels knots of love and duty stretch and give. As the plane rises, he sees the white fragment of his sister between wisps of cloud and feels an ache at the thought of leaving her with her illness, with their parents. He turns towards the yellow smear above London, the vastness of the sky stretching away to the south, and again, a low whoop.

He fingers the collar of his black tunic – his father had insisted he travel in full British Union get-up – and undoes his seatbelt. It is warmer in the plane than he'd imagined. He taps out and lights a cigarette from a soft black packet bearing the Party's lightning fork. The engines seem quieter up here in the wide air, and he can hear the wind against the fuselage, the beat of first one propeller, then the other, until they level out and the sound becomes a continuous, soothing hum. 'You'll enjoy the Dragon Rapide,' Mosley had said. 'Flying and Fascism have a long history, and a long future together.' Sunlight slants into the cabin, thickened by

4

his smoke. A buffeting gust and the plane gives a lurch, and he feels the delicious precariousness beneath him, and realises he hasn't thought of Philip, or Cambridge, for an hour or more.

Anna had pressed something into his hand in the aerodrome. A folded sheet of paper, smudged with fingerprints. It sits on the seat beside him now with *The Wireless Operator's Handbook*. He picks up the paper and unfolds a portrait of himself in gouache, *Anna Lowndes* looped at the bottom. His blond hair is side-parted above wide, long-lashed eyes. His lips are turned down mournfully, cheeks flushed. It is a good likeness, he thinks, if a little tragic, and big-eared. She has drawn a man – given him something to grow into.

A bump and the plane banks to the left. 'Lympne,' the pilot shouts, nodding down to the airfield below. They circle the control tower once and a green light flashes greeting. A waggle of the wings and they are over a cricket ground, dunes, a gaudy litter of bathing huts, strung out in pink, yellow and turquoise along the promenade. The Channel turns in shelves from teal to the deepest blue, and he realises England has gone. He presses his fist to his mouth and stares ahead, over the pilot's shoulder, to Europe.

2

They come in over Boulogne, flat and watery below, then onwards above thick woodland, farmhouses moored in bright fields, steep-roofed chateaux. Esmond had hoped to see Paris, but they pass to the east, and soon the countryside is obscured by a blanket of cloud so dense the earth might have vanished completely. He remembers cricket at West Down and Winchester, deep in the outfield, looking up at the clouds and building great cities of endless light. Now, airborne – and what a beautiful word that is, he thinks – he can dream downwards, spreading his mind across the turning whiteness, smoking cigarette after cigarette, letting his eyes stray to Anna's picture, or his trunk and box of books, stacked beside the lavatory behind him.

He makes an effort to hold the past week in his mind. Cambridge, only seven days earlier, a rap at the door as he and Philip, flushed from bathing, jousted lazily in bed. Without sufficient pause for the repositioning of limbs or the snatching of clothes, Blacker, Master of Emmanuel College, appeared in herringbone, finger extended.

'Vile boys!' Blacker had enjoyed the part, quivering with authentic rage, though his eyes lingered over Esmond's thighs, glimpses of Philip's flesh and hair behind the sheets. 'Keller, pack your bags – it's back to Vienna for you. And you, Lowndes, your father has dealt with people like you before.' In the silence on the way to his digs, Esmond had looked around at the college buildings, the lawns, the oblivious students, and felt his world emptying beneath him.

There is a break in the cloud below, and peering down along rails of sunlight, he sees cathedral spires, the shimmering whip of a river – the Rhône? – and geometrical terraces of vineyards. Blacker, he recalls, had marched him to the station and they'd stood unspeaking on the platform as the train came steaming to a halt. An awkward handshake and Esmond was up into the carriage, and he'd felt as he did climbing the ladder to the aeroplane – stepping from one life into another.

He'd changed trains in London, city of Philip, of literary gatherings and ersatz South African sherry, parties at the Coleherne in Earl's Court where men played piano in just a bow-tie. His father was alone on the platform at Shrewsbury, his breath pluming fast in the night air, his hand scrunching a tweed cap. 'Esmond,' he'd said, and the word seemed to confirm all the bad he'd ever thought of him. He'd limped towards the Humber, Esmond following. In the car, he'd said, 'Sandhurst, then. You start in May.' The thought of himself as a soldier – laughable. He'd lolled back, looking out into the misty darkness, and winced that he'd had the chance to escape and blown it. He saw before him a deep dwindling, the long march of Party rallies and angry speeches, or, if he stayed in the army, colonial wars and booklessness and gin and death.

The Alps rear up from the plain like thunderclouds. It is four o'clock and, as they come into the huddle of the mountains, he sees night clustered in the ravines and crevasses below. They wheel like a cliff-bird over pines and crags, above icy cataracts falling into blackness. 'Monte Blanc,' the pilot says, confusingly, pointing at the great brooding fortress of ice and rock that lowers over them to the east, high as they are.

'The everlasting universe of things flows through the mind, and rolls its rapid waves,' Esmond whispers. He's brought his Shelley with him, one of the few books to survive his mother's libricidal purge. He glances back at the box, tied with string, and thinks ahead to dusty bookshops, libraries, reading the Inferno in the city of Dante's birth.

The engines change pitch and he looks up to see a ridge of rock, a great grey wave coming towards them. The plane lifts, and he feels a little stab of panic. A sublime way to die, he thinks, but still. They crest the ridge, clearing the jagged rocks by a few hundred feet, and the pilot turns, beaming. 'Italia.'

3

The mountains fall as they'd risen, and soon give onto rolling farmland, lakes like spilt mercury, red-roofed towns. 'Your new home,' the pilot shouts. Esmond sees the aeroplane's shadow, which really is like a dragon, harrying the path of a river. He lights a cigarette and presses his cheek against the glass.

'Could I have one?' the pilot calls back, not turning this time. 'Please?'

Esmond looks at the pack in his hand and thinks about throwing it, then pulls himself up, off-kilter until he's in the seat behind the cockpit. He leans over and places a cigarette between the pilot's lips.

'Why do you come to Italy? You are a politician, yes?'

'Not precisely,' Esmond says, lighting a fag for himself. 'My father's Lionel Lowndes, of the British Union.'

'With Mosley. I read the *English Mail*. For your language, you understand.'

'That's right.'

'So you're a Fascist, like your new hosts.'

'I suppose so. I'm setting up a wireless station for the British Union, a commercial enterprise.' The last direct from the mouth of Mosley, who'd kneaded Esmond's shoulder each time he'd said it.

'Bravo,' the pilot says.

'It's the first time for me. Away like this.'

'In Florence, you are lucky. A city of artists, politicians and Englishmen. You are all three, I think.'

'Perhaps.'

Esmond picks up *The Wireless Operator's Handbook* and begins to read about sine waves and resonators, capacitors and inductors. He is half-nodding in the warm cabin when the pilot's voice comes, as if through the doors of a dream. 'Storm over Florence,' he says, showing Esmond his frown. 'Hard landing.'

Esmond shrugs, having given himself up to fate. The dark

clouds paint the whole depth of the sky ahead. Forks of lightning jag downwards, burning themselves out on his eyes. They steer into the clouds and it is as if night has fallen. Rain thrashes the windows, obscuring even the wings, and the aeroplane bobs and yaws, plywood shuddering in the wind, engines muffled. The pilot sends them first one way, then another, trying to cut a path through the storm. Esmond puts his hands behind his head, leans back in his seat and, surprising himself even as it happens, he falls asleep.

He dreams of a Juliet balcony, looking over terracotta roofs towards a dome. His enemy is beside him, torturer's hands folded over the rail. Esmond takes a handful of the coarse black twill of his enemy's shirt, pulls him over the balcony and into the air. In a slow moment, he lets go of the shirt and sees his father and Mosley swinging him between them as a child, his father's good arm full of strength, Mosley's fingers dry and certain. *Here we go, bend a bow, shoot a pigeon and off we go!* They lift him squealing, stomachless into the sunshine. Again he feels he is rising, still rising, into the pale evening. Then he begins to fall, and he hears his enemy's screams, and sees the ground rushing up to meet them. He scents death, impossible in dreams, and opens his eyes, very wide.

'Difficult!' The pilot shouts, stubbing his cigarette on the inside of the window.

They are coming in fast over the runway, yawing horribly, and the screaming is the baying of the wind. A distant green light through the swirling rain, then they drop, bounce once on the ground, are airborne again and careening through the night. The wheels hit the tarmac once more, a blast of rubber, and Esmond's box of books launches into the air and bursts against the cabin roof. He is beaned by a copy of Hamsun's *Hunger*. The back wheel falls to earth with a clunk and Esmond lands hard in his seat, Kipling and Henry James in theirs. The plane comes to a skidding halt, the pilot's shoulders heaving. Esmond sits there for a while, breathing the fusty air of the cabin, the sharp tang of fuel.

'Florence?' he says.

The pilot nods. *'Firenze.'*

≡ Part Two ≡

Palazzo Arcimboldi

FLORENCE, APRIL 1937

1

Esmond wakes to the sound of a bell. He pokes one leg out of bed, then another, hops across tiles to find his dressing-gown and opens the shutters. Watery sunlight falls down on the via Tornabuoni below. There is a church opposite. Old ladies move nimbly up the steps and lean through heavy doors. Cars weave between pony traps, mules, bicycles on the cobbles. A black cat laces along the pavement, licks a patch of fur clean, rubs herself against the wall.

Esmond puts on his watch. It is almost eight. *Dear Philip,* he'd written on a sheet of letter paper before bed. He pulls out the chair, sits at his desk, writes *I miss you* and hears a light knock at the door.

Harold Goad, the Director of the British Institute, stands in the hallway in brisk tweed, the sound of crockery and the smell of coffee behind him. 'I thought you might need these.' He lifts an armful of books to his chest. 'Something to read when you're woken by the bells of San Gaetano. Ugliest church in Florence, I'm afraid.' They exchange their first smile. 'I'm an early riser,' Goad adds. 'I like to walk in the city while it's still quiet. But I've waited for breakfast.'

Esmond takes the books. There is a Baedeker, a thick Italian-to-English dictionary, a thicker *Decameron*, a Modern Library copy of *A Room With a View* and one of Goad's own, *The Making of the Corporate State*. 'That's awfully kind of you,' he says. 'I love Forster. And I'll look forward to reading this.' He holds up Goad's book. 'My father says you're the one true Fascist intellectual.'

'Decent of him.' Goad's cheeks flush a little. 'Splendid fellow, Sir Lionel. Now – hum – we eat breakfast in the kitchen. Nothing too grand, I'm afraid.'

'I'll be along shortly.'

At his desk, Esmond thinks how the Forster, particularly, would bother his parents. The day of his ignominious return from university he'd found gaps like missing teeth in his bookshelves. *Nightwood* was gone and *Ulysses* and all his Forster, and he'd looked down to see his mother feeding book after book into the flames of a bonfire in the field below. She liked her novels like her evenings – light and mannered and smelling faintly of horses; his were fishy and, like Cambridge, to be struck from record.

He dresses, reaching past the stiff twill of the uniform he'd slipped out of the night before, arriving at the Institute late, in the rain, and following Goad up the stairs to the apartment on the third floor. Now he steps out into the corridor, breathing the rich, gloomy air. He closes the door, straightens his tie, and makes for the kitchen.

2

Goad is sitting at a white formica table with a pile of newspapers in front of him: *La Nazione*, *The Times*, *The Italian Mail*. 'Have a seat, have a seat,' he says. '*Gesuina, vi presento Esmond Lowndes.* Esmond, this is Gesuina.'

A lean woman in her fifties turns to Esmond with a quick curtsey.

'*Molto piacere, Signor Lowndes.*'

'How d'you do.' Then, '*Lei ringrazio*,' as she places a coffee cup in front of him.

'And that's one thing you should know,' Goad raises his finger. 'Mussolini has banned the use of *lei* as the formal pronoun. Considers it unmanly. You must use *voi*, d'you see?'

Esmond nods and pours himself coffee.

'You can be arrested for using *lei*.'

Gesuina brings toast and jam. Goad reads, occasionally stopping to snip out an article, inspect it, and place it in an envelope. He tuts, stirring his coffee.

'It's a bad business in Spain, I'm afraid,' he says, folding *The Times*. 'The Falangists have taken an awful beating. Italians dead on both sides. Mussolini shouldn't have begun so soon after Abyssinia, not with the sanctions.'

Esmond shakes his head. 'I've been reading up on persistent oscillators and free radiators.'

'Of course, the wireless. We should have a chat. I could have arranged it myself, of course, but the technology terrifies me rather. Electricity is for the young. Why don't we meet in my study in – hum – half an hour? I need some time after breakfast to allow my digestion to activate. I'm afraid I'm not terribly well. I imagine your father might have told you.'

Goad stands, bows at Gesuina and leaves. After a few minutes of failing to make sense of the front page of *La Nazione*, Esmond gets up from the table and places his plate and coffee cup in the sink, where Gesuina tuts away his attempts to wash them. He walks past his room, past the door Goad had identified as his, and to large, grey-stone stairs.

The apartment is three sides of the top floor of the Institute, the fourth a columned loggia where sheets hang and clothes horses perch on stone benches, draped with shirts and assorted underwear. Esmond notices with interest three small, white brassieres. He makes his way down the steps to the library.

Armchairs are scattered between tables of journals and

ashtrays. Bookshelves line every wall save a large tarnished mirror over the fireplace. Dust and memory in the air. He crosses to the window and looks downwards. The ground floor of the palazzo is given over to offices, including the Florentine branch of Thomas Cook where, Goad had explained, the expats pick up letters, make telephone calls and arrange for goods to come or go home. Already there is a queue out of the door and into the courtyard. An old fellow with a military moustache glances up, raises his hat with one hand and gives Esmond the thumbs-up with the other. He smiles and returns it. Goad had warned him that new taxes for foreigners, anti-English sentiment in Florence and the weakening pound have meant a steady stream of departures. 'You have arrived', he'd said, 'just as everyone is leaving.'

3

Goad's desk seems to have been chosen for its vastness. His present task, gluing cuttings into a scrapbook by the light of a brass desk lamp, is taking place in a small province of it. He looks slighter than the bust of Shelley behind him.

'If I don't do it first thing, it never gets done,' he says. 'With you in a moment.'

Esmond sits in the armchair by the fireplace and examines the bookshelves. Poetry, mostly Italian: d'Annunzio, Foscolo, Ungaretti, Quasimodo. Essays on Shakespeare. An entire shelf of Norman Douglas. He'd read Philip's copy of *South Wind* on the grass by the Cam at Newnham. He spots T. E. Hulme's *Speculations* and thinks of his own attempt at a novel, the fifty-five pages he'd scratched out in his study at Emmanuel, smouldering with the rest on the lawn at home. Even with the embarrassment of his expulsion, those pages had felt like the future. Philip had called it *modern* and *thrilling*. Hulme had been his father's friend at university, his comrade in the war. Now he, and the book, were lost.

'Now then – hum.' Goad is opening drawers and clicking his tongue. 'Here we are.' He holds up a single sheet of writing-paper. 'A letter from *Il Duce* – his blessing to your project. He was much taken with the idea, suggests we name it Radio Firenze – what d'you think?'

Esmond smiles uncertainly.

'They've been doing everything they can to expunge the English language from the Italian consciousness, renaming the Bristol, the Old England Shop, Eden Park Villas, but Mussolini is shrewd enough to realise it's still the language of business. A Fascist wireless programme! Showing that even the English are coming round to his way of seeing the world is – hum – two birds, one brick. Jolly good idea of Sir Oswald's, I must say.'

Esmond stands to take the letter. *BenitoMussolini* is written without spaces, the final 'i's staring above a sulking 'n'. The text – from what he can make out – is plain as a doctor's note, but he can imagine the power of that signature. He folds the letter and holds it.

'This is super,' he says.

'He's an interesting man. A brute, yes, but a poet, too. Everyone knows about his railways – although, in fact, those achievements have been overstated in the British newspapers. It's more that – hum – he has recast the Italian narrative. He has taken the history of the nation, which, remember, is barely seventy-five years old, and made it a myth, the myth of the *Patria*. Ancient Rome, the Renaissance, the Risorgimento—'

Esmond notices that Goad's hands, when they meet the light, are lurid red with a white scurf of skin flaking at the knuckles, which he pauses to scratch.

'Nervous eczema, I'm afraid. Too much work. I keep trying to resign, but they simply won't let me. I feel as if I'm single-handedly putting right the – hum – psychological atmosphere between the British and the Italians. Lord Lloyd has granted a very generous sum to expand the Institute's operations across Italy, but I'm afraid it's unlikely my health will be up to it.'

'I'm sorry to hear that, sir.'

'Can't be helped. I only hope I last long enough to see an end to this silly bitterness.' Goad's eyes smile behind his spectacles. 'Of course, you'll want to get out and explore these many-memoried streets and galleries and churches, as my friend described Florence.'

'You knew Henry James?'

'Oh yes. And Lawrence, of course. Huxley stayed in your room, you know.'

Esmond looks around for the right words. 'And I see you're an admirer of Norman Douglas.'

Goad's face clouds a little.

'Hum. Douglas. I'm sure you'll come across him while you're here. Gerald – my son – enjoys his work. I am not convinced. His novels feel to me like essays padded with sub-Wildean quips and louche philosophy. I buy his books in hope that – hum – bankruptcy doesn't join the many other scandals his lifestyle calls down upon him. He sells them himself, quite shamelessly, you know. Every musical recital or lecture at the Institute, he'll be here, cadging his latest like a tinker. Frightfully expensive and badly printed, but what can one do?'

'I'd love to meet him.'

'That could be arranged.' Goad taps his fingers on the desk. 'Now, what else? You're to see the Podestà, the mayor, at his office at nine-fifteen tomorrow morning. He'll introduce you to the wireless expert, Mario Carità. He's a rogue, but he knows his transmission coil from his— well. Runs an electrical shop just behind Piazza Vittorio Emanuele. Strictly between us, I think the Podestà is hoping that this project will limit some of Carità's – hum – enthusiasms. He's in charge of the MVSN, the voluntary police force, and has been rather too rigorous in addressing anti-Fascist feeling.'

'I see.'

'Your father has established an account for you at the Monte dei Paschi bank. Ten thousand lire to get Radio Firenze started and an allowance of fifty a week. Should be more than enough.' He takes an envelope from a drawer and passes it across the desk. 'Here's a couple of weeks in advance and a chequebook to draw against the bank. Now—' Goad rubs his hands again, making a small haze of skin in the light of the lamp. 'There's the matter of the broadcasts themselves. Sir Oswald has kindly sent out a selection of his speeches recorded onto disc. I think initially it would suffice for me to give a brief introduction to each in Italian, and perhaps a short commentary at the end. And once the station is up and running, when there's an audience, we can see about advertisers, sponsorship, making the thing pay for itself.'

'Fine. Thank you.'

'Not at all. I'm thoroughly excited. Haven't felt this bucked since my fourth edition. And of course when your own Italian is *abbastanza fluido* – it's a very easy language, you know – you'll be able to take over the broadcasts yourself. You should start thinking about which subjects you'd like to discuss.'

'Shall I be having lessons?'

'Let's see how you get on with Carità. There's nothing like learning a language from a native, so to speak. I've never had a lesson in my life, French, German or Italian. If Carità is worth his salt, he'll teach you as you go.'

Esmond half-stands but Goad speaks again, staring down at his hands.

'Since my wife died, I haven't ventured out all that much. When Gerald's here he has his own friends, his own – hum – bustle.'

'Does he get out here often?'

'Not half as much as I'd like, I'm afraid. He's studying for the Bar and rather floats around London. His mother's death touched him very sorely. On the right track now, I think. Imagine he'll be back at some point over the summer, but his movements are – hum – irregular.'

Goad crosses his study and opens the door.

'I'm afraid I haven't arranged an office, a studio. I've been so terribly busy with the start of term. Anyway, there's no rush. Make the most of this time, get to know the place. Use your Baedeker discreetly. What else? Steer clear of the Blackshirt *squadristi* and for goodness' sake salute back if they salute you – arm straight up, Roman style, not like the British Union. And enjoy yourself. It's delightful to have another young person in the building.'

4

Esmond sits on the window-ledge in his room, smoking. He has three cartons of British Union cigarettes in his trunk and feels a sudden surge of fondness for the Party, turning over a black packet and running his thumb over the lightning bolt and golden hoop. Three Blackshirts strut past on the street below, their heels ringing on the cobbles, their yellow fezzes at loose tilts. He watches the crowd outside Caffè Casoni part for them. Grinding out his fag in the ashtray at his bedside, he picks up his panama, forces a pocketbook of wide Italian banknotes into his jacket, steps into the corridor and runs for the stone stairway.

The courtyard is empty now. It is almost eleven when he walks through the entrance-hall of the palazzo, past a large portrait of the late King George and onto the street. The traffic has died down, the rainwater drained from the road. A tramp with a pheasant feather in his cap sits on the steps of San Gaetano, scattering crumbs for the pigeons. Moustachioed men walk arm-in-arm with girls in lace chiffon. Older couples step down from taxis outside Doney's café, its name in gold on frosted windows. Roberts' British Pharmacy, apparently not yet drawing Anglophobic ire, advertises quinine pills and Fleischmann's Yeast. Next door, Pretini the hairdresser waves a white-gloved hand at Esmond through the window. He comes to the intersection where the via Tornabuoni meets the vias Strozzi and Spada.

At a table on the pavement, sipping a spumey cappuccino, is the man Esmond had seen queuing for Cook's. Esmond raises his hat and the old man lets out a whinny. 'Good morning,' he says.

'Is it so obvious I'm English?'

'Bloody right. It's the panama. An Italian fellow your age wouldn't be seen dead in one. It's the Fascist fez or a fedora here. And that's a Wykehamist's tie, if I'm not mistaken. Esmond, isn't it?'

'That's right.'

'Goad told us about you. You're coming to lunch on Sunday after church. I'm Colonel Keppel – George. Pleased to meet you. Off to the galleries?'

'I think so. I was going to wander—'

'Don't wander. Too much to see. The Uffizi closes for lunch at one. You should eat at the Nuova Toscana in the Piazza della

21

Signoria. Say I sent you. Then back to the Uffizi for a couple of hours and then the Bargello. See you Sunday.'

'Thanks!' Esmond is chased across the street by a bicycle. He passes in front of stone and stucco palazzos, their faces coloured cream or ochre, saffron, apricot, or white with terracotta crenellation. He strides through a piazza where restaurateurs set out their tables in spots of sun, then down the via Calimala. The Blackshirts he'd seen from his window pass him and he returns their straight-arm salute, conscious of his foreigner's hat. He resolves to buy a fedora at the first opportunity. He hears the Blackshirts' laughter echoing down the street behind him.

Esmond turns the corner into the Piazza della Signoria and his breath catches in his throat. Bare brick, parapets, the clock tower, Michelangelo's *David*. The palazzo looks like a castle; beside it sculptures cluster on the terrace of the loggia, guarded by stone lions. His eye falls immediately on Perseus holding the Gorgon's head, tendons and gore streaming from the neck.

A tram clatters past, swaying on its rails, heading down into the narrow streets beside the palace. Electronic speakers mounted on the corners of buildings squawk out military anthems. Esmond makes his way past David, whose comely half-turn and tight pubic hair remind him of Philip, and down towards the river and into the arcade of the Uffizi. *And he felt* – he remembers D. H. Lawrence – *that here he was in one of the world's living centres, in the Piazza della Signoria. The sense of having arrived – of having reached the perfect centre of the human world.* He grins foolishly.

5

He had read of Stendhal's collapse on leaving the church of Santa Croce, a fit of panic brought on by the presence of too much beauty, too much history. It is not exactly panic he feels now, coming out of the gallery, but an anguished and somnolent wonder. He cannot remember having lunch, whether he took Colonel Keppel's advice or not. He didn't make it to the Bargello. He walks past a group of Blackshirts who stand on a street corner, eyeing passers-by, the death's heads on their shirts polished to a shine, but he barely sees them. They call after him when he fails to return their salute but he carries on, oblivious.

He pauses for a moment in the centre of a piazza and closes his eyes. Filippo Lippi's *Madonna with Child and Two Angels*, his son Filippino's *Adoration of the Magi*. Then the Botticellis – *Primavera* and the *Birth of Venus*, of course, but also *Pallas and the Centaur*, the *Madonna of the Pomegranate*. He tries to summon every detail to mind. The purity and humanity of the Madonna. Venus's toes, he remembers, long and prehensile, the way her head cocks to one side, the tress of golden hair she presses to her groin.

He'd spent an hour in front of Filippino's *St Jerome*. It had seemed an antidote to the easy pleasure he drew from Botticelli. This was a painting his father could love: the saint's skin was grey-green, his eyes hollow. This, Esmond thought, was what came after. When one has lived with Venus and Flora for long enough, there is only the hillside, the penitence, the twisted branches and dank grottoes. He walks on as the sun dips behind buildings and a breeze sweeps up from the river and he imagines a lifetime of this, being breathed by Florence.

Back at the Institute, the courtyard is dark. A square of light from the window of Goad's study falls onto the flagstones, otherwise all is shadow. He climbs the steps to the apartment and opens the door. He looks for a light switch, can't find one, and edges carefully along until he comes to his door. He pushes and gasps. A young girl, long tanned back to the door, sits naked at a dressing table, combing her hair. There are books on the floor, drowsy jazz on the gramophone, dresses laid out on the bed. In the instant before he shuts the door, he sees the pale undersides of raised arms, the reflection of smiling, startled eyes.

He hurries along the corridor, realising he has confused the three sides of the apartment. He turns a corner to the kitchen, the smell of roast meat, the spitting of a pan and Gesuina's low humming. He finds his door in the half-light, walks in and fumbles for a cigarette. Gesuina has made up his bed, the windows are closed and the ashtray empty. He slips off his shoes, pulls off his tie, tries to force his mind back to the Uffizi, but sees only that long back and dark-freckled shoulders, a coral bangle fallen halfway down a bare arm.

He opens the windows to the street. The tramp with the pheasant feather cap is still sitting on the steps of the church, in the edges of a pool of light that falls from the streetlamp. A military truck, its bonnet painted with the fasces, roars down the road. Esmond watches the tramp's eyes following it. There is a knock at the door.

'Come in,' he says.

In a plain, yellow cotton dress, no shoes or stockings, she is as astonishing dressed as she was naked. Her black hair is pinned in a high pony-tail. She smiles but her eyes remain cool. 'I am Fiamma Ricci. The daughter of Gesuina.' The accent is heavy, her English hesitant but precise. 'I live here with Mr Goad while I study at Florence University.'

'Pleased to meet you. Listen, I'm awfully sorry—' Esmond gets up, lifts a pile of shirts from the chair at his desk and scrapes it towards her. She folds one foot beneath her as she sits.

'Please, don't worry. It is easy to be lost here.'

Esmond grinds out his cigarette in the ashtray and offers her the packet. She shakes her head.

'So how long do you stay with Mr Goad, Esmond?'

'I'm not sure. As long as it takes. I'm here to set up a radio station. For the British Union.'

She looks up at him with a sly smile. 'This is Fascist, right? You do not look like a Fascist. A Nazi, maybe, all that blond hair. But not a Fascist.'

He swallows and sits, straight-backed, on the edge of the bed.

'You are a Fascist like Mr Goad is a Fascist, perhaps?' she says. 'He is an intellectual gentleman. Not like the brutes we have here.'

'Oh, we have our share of brutes,' he says, thinking of William Joyce, Mosley's right-hand man, breaking windows in the Jewish East End. 'And you have noble Fascists, too. What about Ungaretti, d'Annunzio?'

'You like poetry? I am glad. Then you will be a friend for Mr Goad. He is lonely, I think, since his wife died. Too much work.'

There is silence between them. They hear footsteps pass in the corridor.

'Listen, mightn't you show me some of the city? It would be super to have a local guide.'

Her smile fades as she stands.

'I am not a local. We are from Milan, my mother and I.'

'Oh. Right then.'

She walks to the door and opens it, turning back to address him from the hallway. 'My father is in the gaol there. He is a Socialist, a political man. He wrote for *L'Ordine Nuovo*. He has been in exile, on an island. Now he is back in Milan, like a common prisoner. I haven't seen him since I was ten.'

'I'm sorry.'

'It is not your fault. If you have to be a Fascist, just make sure you are the right kind, not like that fat frog who calls himself our leader. Now I go out. Good night.'

She closes the door behind her. Esmond lights another cigarette and sits on the windowsill, looking down at the young people gathering outside Casoni and Doney's. A motorcycle engine revs and the bell of San Gaetano tolls eight. He sees Fiamma come out into the street. She is wearing a dark blue jacket over her dress, a pair of high-heeled sandals, her hair wrapped inside a crocheted yellow snood. As she walks south towards the Arno, he sees her, bright and bobbing in the pale streetlamps, in the light from the doorways of cafés. She turns the corner, glances back up the via Tornabuoni, and is gone.

6

Dinner is cold meat, a bowl of salad, some bread. A single glass sits at Esmond's place. When he enters the dining room he sees Goad struggling to pull a cork from a bottle of wine.

'Ah, I thought you might – huh –' He stifles a shout and frees the cork, sending a short crescent of dark wine into the air. 'Blast. I thought you might like some wine. This is Arcimboldi Chianti, made by the family from whom we rent the palazzo. Beautiful vineyards at their villa in Val di Pesa.'

'I'd love some, thanks.'

Goad half-fills the glass and then painstakingly reintroduces the cork.

'I can't stomach alcohol, myself. Brings on my black dog.'

He watches as Goad slices and chews carefully, eyes closing. Esmond finishes his wine in a couple of gulps and glances meaningfully at the bottle on the table. When Goad has eaten the last of his ham he pours himself some water and, finally seeing Esmond's empty glass, passes the wine.

'Do help yourself, dear boy. We don't stand on ceremony here.

I'm afraid these evening meals will seem rather drab to you. I don't like to ask Gesuina to work too late, particularly when it's only the two of us dining.'

Goad peels and cores an apple with his pocket-knife. Esmond sips wine and clears his throat. 'I met Fiamma earlier.'

'Ah, did you. And how did you find her?'

'Very charming. It's good of you to provide for her.'

'Hum – Did she tell you her story?'

'That her father is in prison.'

'It's rather more complicated. You see, Gesuina, her mother, is the half-sister of Niccolò Arcimboldi, from whom we rent this palazzo. She married a Milanese.'

'A journalist, she said.'

'Although he's not published a word, at least in any news-paper worth the name, for some time. In and out of gaol, exiled to Ustica and Lipari for sedition. He's a member of *Giustizia e Libertà,* the anti-Fascist movement. A thoroughly bad egg. He was arrested for helping Socialists escape from prison. Not a thought for his wife and daughter. After a year in squalor in Milan, Gesuina came home and threw herself on her brother's mercy.'

'And he asked you to take them in?'

'Niccolò Arcimboldi is one of the hardliners. Believes Musso-lini isn't going far enough, that Italy should round up the Jews, purge the factories, shoot the Communists. He's chums with Carità at the MVSN, marches around looking for Reds to set about. Gesuina marrying a Socialist riled him terribly. So when she and her daughter came back to Florence, Niccolò reluctantly agreed to put them up. Asked me if I could use her as a house-maid. And since the apartment isn't full, even when Gerald is here, and it reduces our overheads—'

'Doesn't she resent it, Gesuina?'

Goad scratches his hands.

'She is here as a guest, she knows that. Over the past few years we have grown – hum – comfortable. Since my wife died she runs the household. I believe it suits her very well. Fiamma is different. She was horribly impertinent at first. Rather trite, adolescent talk. Now she's a closed book. Not unruly any more so much as – hum – inaccessible.'

'It must be hard for her, not knowing how her father is. And she's studying?'

'Literature, or so she says. Dante and Boccaccio this year, but you wouldn't know it to speak to her. She's out at dances most of the time, home late, connecting with heaven knows whom.'

He looks more closely at Esmond, a slice of apple paused on the approach to thin lips.

'You might befriend her, Esmond. I feared you wouldn't encounter enough young people, cooped up here with – hum – the aged adviser. And she would surely benefit from the company of someone as sensible and purposeful as you. Yes, this really is very good.' He smiles and pops the apple into his mouth.

'I'll do my best.'

'Capital.' Goad rises. 'I must prepare my lessons. Our students return from their Easter vacation on Monday. You'll find the place quite different when they're around. Serious young fellows, most of them, but I do enjoy the peace of the holidays. Good night.'

Esmond waits for a few minutes and then, careful to ensure that no one sees him, makes his way up, the three-quarters full bottle of wine in one hand, glass in the other. He closes his door, fastens the shutters and windows and switches on his desk lamp. Pouring out a glass, he sits at the desk and picks up his pen.

Florence is beautiful, he writes, imagining Philip in a Viennese tearoom, white marble tables and clever laughter. *I'm staying at the British Institute. It's in the heart of the city, a fifteenth-century palace. Lots of dark passageways and tapestries. You imagine turning a corner and finding Michelangelo arguing with Ficino.* He takes a sip of his wine and lights a cigarette. *I can't tell you how glorious the Uffizi is.* He wonders where Fiamma is now. On the dancefloor of some half-lit nightclub, a pack of wolfish boys around her. *I worry about you. I always look out for Vienna in the newspaper. If you get a chance to leave, you should. Tanti auguri (as the locals say!), Esmond.*

He folds the letter into an envelope. Pouring another glass of wine and picking up his towel, he makes for the bathroom. Filling the bath so hot that a bank of steam hovers above it, he lowers himself into the water, cups his glass and reclines. He feels Philip's absence in the groan of his stomach. He remembers a day in May when they'd cycled to Grantchester, the sun on Philip's tanned shoulders, the sudden shower that sent them into the cover of bushes, the damp grasping for each other as the rain pounded around them and their lips became two wet, living things. He remembers sitting with Philip in F. R. Leavis's lectures, the older boy with his hand on Esmond's thigh, and then in the saloon bar of the Pickerel, where they drank with Leavis and talked until closing about Russian novels and the book-buttressed adventure their lives would be.

With Philip, something had loosened within him, his childhood lifting under the beam of the older boy's careful love. Until then he'd felt himself, before anything else, his father's son. At Cambridge he was pointed out as Sir Lionel Lowndes's boy, scion of the second family of the British Union. People were surprised he wasn't in black. On Philip's arm, he felt himself different, decent.

He lets the bath run out with a gurgle and goes back to his room. He puts on his nightshirt, reads for an hour and then sleeps. In his dream, Fiamma and Philip are together, dancing with the clever, cautious footsteps of the cat on the pavement outside San Gaetano.

7

At a quarter to nine, Esmond walks through the courtyard of the Institute, past the portrait of the dead King, out onto via Tornabuoni. A light drizzle, little more than mist, pearls on the manes and tails of the horses. Bicyclists pass with umbrellas held high and the window of Doney's is steamy with breakfast. An old woman steps from a cab into Pretini's hair salon, tutting. Esmond turns up the collar of his mackintosh and makes his way onto the via degli Strozzi.

By the time he gets to the Piazza della Signoria, the shower has passed and a tentative sun emerges. People come out of shop doorways, furl their umbrellas and wait for their trams. He wafts his letter from *Il Duce* and is ushered through a silent inner courtyard where gargoyles spew from the capitals of columns, then to a wooden bench in a gilded hall, where the guard asks him to wait.

Small, well-dressed men hurry back and forth, heads down. Occasionally a Blackshirt, skull and crossbones on his chest, marches past. Esmond draws *A Room With a View* from his pocket and begins to read. After a few minutes, a peroxidial secretary shows him into the mayor's office. The Podestà sits at a large desk between two windows, one of which is open to the morning. Over his right shoulder, against the brightening sky, stands a stocky figure with his back to the room, looking down to the banks of the Arno. The mayor gestures towards one of the armchairs facing him.

'Please, Mr Lowndes, have a seat.' He opens a silver cigarette case and holds it out.

Esmond takes one, tilts forward to accept a flame and sits. The Podestà lights his own cigarette and leans back.

'My name', he says, 'is Count Alfonso Gaetano.'

Esmond smiles shyly. 'Like the church,' he says.

The mayor raises an eyebrow. 'I had the pleasure of meeting Sir Oswald when he and his late wife came to visit some years ago. A most remarkable man. Now this project of a wireless broadcast to educate our citizens, to forge ties between the right-thinking men of your country and ours. Bravo! Mussolini himself has given his full support. If I, humbly, may be of any assistance at all, you must tell me.' He reaches across and presents a creamy card with his full title in loping cursive.

'Decent of you,' Esmond says. At this moment, a butterfly, a cabbage white, flutters blithely into the room, borne up on a breeze from the river. It pauses for a moment on the window-pane, opening and closing its wings. The stocky figure at the window shoots out a plump hand and crushes the insect against the glass with his thumb, leaving a green smear. The mayor turns at the sound.

'I must introduce you to our local communications expert, Mario Carità.' The man, unhealthy-looking in black shirt and grey flannel shorts, inspects his thumb for a moment and turns to face them. He looks, Esmond thinks, like a pickled schoolboy, save for a streak of white in quiffed hair and his eyes, hard and black and glassy.

'Carità will fix you up with your studio, with all the equipment you need. He's one of the coming men in this town. Doing business in Italy, you'll find, is all about whom you know, and Carità knows everybody.'

The little man steps forward. His palm is damp. 'I happy to

meet you—' He pauses, holding Esmond's hand, smiling blood-lessly. 'You and me, we make radio big success.'

The Podestà looks at his watch. 'I have a committee meet-ing. Please do feel free to stay here and get acquainted.' He gives a bow, collects some papers from the desk and leaves. After a pause, Carità pulls out the mayor's chair and sits down, reaching for the floor with the balls of his feet.

'We need make things straight,' he says. 'I no like English. We not need English here. For too long English treat Florence like a home. But' – he gives a reluctant grin – 'Podestà says you good Fascist. For me, nationality not so important, Fascism important.' He stands, walks over to Esmond and leans down to embrace him. He smells of wet vegetation.

'Hey,' Carità stands back waggling his finger. 'You tell Goad, he not pay enough for translation *and* radio work. I not a teacher. I a soldier first' – he points to the death's head on the breast of his shirt – 'second electrician.'

'Fine,' says Esmond. 'When do you think we can start?'

Carità lifts himself to sit on the desk, picks up the Podestà's fountain pen and begins to play with it, tutting. 'I'm not so sure. I very busy man. You wait to hear from me, *va bene*?' he says finally. Esmond nods. 'Good boy. We work very well together, I know this. *Arrivederci.*'

Esmond walks out into the morning. The rain has returned, settling in puddles. He pulls his mackintosh up over his head. At the entrance to Doney's some girls laugh under an umbrella as a boy steps into the road to flag down a taxi. They tumble in, the boy holding the door and another taking the brolly. Esmond watches as the girls pat their hair and the boys call orders to the driver. The girl nearest turns her face and he sees it is Fiamma. She smiles and presses a hand to the glass, her breath misting it as she laughs. Esmond waves, feeling foolish, as one of the other girls leans over to look at him, tented under his raincoat. Now both girls laugh and the taxi pulls away. He drops his hand and walks back towards the palazzo.

He starts another letter to Philip. *Perhaps this is all for the best*, he lies. *Perhaps I'll find someone else who'll make me feel as good, as loved as you did. You invented my heart, you know.* A postcard of *Primavera* to his father. *I am doing my best for the Party. Give my love to mother.* To Anna, the Gorgon shield by Caravaggio. *I miss you. Have decided to restart my novel. How are you?* He closes his eyes and thinks of Anna. She has weak lungs, her childhood one long, soft handshake with death. He remembers sitting beside her, pressing her burning skin, reading to her. In turn, she'd loved him, and her love was the thread that led him out of the labyrinth of spite and recrimination that was his family. He kisses the Gorgon's head as he steps down to the postbox at Cook's.

He eats dinner alone – Goad is at the German Consulate, Gesuina says – then goes to his room and lies on his bed. He opens a notebook on his knees and writes *Chapter One*. Music rises from the street, happy voices, the clatter of plates from Doney's. He throws the notebook to the floor, strips off and crawls under the covers. He thinks of the look of mock absorption he and Philip would shoot discreetly at one another whenever someone nearby was being particularly dull. He pulls the pillow over his head. Later that night, he wakes as a door bangs. He wonders if it is Fiamma coming home. He listens for a moment to the night, to a disappointed silence. He turns over and falls into a deep, blank sleep.

8

On Sunday morning, Esmond pulls on a green jumper and tweed jacket. He and Goad meet at a quarter to ten in front of the late King and walk together through the mist, down the via Tornabuoni to the Ponte Santa Trinità. The bells ring across the city, people hurry to secure the best pew in the best church.

'The ignominy of the side-aisle,' Goad cautions, 'and the Lady Chapel.'

Mist cushions the river, thick and white. When they reach the centre of the bridge, the bells of the town begin to muffle, and Goad peers nervously over the stone bulwarks. Sounds creep up through the mist towards them: the slop of the river, fishermen on the banks downstream, the distant bellow of the weir.

'It's as if we were underwater,' Esmond says.

'Or lost in time.'

They reach the south side of the river and walk down the via Maggio towards an old palazzo. There is no spire, only a small gold sign: *St Mark's English Church*. The front is weather-beaten, the wash on the *pietra serena* chipped and flaking. Wire bird-cages hang at eye height outside the shops and cafés on the street. None of the birds – canaries, zebra finches, parakeets, bullfinches – are singing. They stand in front of the church and Esmond looks down the line of silent cages. Goad makes his way through a wicket gate set in the large oak doors; Esmond ducks to follow.

In the entrance hall a flight of stone steps rises ahead of them, passing through an arch and curling out of sight. Green baize notice boards: *Italian Lessons Offered, Vieusseux's Circulating Library* and *Christian Lady Lodger Seeks Room in Central Location*. The cards have yellowed and curled at the edges. They remind Esmond of the boards on the walls of the common room at Winchester, scholarships to Oxford and rowing blues, messages of triumph from the world to come. A crackling organ begins, and Goad leads them through a small door to the left.

In near-darkness, they make their way down the aisle towards the altar, a block of white marble with lambs and palm trees in alabaster bas-relief. It looks ancient and sacrificial, scrubbed of blood each night, Esmond thinks, as they shuffle into a pew near the front. On the wall behind the altar is a triptych of the crucifixion. Christ's crown of thorns draws blood at every needle, his ribs press closely against his skin. Blood seeps and clots at the wounds in his hands and feet, where the nails are thick and twisted. The left-hand panel of the triptych shows Mary Magdalene, mourning, just as withered and undone. On the right is John the Baptist clinging to a gold cross. All three have grey-green skin, faces gaunt and horrified, every tendon and muscle risen. Esmond thinks of Filippino's painting of St Jerome in the Uffizi. The same leached skin, the hopeless terror.

'Rather brutal, hum?' says Goad.

'It's ghastly. Is it Filippino Lippi?'

'Ha! Bernard Berenson thinks so. Art expert, lives at I Tatti, up towards Fiesole. The triptych was owned by Charles Tooth, queer fish, by all accounts. He was the first vicar here and the triptych just hung around, so to speak. It was only when Berenson came for a lunchtime recital that we realised it was, that it might be, something rather special.'

'I must write to my father and tell him. He adores Filippino.'

'Had quite a collection, didn't he?'

Esmond thinks of the chapel at Aston Magna, the family home seized by the banks after the Crash. There was no altar, no pews or promises, just his father's paintings, stained glass replaced by clear panes to better light the cheeks of a Bronzino goldfinch, the pietà by Filippino Lippi, the Gentileschi *Judith*. His father had felt the loss of the paintings more than the house or the family firm. He'd blamed the unions in the factories, the Jews in the banks and the courts. Above all he blamed the Socialists, who'd pushed him from conservatism into full-blooded Fascism. Communism was a red rash on the mind of the family.

St Mark's is like the chapel at Aston: secular, cluttered, flannelled with dust. A great-aunt's attic. A grand piano sits at the back with a sheet over it. A sofa supports three peeling pictures of the Madonna. Chairs stacked down the side-aisles. A smell of damp and plaster, the sense of benign but terminal neglect. The darkness is partly due to the narrow clerestory windows at either end, and partly because everything is painted a light-eating crimson: the walls, the pillars, even some of the pews.

Goad bows his head to pray and Esmond looks around. He hadn't realised how many worshippers had crowded into the darkness – all of them old, obviously British in their twill and tweed, floral hats and medals. Colonel Keppel is bolt upright in the front row beside a martial woman with a large nose. Behind them, on his own, is an old man in a double-breasted suit, a single comb of hair across his head. Goad looks up and the old man waggles thick eyebrows.

'Reggie,' whispers Goad.

'Wotcha,' the man says.

Another old man steps jauntily down the aisle. He wears a high-buttoned jacket, Edwardian-style, with turn-ups to the cuffs, a grey shirt and vermilion handkerchief. He stoops and crosses himself in the aisle, then edges into the pew behind Esmond and Goad. He leans his face between them.

'Goad.' His voice is a whispered quiver. Esmond can feel his breath – peppermint – on his cheek. 'And I don't believe we've met—'

'Esmond Lowndes,' Goad says. 'Reggie Temple. One of our two Reggies. The other is Turner.'

'How confusing,' Esmond says.

'Not at all, my dear,' says the nearer Reggie. 'Other Reggie looks like a Turner. All washed out. And I've still got hair at the temples.' He gives a dry giggle. 'Going to the Keppels' later? Lunch?' The organ grows louder and his head retreats. The congregation stands and heavy footsteps sound in the aisle.

'In the name of the Father, and of the Son and of the Holy Ghost, Amen.'

The priest is tall, in a black cassock with a white lace smock on his shoulders. He is handsome – narrow black moustache, sharp blue eyes, a heaviness around the jowls, the creeping solidness of age. His voice is deep with a faint Scottish burr.

'Welcome, all of you. Jolly good to see so many here. Those that have gone, go with our blessing, of course, but while there's a single one of you left in Florence, I'll be here every morning, twice on Sundays.' He gives a sad smile. 'I'm afraid Walter Goodwin was among the latest exodus, so I shall need a new sacristan. A Reggie, perhaps?'

Turner looks at Temple. 'You wouldn't be able to reach,' he whispers sharply, rising to walk down the aisle.

'Thank you, Reggie. Now, we've had an approach from Holy Trinity to combine services. Father Hywell-Jones wishes to take his family back to Wales. Given that their congregation has held up rather worse than ours, we shall welcome all eight or nine of them next week. Remember that they are more sombre in their worship than we are, and be kind.

'In better news, and against the general trend, we have a guest with us. I'd like to welcome Esmond Lowndes, who is staying with Harold Goad at the British Institute. He's over here to set up, of all things, a radio station, with the aim of building bridges between the British and Italians. All I can say is jolly good luck to you, Esmond, God bless, and if there's anything any of us here at St Mark's can do to help, then do let us know.' Everyone turns to look at Esmond and he raises a shy hand towards the priest and nods. 'Now let us pray—'.

There is no service sheet and Esmond has trouble remembering the words. At school he'd spent his time in chapel looking at the backs of the younger boys, soft blond napes that shimmered in the stained light. Sometimes he'd humour baroque sexual fantasies of the barmaid at The Wykeham Arms, so that he'd have to struggle his erection into place before walking up to receive his blessing. Here, though, he can't drag his eyes from the triptych. He feels the pressure of Mary Magdalene's desert gaze, the heft of the russet hair that tumbles down over her back like a pelt. She holds her arms across her chest as if, were she to let go, she'd burst forth, ruptured by the weight of her sorrow. John's eyes, deep in sallow cheeks, peer up to his crucified God in appalled disbelief. Their bodies are chicken-thin and painful to look at. When he goes up to the altar rail beside Goad and bows his head, he shudders at his nearness to the painting.

After the service, Goad prays for a long time. Colonel Keppel and his wife stride down the aisle, nodding sternly at Esmond as they pass. Other expatriates step away, pausing only to genuflect broadly. The women are artistic and nervous, hanging onto the last vestiges of girlhood, or rather finding them again, turning up in their late-life bodies something gamine, playful, fragile. Their husbands march stiffly behind them, hands behind their backs. Finally Goad shakes his head and stands. The priest, who has taken off his smock and cassock and stands in a grey suit, is extinguishing candles at the back of the church with a brass snuffer. When he sees Esmond and Goad coming towards him, he puts it down and rubs his hands together, smiling.

'Now then, Esmond.' His palm is smooth and cool. 'Harold, good morning.'

'I thought we might show Esmond the room, if you have a moment,' Goad says.

'Of course. Perhaps I could drive you up to Bellosguardo afterwards.'

They make their way back through the entrance and follow Father Bailey up the dark stairwell. The priest takes the steps two at a time and Goad is soon panting, reaching for the support of Esmond's elbow. Bailey stops to wait for them.

'Here we are.' Bailey turns through a bunch of keys, selects one and opens the door onto a corridor, dimly lit by a window at the far end.

'It was the Machiavelli family palazzo,' Bailey says. 'He was born in one of these rooms. Amazing, isn't it?' He throws open doors as he passes, showing empty rooms thick with dust. They come to the end of the corridor. 'Now tell me what you think of this.' He opens the last door on the left and they step into a large, white space. It reminds Esmond for a moment of the ballroom at Aston Magna. Four French windows open onto a narrow balcony overlooking the church of Santo Spirito. He can see young men playing football in the piazza, doves in a gossipy cluster on the tiled roof.

'I spoke to Father Bailey,' Goad puffs, 'about a studio. He suggested you might use this. For a small contribution to the upkeep of the church, of course, but—'

'You'd be welcome to have it for nothing, Esmond. Far too quiet around here recently and what you're doing is more good than harm. If Harold's behind you, that's endorsement enough for me.'

Esmond can see fingers of damp creeping up the walls, patches of mould that fur the far corner. Parquet tiles are chipped, missing in places. Dust covers the stone mantelpiece at the far end. He breathes the smell and lets out his breath in a low whistle.

'This is smashing.'

'Glad you approve. Now, oughtn't we get going? I'm ruddy terrified of Alice Keppel.'

With a last look at the room, Esmond follows Goad and Bailey back along the corridor, down the steps and through a side door into the garage and Bailey's old, rather dazzling, red Alfa Romeo. They drive out into the misty square, along streets so narrow that rugs touch as the women shake them from high windows. Finally, with a careless roar from the car, they wind up into the hills and out of the city.

9

The Villa dell'Ombrellino takes three terraced steps down the hillside. The uppermost has a gravel path between lemon trees, plumbago and gardenia. There is a vegetable garden further down growing beefsteak tomatoes. Fountains babble in the shade of umbrella pines. The house is large and symmetrical with a loggia running the length of the ground floor. Most of the lunch guests are sitting here smoking and sipping sherry.

Esmond is at the front of the upper terrace with Colonel Keppel. His hand rests on the metal pole that supports the brass parasol, the *ombrellino*, and they look down across the mist to the tower of the Palazzo Vecchio, and beyond it the plump dome of the cathedral. Otherwise Florence is obscured.

Colonel Keppel is smoking a pipe, nestling the stem under his moustache and drawing deeply. He steps forward to the stone wall that marks the edge of the uppermost terrace.

'Have you seen the pool?' he asks, pointing downwards with his pipe.

Esmond joins him at the balcony and looks over. A camphor tree grows at the top of a rocky grotto where a shadowy swimming pool crags under ferns and hostas. Over the shallow end are bronze statues, two dodos, covered in verdigris. He thinks of Philip floating star-shaped in the pool at Emmanuel College, misquoting Byron, paddling with his hands.

'Modelled on the Roman baths at Caracalla. Same chap who did the garden, Cecil Pinsel.'

'It's beautiful. Why the dodos?'

'Reminder that we're all dying and all stupid. It's why I built the pool. Attracts the young, or used to, until they buggered off back to London. Important, when you get to my age, to surround yourself with young people. You must come and swim here when the weather improves. It'd make Alice happy.' He pauses. 'D'you enjoy the service?'

'Yes. It's a funny little church.'

'Funny priest, too. Goad tell you about Bailey?'

'No.'

Colonel Keppel glances over his shoulder.

'Confidentially, he's a spy. Intelligence Corps during the last war and now reporting back to Whitehall on Musso.'

'He's not a priest?'

'Oh, he's an amen-wallah all right – it's his cover. He got me to carry a few packages to London when we went to heave Violet, that's our daughter, down the aisle. Very hush-hush.' He touches his nose. 'Disappears for days in that sports car of his. Up to the mountains. *Giustizia e Libertà*, I shouldn't wonder. Now, not a word of this. Scout's honour?'

'Scout's honour.'

Alice Keppel comes down the path from the house. Goad, on

41

her arm, looks shrunken, doll-like. The four of them face over towards the hills of the Sienese Clavey that billow up out of the mist.

'I hope I didn't embarrass you at lunch, young man,' she says, without turning. 'Out here, one assumes that every*one* knows every*thing*.'

'It'll take more than your youthful indiscretions to make Esmond blush.' Colonel Keppel pats her buttock. 'Hasn't heard about me and dear old Victoria yet. Not for nothing were they called the naughty nineties.'

Over lunch, leaning closely, Mrs Keppel had told Esmond how dreadfully sorry she was for Wallis. The problem was, she said, Mrs Simpson didn't know what she wanted. When she, Mrs Keppel, had been the mistress of Edward's grandfather, she'd been very clear. She wanted money. Money so that she might live in the style that her ancestors had enjoyed. Money so that she might take her husband away to a place like this – she'd waved her hand across the dinner table, the plates of food and silver candlesticks. And when the King had come to stay, George had gone shooting, or riding, and the King had ridden her. Here she laughed breathily.

Now, on the terrace, she wraps a heavy arm around his shoulder.

'It's divine to have you here, Esmond. I'm always saying to Harold that he must get Fiamma and Gerald, when he's over, to come up and swim, but I'm afraid he disapproves of us.'

Goad clucks. 'Not at all, Alice. It's just that – hum – young people—'

'But the young are what George and I live for. I insist that Esmond come up to bathe soon.'

Goad looks doubtfully at the water below.

'I'd love to,' Esmond says, aware of the weight of her arm.

A gust of wind rattles the pines around the house. Mrs Keppel finally lifts her arm and begins to shiver. Father Bailey crunches down from the house with a shawl, which he wraps around her shoulders.

'We should leave you,' Goad says.

'Oh, do stay a little longer.'

The mist begins to clear beneath them. Gradually, in little plots and then in larger pools of light, Florence reveals the dome of San Lorenzo, Santa Croce to the east, the Badia Fiorentina, Santo Spirito. As the sun strolls from rooftop to rooftop, rusticated brickwork and cool white facades appear, the huge teal egg of the synagogue, and villas like a loose necklace across the hills.

'It must be difficult, at moments like this,' Goad says, 'not to believe in God.'

'Amen,' says Bailey.

Esmond feels weightless, as if he could sail down over the currents of air.

'Harold. You and your sublime,' Colonel Keppel says, turning and leading them back to the house. Esmond takes a last look at the pool, the city beyond, and follows.

In Bailey's car on the way home, the priest leans over his shoulder and speaks to Esmond, who is perched in the cramped rear.

'Did you realise that your host was a holy man too?' he says.

'Colonel Keppel?'

'Your real host, Harold here.'

Goad looks out at the landscape. 'Oh, come now.'

'I'm entirely serious. If he hadn't been so taken with politics, he'd have made a sparkling priest. Is that not so, Harold?'

Goad shakes his head. Esmond sees a half-smile on his lips. 'I wanted to find a way of – hum – doing some good.'

'He'd cut his tongue out before telling you this, but he used his inheritance to found an orphanage at Assisi. Eighteen years old. A year in a Franciscan monastery in the Apennines after that. He's done more good than most saints I know.'

'You're too kind, Father Bailey.'

'I just want young Esmond to know what sort of man he's living with.'

'I do,' Esmond says. 'Really.'

10

The next day, just before lunch, Esmond is in the library with Goad. The older man sits in a high-backed armchair reading Browning. Every so often he rolls out a warm chuckle, or mutters 'Yes, yes,' to himself. Esmond watches dust riding the beams of light from the windows. They hear the front door clang and footsteps on the stairs. Goad looks at his watch and stands, Esmond with him.

'Here she is,' says Goad, as a woman, mid-twenties, Esmond guesses, with a hard, grown-up air, walks in. Her knotted hair is deep red, the colour of Mary Magdalene's in the triptych. Goad crosses to kiss her. As he reaches up to take her by the shoulders, on tiptoe, and place a kiss on each pale cheek, she stoops a little to meet him, and Esmond sees how thin she is, barely filling her tunic and slacks.

'Harold,' she says. 'I'm late.'

'Not at all. Ada Liuzzi, Esmond Lowndes. Ada's father, Guido, edits the Florentine edition of *La Nostra Bandiera*.'

Esmond takes her hand and notices a mole, a dark moon in the orbit of her left eye.

'Pleasure to meet you,' he says.

Gesuina places a tray on the table beside Goad's armchair. Goad picks up the teapot and fills three china cups.

'From England,' he says. 'One simply can't get good tea out here. Milk?'

Ada looks from one of them to the other. She raises the tea carefully to her lips and sips. There is something almost manly about her face, Esmond thinks. She is not beautiful. Striking perhaps, even startling, but never beautiful.

'I told Ada about Radio Firenze. I knew, you see, that she was at a loose end, and I thought she might be a good person to have aboard.'

'I studied English in Bologna,' Ada says quietly. 'I have been looking for a job here in Florence, but with the sanctions and the war in Spain – I thought, perhaps, of America. But for the moment, I would be very happy to help you.'

'That's excellent, Ada. I'm sure you'll find it terribly easy. Some research, some translation with Carità, the wireless man—'

'I know Carità,' she says, and Esmond feels a momentary curdling of the atmosphere.

'Splendid.' Goad rubs his hands. 'And I wonder if you might come along for a drink here on Thursday night, for the Coronation. We'll take the opportunity to halloo those Brits who have – hum – persevered. A bottle of Asti spumante or two, a picture of the new King in the hallway. You'd be very welcome.'

'I should be delighted,' Ada says, her face softening. Esmond finds himself grinning back as he and Goad walk her to the door. She kisses him; lavender in her hair and on her pale skin. The two men stand at the top of the stairs, watch her descend and turn out of sight.

Back in the library, Esmond smells the lavender, thinks of her cat's eyes, her heavy jaw.

'She'll be super,' he says. 'Her English is excellent.'

'Yes. She's a terribly nice girl. Fascinating family. Her father's a Jew, would you believe? He and Ettore Ovazza, the banker, founded *La Nostra Bandiera* in Turin. Hugely pro-Fascist, all of them.'

'But Jews?'

'Indeed. It's folly to think the Jews are all Communists and agitators. One which leads some of the British Union chaps in entirely the wrong direction. *Il Duce* understands that, whatever the racial origins, whatever the dress, the gods, human beings are all about connection, and if you throw people together for long enough, they'll rub along. Mussolini refuses to implement racial laws because Jews have been here since the days of Ancient Rome. Lorenzo the Magnificent's doctor was a Jew.'

'Didn't Mussolini have a Jewish mistress?'

'Margherita Sarfatti. Jews here are firstly Italians. What they choose to do in their temples is no concern of ours.' He looks worried. 'I hope that isn't a problem for you? Ada being Jewish. I presumed, like your father, you had no truck with this racialist nonsense.'

'None at all,' Esmond replies. 'I'm just surprised. With everything that's going on in Germany, and the Italians cosying up to Hitler, the Rome–Berlin Axis and all that.'

'I can't help but think', Goad says, 'that there's a degree of exaggeration in what we hear of Germany. The Germans I know are the most civilised people on earth. Simply couldn't imagine them putting up with that kind of – hum – savagery. I should like, perhaps, to go and see for myself. But now, I must prepare for my lessons.'

Later that evening, from the window of his room, Esmond watches a stream of earnest, dark-suited young men enter the palazzo. He sits down to write Anna a postcard of *St Jerome*, recalling the two of them sitting in their father's chapel at Aston Magna, staring up at the paintings, swooning themselves into

46

the future. In art, in books, they'd built a bubble around themselves, impervious to their family, to Fascism. Her illness gave them an excuse for this, for long hours in her room with *Middlemarch* or *The Eustace Diamonds* or *Tristram Shandy*. *Whenever I read*, he writes, *part of me is always reading to you, out loud*. He finishes the letter and then sits with his legs on the windowsill, *The Decameron* in his lap. Bats begin to flutter past like thoughts, sweeping and circling over the streetlights. Just after nine-thirty, he hears voices below and watches as the young men come out, laughing, carrying books, shouting as they scatter into the lamplit streets of the city.

Before going to bed, feeling indulgent, nostalgic, he opens his cupboard. Already, his British Union uniform has taken on a historical air, and he's surprised at the familiar scratch of the twill as he runs a thumb over the collar of the shirt. A sudden keen memory of coming back to Cambridge, important in his uniform after a march in the East End. He'd found Philip in his room and the older boy, silent and ritualistic, had unbuttoned Esmond's tunic, opened his belt, slipped off the jackboots. He knew that in the silence was a question, and in the hot press of their bare bodies in the frantic hours that followed, a response. Now, concussed by memory, he sleeps.

11

On Thursday night, the entrance hall of the Institute is lit by two standard lamps from the library. The front door is open to the evening. Gesuina, in a sober black smock, is next to a table with the wine. Esmond stands smoking, watching Fiamma balancing her tray of fizzing glasses carefully, proudly, like a completed jigsaw. He is already a little drunk. Goad places a hand in the small of his back and moves him towards a white-bearded man in a smoking jacket.

'Esmond, let me introduce you to our most celebrated resident, an honorary Brit, Bernard Berenson. Esmond was rather taken by the triptych in the English church. That's a Filippino, he said, without a blink.'

'It's a sin they didn't sell the thing,' Berenson says, a faint American twang in his voice. 'I had the Italian government baying for it, three pages of authentication, and this new priest good as tore it up. Maddening.' He shakes his head. He reminds Esmond of the photograph of Freud that Philip had pinned to the wall of his study.

'They are astonishing paintings.'

'Yes? One refers to a triptych in the singular. But it is special, there's no doubt.'

'The colour of the skin. It's almost alien.'

'It wouldn't have been like that at the time, of course. It's *verdaccio*, the green undercoat coming through. But it is striking, isn't it? Filippino was always in the shadow of his mentor, Botticelli, but with the triptych, and his *St Jerome* in the Uffizi—'

'Yes, of course.'

'They're a whole new mode, as if he were trying to unpaint all the flippant beauty of his earlier work. He's not studied widely enough, I'm afraid.'

There is a stir at the door, a few shouts of welcome. Esmond sees Gesuina turn and whisper something in her daughter's ear.

'Here's trouble,' says Berenson. 'Don't block the path to the wine. Like getting between a hippo and her young.' He stands back to let a red-faced man tap through on a silver-topped cane. Behind him comes a smaller fellow, fortyish and chubby, with round spectacles and cheeks.

'*La Signora e la Signorina Ricci, che belle regazze,*' the first man says, bowing to Gesuina and Fiamma behind the table. '*Come mi fa contento di vedervi.*' He takes two glasses, passes one to his friend and tastes his own. 'Asti spumante,' he says, letting out a sigh, '*il champagne italiano, il nettare degli dei.* And who might you be, my angel?' Sea-grey eyes fix upon Esmond, widening with slow delight. He holds out his hand.

'Esmond Lowndes. Pleased to meet you.'

'Norman Douglas,' the man says with another bow. 'This is my dear friend Pino Orioli. Is there any particular book of mine you'd like?'

Esmond feels himself blushing. 'I believe I've read most of them, sir.'

'Oh really? And which is your favourite?'

'*South Wind,*' Esmond says, then, seeing Douglas's face fall, 'but, of course, *Alone* was magnificent, and *Old Calabria*. Some of the best travel writing I've read.'

'Some of it, eh?' Douglas frowns at him. 'I'm not a travel writer. I'm a writer who happens to rush about. Have you read *Together*?'

'Yes. I had a great friend at Cambridge from Austria. He said … that you described the country in a way that made it feel more real than his clearest memories.'

'And you?' Douglas asks, jabbing a finger towards him. 'What about you?'

Esmond hesitates. Then, in a small voice, 'It made me feel like I knew my friend much better than before. That I could understand where he'd come from.'

Douglas twitches his nose. 'I think we shall be seeing young Mr Lowndes again, don't you, Pino?'

Orioli grins, waggling his eyebrows and reaching for another glass of wine. Douglas places a hand on Esmond's shoulder and squeezes. 'He's all right, this one.' With a nod, he drops his hand and speaks again in Italian.

Esmond looks around and realises that Ada isn't there. He wonders what it will be like to work with her, what closeness might grow between them. He glances sideways at Fiamma. It is a shame, he thinks, that Ada looks so un-Italian, has none of Fiamma's fine grace. It's not her Jewishness, rather the square-ness of her jaw, the gas-blue skin that make him shiver when he pictures her.

The ting-ting of a fork on glass. Goad stands on the first step of the staircase, pulling at his hands. Esmond sees Berenson and a Reggie, George and Alice Keppel turn and straighten, Father Bailey towering over another Reggie in the corner. Others he doesn't recognise. He counts eighteen people in the entrance hall.

'Ladies and gentlemen,' Goad says. 'The coronation of George V took place in my first year as Director of the Institute. A gala dinner for eighty guests in the Palazzo Vecchio, bunting stretched across the via Tornabuoni, dancing and fireworks late into the night. Public occasions like this one are a rock in the fluid currents of history, that we may look back and see how far we've come. So few of us left in this most English of Italian cities. So many gone.' He takes a sip of water. 'For all its roughness, its – hum – youth, we have seen a brave new power driving the history of this country, and it won't be long before England is the odd man out of Europe. Democracy is dying. Kemal, Horthy, Pisudki in Poland, Salazar in Portugal, Franco in Spain. Herr Hitler.

'These rumours of war between Britain and Italy – put them from your minds.' A *hear, hear,* from Alice Keppel. 'When the statesmen of Europe fix the mess bequeathed them by the Treaty of Versailles, everything will go on as before. The British and Italians could never be any serious enemies. We are in the middle of a – hum – tiff, nothing more.'

He holds up a framed photograph of the new King, crosses the room, lifts down the picture of George V and smiles at the applause. He stretches up to hook George VI in its place. Esmond looks to see if Ada has arrived, but sees blackness on the street.

'Most of you have met Esmond Lowndes,' Goad continues, back at the step. 'His wireless programme will be broadcast throughout Tuscany. Do go over and say hello. Esmond, stick up a hand. Yes. And if any of you have an idea for a transmission, something we might send out for the instruction of our listeners, don't – hum – keep it a secret.'

Through the crowd Esmond can see bodies in the street, black-shirted figures outside the doorway.

'It only remains for me to ask you to charge your glasses and raise them to our new King.'

Alice Keppel lets out a high scream. Two men are inside, stockings pulled over their faces. Douglas and Orioli squeeze past Esmond and head down the corridor to the inner courtyard. Esmond feels Fiamma tense beside him. More black figures enter, six in all, faces smudged like ghosts. One shoves at Reggie Temple, who lands in a heap, breathing heavily. Father Bailey steps forward and the Blackshirt nearest him pulls out a revolver.

The room takes a breath. Two men rush to the table and tip it over. The musical shattering of glasses. A bottle fizzes to Gesuina's feet and Esmond reaches down to right it. Fiamma, a slash of wine across her blouse, looks towards Esmond. He feels breathless, a shameful excitement in his chest, and meets her dark eyes.

One Blackshirt stands in the door, another in the passageway. The smallest, whom Esmond recognises with swift certainty as Carità, crosses to the photograph of the King, pulls a dagger from his belt. Alice Keppel lets out a whimper. Taking the picture with one hand, he breaks the glass with the hilt of the dagger. He draws the blade carefully across the photograph, opening up long white scars in the King's uneasy face, and lets it fall. Goad has stepped from the platform towards the Blackshirt.

'Look here,' he says. '*Sapete qui sono io?*'

One pulls out a package in brown paper. He hands it to the small man, who slips the blade under the paper and holds up another photograph. In a plain wooden frame, it is a portrait of Victor Emmanuel III, with his absurdly curling moustache and slow-witted eyes.

'You in Italy,' the small man says, his voice muffled by the stocking. 'You have Italian King now.' He places Victor Emmanuel on the hook and squares it on the wall. 'Always here. We will come back to check.'

Goad steps towards him, smiling hesitantly.

'I quite understand, although I'm not sure that we needed the point made quite so dramatically. What would you say to having portraits of both kings together, or perhaps—'

The small man raises his dagger. Esmond feels a lurch. He leaps forward over the upended table, his feet crunching on the glass. The man brings the dagger down hard, landing two sharp blows on Goad's head, hilt-first. Goad doesn't pass out, but lowers himself carefully to the ground, a plume of blood darkening his hair. The small man brings his dagger up again as Esmond reaches him, seizing his arm from behind. The man wheels around. His hand is hot and damp.

'Carità,' Esmond says.

A pause, and the man takes the opportunity to drive a knee into Esmond's groin. A sour pain spreads through his body to his throat. He lets go of Carità's arm and bends double, tears springing to his eyes. He thinks he might vomit. A soft hand on his back and he turns to see Fiamma standing beside him.

'*Basta così!*' she shouts, jutting her chin towards the little man. He regards her for a moment and then lets the dagger fall to his side.

'*Allora, andiamo,*' Carità says. Then, bending over Goad. 'You think your friends protect you? You tell anyone in Rome and we start to kill English people. Your time has run out. *Me ne frego!*' The last is shouted and repeated by the others as they file out. They listen to the Blackshirts singing as they make their way down the via Tornabuoni.

Fiamma is still next to him, her hand on his back. Gesuina is crouched over Goad, speaking softly. Someone has balled a jacket beneath the older man's head. His cheeks are grey, his eyes closed. Gesuina holds a cloth to the wound. Bailey goes to stand above him.

'We need an ambulance. Can someone call the Golden Cross?'

'I'll go,' says Fiamma, 'the telephone is in the library.'

Esmond stands, wincing. He sees Douglas and Orioli appear from the corridor.

'Everything all right?' Douglas asks, and looks at Goad.

The Reggies take Douglas and Orioli outside. Father Bailey and Colonel Keppel turn to Esmond. 'How d'you feel?' the priest asks.

'I should have thumped them, I really should,' says Keppel, jabbing in the air.

'Esmond did more than enough. You'd have ended up like Goad.'

'I'd like to have seen them try.' The Colonel pinches his moustache and lets out a gravelled whinny.

'I'm fine,' says Esmond. 'How's Harold?'

'He'll live, lucky fellow. Here they are.'

Two men in blue uniforms come through the door, golden crosses embroidered on their backs. They lift Goad's arms to their shoulders and carry him to the door.

'I'll go along,' says Bailey. 'Perhaps, Esmond, you could wire Gerald in the morning. Tell him his father's had a spot of trouble. He'll want to know. Gesuina will give you his details.'

12

He and Fiamma are in the kitchen drinking tea. She has changed into green silk pyjamas and looks, Esmond thinks, like a princess from the *Arabian Nights*. They'd cleared up the entrance hall together, sweeping glass and mopping the sticky floor. It had grown dark and they worked in the light between standard lamps, under the dull gaze of Victor Emmanuel. Now San Gaetano chimes ten o'clock. The pain in his groin has finally lifted. Fiamma fishes a slice of lemon out of her tea with a spoon, sucks it, drops it back into her cup.

'Where have they taken him, do you think?'

'Santa Maria Nuova. It's not far.' She blows on her tea. 'How are you feeling?'

'Rum,' says Esmond. 'Worried about Harold.'

'Me too. He looked so unwell on the floor. *Bastardi.*' She places her cup in the sink with a crash. 'You were a good man tonight,' she says, stepping towards him and walking her fingers across his head. 'You were brave. Now I must go to bed.' Esmond's scalp tingles as he finishes his tea and makes his way along the corridor to his room.

The next morning he breakfasts alone and then wires Gerald from Cook's. He pictures Gerald as a younger version of his father: thinning, hesitant, hands a patchwork of scabs and raw skin. Afterwards he climbs the stairs and knocks on the door to Fiamma's room.

54

'*Sì, entra!*' she says. A gramophone plays 'Summertime'. *The Decameron* is face down on the dressing table, dresses and jackets on the bed and the doors of her wardrobe. 'It's such a mess,' she says, smiling, picking up her handbag and placing a navy shawl around her shoulders. 'Let's go.'

Goad is in a ward with elderly people, all of whom appear to be more or less dead. There is an occasional groan from one of the beds, otherwise silence. Goad's head is heavily bandaged, his face grey and drawn under the white turban. Bailey sits in a chair beside him, Gesuina in another.

'How is he?' Esmond asks. Fiamma takes Goad's hand, running her thumbs over the skin. Goad opens his eyes narrowly and attempts a smile.

'I'll be fine,' he says.

'He'll be fine if he gets some rest,' says Bailey, firmly. 'The head seems to be in reasonable condition, nothing broken. But the blood pressure's terribly high, his heart is not in good shape at all. The doctors have insisted on at least a month of rest.'

'The shock?'

'They don't know, I'm afraid. One suggested—'

'I've told you, Frederick, I simply can't take the time off. My students rely upon me. And Radio Firenze—'

'You don't have the option.' The priest's voice is tired and Esmond realises he has been here all night. Gesuina has a basket of food by her feet, a steaming flask of coffee in her hands. Her eyes are red.

'What about the people who did this, what about Carità?' Esmond asks.

Goad sighs and shakes his head. 'Anything we do will just drive a deeper wedge between us. It's my fault. I should have known, brandishing the picture of the King through the open door. Idiotic. I'm surprised it didn't happen sooner.'

'But Mussolini should know about this. We should write to him.'

'We need to work with Carità, not against him. This is something you must understand, Esmond. We live according to different rules here. Violence is the blood of this new Fascism. I don't hold it against Carità for a moment, what he did. We were in the wrong and were punished. It's him I ought to write to – a note of apology.'

A nurse comes in, gently removes Goad's hand from Fiamma's and takes his pulse.

'*Signor Goad dovrette dormire,*' she says.

Fiamma kisses Goad on the cheek and squeezes his hand again.

'Will you let my students know when they arrive this evening? Tell them in person. I don't think a sign—'

'Of course,' Esmond says. 'I'll deal with it.'

'As for the station, it's down to you now. Prepare, Esmond. Go and see Carità. Square things up with him. Make sure the studio's ready for when I'm back on my feet.'

Bailey walks with them to the corridor. 'He's really very sick,' the priest says. 'They were talking about operating, but he's not well enough for that. He'll be here for at least another week. I'd like him to take the waters at Bagni di Lucca. I think I'll be able to persuade Gesuina to go with him, but he's in no state to travel yet. You'll hold the fort at the palazzo, you two?'

'Of course,' Esmond nods.

'We'll manage,' Fiamma says.

At the Institute, Esmond stands at the door and meets the clerks and university students, shop workers and salesmen arriving for Goad's English lesson. 'I'm afraid the lessons will have to be postponed. Signor Goad has had an accident. He's in hospital.

I'm terribly sorry.' He repeats it to each of them. They ask after Goad, if they might visit him, offer their condolences, pressing Esmond's hands with theirs. When the last has left, Esmond walks into the courtyard, looks up and feels the old building breathing around him. He sees a light flickering against the pale roof of the loggia. He climbs the stairs to the top floor and, instead of turning left towards the bedrooms and the kitchen, he turns right.

He tries the door at the end of the passage. It opens with a creak. There on the loggia, again in green pyjamas, this time with a woollen shawl around her shoulders, sits Fiamma, reading by candlelight, making notes in a pad on her knee. She has found a rusty garden chair to sit on. Esmond steps out onto the pathway between railings and she looks up at him.

'It's better to read outside,' she says. 'You can hear the city, see the sky, the mountains.'

'*The Decameron*?' he asks.

She holds up the cover and then goes back to her reading.

He looks around. The hills that circle Florence are purpled by the night. Thin feathers of noctilucent cloud sit in the air to the west. To the east, the hills are dark, marked here and there by the lights of villages, the solitary glow of villas.

'Could I join you?' he asks.

'Of course. Do you have any food? My mother's still at the hospital.'

He crosses to the apartment, finds a loaf of bread and some salami in the pantry, a bottle of red wine and two glasses from the kitchen cupboard. He pulls on a jumper, puts his own copy of *The Decameron* under his arm and heads back out onto the loggia. Fiamma has unfolded another green chair. They sit, each reading the same book in different languages, each sipping, munching, smiling, sighing as they follow the stories of ten young people, six hundred years earlier, in the very hills which tend them now. When San Gaetano has tolled twelve and the wine is finished, the candle almost down to its holder, Fiamma draws in a sharp breath, shivers and reaches out for Esmond's hand.

'My uncle was one of them,' Fiamma says.

'One of what?'

'The men, last night. He passed Carità the portrait of Vittorio Emanuele.'

He can feel her pulse in her palm. Her hands are cold and he seizes them both between his. She looks at him with wide, frank eyes.

'I can't believe he could do this to Mr Goad. They have lunch, they are friends even. Something has happened to the people in this city. They are turning against themselves.' She takes her hands from his and stands up. 'I must go to bed. I have classes tomorrow.' He can barely see her eyes in the candlelight. 'It is good to have you here.'

She bends over and places a kiss on his cheek. He watches her cross the loggia to the door and out of sight. He stays for a while on the rooftop, turning with the drifting stars. Later, in bed, he imagines he can feel the moist press of her lips with his fingertip.

13

They live the next week like a holiday. They get up later, dine longer, fall asleep or into books in the afternoons. Gesuina is in and out of the apartment, leaving meals under muslin cloths on the sideboard in the kitchen, salads in deep glazed bowls in the icebox, loaves of bread on the table. She seems unwilling to quit Goad's side, particularly at night, when she says he grinds his teeth and calls out, his heart a skipping trot in his chest. She's usually there at breakfast, looking rinsed but satisfied, her hair in a fretful bun. After Fiamma has left for lectures at the university, Gesuina puts together a basket of food and she and Esmond walk up to Santa Maria Nuova to visit Goad.

Bailey is often at the hospital, his cool assurance a comfort in the wheezing closeness of the ward. His Italian indulges no accent and is garnished with English words and suspect Italianate endings: *stethoscopio*, for instance. He and Gesuina together, though, are a formidable pairing, and the doctors and nurses soon scurry at their command. Goad is moved into a private room overlooking a flagstoned courtyard, the bluff back of the church and the railway station visible through a gap between hospital buildings.

'They call it a *scorcio*,' Goad says. 'A view you glimpse, all of a sudden, that leaps inside you. Florence is the city of *scorci*.' Pale blue curtains belly in the breeze as they stare out into the bright day. Esmond has brought Goad's Tennyson, his Foscolo, his Browning, but feels useless now, gently gripping the old man's hand. He has done nothing about the wireless station, about Carità, and the thought presses upon him. There has also been no word from Gerald.

In the evenings, he and Fiamma have dinner on the loggia. They drink and read, closeness creeping between them as the night inks the hills, bells tolling in the darkness around them. They bring cushions and rugs onto the loggia like tender colonisers, giving it back the purpose of its design. He plans his novel, with Fiamma a new Philip, listening to his ideas, laughing encouragement. *Hulme at Cambridge – sent down – then in London*, he writes. *After a row over a girl, he hangs Wyndham Lewis upside-down on the railings of Soho Square. Henri Gaudier-Brzeska, the artist, forges him a pair of brass knuckle-dusters which he uses to drive home philosophical arguments.*

One evening they go down to Doney's for a *digestivo*. Fiamma drinks three glasses of Frangelico as the white-coated waiters dip and bend around them. The room glitters with marble tables and chandeliers, coruscating brightness. Everyone seems to know Fiamma, who is wearing the same yellow dress she wore the first time Esmond saw her. Late on, just as the waiters are beginning to stack chairs, one of them performing a *pas de deux* with his broom, Fiamma reaches across to take Esmond's hand on the silver-topped table.

'When I was young,' she says, 'I was hungry. My father couldn't get work – it was the first years of Mussolini's reign and the papers suddenly refused to take articles from a Communist, even one who'd fought in the war, and who wrote so beautifully.' She reaches up to draw her fingers down the sleek curve of her hair. 'My early memories are of being cold and hungry, and of there never being any money, of having to go to our neighbours to beg food.' They both lift their feet as the dancing waiter sweeps beneath their table. Fiamma lets out a little sigh. 'We'd come to Florence for holidays, my mother and I, and there'd be food and soft sheets and my Fascist uncle, and I hated myself for loving it, for not staying in the apartment in Milan with my father. I still feel that, here, a little.' She shrugs, swirls her glass and drinks it down.

When they get back to the apartment there is a moment of awkwardness at the door to her room. He leans to kiss her cheek, they move their heads the same way, then again, and their lips brush together. They draw apart, eyes wide. Fiamma smiles, and moves to place another swift kiss on his mouth. He is wordless, all lips, staring at the blank face of her door.

14

He wakes at dawn, the air in his bedroom close and stale. The rumble of a taxi below. A muttered conversation, banging doors, footsteps on the stairs, then silence. He dozes again and wakes with a start as his door bursts open. In the dim light he makes out a tall figure with thick chestnut hair. Fiamma stands behind him, her arm on the doorframe.

'Well, turn the light on then. Let's get a look at you.' The voice is warmly amused.

Esmond sticks out a hand for the light and looks blinkingly towards the doorway. The young man is *sportif* in a white boating jacket and slacks, a loose tie. He smiles, and it is like a growl. Fiamma's nightdress shows the darkness of her skin as she steals happily behind the stranger. Beautiful, Esmond thinks, sitting up.

'May we come in?' The young man crosses to the window and throws open the shutters. The world stirs shyly outside. He pulls out the chair, turns it towards the bed and sits. Fiamma perches on the desk behind him, looking first at Esmond, then at him. Esmond is aware that an incipient morning erection is prodding his sheets. He feels childish and Victorian in his nightshirt, his father's, too large and threadbare at the armpits.

'Listen,' the boy says in a loud voice. 'I want you to know how bloody good you've been. Standing to attention at the old man's bedside, keeping the pip from his tooth and all that. I've spoken to Bailey and he says you've been a sainted hero. So thanks a million, pal.'

'You're Gerald.' Esmond says, looking for a trace of Goad in the elegant, almost oriental eyes.

'S'right,' Gerald says. 'Bloody good to be back here. And to see this little one.' He slaps a hand on Fiamma's thigh and she smiles out a squeal. 'Too early for breakfast? Procacci'll open in twenty minutes. Milk rolls and jam. My treat.'

Gerald and Fiamma leave and Esmond sits muddled and sleepy, listening to their voices and laughter echoing through the corridor. He gets up and picks his clothes more carefully than he has all week – a pale lawn shirt and sponge-bag trousers.

He finds them in the courtyard. It is light now, a lemony brightness in the air. As they stroll out into the street, Gerald throws his arm around Esmond's shoulders.

'We're going to have a high old time this summer. No idea what I'll do when I get back to London, but I intend to be thoroughly debased before I go.'

They walk through the doors to Procacci, whose stooped, trembling owner is letting up the blinds. He nods them in, tucks a dishcloth into his belt and stands behind the counter.

'*Tre panini con confettura, tre caffè, per favore,*' Gerald says. He pulls out a chair from the round marble table for Fiamma and sits down himself, rocking backwards as he draws out his cigarette case. 'Smoke?' he asks, holding it towards Esmond. Esmond takes one and leans forward to light it as the owner brings their breakfasts.

'You're studying for the bar, aren't you?' Esmond says.

'Rather flunked, I'm afraid. Have you seen inside a law court, Esmond? There's always one bird looks as if he's about to split the atom when all he's thought about for twenty years is roast beef and gravy. A cemetery for the mind, law.'

Later that morning they visit Goad. Gesuina sits knitting as the old man sleeps. She stands up when she sees Gerald, letting out a whimper of pleasure as they embrace. He tilts backwards and lifts her from the floor. Goad wakes, looks over at them and breaks into a smile.

'You came,' he says.

Gerald sits by his father and they talk for some minutes in low voices. Then he turns towards them. 'I think I'll sit and read to the old man for a while. Listen, it's going to be a scorcher. Why don't we head up to L'Ombrellino for a swim later? I'll meet you chaps up there, say, three?'

Outside, Fiamma reaches into her clutch and draws out a pair of round, wire-framed sunglasses. Esmond takes her arm. As they walk down past the train station, past Santa Maria Novella, he can feel the heat rising from the paving stones. There are speakers mounted around the piazza and Mussolini's voice cries out as they pass. Fiamma stops, and he watches a group of boatered schoolgirls giggle past in the mirrors of her lenses. Mussolini ends with a shout that is almost a scream. Fiamma walks on, shaking her head.

'*Che palle*,' she says.

15

Esmond lowers himself down between the dodos and into the water. The steps are slick beneath his feet and he moves carefully, spreading the water, deepening the blue and white stripes of his costume. The sun flings across the pool, sparking off the shadowy nooks of the cliff that climbs towards the house. He leans forward, kicks into a breaststroke and opens his eyes. He can see the mosaics on the bottom, a dolphin in turquoise tiles, mermaids, seahorses, starfish. He turns over, surfaces and looks up. Alice Keppel gazes down on him from the terrace, her hands on the parapet wall. She raises an arm.

'Is it glorious?'

'I'll say,' he agrees, swimming to the edge of the pool. He rests his elbows on the side, looking down over the city, across to where the valley funnels up into the mountains.

Colonel Keppel is coming down from the terrace above, his hand on Fiamma's back. She is wearing a red bathing costume with a belt of gold rings. She dives into the pool and swims to join Esmond, her hair fanning out behind her. Colonel Keppel sits on the steps at the other end, his barrel chest inside a black costume of coarse wool, his face reddening in the sun.

'It's beautiful, isn't it?' Fiamma says, kicking her legs. 'The only place on a day like this. I hope Gerald comes soon.'

They swim for half an hour and then sit in the shadow of the camphor tree by the pool. The butler brings drinks – Negronis, tomato juice, lemonade – and the sun begins to lose some fierceness. Mrs Keppel sits on one of the white iron chairs beside the pool. The city's bells are tolling four when finally Gerald arrives, his hair damp with sweat, his boating jacket swung over his shoulder and large dark patches at the armpits of his shirt.

'Darling Gerald,' Mrs Keppel says, 'we've been waiting for you. You didn't walk up, did you?'

He smiles bashfully at Esmond and Fiamma and then at Mrs Keppel.

'I wanted it to be just like the old days.'

'Every afternoon, all summer long,' Mrs Keppel sings.

'I remember running up that hill as if it wasn't there. *Eheu fugaces labuntur anni*, eh?'

Mrs Keppel gives him a firm embrace, clutching him to her chest. The Colonel comes and seizes his hand.

'Do you the deuce of good to walk. Too many soft young chaps – no disrespect, Esmond – think a taxi's the only way to move. In my day, we'd walk to Bristol to get an appetite for lunch. Now, how's the old man?'

'He's fine, sleeping. He and Gesuina are heading up to Bagni di Lucca tomorrow. A few weeks' rest and he'll be back to his old self.'

Mrs Keppel presses a Negroni into his hand and he drinks it, puts his jacket over the back of one of the chairs and begins to unbutton his shirt.

'I hope you don't mind, Esmond,' he says, shrugging off his shirt and beginning to lower his trousers. 'I have never worn clothes to swim and I don't intend to start now.' He takes off his socks and stands in his undershorts. Mrs Keppel looks at him as she looks at the rest of Florence.

'I remember you swimming here, oh, you must have been thirteen. Length after length, utterly tireless. Mesmerising to watch your skinny body plunging through the water like a mer-prince.' Gerald drops his white undershorts, makes his way to the steps and lunges forward. He arrows beneath the surface, a trail of bubbles fizzing behind him, shooting up from the far end with a roar.

'Oh this *is* the life! Come on, George, come and have a swim. It's bloody exquisite.'

With a slap, Colonel Keppel throws himself into the pool and, thrashing the water, swims in a fierce crawl to where Gerald is stretched out on his back in the leafy light. Esmond looks across at Fiamma, who watches them both with faint amusement.

'We came here all the time as children, Gerald and I. Sometimes we'd swim in the Arno, up past Pontassieve. You think this is hot now, you'll see in the summer. People drop dead in the street. The tarmac bubbles.'

Gerald comes up and begins to splash Fiamma. They swim off together, and Esmond is left looking down over the trees on the terrace below. He paddles to the shallow end, walks up the steps, and pours himself another Negroni. Fiamma and Gerald and Colonel Keppel are having races in the water,

Mrs Keppel watching, laughing and clapping her hands. A few clouds appear over the hills of Fiesole as the sun sinks lower. Church bells toll and, behind them, the tinkle of goat-bells. Esmond watches an aeroplane cut through the sky to the west, extraordinarily high above the mouth of the valley. He downs his drink and looks at the pool. Gerald is balancing Fiamma on his shoulders and turning, both of them shrieking with pleasure, Colonel and Mrs Keppel cheering as they circle. Finally Gerald stumbles, topples, and they disappear with a howling splash under the water.

16

That evening, they step out for dinner as the city's clerks and secretaries are leaving their offices, calling to one another across the via Tornabuoni, heading for their trams, swinging their briefcases and satchels, laughing and talking.

'Norman Douglas is the finest mind I've met,' Gerald says as they walk down the hill from L'Ombrellino, their hair still wet, still humming from the Negronis but changed and scented. 'He's coming to Piccolo's,' he adds, pointing ahead. 'I just wish I'd known him when he was younger. He's nearly seventy, you know. Orioli is bloody good value, too. Pinorman, we call them. Inseparable.'

The sun has dropped below the rooftops and Fiamma has her shawl around her shoulders. Esmond watches her hair flow from shop window to shop window as they pass. Gerald is in his suit, pink handkerchief spilling from his breast pocket. He stands aside to let two *carabinieri* march by, their swords clacking, capes puffed out by the breeze off the river.

They take the swaying tram to the Piazza Costanzo Ciano,

Fiamma wishing the driver a *buona sera* as they descend. Children are noisily playing, someone is listening to a wireless in one of the apartments above, windows and shutters open to the evening.

'It'll be dreadful grub,' Gerald says as they enter the square. 'Douglas grew up in Austria, no idea of good food. Only reason he comes to this place is because the chef was trained in the Vorarlberg.'

'It is worth it for the company,' Fiamma says, and they smile at each other.

They make their way down a narrow alley and into a courtyard where a sign sways gently above an oleander hedge. A sad-faced maître d' greets them at the door, bowing deeply to Fiamma. Despite the heat, he leads them into the stuffy, candlelit room where Douglas and Orioli sit at one end of a long table. Reggie Temple is with them. A waiter hovers over Douglas with a dish in his hand whose contents the old man inspects carefully. He looks up as they enter.

'Ah. All right! Come on, sit down. I'm bartering with this crook over the scampi. Fresh today from Forte dei Marmi. Look like a little boy's tom tiddler, don't they?' He bangs the table and gives a nod of his head. '*Va bene!*' He lights a Toscano cigarillo and grins.

Esmond sits down between Orioli and Reggie. Douglas is embracing Gerald with a cry of 'He's all right, this man!' Fiamma sits at the end of the table and lifts the shawl from her shoulders, bare skin above a green and white polka-dot dress. She looks a little nervous, and very beautiful. Esmond smiles at her, feels a blush.

'I bet you're glad to have young Gerald out here now, eh?' Douglas says, fixing Esmond in a stare. 'Must have been hellish boring in that place with only old Goad for company.'

'Fiamma was there,' says Esmond, looking down the table at her again.

'Ah yes, but not the same as having a man there. You know Pino and I have a walkie-talkie system between our rooms? Sort of speaking funnel at the head of each bed. Means if we wake in the night with some 4 a.m. satori, we can yell it out to the other before it's lost.'

There are two bottles of cheap Soave on the table and Orioli fills all of their glasses to the brim. He never stops smiling, looking first at Douglas, then Gerald, then off into the distance, an expression of constant, wistful benevolence. Reggie has drawn out a little sandalwood box and is showing it to Fiamma, who peers in and pulls a face.

'I design these,' he says, holding the box up to Esmond. Painted inside the lid is the scene of a medieval torture chamber, a young boy stretched out on a rack, the masked torturer attacking his groin with pincers. 'I sell them to tourists.'

'Gosh,' Esmond says, passing it carefully back.

'Oscar Wilde was a dear, dear friend of mine, you know. I had a small but not inconsequential part in *The Ideal Husband*.' Reggie opens one of the buttons of his high-necked serge jacket and looks appealingly at Esmond.

The food arrives. Scampi in breadcrumbs; a *bollito misto* of tongue, beef, capon, sausage; saltimbocca; grey truffles in cheese sauce in sizzling pannikins; wild boar *agrodolce*. The tragic-looking maître d' appears with a pepper pot that he grinds as if he were wringing a man's neck. Douglas's appetite is vast; half-standing and arcing genially across the table, he makes sure to snare the best cuts of meat, the juiciest prawns. He takes long swigs of his wine as he eats, his nose growing redder, and he begins to talk in close whispers to Gerald, who eats little and places his hand on Douglas's every so often.

After a while, a pale man in his thirties comes to the restaurant, frayed and shiny as his suit. He looks around the room and then over at their table with a desperate beam.

'Oh, Christ,' Douglas mutters. 'Eric, dear boy, come and join us, won't you?'

The man takes a seat next to Gerald and nods doubtfully around the table.

'Eric Wolton's an old pal. Back when I had a wife.' He claps his hands together. 'Happiest day of my life, the day my wife died. Did I ever tell you I danced on her grave? A Scottish jig. Don't tell my sons that, if you see them. Do you ever see them, in London?'

When they finish eating, Orioli turns to Esmond and puts his hand on his knee. His breath is sweet and heavy on Esmond's cheek.

'I think we will be very good friends,' he says. 'Norman likes you. I like you. It is so nice to have you and Gerald here. Tell me all about Esmond.'

Esmond stutters, looking across at the round spectacles, the tubby cheeks.

'I went to school at Winchester, then Cambridge, though only for a year and a half—'

'Winchester?' Douglas shouts down the table, breaking off his conversation with Gerald. 'I loathe the public school system. Creates kinds, not characters. Dr Arnold has a lot to answer for. That merciless pruner of the spirit prevented the upper classes, who were barmy, from feeling comfortable in their skins. We have ceased to be mad, the English. None but a flatterer would still call us eccentric.'

'I thought Winchester was ghastly,' Esmond replies, looking straight at Douglas. 'Full of ugly, small-minded teachers, tuppeny tyrants, taking out their disappointments on the sons of

69

equally catastrophic minor aristocrats and merchant bankers and retired colonels.'

'Why d'you still wear a Wykehamist's tie then?'

'So when I hang myself, they'll know why I did it.'

'Hear, hear!' Douglas shouts and the table laughs. 'He's all right!' Douglas lifts his glass as Esmond turns back to Orioli.

'I'm here to help Mr Goad set up a radio station. To finance my father's political party. He's the Chairman of the British Union.'

Orioli raises his eyebrows.

'And you're a Fascist, too?'

'I'm not really sure, these days.'

Orioli removes his hand from Esmond's knee and polishes his spectacles on his napkin. More wine is poured. The restaurant begins to fill with young couples staring at each other over candlelight; a family of grandparents, parents and a boy of six or seven in a sailor costume; an old man reading *La Nazione* with a plate of cannelloni.

'Strindberg!' Douglas shouts and bangs the table. 'That's what I call the maître d'. Because he looks so dashed mournful, worse than Eric over here. Strindberg, bring us the bill.'

When it comes, Douglas holds it under a candle and makes a few marks with his pencil. 'Twelve lire each,' he says. 'I'd love to treat you all, of course, but money is very tight at the minute.'

Wolton, who has neither eaten nor drunk, passes a handful of notes towards them. On the way out, they stop at the table where the young boy in his sailor's suit sits, looking pleased to be out with the adults, listening carefully to something his grandmother is saying. Douglas pulls over a chair to sit beside him and, quite naturally, lifts him onto his knee.

'*Permesso?*' he says, smiling at the boy's father.

'*Si, Professore,*' the man replies.

The little boy looks up at Douglas with wide, delighted eyes.
'*Ma come ti chiami?*'

'*Dante,*' the little boy replies, grinning bashfully.

'*Magnifico! Ma dov'è Beatrice?*' Douglas pretends to look under the table, and now in the little boy's pockets. The boy giggles and simpers up at him.

Reggie Temple leans over and whispers to Esmond with a hiss.

'It's frightful. He's like the Pied Piper. Wherever he goes, the boys just flock to him. One of the reasons he's so short of money.'

'What do you mean?'

'The queue of parents wanting restitution. He holds competitions for the gypsy kids under the arches of the Ponte alle Grazie. Fifty centimes to whoever can gism first. It's not dignified, a man of his age.'

Orioli, who has been listening, elbows Temple in the ribs. 'You're just jealous. It's been a long time since anyone looked your way. And Norman is older than you, is he not?'

Douglas presents the father with his card and rests his hands on Dante's shoulders. The man beams gratefully and insists on introducing his wife and her parents. Reggie tuts and shakes his head while Douglas bows and coos in a Florentine dialect. Finally, the group make their way out and hail taxis on the Piazza.

An hour later, Esmond is sitting on the little balcony of Douglas's top-floor flat on the Lungarno delle Grazie, looking at the villas on the opposite bank of the Arno, the outline of cypress trees like feathers in the caps of the hills. He is smoking, tapping his ash onto the awning of the Davis & Orioli bookshop two floors below. Douglas comes out of the drawing room, where Schubert is playing on the gramophone.

'*Ma la notte sperde le lontananze,*' he says, sitting down beside Esmond and lighting a Toscano. 'Night dispels distances. Ungaretti. Will you be with us in Florence for some time?'

'It depends, I suppose, on how long it takes to set up the radio station. A year or two, perhaps more if it's a success.'

'How terribly dull for you. I can't stay in one place for more than a few months. I am bored stiff with Florence. I should like to get further away, out of Europe, but money is very tight just now. You wouldn't like to buy one of my books, by any chance?'

He reaches into the breast pocket of his jacket and pulls out a slim volume with a mottled gold-brown cover.

'*Paneros,*' he says. 'Aphrodisiacs. The search for an elixir of youth and of sex. It's about death, too. Because without death there would be no sex, d'you see?'

'I think so.' A gibbous moon is rising over the hills, reflected in the fast waters of the Arno.

'Thirty-five lire usually, but twenty to you.'

Esmond opens his wallet and counts out the notes.

'Jolly good,' Douglas says, handing him the book. 'Gerald tells me you're a writer yourself.'

'Actually, I'm trying to use this time to work out if I'm any good.'

'I didn't write a novel until I was forty-two. Would have been no point, I hadn't lived enough. Before that I was all biology, geography, a paper on the pumice stone industry.'

Esmond smiles.

'Oh, yes. Helped to gaol a gang of child labour racketeers, that one. It was read aloud at the trials in Messina. But fiction? No, you need money in the bank for fiction.'

He turns his head, which seems to Esmond like a statue in the moonlight: hewn and marmoreal.

'Forsake books,' he says. 'Go out among people and nature and think it through for yourself. Keep a diary, if only dates and places. But more than anything, don't scatter the gold of your youth. Don't lose your life in books. Get out and live. Michael

Arlen said of me – or was it Ronald Firbank? One of them said I was the least literary writer they'd ever met. That I might as well have been a lumberjack.'

Esmond smiles again. 'I used to write with a friend of mine, the one in Austria. I find it very hard to know if anything I write's any good without showing it to him. He gave me the necessary confidence.'

He pictures Philip in his digs in Park Terrace, chopping ben-zedrine tablets into the wine on the desk. The electric moment when he handed over the notebook, and Philip sprawled on the bed, whistling and smiling, his Cambridge-blue eyes galloping over the pages as he read.

'I never show my work to anyone,' Douglas says. 'Writing's like shitting. If someone's cheering you on, it's hard to get going, but give it time and space and it'll come. And by the way, if you don't eat well, you won't shit well.' He pauses. 'Did you love this chap?'

Esmond turns to look out over the river. It is past eleven. A gentle breeze is blowing, stirring the hillside and making tight waves on the surface of the water.

'I still do, I suppose,' he says.

'And where is he now?' Douglas's voice is suddenly very soft, very kind, like the breeze.

'He went back to Austria. I think his parents were trying to emigrate to America. I haven't heard from him for a little while.'

'Ah, a Jew? Rotten business this. Shames a once-great nation. Hitlerism has its roots in the Old Testament, of course. All that pure race nonsense in Ezra and Nehemiah. Germans are dread-ful Bible readers. Don't give up on him, though. It's good to be in love while you're writing. Each of my books ripened under the rays of some attachment or other. Unless I am in love I have no impulse to write.'

They are silent for a while, smoking and watching the river.

73

Then Douglas sits forward slowly and puts an arm around Esmond's shoulders.

'Are you sure you're not throwing your lot in with the wrong side?'

'The station? It's for my father, for his Party.'

'Must you?'

'What's the alternative? Communism? I'd rather Mussolini than Stalin.'

'Break free from what you were born into, Esmond. This isn't you, the politics. Embrace your freedom, embrace the flesh. You should go to Goa. Astonishing place. Why don't you sail to Goa and write a life of St Francis Xavier? Dee-lish curries. Find yourself an ebony youngling and write in a little timber-framed hut under palm trees. Don't let your family write the script of your life.'

They sit for a while longer, then go in to join the party. A bottle of Punt e Mes is passed around. Reggie Temple is asleep on the sofa, Pino talking in Italian to Fiamma and Gerald. Wolton sits on his own, hands on knees. Douglas looks down at him and lets out a snort.

'Why do you insist on coming here, Eric? For God's sake can't you see you're wasting space.'

Wolton's grey skin colours momentarily but he stares at his hands.

'Because I love you,' he says, so softly that he has to repeat it. 'I love you, Norman.'

'So you come running after me as if I were a ballet girl? Not on your life! Clear out!' Douglas picks up his stick and raps it hard against the floor. 'You were worth talking to twenty years ago. But now? I simply don't want to see you. Clear out!'

Wolton staggers to his feet. Reggie Temple has woken up and looks out blearily. Wolton moves for the door.

'Norman, I—'

'Clear out!'

Ten minutes later, Esmond and the others leave too, Reggie Temple walking with them as far as the Ponte Santa Trinità. 'Such a sad figure, the Wolton feller,' he says, as they make their way along the deserted Lungarno. 'Norman's frightful to him, but I can't blame him. Shows up here after so many years.'

'What's his story?'

'He was one of Norman's boys. Norman's wife caught them buggering in the marital bed some twenty years ago. But he was old for Norman even then. He has a theory, you see, that boys after puberty suffer a loss of body heat. That he ought to sodomise only the very young in order to keep himself youthful.' He lets out a low chuckle. 'It's all in that book of his, *Paneros*. Quite barmy.'

'And now Eric's back.'

'Yes, after a failed marriage and some kind of collapse, he seemed to think Norman would find him irresistible. Really it is *too* sad.'

They leave him at the bridge and walk up to the Institute. It is dark and silent inside. They say good night, each of them a little drunk, a little sombre, and fall asleep, the bats riding the cool air outside their windows.

17

Esmond realises he has been putting off seeing Carità, disgusted and, he admits to himself, scared by what the little man did to Goad. He would rather face his father and Mosley at once than a brute like Carità. But there is no word from England, nothing from Goad, and so he keeps his head down, waiting, thumbing through *The Wireless Operator's Handbook* whenever he feels particularly guilt-stricken.

One morning, a Saturday, Fiamma comes into Esmond's room early. She sits at the end of the bed in the darkness. He sees that she's crying as he pulls himself awake.

'What is it?'

'They've killed Carlo and Nello in Paris. Oh, Esmond—' She reaches over to take him in her arms and begins to sob. After a while he regretfully disentangles himself, stands to open the window, and looks back to see her slumped on the bed with her fingers in her hair. It is another hot day; the room is close, the breeze warm and dusty from the street. He sits beside her in his nightshirt and places an arm around her, whispering softly.

'Who were they? Died how?'

'Friends of my father. They founded *Giustizia e Libertà*. Heroes—' She unravels into tears. Esmond finds a handkerchief in a drawer and offers it to her, but she pushes it away, drawing her arm across her face. He picks up her hand and clasps it between his own.

'Who killed them?'

'Fascists,' she spits at him. She begins to speak very swiftly. 'They are taking everything from me,' she says. 'First my father, then the house I grew up in. My friends, who are either running off to join them, or in gaol because they won't. They took dear, gentle Goad. Now Carlo and Nello.' She bangs her hand down on the bed and turns to him. 'I never understood what it meant, totalitarianism. You have this word in English, too?' He nods uncertainly. 'They are intruding into every aspect of my life, taking over all the things that are dear to me just as they took over Libya and Abyssinia. I hate them, Esmond.'

Gerald comes into the room. Fiamma looks up at him damply.

'Where were you?' she says. 'I came looking for you this morning but you weren't in bed.'

He kneels down beside her.

'I'm so bloody sorry. I saw it on the front page of the *Nazione*. It was the Cagoule, of course, the French Fascists. On Musso's orders. Bastards.'

She wipes her face again with a slippery arm.

'Listen,' he says, with a doggish grin, 'I've something to cheer you up. Get dressed and meet me in the courtyard. Come on, Fiamma. There you go.'

Esmond pulls on shorts and an Aertex shirt, brushes his teeth and knocks on Fiamma's door. They make their way down the stone steps to the courtyard as darkness lifts off the city. Gerald is standing in the cloister opposite the entrance to Cook's, a large canvas bag at his feet. Behind him, leaning on their stands, are three bicycles. One is a racer – a Romeo – the other two are Peugeot tourers. Gerald stands back with a flourish.

'Thought we could use them to get out of town, find a cool spot along the river. I saw them in the barn at L'Ombrellino and knew George wouldn't miss them. Couple of the gardeners helped me wheel them down this morning. D'you want the racer, Esmond?'

Esmond holds its lean, crouched frame, grey with red livery. He pats the leather seat.

'It's super,' he says.

The three of them set off wobblingly towards the river. Fiamma is still crying quietly, hiccoughs escaping as she pedals. It is before nine, but already the sun is powerful overhead, searing as they gather pace along the Lungarno. At the Ponte Vecchio they pass tinkers with fly-bothered mules, beggars in the shadows, fishermen pushing ice-filled trolleys of their catch towards the Mercato Nuovo. The rich have left for their out-of-town villas or the Alps, the poor sit indoors with their fans, their windows open, their feet in tubs of ice-water. A group of Fascist Youth walk along the river in a bedraggled crocodile behind a little man in a heavy black shirt. He is sweating so much he barely sees the bicycles coming and has to leap, cursing. The boys behind him laugh.

'My uncle,' Fiamma shouts over her shoulder. 'He is in charge of the *Sabato Fascista* today. Poor boys—'

On the towpath of the river the air is cooler, the wind fresh from the Apennine peaks, finding its way into the folds of their clothing, the nooks of their bodies. Esmond races ahead, pumping his legs, head down, lets out a joyful shout that's muffled by the wind. Gerald rides with no hands, arms held up, cupping the breeze. They stop for a drink of water before crossing the river at the ford at San Jacopo al Girone, poppies in the wheat field behind them.

Fiamma, wheat-dust blanching her lips, walks waist-high to the fragile flowers and picks a handful. She puts them into the basket of her bicycle and, halfway across the stony rise of the ford, she drops them into the water.

'For Carlo and Nello,' she says.

Along the south bank of the river, through more wheat and corn and maize, then steeper ground, vineyards stretching up into the low reaches of the hills. They join the road, through small villages – Candelli, Santa Monica, Vallina – where old men sit on the stoops of their houses watching them pass, their eyes crinkled from contemplating the long moment of their lives. Under every roadside tree stands a mule, swatting its tail placidly against the flies. In the fields heavy cattle swing their heads like slow church bells. They buy apricots from a stall where a young woman with a baby on her hip chews a stalk of grass beneath her hat and addresses them in Florentine dialect so thick that even Fiamma can't understand her.

Finally, they turn off the road and down a track to the river. They come to an abandoned watermill with a crenellated roof like a castle. Martins have nested in its walls, opening large clefts. The whole building looks about to crumble down the bank into the Arno.

'The Gualchiere di Remole,' Gerald says. 'This would have turned wool into cloth. Hugely important to Florence in the Middle Ages. The *Comune* is always promising to turn it into a museum but, I mean, look at it.'

Past the mill, they cycle carefully along an overgrown path to the river. Brambles tear at Esmond's legs as he follows. He stops to help Fiamma unhook her dress from a thorn that snags it and sees the white and red scratches the brambles have raised on her legs. They come out on fine yellow sand beneath the lip of the bank. Upstream of the mill, the river is pocked with small islands and the Arno is wide and clear. They lay their bicycles down in the grass.

Gerald unpacks the canvas bag: a thermos of Soave, two bottles of red, some bread and salami. He takes a knife and cuts the salami as Esmond and Fiamma paddle, looking across the river to where *contadini* labour in the fields, their backs pomegranate brown. The river is hard and sandy on their feet and slopes towards the middle where fish flicker like shadows.

'Lunch is served, you two. Come and get it.'

An hour later they lie lazily fuddled on the sand. The thermos is empty, and they have started on the red. Esmond is aware that he is sunburning, his head beginning to throb in the heat, but he can barely lift his arm to cover it. Gerald has taken off his top and is using it for a pillow, lifting himself up on his elbow to take a gulp of wine every so often. Fiamma is sleeping, twitching, sometimes turning. Only the electric thrum of cicadas stirs the air, the bray of a mule or the shouts of *contadini*.

'We should swim or we'll boil here,' Gerald says. As he stands, Esmond can see sweat in the tufts of dark hair beneath his arms, across his chest. He walks down to the water. Fiamma has woken and stretches, frowning. Gerald drops his shorts and underpants, leaving them in a coil on the bank, and plunges into the water. He comes up in the centre of the river, blowing gouts of water out of his mouth and laughing.

'You should come in! It's marvellous.'

Esmond looks over at Fiamma. She stares, unfocused, a hectic flush to her cheeks.

'It *is* hot,' he says.

'Go on, then.'

He walks down to the edge of the water. His shirt is sticking to his back. He lifts it off with difficulty, takes down his shorts and then, suddenly delighted to think of his body immersed in the cool water, strips naked and leaps forward into the river. He swims towards Gerald who is floating, spreadeagled. He dives and opens his eyes: it is clear and green and as he goes deeper, icy. Sunlight arrows down and he can make out Gerald floating above, the smooth curve of his back, his hair flaming out, his arms and legs paddling him gently afloat. He comes up beside him, laughing.

'There's nothing like it, is there?' Gerald says. 'Come on, Fiamma! Come and cool down.'

She takes a final swig of wine, stands and shakes her head, then steps down to the river's edge. She unpins her hair and it tumbles down to her shoulders. She lifts the skirt of her dress up over her head and stands for a moment in her bra and smalls.

'Nello', she says, 'used to take me swimming. When I was still a little girl.' Esmond and Gerald watch her and she meets their gaze. She steps in, the whiteness of her underclothes striking against the darkness of her arms and legs. She swims towards them.

They are careful of each other at first. Esmond looks down at his body, caressed by the same water, swimming in the wake of skin scurf and sweat that links them. He and Gerald dive underwater. They all know these submarine plunges are intended to catch better glimpses of each other, the arrangement of limbs. Gerald's nakedness, which had come to seem natural by the swimming pool at L'Ombrellino, is changed by the fact that he, Esmond, is naked himself. He thinks his friend looks like a Greek sea god, Proteus or Glaucus, and Fiamma a nereid.

They swim downstream to one of the islands that prods up from the river near the mill. Gerald is the first to pull himself out onto the sand. Esmond does his best to leave the water gracefully and sits down, the sand warm and soft beneath him. Then Fiamma joins them, elbowing herself a place between them. At the touch of her skin, Esmond feels a warm jolt of longing in his groin and has to turn over and lie on his front. The water evaporates from their bodies as the sun moves across the sky.

'It must be nearly four,' Esmond says.

'I'm going to swim to the other bank,' says Gerald. 'See what's over there.'

Esmond watches Fiamma through half-closed eyes and the strong sound of Gerald's strokes. There is a slight reddening under her brassiere, on the tops of her thighs where she has allowed the sun to catch her. He realises she is looking back at him, that she can tell he is watching her. He reaches up and moves his finger over her lips; she smiles at the contact and then bites him.

'Turn over,' she says.

He opens his eyes. 'No.'

'Turn over, Esmond. I've had a terrible day.'

81

He lifts his head and sees that Gerald is much further upstream, bobbing in the silver reflection of the sun. He turns. He and Fiamma stare downwards. She smiles, not taking her eyes from his gently pulsing cock. Carefully, she lays a soft hand on it, closes her fingers and leans over to kiss him. Her lips have the warm tackiness of a child's. She draws back and then bows to place a kiss at the place where his cock emerges from her clenched fist. She leaves her lips there. A long slice of time. He hears voices, splashing. Fiamma raises her head and they look upstream.

Gerald is swimming towards them. On the bank, running and waddling, red-faced and bellowing, holding what look like branches, comes a group of seven or eight *contadini*.

'Swim for the shore, you two,' Gerald shouts. 'Quickly!'

Esmond helps Fiamma to her feet and they move swiftly into the river and towards the beach. Gerald is already there, pulling on his clothes and filling the canvas bag with their picnic. Esmond takes great handfuls of water and is on the bank, his cock still half-hard. He turns to see Fiamma ten metres from shore. In the other direction, the red-faced *contadini* are almost upon them, shouting and cursing.

'Get on your bike,' says Gerald, 'I've got your clothes.'

Fiamma is staggering up the beach and Gerald puts the bike in her hands. The *contadini* stop for a moment, nonplussed to have landed their quarry so easily. Esmond realises they are not holding branches but nettles, grasped at the stem. The leader, a squat, paunchy fellow of fifty or so, steps towards them.

'*Deliquenti! Furfanti!*' he shouts, and whips one of the nettles across Esmond's back.

Another steps towards Fiamma and slashes at her thighs as she tries to mount her bike. '*Putana!*' he cries. Esmond makes to get down from his bicycle.

'No, Esmond. Just go!' Gerald is already heading up the path towards the mill.

'You first,' Esmond shouts to Fiamma, and she pedals furiously up the rocky slope, brambles scything at her legs.

Esmond is last, nettle-whips raining on his back until he crests the hill to the mill's forecourt. They pick up speed and pull away. Only when they are back on the main road, cycling past the woman selling peaches at her stall, does Esmond realise he is still naked, Fiamma in her damp and muddy underwear. He looks ahead to see the muscles of her thighs working, the jounce of her breasts as she pedals, and he cycles up beside her with a long whoop of pleasure. Soon Fiamma is laughing too and they race along the road, the wind and warm sun bathing them, Fiamma's hair streaming behind her like steam.

18

Back at the Institute, they sit out on the loggia as the sky fades around them.

'Vodka and the last of Gesuina's lemonade, doctor's orders,' Gerald says, and they sip, stretching their tingling limbs, Gerald swirling his drink and looking out over the rooftops.

'It's easy to forget how conservative they are, the *contadini*. They couldn't care less about a revolutionary government. It's why the aristocrats are still so popular.'

'Hasn't Mussolini banned indentured labour?' Esmond asks, reaching to touch his shoulders with his glass.

Gerald considers his drink. 'The spirit lingers.'

'I thought they were going to kill us,' Fiamma says.

'Did one of them have a pitchfork?' Esmond laughs. 'Or did I imagine it?'

Gerald stands up. 'I need a piss.'

Esmond and Fiamma are left on the terrace. She leans and looks at the sky.

'I keep thinking about them,' she says.

'The *contadini*?'

'Carlo and Nello. They were stabbed to death, you know.' She's silent for a while. 'How hard they must have fought. I keep trying to imagine how their faces looked.' She looks at him. 'Promise me one thing, Esmond.'

'Anything,' he says.

'Promise me that you're not one of them, not one of the *bastardi* who did this to my friends.'

'Of course I'm not.'

'You know what I mean.'

He pauses for a moment and then takes her hand. 'I do know, of course. I grew up with it, you understand.'

'That's not enough. It's not right, or decent. It's not you.'

Gerald comes back and they sit under the swooping bats and the stars until San Gaetano strikes twelve and, drunk, they stumble towards bed. Outside her room, Fiamma pauses.

'I'm never going to sleep in this heat. Will someone rub some Pond's Cream on my shoulders? I feel like I'm on fire.'

'Yes,' say Esmond and Gerald at the same time, stepping forward and following her into her room. Esmond remembers seeing her at her dressing table, the way her hair fell down her back, the reflection of her breasts in the mirror. Then he thinks of her body earlier on the sand, her lips. She has turned on the bedside lamp and her skin looks extraordinarily dark in the light.

'Do this, will you?' she says to Gerald, turning so he can unzip her dress at the back. Esmond watches her slip out of the straps and pull it down to her waist. She sits at the table of her dresser and he wonders if she's deliberately recreating that initial glimpse, the *scorcio* he'd caught through the door three months ago. She unhooks the clasp of her brassiere, crossing her arms over her chest and smiling coyly over her shoulder.

'Now, Gerald.' She reaches back and hands him the cream then leans forward, her hands on the dresser. Esmond can see the heavy curve of her breasts in the mirror, dark circled nipples, the beginning of a grin on her face as Gerald rubs the cream into her neck and her back. She lets out a long sigh, which begins as a shiver, and ends in a definite moan.

After a few minutes, she raises her head, stands up and turns around. Her eyes are bright, her hair falling in sweat-damp tails to her shoulders. She looks like a goddess, with her burnished skin and bare breasts, a dark Venus.

'I think Esmond is the most sunburnt,' she says, looking over at him.

Gerald grins. 'I agree. Kit off, Lowndes. Come and lie on the bed.'

Stumbling, laughing, Esmond takes his shirt and trousers off. He lies down on the bedspread in his briefs, his face pressed into Fiamma's pillow, smelling her scent and hair. The first of the cream is almost painfully cold against his skin. But then the hands, indistinguishable and swift across his body, begin to smooth and caress and he closes his eyes and gives himself over to the pleasure.

When he opens them again, he realises he has been asleep. The lamp is extinguished and there is only the low light of the moon from the door to the corridor. His briefs have been removed and his cock stirs gently between his legs. He is lying against the wall and beside him on the bed, Gerald is naked on his back, Fiamma pressing cream along him. Gerald groans every so often. Esmond lies there, hardly breathing, eyes half-closed, watching. Fiamma sucks in her lower lip, pausing when her hands reach the centre of Gerald's body. Esmond realises she has taken the dress off completely and shifts to get a better look. She stops, Gerald turns, Esmond smiles foolishly.

'I fell asleep,' he says, but Gerald pushes a finger to his lips and then reaches across to kiss him. Fiamma clambers over to lie on top of the two boys and Esmond feels her fingers close around his cock again. She slides downwards, guiding him into the damp warmth of her and then it is just flesh and sweat and spit, the warm breach of a mouth, the slippery press of a tongue, hot breath panting, laughing, groaning. They melt into the sweating night and into each other. By dawn, they are nothing but husks of bodies on the bed, burnished with sweat, sheets torn to the floor. A jug of water lies shattered on the tiles, its contents soaking into the sheets. Fiamma sleeps with her mouth open, her head on Gerald's chest, one arm around Esmond. Their limbs have been shuffled, redistributed; they might be one spiritless creature. The bells of San Gaetano chime for matins, but they sleep on in sluggard happiness.

19

'Come on Esmond, up we get.' Gerald has opened the blinds and sunlight streaks into the room. Fiamma rubs her eyes and stares down at the wreckage on the floor. Esmond stretches, looks over at Gerald, who is dressed and carrying a mug of coffee.

'Leave us alone,' he says, trying to pull the pillow over his head.

'Not a chance. You and I are going to church. Bailey was a real brick to the old man while he was in hospital and we haven't so much as glanced at him since. You've got twenty minutes to get vertical.'

Esmond bathes in cold water, his head pounding, mouth dry. He sinks down beneath the surface for a moment and blows bubbles out of his nose. He dresses quickly, hands shaking as he knots his tie. He looks into Fiamma's room, whispers goodbye to her sleeping body and then walks down to meet Gerald in the courtyard.

The church is emptier than the last time, despite the worshippers from Holy Trinity. As he steps through the wicket gate and down the aisle, Esmond discovers in himself an affection for the gloomy place, for its tortured paintings. Gerald bows deeply before the altar, crossing himself, and then takes a seat near the front, Esmond beside him.

'Love the decor,' Gerald says, nodding towards the triptych. 'Fucking terrifying. Just what you need in church.'

Esmond smiles. He makes a rough calculation: their combined age, he thinks, still less than half that of anyone else in the congregation. Bailey beams when he sees them, and Esmond senses a verve and bluster to the sermon, a twinkle as they go up to take communion.

During the slow, prayerful parts of the service, Esmond feels Gerald breathing beside him and, looking at the slim-fitting suit on his thigh, remembers his head in Esmond's lap, grinning wolfishly; Fiamma perched above them, her legs apart showing slick darkness, swaying; he remembers how, at one point, the two of them had pinned him down, taken turns to have him inside them, Gerald letting a silver string of spit down onto the tip of his cock beforehand. He feels a hot rush to his face as he realises he must stand for the Peace and carefully adjusts himself through the fabric of his pocket. Gerald looks at him and grins.

After the service, they wait for Bailey while he and Reggie Turner clear up. Gerald stands looking at the triptych, a warm detachment on his face. Esmond lounges in the pew, longing for his bed, wondering what it will be like to see Fiamma again. Now Bailey bounces down towards them from the sacristy, rubbing his hands. Esmond had forgotten how big he was, how his body seemed out of place in the small, dark church.

'How've you chaps been? Any word from your father, Gerald?'

They walk out and into the entrance hall with its faded notices and plaques.

'I telephoned him on Friday. He says he's better, although he sounded awfully tired. Gesuina tells Fiamma that the doctors are still in a dither. I'm going to catch the bus up there next week, see for myself.'

'Why don't you let me drive you? Always good to give the Alfa a run. Hold on a minute, Esmond.' Bailey takes him by the elbow. He can smell the priest's cologne, feel the strength in the fingers that close around him. 'There's something I wanted to show you,' he says, guiding him up the stairs. 'You come too, Gerald. It'll give you something to tell your father, buck him up.'

They make their way up the stone steps and then along the corridor to the room overlooking the Piazza Santo Spirito. Esmond pauses for a moment, allowing Bailey and Gerald to pass in front of him. He thinks of the airless feel of Aston Magna, the ancient dust of his prep school at West Down.

'*Ecco là,*' Bailey says, opening the door to the studio.

Esmond steps into the room and lets out a gasp. The studio is no longer empty. A walnut desk, a pair of microphones. A silver cross-hatch BBC standard, a direct-to-disc recorder. An RCA sound-mixing desk and reel-to-reel electromagnetic tape machine sit on a chest of drawers. Against the far wall, hiding the mould patches Esmond had noticed before, stands a large cupboard with what looks like a transmitter. There are wires spewing out from the front, a series of parts, screwdrivers, spanners and a hammer on the mantelpiece.

'What do you think?' Bailey asks, smiling broadly at him.

'This is amazing, bloody brilliant. How did you manage—'

'Not my doing at all. Ada's the miracle worker. She rounded up some engineer friends at the university. They did this for next to nothing. It's her you should thank.'

Esmond runs his hand along the desk, looks at the reels on the tape machine, lifts the needle on the recorder, blows dust from the disc.

'How fabulous.' And then, grinning as it dawns on him, 'We never have to see Carità again.'

'Exactly.'

'I must— Do you know where Ada lives?'

'The Liuzzis are over in Le Cure. I'll have the address downstairs.'

'I'll go and see her now. This is just— It's perfect.'

He leaves Gerald at the Institute and makes his way alone along the via dei Cerretani, past the Duomo and up towards Le Cure. As he strolls through the warm afternoon, he realises how much Carità had been casting his angry shadow over things. He feels a swell of gratitude for Ada.

The Liuzzi apartment is at the top of a glum, grey house overlooking the gardens of the Villa Ventaglio. A tall man stoops to the door. He carries a book in one hand and looks at Esmond over half-moon glasses.

'*Si, posso aiutarvi?*' he says.

'*Buongiorno,*' says Esmond. 'I'm here to see Ada. I'm Esmond Lowndes.'

'Come, please,' the man says, opening the door. 'I will call her. I have heard a great deal about you. About Radio Firenze. Ada! *Vieni qui!*'

There is the sound of hurried footsteps and Ada appears. She is wearing the same peasant's linen tunic, her red hair reminds him again of Mary Magdalene in the triptych. She runs a hand through it, pulling strands behind her ears, and looks suddenly bashful, a flush flooding her cheeks. He notices the small, fragile mole below her left eye. Her father clears his throat.

'I wanted to say—' he says, 'I am sorry about Mr Goad. But you British must understand. This is not your city. We will not be another pink-shaded nation. Excuse me, I must get back to work. Ring the bell for Lydia if you need anything.' Ada leads Esmond into a gloomy, book-cluttered drawing room. Copies of *La Nostra Bandiera*, the newspaper her father publishes, are stacked by the French windows, cuttings spread out on the coffee table, on the floor. Ada sits down primly, hands on her knees. Esmond goes to the window and looks out over the trees of the park in front of the house.

'Listen, what you did at St Mark's—'

'No,' she interrupts him. 'Let me speak first.' She looks at him nervously again. 'It was my fault,' she says. 'What happened to Signor Goad.'

Her voice drops to a whisper. 'I told my father that I had been invited to the drinks party at the Institute. I was going to celebrate the coronation with you. He was very angry. He doesn't approve of the British Institute. Hates the British. I'm so sorry, I should have thought—'

'He wasn't one of them, your father?'

'No, he didn't go, but I know he telephoned Niccolò Arcimboldi. He does everything he can to please. It isn't as easy for him here as it was in Turin. There is more resistance, you know? To a Jewish Fascist. I should have seen this. Signor Goad, is he very bad?'

She turns, biting her thin upper lip. He thinks about putting

90

his arms around her but sits beside her on the divan with a hand in the small of her back.

'Don't worry,' he says. 'Goad will be fine. You couldn't have known this would happen. And what you've done at the church, it's amazing. We won't need to see Carità again.'

She smiles. 'I have some very capable friends. They saw it as a challenge. I was mostly standing around passing tools.'

'You must tell me how much I owe you.'

'It was really nothing. We salvaged most of it from the university. Parts no one was using. What I did spend, counts as penance for what happened to Mr Goad. We have another few days' work before it's ready—'

'You're too kind. We'll be able to start as soon as Goad returns from hospital. I do hope you'll be involved. I mean, not just translating, but in the whole project.'

'I'd like to,' she says. They sit quietly for a few moments, then he rises, kisses her cheeks and walks out into the hallway. As he makes his way to the front door, she stands looking after him. In the shadows of the corridor behind her he makes out her father, watching him over her shoulder.

That evening, after dinner on the loggia, Gerald and Fiamma and Esmond drink a bottle of wine, a few glasses of grappa. Without speaking much, they bathe together in the large, cool bathroom, splashing about like children and taking turns to soap each other. Esmond had been expecting awkwardness between them, a sense of shame. Instead they fall into bed again like they fall into the water. He feels, with them, rather like the triptych: an obscure work newly attributed to a master. When he finally sleeps, he sleeps with a hollow sound to his gentle snores, utterly quenched, content, dreaming of Gerald and Fiamma.

They arrange to meet Pino and Norman at Piccolo's again and, as they make their way into the restaurant, Esmond wonders if their secret is visible on their faces. If Douglas or Orioli will be able to scent out the change in atmosphere that feels, to him, as if it is banked up in the room around them, a wave about to break. Certainly there had been a coldness in Mrs Keppel's attitude that afternoon, although the Colonel was delighted when, rather than just Gerald, all three had decided to peel off their clothes and plunge naked into the pool at L'Ombrellino.

They stop going to the galleries in the mornings, choosing instead to lie in bed and recover from the drinking and carousing with Douglas and Orioli; further drinks and dancing with their younger friends at Doney's or the Circolo Unione in the Palazzo Corsi; then the frantic grasping and thrusting and sucking and biting that, sustained perhaps by the triangulation of their urges, the seemingly limitless possibilities provided by three young bodies equally desired, equally possessed, keep them lost in the hot heaven of Fiamma's room until the roosters crow over by the Cascine and the swallows start cheeping outside the window.

Gerald goes up to Bagni di Lucca to visit Goad and comes back grim-faced and quiet. Gesuina, he says, pushes his father up and down the streets of the town, from the sanatorium to the baths, from the baths to the sulphur springs, walking the steep streets tirelessly so that Goad might get the freshest, cleanest air. But the old man is still skeletal, eyes shadowed, breath quick and ragged. The doctors have found nothing more than 'nerves', a word they repeat in various tones of exasperation and wonder, in a range of evasive accents, shaking their heads.

Esmond continues his novel. *Hulme at war. Heroism. Boredom.* He has heard his father speak so many times about the deep-throated booming of the guns, the burst of star-shells, trench-foot, trench-mouth, sorties that might as well have been suicides. But he can't make it come alive. The letters on the page are like bones in a vault, dusty and lifeless. He fills his notebooks, buys more, revises and rewrites, imagining all the time his father reading over his shoulder, tutting and shaking his head and muttering. 'No. It wasn't like that. It wasn't like that at all.'

One evening towards the end of August, they are dining with Douglas and Orioli again at Piccolo's. Both of the Reggies are there, and a new face, offered by Douglas with a sweep of his arm.

'Prince Heinrich,' he says of the tall, dashing young man in a suit of blue serge. Esmond shakes his hand. The Prince, fortyish, speaks perfect English, but seems reserved, otherworldly, sitting back and watching as they bellow at each other over the table. Douglas is on coruscating form, bristling when Esmond, who has been reading *Paneros*, suggests it reminds him of Wilde.

'Can't stand the man. Wrong type of sod. I know the Reggies here fight a posthumous battle over who has the misfortune of being the poor bugger's widow, but he was nothing but words, words and old maid's ways.'

Esmond learns that Prince Heinrich is the son of the Crown Prince of Bavaria, exiled by Hitler for not agreeing to support a south German military alliance between Bavaria and Austria.

After dinner, Douglas puts his arm around Esmond and guides him away from the others.

'You're enjoying *Paneros*, then?'

'I've almost finished it. And yes, very much.'

'Good. It's really, if you like, a hymn to the sexual act. What ecstasy, of all of them, is more fervid than that of young lovers locked in lush embraces? I wanted to put that on the page, to make you feel it as you read it. I can't read that book without a stiffy, all right!'

Orioli had looked a little jaded during dinner, eating and drinking less than usual. He'd asked Strindberg for a mineral water and drunk it, burping loudly and proffering swift, embarrassed apologies. He trots to catch up with them.

'I'm not so much tonight. It's my *fegato*, my bad liver. I need to go on a diet. Maybe I should go home.'

Douglas gives him a swipe on the buttocks with his walking cane.

'No slacking. We're going to join these young ones at their nightclubs. I want to see what they do after leaving us. They've been secretive recently. We ought to know what we're missing.'

They make their way towards the orange dome of the cathedral. Beside the main steps of the Duomo, where indifferent hawkers hold out black-market cigarettes and saucy postcards, Douglas gives a little bark.

'Let's go in,' he says. 'I want to look at Sir John.'

The Prince and Colonel Keppel wait outside with the Reggies as the three friends follow Douglas and Orioli into the cathedral. It is very dark inside, barely any light through the stained glass from the streetlamps in the square.

'Bugger,' Gerald whispers, stubbing his toe on an unseen step. They walk down a side-aisle until they come to a small chapel. Douglas speaks, his voice terribly loud in the echoing church.

'You see there?' he says, lighting a match and holding it to one of the prayer candles. 'Let's fire up some of these, get a better look.'

As Douglas and Orioli light the candles to the side of the chapel, the fresco on the wall is illuminated. It is the painting in *terra verde*, the colour of the patina on bronze. A cruel-looking man on a horse atop a triumphant plinth.

'Sir John Hawkwood,' Douglas booms. 'By Uccello. This is my favourite Florentine Englishman. Better than the soft-souls who live here now. A *condottiero*, a mercenary, in the twelfth century. They couldn't pronounce his name, so they called him Giovanni Accuto. Fought mainly against Florence, actually, but chose to settle and die here. Bloody tough. Would have taught these Italians a thing or two about war. They could do with him in Spain, in Abyssinia. Bloody wet, the Italians.'

Esmond hears someone clear their throat, the sound of rustling papers. He looks around and, with a start, realises that the nave of the cathedral contains some dozen people, dressed in black. A priest comes hurrying towards them.

'Signori,' he says, 'I really must insist—'

Esmond starts to apologise, but Douglas lifts his chin belligerently to the priest.

'Lining your pockets with pelf from these sentimental fools. Irrational dunces praying for magic and redemption and hope. God, how I hate the clergy.' He turns towards the congregation, mainly frightened-looking old women, and booms. 'It's all claptrap! Don't you see it? Making you feel corrupt for the few real pleasures of your miserable lives. Go out and live, don't waste your final days in here!' By this time Gerald is hurrying him towards the door and Esmond, mumbled apology, places a five lire note in the collection plate.

In Doney's, Douglas is loud and quarrelsome, ordering bottle after bottle of cheap Chianti and banging his fist on the table with every detail. He smokes incessantly, his large pale face moving behind the smoke like a moon behind clouds. Prince Heinrich, previously vaguely amused by Douglas, now looks on with a kind of fascinated horror.

'I switched from girls to boys,' Douglas says, a group of elderly English spinsters at the table next door nodding to one another, 'in Naples in '97. I was bartering with some street girl's mother. A gypsy girl, up near Scampia.' He inclines his head to Prince Heinrich. 'Have you ever undressed a gypsy? They're always perfectly clean.' He turns back to the table, making sure the old ladies can hear him. 'So, I was bargaining with this woman over her daughter when the girl's brother turned up and gave me the most tremendous clout with a cosh. When I woke, he was covering my face with kisses and tears and I quite forgot about the girl. Disappeared with the boy for a fortnight.'

There is a bustle at the back of the room and Esmond can see Fiamma's uncle Niccolò with a group of other Blackshirts at the bar, arguing with the bartender. With a lurch, he sees that Carità is amongst them. 'We should go,' he says quietly.

A younger Blackshirt, whom Esmond hasn't seen before, walks slowly to their table. He leans over carefully and picks up Douglas's glass.

'You drink too much,' he says, draining the wine himself and placing it back on the table. '*Basta così.*'

'Damn fool!' Douglas yells, his face softened and inflamed. The other Blackshirts gather behind their crony. Esmond sees a look of cold rage on Niccolò Arcimboldi's face, a smirk on Carità's, as Douglas begins to shout. 'Look at you, stuffed up and delighted with yourselves, playing at soldiers. Italians make rotten soldiers, d'you know that? Halfway into an attack and they're writing to their mothers.'

The young Blackshirt pauses for a moment, as if in thought, then swings a punch at Douglas. The old man topples back, knocking over the table, breaking glass and plates. The English women scream. Esmond thinks of Goad at the unveiling of the portrait, a reeling sense of déjà vu. He aims a swift kick at Niccolò Arcimboldi's shin. Fiamma has picked up her butter knife and sweeps it wildly at Carità, who ducks. Gerald tries to get

Douglas to the door while Pino beats frantically at a wide black back with his friend's cane, his spectacles misting, a stream of curses in English and Italian. More punches reach Douglas as he staggers towards the door with Gerald. Esmond sees Carità draw a dagger from his belt and, before he has a chance to feel afraid, he picks up one of the empty wine bottles from the table and brings it down over the little man's head. The bottle shatters, Carità stumbles forward, another Blackshirt takes out a pistol and holds it up. 'A gun!' More screaming; the Prince and the Reggies cower in the far corner.

Grabbing Fiamma's hand, Esmond hustles them towards the door and into the night. Gerald and Douglas are disappearing into the Institute, twenty yards ahead. He looks back and sees the Blackshirts lifting their weapons in the air, shouting, Carità leading them. He drags Fiamma after him, stumbling through the doors of the Institute, which he slams and bolts. Panting, they lean against one another until their breathing slows.

'We just can't behave like that any more,' Fiamma says, shaking her head. 'Norman is out of control. I felt like hitting him myself.'

When they reach the library, Douglas is sitting in an armchair while Gerald pours him a scotch. The old man's eyes are bloodshot, a bruise ripening on one cheek, his hands shaking.

'They're beasts,' he says. 'Brutes. See what they've done to my little boys, dressing them up as soldiers, marching and drilling when they should be lying in the sun.'

'Where's Pino?' Fiamma asks.

'The problem is that Musso's foisted a political system designed for sober Northern temperaments onto a race of lovers. The Italians are all heart, too much compassion for Fascism—'

He lights a Toscano. Esmond crosses to the window. The Blackshirts aren't waiting for them, only the old man in the pheasant feather cap sits on the steps of the church opposite, watching. A small crowd stands further up, in the pool of a streetlight outside Pretini's salon, looking down at a pile of clothes on the ground. When it moves, Esmond wonders if a dog has been hit by a car. Then he sees the hands and arms, and runs for the door with Gerald and Fiamma following behind.

Orioli is lying buckled in the road. The Prince and the Reggies are there, Temple keening quietly. Pretini, a pair of scissors in his top pocket, has Pino's head in his lap. Esmond kneels beside them and looks down at Pino, who attempts a smile. His spectacles are empty of glass, his eyes flooded with blood, shards sticking through in the soft red flesh.

'Norman? Is that you? I can't see you.'

Esmond takes his hand.

'Norman?'

They ride with him in the ambulance, Douglas following with the Reggies in a taxi. Esmond feels he is somehow to blame, first Goad and now Orioli savaged in his presence. In the ambulance, bandages are wrapped around Orioli's eyes. He begins to sob, calling out for his mother, and Esmond looks away into the night. He is lowered into a wheelchair at the hospital, still sobbing, and rushed into an operating room through double doors from which, two hours later, a white-coated doctor appears.

He speaks to Douglas in Italian for a while and then cups the old man's arm with his hand, as if to show that he knows Orioli is more than a friend. With a shrug, Douglas turns to Esmond.

'They're taking him to Venice. There's an expert there they think may be able to save his sight.'

He slumps down into a chair and lowers his great marble head into his hands. Fiamma crosses to put an arm around his shoulder. She whispers to him in Italian and he nods and mumbles in response. Esmond joins them.

'You'd better stay with us,' he says. 'You don't want to be alone, not after all this. He can have your father's room can't he, Gerald?'

'Of course.'

Douglas is with them for three nights, a sad, sleepless figure in the house. He sits in the library, drinking all day, and out on the loggia in the evenings. They do their best to entertain him, invite him to L'Ombrellino to swim, offer to drive him over to Piccolo's for dinner, but he declines. His face is a patchwork of bruises, and the only time they hear him speak more than a few words is when he calls the hospital in Venice to speak to Pino. One afternoon, they come home from swimming and he is gone, a polite note on the bed, two bottles of whisky missing from the cabinet in the library.

21

They haven't seen Douglas for a week. Strindberg has gone back to Austria for a fortnight's walking tour and Piccolo's is boarded up. When they cycle past Davis & Orioli on the way to the woods at Lungarno Colombo, they look up at the shuttered windows on the second floor, peer through the blinds of the bookshop, hoping to catch a flash of white hair. Gerald has rung the door-bell several times without answer. They ask at Betti's and Vieus-seux's Library, but nobody has seen him. Esmond talks of him often, of his stern eyes, the catty dazzle of his smile; 'He's all right!' they mimic and laugh.

One afternoon Esmond visits the English Cemetery while Gerald and Fiamma climb the hill to swim at L'Ombrellino. He knows that Elizabeth Barrett Browning is buried there, and Clough, and Landor, and feels it's a pilgrimage he should make, a way of touching the England he's left behind. He reads in

Forster that the English had once spent their Sunday afternoons strolling through the bosky graveyard, admiring the tombs by Holman Hunt and Stanhope.

It is crushingly hot in the graveyard. Weeds have grown up over the paths, some of the stones have shifted and fallen and lean on each other like ancient, lichen-covered drunks. He walks aimless diagonals across the cemetery, from the shadow of one tree to the next, trying to find Clough's grave and remembering lines from *Amours de Voyage*. 'St Peter's disappoints me,' he half-sings to himself, 'Rome in general might be called a rubbishy place—' The cemetery is stuffy with an English melancholy, prim and out of sorts with the swooning, histrionic tombs of the Italians that stretch up the hillside behind San Miniato. He leaves feeling embarrassed, parched and damp with sweat.

On the way back from the cemetery, walking down the via Laura, is Douglas. One hand taps his silver cane on the cobbles, the other holds the arm of a young girl. Esmond hurries to catch them.

'Norman!'

Douglas turns around with an irritated sheen. His eyes soften when he sees Esmond and he attempts a smile. He looks shaky, unsteady on his feet. Little deltas of red and blue snake out from his nose and cheeks. He reaches into his pocket for a Toscano, lights it, inhales slowly.

'Morning, Esmond. Well met. Let me present a young friend of mine, Roberta Drago. She's all right, this one.'

The girl is perhaps eleven years old, smartly dressed with long, dark, serious hair. He gives her a little pat on the backside. She holds out a thin, gloved hand to Esmond, who shakes it.

'We were just heading up to the gelato place by the station, care to join us?'

The girl runs ahead as Douglas takes Esmond's arm. He can

feel the occasional shudder passing through him. The old man speaks in a low, confidential voice, his breath sour with smoke.

'It's a miracle. Never thought I'd look at a girl again, but this one? Heavenly little thing.' He winks at Esmond. 'She's run away from home, you know. This is our first trip out for a week.'

Esmond looks ahead to the girl, who now breaks into a skip across the drain covers. Douglas stumbles and clutches at his chest, breathing heavily.

'Do you want to sit down?'

Douglas shakes his head and allows his lips to open into a damp smile.

'One gets a little groggy at my age. If it isn't heart, it's liver, it's kidneys. These doctors, I don't know whether they're discussing me or their breakfast.'

They eat their ices on a bench in the Piazza Santa Maria Novella. A group of Fascist Youth is carrying out exercises in the square, weapons to their shoulders, black boots stamping on the paving stones. The girl runs with her ice-cream to look in the window of the perfumery on the other side of the square. Douglas watches her as his short, fleshy tongue darts out to lap at his ice.

Esmond feels suddenly nauseous and leans forward. He thinks of Fiamma and Gerald in the cool air above the city, the water on their skin. He stands. 'Any word of Pino?'

'He's being operated on tomorrow in Venice. They're hopeful.' A pause. 'Come and see me some time,' Douglas says, shrugging his shoulders. 'If you like. Bring some of your writing, perhaps. Can't write a word myself these days. It's no good.'

Esmond leaves him on the bench, staring towards the girl pressed against the window of the shop. He looks back at Douglas, his careful white hair, his once-handsome face now untying into papery jowls. Lawrence had described him as a fallen angel in *Aaron's Rod*, Esmond remembers. Thinking himself unobserved, Douglas allows a tremor to seize hold of him. His ice-cream drops to the ground, cone-up. The girl turns back, skips across the square and sits beside him, taking his hand in hers. The two of them sit there, in the monstrous sunlight, like a long-married couple until Esmond tires of watching and heads back to the via Tornabuoni.

22

He is aware of a sound creeping into his dreams. It is the darkest heart of the night, so hot he'd left the windows and shutters open. He drags himself slowly from sleep and opens his eyes, searching the darkness until he recognises the trilling of the telephone in the library, echoing up the stone steps and into the apartment. He slips from bed, sticky and fuzzy-headed, and pads down the corridor. Gerald is standing in the doorway of his room.

'What time is it?' he asks, yawning.

'Search me. Two?'

Fiamma joins them in her nightdress. It seems to Esmond that every door and window in the house has been left ajar, all of the fans turning, but there is still no air. They walk down the steps and enter the library together, the old-fashioned stick phone shrieking on a desk beside the window. Gerald crosses to pick it up.

'Hullo. Yes. Right. Bugger. We'll be over shortly.'

He hangs up and pinches his fingers at his forehead.

'Bugger,' he says.

'What is it?' Fiamma asks.

'No time,' he says, striding back towards the doorway. 'It's Norman, he needs us. Meet in the courtyard in five minutes.'

Wearing shorts and a linen shirt, Esmond stands in the moonlight watching moths as big as hummingbirds circle the lit windows of the apartment. Occasionally a bat swoops down to snatch one from the air. Gerald and Fiamma come down together.

'We need a car. Norman's in a fix and we must get him out of Florence. We could head up to L'Ombrellino and borrow George's but it's a hell of a way.'

Esmond pats his pocket.

'I've got the keys to the church. Father Bailey keeps his Alfa in the garage at the back. I'm sure he wouldn't mind. If it's an emergency, I mean.'

They cross the Ponte Santa Trinità, then down the via Maggio, past the sleeping birdcages and quietly through the wicket gate of the church, tiptoeing along a passageway and into the garage. The room is full of half-assembled engines, bicycles without wheels, a pony trap resting on its haunches. Esmond slides open the doors which give onto the Piazza Santo Spirito. The square is empty, cardboard boxes by the roadside for the dustbin men, a small pyramid of wine bottles leaking onto the earth outside a bar.

The key is in the ignition. Esmond sits beside Gerald in the front while Fiamma squeezes into the seats at the back. The engine starts with a roar that makes them all jump.

'I haven't driven in a while,' Gerald shouts over the noise.

As they edge out into the square, Esmond looks back to see that a light has come on in the apartments next to the church. He thinks he sees Bailey outlined in the window, looking at them. They pull through the square and through the silent streets of the Oltrarno, along the south side of the river. Moonlight has turned the city to bone. Finally, they drive across the cobbles of the Ponte alle Grazie and pull up outside Davis & Orioli.

Douglas steps from the shadows of the alleyway beside the shop. He is wearing a lady's straw sunhat and a neckerchief pulled up over his face like an outlaw. He carries a small pigskin travelling case and looks nervously up and down the road. The tremors that Esmond had seen outside Santa Maria Novella now cause the old man to quiver like a mystic, surprised by the truthfulness of his vision. Esmond climbs over to sit alongside Fiamma while Douglas sinks down beside Gerald in front.

'Where do we go?' Gerald asks.

'Pisa,' Douglas says, pulling the neckerchief down around his neck and clamping the hat on his head with one hand. 'One of Pino's friends will put me up for a few nights. Then they'll bung me in the back of a lorry to Menton. It's all part of the game, isn't it? What I always say. Everything's interesting. All right!'

Gerald turns the car back towards the bridge, through the Oltrarno and past the basilica of San Frediano. Soon they are on the viale Etruria and moving at a smart pace through dark hills, shadow-clad cypresses rising and falling beside them with the swell and sink of the land. Douglas turns round to speak to Esmond, the red coal of a Toscano glowing at his lips.

'Filly you spotted me with earlier,' he says, raising his voice over the wind. 'Turns out her father is a *Centurione* in the MVSN. Someone saw us walking back from our gelato.' He rolls his eyes at Esmond. 'Knew I shouldn't have let her out of the house.'

Fiamma's hair is streaming out behind her and Esmond grows cold as they hit fifty miles per hour on the empty road. There is a tartan rug on the floor and he pulls it over their laps and puts his arm around her shoulders. She nestles her head in the crook of his neck and closes her eyes.

'Probably a good thing,' Douglas says, throwing his cigarillo into the night and forcing the hat down with both hands. 'Needed to get moving. Can't stop in one place for too long.

Florence is a drag without Pino. I haven't been able to write for weeks.' He prods at the bag in his lap. 'Latest book. Cultural history of Paphian love. Start off with the Greeks. Theognis, Solon, Anacreon, Alcaeus, Ibycus. Know any of them?' He doesn't seem to expect a reply. 'Magnificent stuff. Meeting the girl caused a blockage. Good to be shot of her.'

It is as they are passing the lights of Empoli to the north that Esmond is first aware of the cars behind them. There is, before anything, a sense that they are being followed. Then, coming up very fast out of the darkness, two sets of headlights. Soon their engines are audible even over the growl of the Alfa and the rush of air. They are moving up into hill country around San Miniato. The car shudders as they accelerate up a long, steep incline. Fiamma looks back, her hand held to her eyes as if shading them against sunlight.

'The cars,' she says.

'I've seen them,' Gerald replies, putting his foot down. 'Bugger.'

They have reached the crest of the hill and are now coasting into the valley. For the moment the cars are out of sight and Esmond hugs Fiamma to him. He can see that Douglas is shuddering in the front seat, his arms on the dashboard, his head on his arms.

'Pull yourself together, Norman,' Gerald says. 'I'll need you to navigate once we hit Pisa.'

The Alfa seems to skim the surface of the road, riding the trail of moonlight before them. Gerald drives with one hand, his elbow on the windowsill, a cigarette between his lips. Fiamma is sleeping, breathing softly into the hollow of his neck.

'I'm sorry, you chaps,' Douglas says quietly, barely audible to Esmond. 'It seems I can't help myself. You see I still think of myself as your age, hale and hot-blooded. Shocks me to look in the mirror sometimes. Expect to see a strapping young bounder and instead—' He turns to Esmond with grey eyes, swinging jowls. 'I'd have liked to die in Italy, but France won't be so bad.' He begins to sing. '*It'll all be the same in a hundred years.*'

Villages appear and vanish, dark and dreamlike. Douglas smokes constantly, throwing the stubs of his Toscanos out into the air. Esmond leans back and looks at the moon, remembers floating in the pool at Emmanuel with Philip. He takes a deep breath and feels Fiamma stirring against him. 'Where are we?' she asks sleepily.

The engine begins to sputter around Pontedera. At first a wheeze, then a definite cough. There has been no sign of the pursuing cars for half an hour or so, and they are approaching the turn-off for Pisa. Now the Alfa begins to bark and a cloud of blue smoke plumes out behind them.

'What's wrong?' Esmond asks.

'I don't know,' Gerald says. 'We have a quarter tank of petrol, so it can't be that.' There is a thud from the engine and the car shudders. Gerald slows and pulls over. 'I know nothing about cars,' he says, getting out and walking round to open the bonnet. 'Bugger. It's hot.'

After a few minutes, a throb of engines is audible in the distance. Esmond looks back towards Florence and sees the first faint brightening of the horizon at the end of a long stretch of road. It is quarter to five by his watch. He gets out and goes to stand at the open bonnet of the car. Fine steam is rising from the engine. Gerald pulls his hand inside the sleeve of his jacket to unfasten the radiator cap.

'It's the water, I think,' says Gerald. 'Look in there.'

Esmond looks. The tank is empty. The roar of engines is closer and, looking back down, he can make out that the cars are Fiats, in procession, coming out of the sky to the east.

'Let me see if there's anything in the back.'

He opens the boot and finds only a small can of petrol, a few maps. 'Nothing,' he says. Douglas is staring backwards, down the road to where the Fiats are, closer now, their rumble building with each turn. 'Piss in it,' he says.

'What?'

'Piss in the tank. Always works. Had a Siddeley Special Six back in Blighty. Was forever blowing up. Piss, I tell you.'

'Are you sure?' Gerald asks, looking at Esmond. He shrugs and closes the boot. They stand, side by side, cocks out, watching the Fiats approach. Esmond whistles, trying to drown out the sound of the engines. Gerald is the first to send down a heavy stream onto the hot metal, splashing and fizzing around the mouth of the radiator tank. Esmond follows shortly after. Fiamma has her hand to her mouth. Douglas is watching around the side of the raised bonnet. They finish, shake and leap inside the car. Gerald turns the key in the ignition.

The Fiats have pulled abreast of one another and are perhaps two hundred yards away. Blackshirts lean from the windows of each car and Esmond can see revolvers in their hands; one of them carries a shotgun that he waves from side to side like a baton. The Alfa's engine turns over, fails. The sun has begun to rise behind them as the cars close in. The engine turns over again and fires a plume from the exhaust. Gerald stamps on the accelerator and, with a spray of pebbles, they pull away.

The Fiats are yards behind them. The Alfa is heading up a slope towards a coppice, harried by the two cars. The sun appears above the dark mass of the Sienese Clavey and light floods the plain, pouring down like water from the peaks. There is a sound like a sharp intake of breath followed by a high whistle. Esmond looks back at the cars and, as he does, there is another whistle and the front windscreen of the Alfa shatters, sending shards of glass splintering over hands and faces. He can see that Douglas is badly cut: a wide gash has opened above one eye, his cheeks flecked with blood. The old man sinks down, trying to curl into the footwell, shivering and sobbing.

Bullets ping off the bodywork of the car, fizz overhead, explode in the tarmac on the road beside them. The Blackshirts shout and one of the cars pulls alongside the Alfa. Esmond looks over and sees Carità at the wheel, a snub pistol in one hand, the white tuft in his quiff fluttering in the wind. He grins eagerly and steers the Fiat into the side of the Alfa. There is a crunch of bent metal, a shudder as the two cars scour and then the Alfa lurches on. Carità is standing up in his seat, steering with one hand and popping at them with his Beretta. Esmond puts his arm around Fiamma and hauls her down into the cramped space behind the front seats, pulling the tartan rug across their backs. Fiamma is moaning quietly, her cheek pressed against his in the rumbling darkness, her breath in quick pants.

'Fascist bastards,' she mumbles.

They are down there for what seems like hours. Esmond thinks of trips to London with his parents as a child, when Anna and he would curl up in the back seat of the car as their father drove the Lagonda home to Aston. He remembers the feeling of weightlessness, the sense of flying through the night as they snuggled under blankets, his sister's head on his shoulder. And then, pulling into the gravel of the house's turning circle, he would pretend to be asleep so that his father would have to carry him from the car, hauling him over his shoulder like a fireman and gripping him with his good arm until he laid him out on the bed, helped him from his clothes and smoothed his hair.

The car slows. He hears Gerald and Norman speaking and lifts himself carefully onto the seat. They are coming into the outskirts of Pisa. There are other cars on the street, a bus taking workers to their offices, but no sign of the Fiats. The car is covered in scratches and pocks. A few pieces of glass hang trem-blingly from the metal frame of the windscreen. Gerald and Douglas are ashen, their hair clumped with blood, their mouths and teeth stained with it.

'Turn here,' Douglas says. 'Now there. On the left.'

They make their way through a gateway into the courtyard of a long house. Gerald brings the car to a halt and turns off the engine. There is a mulberry tree in the centre of the yard with a car parked beneath it. Gerald begins to laugh.

'Christ. I mean, Norman, bugger. I thought we were goners. What in God's name are we going to tell the priest about his car?'

Douglas begins to laugh, too, and Esmond joins him, reaching down to draw back the blanket from where Fiamma is crouched in a terrified huddle on the floor, her face pressed into Gerald's seat.

'You can come out now,' he says. 'We're safe. We're all safe.'

He leans down to help her, reaching behind her head. He feels wetness.

'Fiamma?' he says, with a sudden lurch in his chest. 'Fiamma?' He turns her over and sees the whiteness of her face, the dark red, almost black pool formed beneath her. Gerald has turned and looks down at the girl now stretched out on the seat as Esmond searches her neck for a pulse.

'What do we do?' Esmond asks, looking first at Gerald and then at Douglas. She is not breathing, there is no heartbeat, just a small hole in the nape of her neck through which blood is seeping in a slow trickle. Esmond reaches round and puts his finger into the hole, but there is little blood left, and he prods through to tendons, wet gristle. His mind feels as if it has lost its surface, its ability to grasp hold of the car, the dusty courtyard, Douglas or Gerald. It is all depths, horror, and he lowers himself down to lie against her frail, sunken body.

Douglas turns to get out of the car.

'I can't have anything to do with this,' he says. 'After everything else. They'd kill me.' He backs away towards the house, leaving the boys with the body of their friend. They hear a door slam, the sound of conversation. Douglas comes out of the house followed by a small man with yellowed hair and thick-rimmed spectacles. They get into a Topolino parked underneath the mulberry tree. Neither of them looks at the Alfa or its contents as they pass.

Esmond presses himself against Fiamma's chest, Gerald reaches over to stroke her blood-matted hair. They stay like this for a long time as the city wakes around them and, even in the warmth of the morning, her body is so cold that Esmond begins to shudder. Gerald is crying and the tears clear furrows in the blood on his cheeks. Someone in the house turns a radio on and there is the sound of a ukulele. The voices of the Trio Lescano seep out into the still air of the courtyard. Finally, hopelessly, Esmond turns to Gerald and asks again, 'What do we do now?'

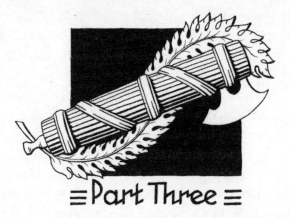

≡ Part Three ≡

Esmond Lowndes, Selected Correspondence,
1937–1939

(*Italian translation by Ada Liuzzi*)

Shrewsbury, Salop.
13/10/37

Dearest E -
It's all just too horrifying for words. You must
be undone. The poor girl; her poor mother. I wish I
were out there to help you, darling. I had no idea the
Blackshirts in Italy were such monsters. This Carità
fellow sounds like a fiend - do watch out for him. Did
you love her, this Fiamma? I imagine you did. At least
Goad sounds like he's been a brick. I do think you
ought to write to daddy about it all. Goad is sure to
let him know why you aren't at the Institute any more.
Sorry this is rushed. I'm back in the cursed
hospital. First cold snap of the autumn and I'm
gurgling like a drain. Perhaps they should send me
out to join you in the sunny South!
Much love to you and chin up,
Anna xx.

Welsh Frankton,
Shropshire.
October 21st '37

Dear Esmond -
Your letter arrived in the same post as one from
Harold Goad outlining the events of the end of
September. The stories tally, more or less, for

which you should be bloody thankful. I would have thought you might have written to me sooner - you need to face up to your misdeeds and take any punishment on the chin. I believe I've told you this before.

As it turns out, it sounds like you might get away with this one. The girl's father is persona non grata, which helps. You're lucky that the Blackshirts seem so keen to sweep the whole mess under the rug. You understand the kind of trouble you might have been in? Beyond our powers of help. I want you to be careful now. Concentrate on getting this station going and stop palling up with blasted sods and degenerates. I thought I made that clear to you before you left. This Douglas fellow sounds like the lowest of the low, one of these parasitical aesthetes happy to see the lives of others crumble to ruin as long as their own base interests are catered for. A bloody swine, and below you.

So you're to live at the English Church? Goad explained the move in his letter. He can't have someone under his roof who has betrayed his trust so completely. You see that, I'm sure. In exchange for him continuing to sponsor your undertakings in Florence, I've agreed to find his son a place at the Party headquarters. Is he a good chap, this Gerald? A solid Fascist like his father?

I understand that the studio is operational - well done for this. The stations in Heligoland and Sark are bringing in a not insubstantial amount of cash. It's imperative that Florence begins to make its own contribution. Goad tells me he has plans for two

114

hours of programming a day. Harder to fill than you might think, or so I'd imagine. Have you thought about contacting Ezra Pound? He's been writing for _The Blackshirt_ and _Action_, a new newspaper Mosley has set up. He's in Rapallo, near Genoa. I think he's probably insane, but his ideas about Social Credit are not so far from the Corporate State, and he can certainly string together a sentence. I enclose some recent discs of Mosley's speeches that you might like to broadcast.

You will also find enclosed a list of Italian businessmen Rothermere has sounded out as potential advertisers for the wireless station. They will expect you to contact them over the next few weeks. Make sure that you do. Seize the hour, Esmond! Things are looking up for you now - all the nonsense is behind you. Get your head down and put your back into it. Good luck and be a bloody man!

Your mother sends her love,

Your Father.

P.S. You asked if you might draw upon the wireless funds to pay for repairs to the automobile you damaged during your hapless trip to Pisa. No.

P.P.S. The priest you're staying with is Frederick Bailey, isn't he? I met a God-botherer called Bailey in the First Battle of the Marne. Brave fellow if it's the same chap (and you know what I think of priests as a species).

MINISTRY FOR POPULAR CULTURE
VIA VITTORIO VENETO, ROMA
2/11/1937

Dear Mr Lowndes,

It is my pleasure to announce that Il Duce
himself has asked me to write to you regarding
Radio Firenze. We view this radio enterprise as
having two heads - to school the Italian shopkeeper,
clerk and artisan in the English language, so that
the temporary cooling-off in the relationship
between our countries does not lead to a loss of
that particular feel for the language of business
that marks out the Italian from his Mediterranean
cousin; and to link up the right-thinking men of
each country, so that the Italian realises that not
all Englishmen are like Mr Eden, and the Englishman
knows of the success of our glorious revolution, the
real changes that have been effected in the lives of
the ordinary people here, and the powerful muscle
with which Il Duce is leading us into the future.

As such, Il Duce suggests you might broadcast on
the Radio Roma network, meaning that Radio Firenze
will be audible not only throughout Italy and the
Greater Italian Empire, but also across the whole
of Europe, including Great Britain. I hope that you
understand the faith we are putting in the British
Union here. Had Harold Goad not always been such
an intelligent and loyal friend of our work, this
project could scarcely have been contemplated.

Do pass on my very warmest wishes to Mr Goad,
whom I have always held in the greatest admiration.

Perhaps - with your permission - I might come and
visit the studio next time I am in Florence. I
could even prepare a small speech of an informative
nature.

Cordial salutes,

Alessandro Pavolini, Minister for Popular Culture.

He stands on the Ponte Santa Trinità thinking of Fiamma, a sob in his heart. Carità has taken to parading his squads of MVSN up and down the Lungarno degli Acciaiouli and their jackboots echo between the buildings either side of the river. The city grows darker with every passing day as the Blackshirts locate dissenters, arrest Communists, round up pacifists. Fasces are carved into walls that once housed tabernacles to the Virgin. Everywhere is the slogan *Credere, Obbedire, Combattere.* The MVSN swarm like flies over the streets of the town, wringing money from shopkeepers, threatening and swindling, and always the marching, marching. It's easy to see Carità out front, he's the only one wearing shorts. He has a horse-whip in one hand which he beats against his bare leg as he shouts – *Sinister, dexter, sinister, dexter.*

Esmond imagines a gun in his hand as he stands there, imagines pointing it at Carità and pulling the trigger. He pictures Carità stumbling forward, over the parapet and into the Arno, the yellow water filling his lungs. He shakes his head. Goad was right – men like Carità, like William Joyce, these are the men of the violent future. He's a relic, like Douglas, like his father. He strolls back along the bridge towards the Oltrarno, away from the Institute, the via Tornabuoni, Doney's and the bells of San Gaetano, and south towards St Mark's, the studio, the small room in the church apartments where he spends his nights, where his days are filled with disc recorder switches, the knobs and dials of the transmitter, the quiet precision of Goad's voice outlining the differences between stress-timed and syllable-timed languages, the mysteries of the modal verb.

He pays melancholy visits to the triptych downstairs, and then upstairs to the lonely studio. – *Work is the best antidote to sorrow, my dear Watson*, Ada tells him, and they both smile. He and Goad have broadcast on Shakespeare, Dante, Corporatism, Fascist art, and the programmes have been well received. He pictures his father, listening on his ancient Philco Easytune and hearing his, Esmond's, voice, beamed across the Alps, across France, into the South Downs and breaking over the Midland towns into Shropshire. He imagines the smile on his father's face and feels himself blush with pleasure.

Telegram: 26/10/37

Arrived in Ldn STOP 1st day at BUF HQ STOP Utterly mad all of them STOP Hope not 2 ghastly for you STOP Gerald

Rinaldo Piaggio, SpA
Genoa Sestri
1/11/1937

Dear Mr Lowndes,

Since my father is in ill health, I take the opportunity to reply to you in his stead. We would certainly be interested in purchasing three two-minute advertising slots on Radio Firenze. One of our employees will send you disc recordings

directly, where we present the great aeronaut and
Governor of Libya, Italo Balbo, praising the skills
of Italian aircraft manufacturers and, particularly,
the Piaggio P.16 heavy bomber, with which I'm sure
you are familiar.

We agree your terms, namely five hundred lire per
advertisement. Please find a cheque enclosed and
we take this opportunity to wish you luck with your
sensible venture.

Evviva Il Duce!

Sincerely,

Enrico Piaggio.

Isotta Fraschini Automobiles,
12845 Milano
7 November

MR LOWNDES

FIND ENCLOSED BANKER'S DRAFT FOR L2500 AND ONE
DISC RECORDING OF PROMOTIONAL MATERIAL FOR THE
ISOTTA FRASCHINI TIPO 8B. WE ARE DELIGHTED TO HEAR
OF IL DUCE'S INTEREST IN YOUR UNDERTAKING AND
PLEDGE OUR CONTINUED SUPPORT FOR RADIO FIRENZE.
PLEASE GIVE OUR REGARDS TO LORD ROTHERMERE.

VIVA IL DUCE!

ORESTE FRASCHINI ON BEHALF OF ISOTTA FRASCHINI
AUTOMOBILES.

Café Rapallo
Rapallo
27th November 1937

Mr Lowndes -

YES! in a word. In rather more, I might say to
you how long I have been waiting for an opportunity
of this sort. I first suggested that I broadcast my
views regarding the SCOURGE of usury and the sole
solution - that of C. H. Douglas's SOCIAL CREDIT
- some five years ago at a dinner I happened to
attend with, amongst others, Signor Achille Starace.
Unfortunately, the Italian administration has not
seen fit to take me up on this offer. I am delighted,
therefore, that you have made contact, and that I
might continue my association with the laudable
efforts of the British Union to repel the threat of
Communism.

I will talk about the JEW. For centuries, since
the brute Cromwell brought them back into England,
the kikes have sucked the English marrow from its
bones. And now even those last remnants of the WHITE
RACE, the proper, intrepid Brits each of them the
right blend of Saxon warrior and Norman noble, find
themselves kowtowing to international financiers,
the houses of Rothschild and Raphael and Samuel,
usurers in London and New York. I will speak, and
when I have finished speaking, it will be as when
the storm passes, and the sky is crystalline.

I am afraid that I am not able to come to meet
you in Florence as I am currently rather diminished
of capital. If you should like to visit us in

Rapallo (we could put you up at my good friend
Olga Rudge's place - we are far too cramped here)
and bring your recording materials, I will be
delighted, for a small fee, to deliver you several
hours of DYNAMITE.

Give my best to Sir Oswald and your father.

Sincerely yours,

Ezra Pound.

Wooton Lodge, Staffs.
20/12/37

Dear Esmond -

All the best for a magnifico natale from Diana
and me. I'm bloody proud of you, young man. I think
you still smoke: here's a couple of cartons from our
doomed attempt to take on Philip Morris! Hope they
aren't too stale . . .

Warmest wishes,

Oswald.

[Card: Blake's *Newton*]

Happy Christmas Darling E! Miss you masses. I'm in
hospital again, worse luck. Any chance of you coming
back for a visit? A xxx.

[Card: Winter scene, English landscape.]
Dec '37

Dear Esmond -
  Wishing you a very Happy Christmas. Sorry you're
not with us. Cheque inside as I'm sure you can buy
much finer things out there than we'd be able to
send you from Shropshire.
  Your mother sends her love,
  Your Father.

The mince pies have been crushed in transit from England. Alice Keppel looks down at them apologetically as she serves coffee at the end of Christmas lunch. Reggie Temple has drunk too much and is lolling back in his chair, snoring. Bailey and Goad are wearing paper crowns and discussing the Nanking Massacre. Colonel Keppel alone seems cheerful. – *I'm dashed if I'm too old to fight*, he says to anyone that will listen. – *Just let me at the bounders. Russians, Germans, all the same to me.*

Esmond had unwrapped his presents alone, in bed. Two Old Wykehamist ties from his father, the Dugdale abridgement of *Mein Kampf* from his mother. His sister has sent him a bundle of Everyman editions of the great Russian novels: Tolstoy, Dostoevsky, Turgenev. He lays them on his dresser alongside the box of gaudy handkerchiefs from Gerald via Goad. *Missing you*, the card read.

He decides to walk back from L'Ombrellino alone. It's cold and he's wrapped in an overcoat. The wind brings tears to his eyes as he makes his way down into the city, lustrous under her lamps. Bells chime here and there, children play with spinning tops, yoyos, push-bikes in the street, their scarves tied in stiff knots at their throats. The church is dark and echoing when he lets himself inside. He has a recording to prepare, needs to check supplies of reel-to-reel tape and record needles. He's in the studio until late and then goes to bed, reading three pages of *Mein Kampf* before tossing it aside with a snort.

Telegram: 2/1/38

  Left yr mad politicians in the lurch STOP Wld
rather sleep on street STOP Dad says he's better is
this true STOP Gerald

Via dei Forbici, 35c
Firenze
1.2.38

Dear Esmond -
  It strikes me that we started out on the wrong
note. Ada has enjoyed working with you enormously -
she seems to have found her calling. Her mother and
I listen to the programme with great pride, knowing
the extent to which our daughter is involved in its
production.
  Perhaps you'd like to come for dinner one evening.
If there's one thing that the tribulations of my
co-religionists north of the Alps have taught me,
it's that leaping to assumptions based upon such
broad measures as race or nationality is almost
always to err. I loathed your Mr Eden, I resented
the sense of entitlement I found in the English who
have colonised Florence, much as you have colonised

the rest of the world. But these past few months
have changed my views on many things. Ada's aunt,
my sister, lives in Hamburg. Life for her has become
extraordinarily difficult. Her husband has been
beaten, many of their friends have fled, some have
disappeared.

It is to the credit of the British that you, like
the Italians, are not temperamentally suited to
racialist behaviour. The strength of your cultural
life gives you access to a finer degree of sympathy -
or that, at least, is how I've come to see it. Let's
discuss over dinner. I'll leave it to Ada to agree
the date with you.

With very best wishes,
Guido Liuzzi.

[Enclosed with following letter: article from *Daily Mail* entitled
'Son of Sir Lionel Lowndes in Italian Broadcast Venture'.]
Welsh Frankton,
Shropshire.
February 2nd, 1938

Dearest E -
Thanks for yours. Can't tell you how chuffed they
all are with you. I'm sure others have sent you the
piece from the Mail, but here it is just in case. It
makes you sound like quite the hero. Mosley wrote
a smashing letter to dad about the difference this
has made to the Party's standing in Italy. Is it
true that Musso himself is going to broadcast for

you? Now that would be a coup. In any case, he's
told Grandi that he's thinking of re-starting his
contributions to the Party.

I've been in the Royal Salop again, can't seem to
shake the cough. It's a beastly pain but I've got
through the boredom by thinking about you out there,
and how fabulously you're doing, and what a splendid
time you must be having.

Oodles of love,

Anna xxx.

– *You know the Treaty of Rapallo?* Pound says as they make
their way down from the train station. – *1922, it was. Marked
the renewal of diplomatic relations between Germany and Russia.
Now it looks like they'll carve the world up between them. And it all
started here!* He has a halo of fiery hair turning white at the ends,
a faun's beard. Esmond had expected an American accent. – *I
found Hitler magnificent, when I met him*, Pound says. – *He's the
real thing, has a vision, a sense of history and destiny.* They come
to a small café on the seafront overlooking the gently curving
bay, bobbing boats, terns and gulls following fishing trawlers out
to sea. – *In here*, Pound says. – *I'm upstairs.*

He arranges the recording equipment on the balcony of
Pound's apartment. Inside it is too cramped, crowded with
books, dark. Pound lounges back in a deckchair, occasionally
stroking his beard. It's cold, a jagged wind pouring down from
the hills. He doesn't seem to notice. – *I've been introduced to the
Boss* – Il Duce – *several times now*, Pound says as Esmond checks
levels and adjusts the microphone. – *I've never met anyone who
understood my poems so quickly. He seemed to feel them on an
instinctive, primal level. He's a soldier, of course, but he's also an
intellectual. People forget that here.*

That evening they have dinner at the villa of the violinist Olga Rudge. Pound sits between their host and his wife, Dorothy. Esmond is exhausted, downcast, and the dining room is unheated and chilly. He's not sure he can use any of his conversation with Pound. They'd sat and watched the sun sink over the hills and Pound had spooled out his theories on usury and Social Credit and the Jewish problem and Esmond had felt as if he were back listening to William Joyce address a rally in the East End. There was so little subtlety to his argument, so much anger. They talk about Hulme for a while. – *He was a dear, dear friend*, Pound says. – *Thoroughly brutal. I miss him still.* Throughout, Pound's wife sits in silence, looking over sombrely at Esmond as if he might help her escape along his radio waves to Britain. He retreats to his room as early as he can.

He stands at his window and can see the castle on the bay, patches of darkness on the water where ships are moored, young people walking along the seafront arm-in-arm. He'd brought his novel with him, but he can't write. Perhaps, he thinks, he's not supposed to be a novelist. Perhaps novels won't even be read in the years to come. Maybe his legacy, the thing to make his death less hollow, is the recordings. He imagines a shell whistling down on St Mark's, he and Goad dragging archives down into the crypt. *The best way to speak to the future*, Goad is saying, *is with brilliant ideas.*

The next morning, as the train winds down the coast towards Pisa, he leans from the window of his carriage and sends the discs he'd cut with Pound the previous day spinning out to sparkle for a moment in the winter sunshine and then crash on the rocks below.

Telegram: 10/2/38

Wiring E Lowndes five thousand lire for purchase
twelve advertising slots as per agreement at meeting
in Milan 6 Feb STOP Viva Il Duce STOP Bianchi
Automobiles and Bicycles 7 Via Nirone Milan

MINISTRY FOR POPULAR CULTURE
VIA VITTORIO VENETO, ROMA
10/3/1938

Dear Esmond,
   I was delighted and honoured at the introduction
Mr Goad gave to my short speech on Radio Firenze
last week. I have already written to him directly
and apologise that I haven't been in touch with you
earlier. I very much enjoyed meeting you in Rome and
was delighted to discover so many points of shared
interest. I am sure that Italy (and England) will
thank the day that Esmond Lowndes took an interest
in the rapprochement of our once-close nations.
   You shouldn't let the success of your radio
enterprise distract you from what I feel certain is
your true calling - as novelist. I was fascinated
by our discussion about T. E. Hulme, whose work
I did not know. You are right that it is hard
to find literary figures of the correct type -
perhaps harder in England than in Italy. Here we
have Ungaretti and Pirandello and, of course, the
late d'Annunzio, whose passing we mourn each day

and whose legacy (notwithstanding his regrettable assessment of the Axis alliance) I am now working to assure.

I like the idea of using the novel, with its mutability, its openness and its place at the heart of middle-class life, to address historical figures, situating them in moments of great political unease. Of course this is not new - your George Eliot famously treated the life of our own Savonarola; Manzoni's The Betrothed is one of the great historical novels (have you read it? I enclose a copy in any case). But what seems new to me in your idea is to claim a figure from the very recent past and to use him to illuminate the current political landscape. I look forward very much to reading In Love and War when it is published.

As you can imagine, with d'Annunzio's death, I have been terribly busy. I will try, nonetheless, to make it to Florence before the heat of the summer strikes and, if you will humour me, I would be delighted to continue my musings on the state of contemporary Italian literature.

With warmest wishes,

Alessandro.

Telegram: 1/4/38

Received with thanks four hundred pounds STOP Impressive STOP Mosley

Early morning. Esmond is sitting at his desk in the studio. He can still smell Ada's lavender perfume. Voices rise up from the stalls on the Piazza Santo Spirito. The sound of a street sweeper's broom is like the whetting of long knives. He sits in thought for a few moments, scratches his fountain pen across his notebook. He leans back, looks carefully at the last page, and gives a thin smile. He has finished his novel. With a sigh, he gathers together the pile of notebooks, puts a sheet of paper in his Olivetti, extends two fingers, and begins to type.

There is no such thing as historical fact. It is likely, however, that our hero, Thomas Ernest Hulme, twelve days after his thirty-fourth birthday, was standing in front of the Royal Marine Artillery battery at Oostduinkerke Bad, two hundred yards from the slate flushness of the North Sea. Witnesses - Captain Henry Halahan RN, for instance - say that Hulme appeared lost in contemplation as the shells descended. He'd just begun a book on Epstein, so it may have been this that caused his wood-cut features to smudge over, his ears to close themselves against the whistle of the falling shells, fired from the 15-inch Leugenboom at Ostend. His comrades threw themselves into the trenches, into the gun pit of the Carnac battery. Hulme just stood there, gazing over towards the long barges on the Yser Canal.

We know what the explosion sounded like, at least to Hulme. He'd had enough near-misses during his time in Flanders to know that, as he wrote to Ursula Lowndes, 'It's not the idea of being killed that's alarming, but the idea of being hit by a jagged piece of steel. You hear the whistle of the shell coming, you crouch down as low as you can, and just wait. It doesn't burst merely with a bang, it has a kind of crack with a snap in it, like the crack of a very large whip.' On the 28th September, 1917, though, Hulme didn't crouch. He stood there, in a dreamy moment, and he was killed. When the smoke cleared, some of his comrades were bellowing, others emitting miserable groans. Hulme had simply disappeared. Not a scrap of clothing, nor a shred of that burly, lusty body was left.

Here we move further from the sham certainties of history, deeper into Hulme's beloved speculations. For in that moment before death, between the whistle and the crack, we'd like to imagine his mind cycling back through his short, sharp life, falling now on the figure of Wyndham Lewis, hanging upside-down on the railings at Soho Square after a row over a girl, now on the crow-like visage of Henri Gaudier-Brzeska, his dear friend, dead not yet two years, now on his lover Kate Lechmere's cyanope smile. And as the shells plunge and shriek like buck-shot birds, we imagine his mind going back to the night when, aged nineteen, he was sent down from St John's College, Cambridge.

It was late and the boathouse was on fire, the flames tonguing the black Cam. Two policemen wrung river water from their jackets, shaking their fists and whinnying while a college porter waved his feet in the air, his upper half wedged in a dustbin. A rower stood in the light of the flames, his singlet and shorts dark-spattered, one hand clasped to a bloody nose. Two girls sprawled on the bright grass,

sobbing. Hulme was swimming in the dark water,
pulling his long body through the velvet iciness of
the river, because he knew he had gone too far, and
he would not feel this water, this river, again.
Under the moth-eaten blanket of the sky he swam, and
he felt the vague grief of the night, and the ruddy
face of the moon leant over the fence of trees that
lined the river like a red-faced farmer, watching
him. He swam on.

Esmond stops and sighs again. It is seven in the morning. He stands, stretches and looks out for a moment onto the piazza below. He turns out his desk light and shuts the door of the studio.

Suisso Atlântico Hotel, Lisbon
15/4/38

Dearest Es -

   I wonder if you'd given up on me? There is, I
understand, a small mountain of unopened mail
waiting for me in Praterstraße; whether some are
yours or not I don't know. The house is being looked
after by our neighbours, although the downstairs
windows have been broken and the statues in the
garden smashed. The last letter I read was from early
in your Florentine days. You sounded miserable. I do
hope things have improved. I'm sorry I didn't write
back - I've always been a dreadful correspondent.

   Mutti and papa left for Lisbon two weeks ago.
They'd been in Switzerland waiting to see which way
the wind would blow. It's one thing you can say for

papa - he's careful. Moving out of Leopoldstadt
was my own concession to caution. I bunked up
with Charlie Campbell - do you remember him from
Emmanuel? He's over on some sort of exchange
programme teaching papyrology at the university.
Put me up in his drawing room. Jolly decent of him.
I earned my keep by bowling leg-breaks at him in
the corridors of the Faculty of Ancient History. At
least I took something from my time in England. I
think I loved cricket almost as much as I loved you.
Helps keep off the Kummerspeck too!

We told everyone that I was a cousin of Charlie's
over from the UK. I wore his clothes, spoke bad
German with an English accent, ordered my tea with
milk. But when the worm von Schuschnigg rolled over,
and the true extent of the whole Heim ins Reich
thing came out, it began to get hot. I left Vienna at
night, wrapped in Charlie's ulster, three days after
the Anschluß. I took the train to Innsbruck where I
fell in with a gang of Jewish students with pretty
much the same idea - escape, get away from that vile
little man, his swarm of vile little men. I followed
my parents to Lisbon. There were people on the
border - not good people, no one I could see doing it
for anything but money - and they ferried us across.
A week in St Gallen, then Geneva, then a night train
to Genoa.

Can't tell you how much it bucked me up just to
be in the same country as you. I even dreamed, for a
moment, of hopping off in Milan, taking a train for
Florence and turning up on your doorstep. If only to
see your face. But that hereditary caution . . .

It feels like things are rushing towards a ghastly end, as if everything is coming apart like something from Yeats. 'The best lack all conviction, while the worst / Are full of passionate intensity.' That was it, wasn't it? I watched those violent men on the streets of Vienna, ugly snarls on their faces, and I knew that no good would come of Europe, that we are entering the new Dark Age, and those who would live must flee.

Another quote kept coming to me on the train, and then on the boat from Genoa to Lisbon. It's Shelley - I think from his <u>Defence of Poetry</u>, but I don't have my books with me - 'A man, to be greatly good, must imagine intensely and comprehensively; he must put himself in the place of another and of many others; the pains and pleasures of his species must become his own.' This is what we've lost, our empathy. The Germans used to have it - Hölderlin had it, and Goethe and Rilke. But they don't any more. Poets still have it - Auden does, and Spender, I think. Whatever you lose out there in Florence, Es, keep that. And for God's sake put it into your writing.

Now the last, rather embarrassing thing. My parents are nowhere to be seen here. Presume they've hot-footed it to New York already. But I was rather relying on them for funds. While I was waiting for the clipper to New York, I met a Portuguese sailor in the Bairro Alto. I know, I know, but Lisbon <u>is</u> a rather thrilling place. You'd adore it here. I woke to find my watch and wallet missing. He left me a handful of escudos on the chair but they won't get me far. I wonder if you could wire me a few quid, just

to see me through until the boat leaves. In my name
to the Central Lisbon Post Office, if you don't mind.

   You're a good man, Es. I'll always think awfully
well of the time we spent together.

   Philip.

L'Ombrellino
Piazza di Bellosguardo
Firenze
28/4/38

   Would you like to come for dinner on the 3rd? Just
a few of the old-timers. You might come and bathe
beforehand. Bring Bailey.

   Alice Keppel.

Telegram: 2/5/38

   Money received with thanks STOP Far too generous
STOP Actually now not going to States at all STOP
Will join Charlie in Valencia STOP Always fancied
fighting the good fight STOP Come and join us STOP
Viva las Brigadas Internacionales STOP Philip

[Selection of twenty-first birthday cards, postal orders, a copy
of Fitzgerald's *Tender is the Night*, Yevgeny Zamyatin's *We*, a
fountain pen.]

He hasn't told Goad, or Bailey or Ada that it's his birthday. It's past eleven and he's sitting in the bar of the Excelsior, drunk. He orders a gin fizz and goes to the lavatory where he urinates down the front of his trousers, singing 'Domum' to himself tunelessly. At the bar, he orders another drink and slumps on the stool. Despite the broadcasts, the money, the novel finally finished and typed up and sent off to Faber, he doesn't feel he's made a success of anything in Florence. And yet, he thinks, if he'd been offered this a year and a half ago in Shropshire – to be running the radio station, hosting vibrant cultural discussions with Ezra Pound and Bernard Berenson, invited to parties at Renaissance palaces in the hills of Fiesole – he'd have fainted. It's partly that his expectations move several steps ahead of the events of his life – Goad smiles expectantly at him at the end of every broadcast and the face he returns grows ever more heedful and resigned, as if to say they could do so much better if only they had better equipment, more staff, more luminous interviewees – and partly that he's different now: he walks a little slower, talks more carefully, drifts away during most of the Fascist broadcasts and looks towards the window.

Welsh Frankton,
Shropshire.
1st June.

Dear Esmond,

    I was delighted with your letter, as was your mother.
It seems extraordinary to us, marooned as we are out
here in the wastes, that our son should be at the very
centre of things, hobnobbing with world leaders. We
listened to your programme on Manzoni's The Betrothed
with great interest in the library this evening.

135

Difficult stuff! Pavolini sounds a good sort - well
done for getting him on. I understand that he has Il
Duce's ear, quite the coming man of Italian politics.

Great sense of relief that the problems in
Czechoslovakia appear to have been resolved. Hitler
perhaps not as bellicose as we had feared. Glad also
that Chamberlain was so swift to bat down any talk of
cosying up to the Russians. They're the real enemy:
remember that.

Good work on the latest instalment of advertising
money. Be assured that it's being wisely invested in
the future of this great country.

Your mother sends her love,

Your Father.

P.S. I saw Pound in London - he's barking but seems
to have enjoyed your meeting. When do we hear the
recording you made with him?

[Selection of letters and telegrams from: Birra Moretti, Wilier
Triestina, Snia-Viscosa, Beretta, Danieli, De Agostini, La Stampa, Martini & Rossi, Romeo Motron. All confirm advertising
subscription to Radio Firenze at the new rate of 1,000 lire per
three-minute window.]

Hotel Las Arenas,
Valencia
15th July, '38

Dearest Es,

Of the many things I might have become, I scarcely
thought I'd end up a soldier. But that seems to be

how it's all worked out. Simply thrilling out here.
We travelled up the coast after getting a boat round
the Straits. We could see the shelling of Alicante
- whole place lit up like the sun had toppled down.
Rather beautiful, actually. We came ashore at a kind
of sandy isthmus called El Perellonet and then,
under cover of night, made our way into the city.
Italian warships like glimmering palaces out to sea.
They fire the odd shell every so often but things
seem to have quietened down since we arrived.

I'm driving an ambulance. The Nationalists are
really quite on our doorstep here, so we're always
getting called to dash out and scrape up some poor
chap who's caught one in the head or arm. Charlie
bought me a gun which I fire at pigeons on the roof.
Not much of an aim yet, but I'll need it soon enough,
I would imagine, when the final confrontation comes.
The Republicans are all thoroughly decent sorts.
Lots of Brits, of course, but it's the locals who up
the pulse.

We're staying in a hotel that's been shelled.
I can see the stars from my bed through a hole in
the roof, but it's mild enough and actually rather
romantic. Charlie has insisted on teaching the chaps
cricket. Rather a different game when it's played
between orange trees in the Plaza de la Reina after
a few bottles of Rioja. I scored my first ever fifty
as the light drew in last night, sound of gunfire
and distant shells as I held my bat up to generally
bemused spectators. Spaniards can't play for toffee,
of course. Charlie, who's much better than me, hit
a six that flew so far it ended up over enemy lines.

I'm going to bowl a few grenades at him tomorrow.
It's all just too bloody exciting.

Anyway, I thought you'd want my address, and if
you could spare some cash I'd appreciate it. Think
of it as contributing to the forging of the heroic
new me.

Philip.

One evening, light still trembling outside the windows of the studio. Ada signals the end of the transmission. They've recorded a programme on Murray Constantine's *Swastika Night*, recently translated into Italian. It seems a very daring subject – the novel had, after all, been a choice of the Left Book Club – but it is, thinks Esmond, important that they engage with material like this. The novel imagines a future where the Nazis and Japanese have defeated the heroic Brits, and now squabble with each other over their Fascist empires. It is futuristic, bold, horrifying in the way it takes the unstable present and ramifies it into a vision of the totalitarian world to come. Esmond had enjoyed the book, Goad hadn't.

– *A most engaging debate*, Goad says, standing and stretching, pulling on the blazer which he had hung on the back of his chair. – *Perhaps the best yet.* He smiles at Esmond. – *It wasn't too—?* Goad thinks for a moment, scratching the skin of one hand. – *No, it was fine. Our uncertainty tallies with the culture, I suppose, the uncertainty of the present moment in Europe. I think we did well. Now I must be off, good night, you two.*

Esmond and Ada coil wires, dust the instrument panel, seal up the discs and store them in the rack on one side of the room. He has deliberately avoided speaking to her about the Manifesto of Racial Scientists, about the new laws in place regarding the Jews. Now she wraps her shawl around her neck and stands in the doorway. – *Esmond*, she says. He looks up. – *I don't want any special favours, I don't want you to get in trouble on my behalf, but I want you to know that I enjoy working here.* He lights a cigarette and blows the smoke towards the cornices of ceiling. – *Of course*, he says. – *There's no question. I'll make sure of it.*

When she has left, he sits at the open window, breathes the summer air, smiles peacefully. He thinks of Murray Constantine's words, which he had quoted in the broadcast and which Goad had repeated two or three times in reply: *They will make a world in which it is impossible for a man to love his own daughter.*

```
Ministry of the Interior
Palazzo del Viminale
Rome
21/8/38
```

```
Sir or Madam -
   As the listed employer of Ada Liuzzi, who is
registered as Jewish/other non-Aryan on the Census
dated August 1st, 1938, carried out by the Italian
Office for the Study of Race (under the guidance of
Dr Guido Landra), please advise by return of post if
Ada Liuzzi is employed in a position whereupon her
duties could be described as falling into one of the
following areas:
   a) Government, politics, local or regional council
work, other general administrative role within the
apparatus of the Italian State;
   b) Banking, moneylending, other employment in
which the worker has control over the exchange,
transfer or deployment of sums of money larger than
5,000 lire per calendar month;
```

c) Teaching, lecturing, professorships, any work which brings the named person into regular contact with children or students;

d) Military (including carabinieri), air force, navy, local police, fire service, or any other position requiring access to weapons of any kind;

e) Other educated profession where the named person's Jewish/other non-Aryan status could reasonably be assumed to represent a threat or potential threat to the economic, military, moral or educational health of the nation.

It is your responsibility as employer to ensure that the Jewish/non-Aryan person is correctly employed.

Please also confirm whether Ada Liuzzi has been charged with any crime in the past ten years, and if so the nature of this crime. Please also list any previous or outstanding arrest warrants.

Please inform if Ada Liuzzi became an Italian citizen on or after 31st December, 1919.

Viva Il Duce!

[Enclosed with following letter: article from *The Times* entitled 'Nuremberg and Aussig'.]

Welsh Frankton
Shropshire
12th September

Dear Esmond,

It seems I spoke too soon. Situation in Sudetenland bloody bad. Mosley has put several calls in to the Führer urging him not to act hastily, letting him know that the eyes of the world are upon him, but

I fear they don't have the close relationship they
once did. You'll see I've clipped an article from <u>The
Times</u> calling on the Czechs to cede the territory to
the Germans. Eminently sensible and we can only hope
that it is the view inside Whitehall.

Runciman's attempts to mediate were shambolic, and
Nevile Henderson made a buggery of things in Berlin.
I remember a time when the Brits were known for their
diplomacy. You can just see that bastard Stalin
perched over all of this, rubbing his hands with
glee. Chamberlain flies to Berchtesgaden tomorrow;
he's got a good head, and he'll need it. You could
picture this all unspooling rather quickly, with
the Poles and the Russians and that madman Konrad
Henlein all buttoning their coats. If Germany does
decide to wade in, the Czech will be wiped out in a
flash. It's interesting, Esmond - difficult times,
of course, but interesting.

I was glad to read in your letter that you have
developed such affection for Filippino Lippi. I
don't remember seeing this particular triptych when
I was in Florence. I never really told you about
that tour back in '06. I went with Arthur Fitzroy and
Chummy Little straight from Cambridge. We arrived in
Florence at night, driving into the narrowing throat
of the valley, using the great dome to guide us.
It's strange, but I can only recall small details of
the city from that time. I remember waking the next
morning in our hotel - the Excelsior - and looking
out over the rooftops of the town, but almost
nothing else. The room of Botticellis and Lippis
at the Uffizi, of course, the insides of certain

churches, Cellini's Perseus. But it's as if it was
too much for my mind to hold. Every time your mother
and I returned to Florence, it was like drawing back
a curtain to reveal bright treasures of memory.

Enough of my rambling. You have great things to
do. Mosley is staying with us. He and Diana are
always after news of you. We are both struck by
how well you and Goad work together - a thoroughly
engaging duo. Funny the way in which things work
out, isn't it? That all of this now feels fated -
that you should leave Cambridge, go out to Florence,
make a man of yourself. Then - who knows? - come back
and do great things for the Party at home, or fight
like a lion in the war when and if it comes.

Your mother sends her love,

Your Father.

Faber & Faber
24 Russell Square,
London, WC1

23rd September, 1938

Dear Mr Lowndes -

I greatly enjoyed the draft of In Love and War
that you sent me. A rather good idea to take a
well-known figure like Hulme and re-tell his life
as fiction. I thought you got the essential clash
between his bawdiness, his brutality and his
brilliance absolutely spot-on. I also very much

enjoyed the way you worked his poetry, his letters, his life, into your fiction.

I would like to ask you to take another run at the passages describing his life in battle. It seems to me that these are where the novel stumbles. Ask your father - he was there with him. Read Sassoon (if you haven't already, and your prose rather suggests you haven't). It is a fact that whilst so many of those who know what it was like to fight in the trenches are still with us, there is something of a moral duty for the writer to convey the truth of war as clearly and cleverly as possible. It doesn't seem to me that your novel does this.

If you are able to fix this, I should think there's a good chance that we'd be interested in publishing. It won't hinder things that your father's name, and your own work on the wireless confer upon you a certain celebrity. We won't make you rich, but Faber & Faber is a fine publishing house and we'd be very glad to have you on board.

Sincerely,

Richard de la Mare.

Via dei Forbici, 35c
Firenze
1.10.38

Dear Esmond -

It was most kind of you and Father Bailey to treat us to such an exceptionally good dinner last week. I am only sorry it has taken me such a long time to write and thank you. As you can imagine, things are rather difficult for our family at the moment. I don't like to go into things too deeply in front of Ada (or indeed her mother, who is, as you saw, suffering from a deep sadness at the turn events have taken), but you can imagine the sense of betrayal we are feeling just now. I - who have given everything for this government, for this country - my country - and for the Fascist cause - that I should no longer be thought of as an Italian, that my passport should be confiscated and returned defiled, that La Nostra Bandiera, which has supported Il Duce for more than a decade, should be closed down - All of this seems incredible to me.

I enclose a petition signed by several of my prominent friends - you will note the first name is that of Giovanni Gentile himself - supporting my exclusion from the punitive racial laws which have so hampered my ability to continue in the service of a cause in whose integrity I continue to believe with all my heart. I acknowledge the need for the Charter of Race, given that so many of those who insist on swimming against the tide of history - the members of Giustizia e Libertà, the leaders of the Communist unions - are Jewish. It seems sensible also to deny the great blessing of Italian citizenship to the recent miscegenated product of our African adventures. But to someone like me? It is a great travesty.

As a figure in the public eye, I'd be very grateful if you would sign this petition. I have been let

down by many of those I counted amongst my dearest
companions, but we are lucky to live at times such
as these when the bonds of friendship are put to
the test and we may winnow out the lickspittles and
toadies. Perhaps you'd pass it on to Father Bailey
once you sign it, and ask him to send it the way of
anyone else he thinks might help my cause.

I'm aware that you have been put under some
pressure over Ada's continued employment at Radio
Firenze. I wanted to offer you my sincere thanks,
and that of my wife. We love our daughter and know
she loves working with you. See you for dinner on
Wednesday as usual, I hope.

With my most cordial salutations,
Guido Liuzzi.

[Collection of invitations; visiting cards; concert, cinema and
opera tickets; train tickets to Rome, Milan, Genoa and Venice;
receipts for meals, hotels, taxi journeys.]

He has been on so many train journeys these past months he
feels the rhythm of the shuddering carriages in the patterns of
his thoughts. He suffers a kind of seasickness for the first half-
hour in a new city, until he finds his land legs again. He does
not see enough of Italy on these trips. Often he is taken straight
from the station to some out-of-town office to meet the scions
of wealthy manufacturing families, ambitious executives keen
to toady to *Il Duce*, place a flag in the ground on Radio Firenze.
Advertising money is pouring into the station, eclipsing the
contributions made by the operations in Heligoland and Sark,
and he and Ada open the discs each afternoon and listen to
stoic men in clipped voices talk about the smooth action of

their Beretta, the speed of their Romeo, the refined taste of their Martini. The next day, he is a travelling businessman – he feels modern, useful, as if he has stepped from a dream into real life.

He spends a night in a hotel in Venice overlooking the Piazza San Marco. The city is more ornate, more oriental than Florence, the squares wider and suffused with grey light. It seems to him a more naturally Fascist environment. His taxi driver points out the balcony from which Mussolini and Hitler addressed the crowds when they met there in '34. He is appalled by the stench of the canals. He meets a girl at the foot of the Torre dell'Orologio and takes her back to his hotel. He is surprised when, in the morning, she wants paying.

He finds an England in the landscape. Looking out of the window of the train as he crosses the Po Valley, he sees a coppice of oak and elder that might have been a hillside in Ellesmere. He is reading *War and Peace*, falling in love with Andrei and Natasha in equal measure, but he thinks of England. And the streets of Milan and Turin are as dull as those of London, the people of those busy northern cities as lost in their own affairs, in their own hurried footsteps and urban anxieties.

Whenever he returns to Florence, making his way by foot down the via Tornabuoni and over the Ponte Santa Trinità to the gate of St Mark's, it feels like home.

Roma Reial Hotel, Barcelona
4/11/38

Dearest Es –

Everything's buggered. I'm in Barcelona, looking down over the Plaza Reial. Bloody rain gushing onto

the cobblestones, turning lanes into mud, splashing
up and soaking the few miserable creatures out there
pushing half-empty carts up to the Ramblas markets.
Above the noise of the rain on the roof I can hear
the shells to the south of the city, guns in the
hills. Place I'm in used to be a hotel, but there's
no bed, nothing in the room but dust, my few books,
my revolver, a blanket. I'm hungry and we're all
bloody buggered.

That sod Chamberlain's to blame. We all had so
much hope. We were cheering Hitler on during the
Sudeten Crisis, applauding every act of violence,
every ultimatum ignored. We thought, you see,
that it'd lead to an alliance against Fascism:
the Russians, the Brits and the French. Even the
Americans, perhaps. That as Hitler pushed things
further and further, the democratic powers (well,
and Stalin) would see Fascism for the evil it is
(sorry, Es, but there you have it). They'd turn not
only on Hitler, but on Franco, Mussolini, Horthy -
the whole dark stain wiped from the map. And before
you brace yourself for a wiping, take a good look
in the mirror. You're no more a Fascist than I am.
Anyone who's had his cock in my mouth automatically
unsubscribes himself from the Fascist Cause. It's
one of life's little rules.

Now all we have is this welching appeasement -
'Peace in our time'. There was a real chance for a
better world and we blew it. I'm in such a rage, Es,
I feel like running up into the hills with my gun
and having a go. It's funny, now that we're really
fighting, now that we can see the Falangists with

our field glasses from the look-out on the roof,
I don't feel the least bit windy. Heroism ain't
the word for it either, it's just a kind of placid
acceptance. I'm going to see this out and bugger the
consequences.

Charlie's dead, by the way. We were caught in
an ambush on the way out of Valencia. Italian CTV
troops. Nothing to be done. He died holding his
cricket bat, which I think would've made him happy.
I lay underneath him and Gonzalo (the boy we'd
been travelling with) for an hour, listening to
the Italians picking around in our stuff, feeling
Charlie's breathing getting shallower all the time.
Gonzalo died immediately. They'd mined the road
and the car was flung up and off into a ditch,
everything rolling and tumbling and then a volley
of machine-gun fire that tore through the car and
through Gonzalo, whose body, I think, protected
me. Charlie only took one bullet, but it was in the
eye. Straight through and out the back. He looked
like he was winking, which I felt rotten about
as I thought it. They dragged him and Gonzalo out
from under the rolled car. I hid beneath a tartan
rug. They'd found our stash of whisky in the boot
and seemed more interested in that than in us, the
bodies.

I waited until darkness and then crept out into
the cool air, a waning moon on the water, bats
flapping etc. Took me three nights, only travelling
by dark, sipping the half-bottle of whisky the
Italians left to keep me warm. Finally Barcelona,
where the Republicans have made their new capital

148

and everyone is doggedly optimistic, even under this
bloody rain.

There are a good number of English here, enough
that I've organised a few games of cricket in the
Plaza in Charlie's memory. Pathetic sight, me in the
rain with a group of five or six scrawny, battered
Englishmen crouched around the crease, and me crying
so much to think of playing with Charlie in the
corridors in Vienna, in the squares in Valencia. I
was never much of a cricketer anyway, but I'll keep
playing for his sake, I think. We were in love, you
see.

Send me some money, Es. Anything will do. I need
to get boiled, stinko, lit up like a church and
slopped to the gills, but haven't a peseta to my
name.

Philip.

Welsh Frankton,
Shropshire.
26th November

Darling E -

I haven't slept a wink since I heard you were
coming back for Christmas. Simply too thrilling.
Daddy's the happiest he's been in years - I
swear it. I should imagine the train ride will
be splendid - take some good books and fall into
some frightfully exotic affair with a White
Russian countess. If it were anyone but you

having this glamorous time, turning daddy into
a nervous schoolgirl and generally being the top
of everyone's toast, I might feel a Small Dash of
Envy. As it is, I'm just too, too thrilled for you
darling.

Mick Clarke (who has taken over the nutty side
of the Party since William Joyce left for Germany)
is in a high frenzy over Kristallnacht. His grin
is so wide he risks flipping open like a hatbox. He
and Mosley are down here for a pow-wow with daddy.
They're arguing over whether the Party should cosy
up to Hitler now he's shown his true colours: daddy
is anti, Clarke pro, Mosley increasingly addled and
prone to letting Clarke take control. The Times got
it right on Germany, for once. It seems as if all
the talk of the British Union as the party of peace
has been for nothing. Because we should be fighting
against the Germans, shouldn't we? Kristallnacht
etc.

At least there's Christmas. We'll have masses to
catch up on when you're here. Mother and I went into
Chester yesterday and I saw what I want to get you
for your present. I won't spoil the surprise, but
it's just perfect. Can't wait to sing carols and
roast chestnuts and go for walks in the cold and
generally just bask in your company.

Excited oodles,

Anna xxx.

Villa dell'Ombrellino
Piazza di Bellosguardo
Firenze

2/12/38

Dear Harold, Frederick and Esmond,

It is with some sadness that I write to tell
you that George and I have decided, when we visit
Violet in Sussex this Christmas, to stay with her
into the New Year. Whether it's the position of
L'Ombrellino, perched up here custodial of the city,
or our own status within Anglo-Florentine society,
it is impossible for us to remain. Windows broken at
night, the crudest graffiti on the walls, two cooks
in a row burgling us of food and plate and the police
won't do a thing about it.

We will, of course, be back eventually, whether
after this ghastly looming war or before it. George
is still certain we'll be fighting the Russians. He
has dusted off his uniform in anticipation and is
wandering around looking fairly brutal.

We wanted, before we go, to wish you both a
great deal of luck, and to thank you for all the
entertainment, friendship and joy you have brought
to us these past few years. We'll be leaving many of
our possessions here. I'll send Massimo down with a
key - perhaps you'd pop in and make sure the place
isn't overrun with rats or Italians in our absence.

With love and best wishes,

Alice and George Keppel.

La Palme,
Bast de l'Abbaye,
Le Colle-sur-Loup,
Alpes-Maritimes,
France.
17th December, '38

Dear Esmond -

Tempus fugit! Know I should have written sooner to
thank you for helping with the scrape I got myself
into last year. Inexcusable, really, but I've been
travelling rather a lot. In the hills above Nice
now, but got here via Greece, Morocco, Malta and
I don't know where else. Pino has just joined me.
His eyes are back working, but he's grown horribly
tubby. Can hardly bear to look at him. We're working
on a book of aphrodisiacal recipes together. Have
you ever tried simmered crane? Lambs' testes? Sow's
vulva? Thought not. All of them dee-lish.

A lot of blathering about the war. Nothing like
an expat community to inspire a gaggle of silly
women on the subject of catastrophe. Pino and I
intend to stay gracefully here for a few more
months before returning to Italy. It's the only
place I feel sane, you see. If there is a war, all
the better. The prospect of a gruesome death gives
young men a bit of spritz. Don't go into battle
yourself, though, Esmond. It'd be a crime to risk
that exquisite phiz.

How's the writing coming along? Are you keeping
a diary? You'll thank yourself when it comes to
your autobiog. More than that, reading back over

the early years of this century in my own tattered
journals is one of the few unassailable pleasures
left to me. Affreux being alive at this age, I
tell you. Pity in the eyes of the sailors by the
dock, with their rotten teeth and the reek of
bouillabaisse. Better live in the corridors of your
own memory. To do that: keep a diary.

Love to Gerald. Terribly sorry about Fiamma.
Rotten luck.

Norman.

His father meets him at the train station at Gobowen. He
is standing on the platform as the train pulls in, a silk scarf
around his neck. He is obscured briefly by a cloud of steam
and then reappears, waving his newspaper. He looks old, kind,
eager. The Humber is parked in front of the station. Esmond
lifts his bag into the back and climbs up beside his father. It is
as if the steam from the train follows them onto the road: mist
parts as they motor along the narrow lanes, through Whitting-
ton with its castle and ugly red church and up the hill to Welsh
Frankton.

His family is waiting at the front door when he arrives: the
silhouette of his mother, Rudyard to one side with a dog in
his arms, scratching its ear. Anna pushes past her brother and
comes running out to the car. Her breath is heavy and hot as
she embraces him and he is surprised at his tears. She has lost
weight and he lifts her from the ground with ease, pressing
their damp cheeks together and spinning on the gravel of the
courtyard.

He's only here for four days – he and Goad will be broadcasting again on New Year's Eve – but now, surrounded by his
family, with Christmas to look forward to, the evidence of his

success in the way his father steers him to the drinks cabinet, sits beside him on the sofa in the library, places his hand on Esmond's as if to assure himself of his son's physical presence, he feels weightless, joyous, grown.

On Christmas Eve, Mosley and Diana arrive, on their way to Wooton Lodge. Everyone seems to want to touch Esmond, to congratulate him, to hear from him some story of his time in Italy that can be theirs. Diana drinks too much at lunch and then sits very close to him on the sofa afterwards. – *Kit is so frightfully chuffed*, she whispers. This is what she calls Mosley. – *Not just with the money, darling, but with the way you've made the British Union seem relevant and involved in the great matters of the Continent.* She blows cigarette smoke towards him and laughs. She places a hand on his thigh, moving it in languorous strokes until it brushes the tip of his cock. He feels himself reddening, murmurs an excuse and goes to join Anna and Rudyard in the kitchen.

Mosley grips him by the hand as he leaves. They are all standing in the hallway and he speaks in loud bursts. – *Bloody good stuff, Esmond. A man in his father's image. Knows how to get things done. Make sure you keep it up. We're all relying on you.* Sir Lionel is looking at Esmond with a kind of evangelical glow. His mother comes up behind him and puts a gentle hand on his back. They go out into the courtyard, waving, as Mosley's car disappears down the drive.

On Christmas morning they sit around the tree in front of the fire. The day seems to serve nostalgia, newly minted. As he watches his mother tousle Rudyard's hair, his father unwrap his presents using his arm and his teeth, Anna open the purse he'd bought her on the via Calimala, he begins to miss and grieve for them, as if the picture were gently fading before his eyes. A Jack Russell and a Scottish terrier come bounding in, yapping and worrying the wrapping paper until Rudyard follows, chasing them out.

Esmond saves his present from Anna until last of all. It is large and square and carefully wrapped in brown paper. He opens a wooden frame around a collage of photographs of the family. He holds it in his lap, smiling, letting himself drift downwards into the scenes she has laid out for him: his mother and father by a piper at Loch Katrine, Anna and him in front of the beech tree at Aston Magna, Rudyard with blood-stained cheeks standing high in his stirrups. Anna comes to sit beside him – *It's simply ripping, old thing,* he says. – *Thank you.*

He and Anna go for a walk that afternoon. The wind has picked up, shredding the clouds above, letting down barbs of winter sunshine. Three ducks bob on the canal's glassy back. – *How are you?* he asks. A faltering of her eyes. – *I'm marked for death,* she says. *Like a character in a motion picture.* She laughs and he sees the red-ribbed roof of her mouth. They walk past glumly chewing horses, a pub with smoke drifting from its chimney, the slim elegance of a birch wood. – *I live through you,* she says. *It's not as sad as it sounds. Each of your letters, it's like a clear breath. Keep writing them.* They stop there and the wind leans into them. She shudders. – *I love you,* he says, and he realises it's the truest thing he's said, perhaps ever. They walk back in silence, arms linked.

In his room alone later, slightly drunk after an hour in the library with his father, he places the collage on his dresser and pulls up his chair to look at it again. His life appears, tessellated yet suddenly coherent. The three blond children crouched around the crease during a cricket match on the lawn at Aston Magna. Cook is at bat, a set expression on her face as she waits for Sir Lionel to bowl. Esmond and Anna on a carousel in Hyde Park. She must be four or five, her blonde hair spilling out from beneath the dome of a cloche hat. He is behind her on the horse, looking serious and responsible. A line-up of young Blackshirts, Esmond at one end, smaller and blonder than any of the others, his chest out, chin up. Esmond and Anna and Rudyard in the various arrangements of childhood, their father proudly with them, their mother more distant, always looking off as if keen to get on to some urgent appointment. Towards the bottom of the collage, more recent pictures: the pantechnicon van unloading in front of Welsh Frankton; Esmond in a straw boater by the river in Cambridge. In the very centre, the sun around which the other pictures orbit, is a large photograph of Esmond and his father in full British Union uniform, lightning flashes bright on their chests. They are on-stage at the Royal Albert Hall. It was 1934, Sir Lionel's last great political speech. He'd chosen Esmond to stand with him on the platform beforehand in front of the thousands of faces. – *This is my eldest son*, he'd said, holding his good arm towards Esmond. – *This is who I fought my war for. It's why I'm here now. To build a future for young men like Esmond, a future in which there can never be another war like 14–18, a future where honest, decent folk who want to earn a living may do so. We are moving –* he'd looked around at the massed ranks of Party members – *towards a moment of reckoning. Choose the right side.* He seized Esmond's hand and lifted it into the air. *Choose Esmond!* The crowd let out a roar, Esmond had tried to force a smile, the camera flashed.

The next morning, his father comes into his room early. – *We decided not to hunt*, he says – *Really?* Esmond sits on the side of his bed. – *I know you can't bear it. You're our guest of honour.* Sir Lionel goes to look at the collage on the dresser. – *We lost her for hours making this. Covered herself in glue. I'd forgotten that photograph, you and me at the rally. It's rather good, isn't it?* He comes to sit beside Esmond on the bed. – *Things aren't as easy as they might seem back here*, he says. *I fear Mosley's made some bad decisions. Circumstances are moving against us. Your mother and I— There have been rows. She's been talking to Diana, to Mick Clarke, all of them helping to clarify my faults. I simply won't have us allied with the Germans. Mosley's still on my side, most days.*

He's looking down at his hand, frowning. – *Your success, Esmond, it gives me the advantage in these negotiations for the future of the Party. That we can forge a future that is cultured, civilised, peaceful. I point to the fact that Radio Firenze is ten times more successful – in numbers and in contribution to Party funds – than these lunatic broadcasts coming out of Heligoland and Sark.* He stands, ruffling Esmond's hair. *It also gives me hope*, he says, *to have you, my eldest son, out there, making a difference. It helps me believe there's a future worth hanging around for.*

They all come to see him off at the station. The collage, back in brown paper and string, is on the seat of his compartment. He presses his face to the upper window as the train moves off and he sees the four of them standing there, Anna with her arm around their mother, who is inexplicably crying, his father waving furiously, Rudyard kneeling down with a dog and looking on. It strikes him, as the train gathers speed and moves out of sight, that Rudyard's eyes are the mirror of his own, identical in shape and shade. He sits down, pulls out *The Brothers Karamazov*, and begins to read.

[Postcard from Lyme Regis]

31st January

Dearest E -

Presume you've heard about Auden and Isherwood going off to America. Father is over the moon, as you can imagine. Proves that the younger gen of

leftie writers has no spine. It is rather feeble of
them, don't you think? To flee when we need writers,
poets, men and women who can make sense of the world.
I was reading Auden after you left. I thought: a
poet is a stranger who knows one's secrets.

One of daddy's friends suggested I take the
seaside air for my asthma. It's frightful here. The
unanimous elderly, wandering along the front as if
they might walk themselves away from death. Luscious
to see you at Xmas. Do come back more often.

Brisk, deep-lunged oodles,

Anna xxx.

Faber & Faber
24 Russell Square,
London, WC1

4th February, 1939.

Dear Esmond,

I'm sorry it has taken me so long to get back to
you. I'm very much aware that you've been waiting
for a reply and it is inexcusable that it has taken
us these months to come to a decision.

I'm afraid the war passages haven't much improved
as far as I can see. It's as if, as soon as Hulme
crosses the Channel, a veil comes up over him and
your ability to feel your way into his experience
evaporates. It's really very sad. I showed this
to Tom Eliot - to make sure I wasn't being blind -

and he agreed wholeheartedly. It's difficult for
a writer your age to capture something so raw, so
violent, so far outside his own space. Has your
father read it? What does he think?

There's also the problem of a certain resistance
within some parts of the company to publish an
author so closely associated in many minds with
the Fascists. Things have changed in the national
atmosphere since I first read In Love and War.
Since we became aware of the horrors executed by the
National Socialists, the bloodiness of Mussolini's
regime (so wonderfully set out in Ignazio Silone's
Fontamara - have you read it?), it feels like a
madness to publish a novel which - if we look behind
the curtain of the fiction - is the elevation of a
Fascist (or proto-Fascist) to a position of mythic
heroism.

I'm sorry to be the bearer of bad news. You're
still very young and do please send me your work as
it develops.

Sincerely,

Richard de la Mare.

Via dei Forbici, 35c
Firenze
17.2.39

Dear Esmond -

A thousand thanks for your visit. I know that
Ada put you up to it, and I know what a miserable

and pathetic creature I must seem, but to have
had everything ripped away from me like this--
My good friend Friedrich Kriegbaum, from the
Kunsthistorisches Institut, visited the night
before last and I could barely stand to have him in
the house. 'The annihilation of the Jewish race in
Europe.' It is shameful. It is as if I was walking
in darkness and suddenly a light of impossible
brightness has been shone upon me. I am blinded
again, but this time it is the force of the light
that has taken away my sight.

I'm not sure what will happen to me, Esmond. I
wrote some ill-advised letters in my madness. I
wrote to Il Duce himself, I wrote to the German
Consul, I think I even wrote to Herr Hitler. If
the worst should occur, look after Ada for me. Her
mother has travelled north to stay with relatives in
Switzerland. I'm determined not to be chased out of
this city I love, but I may have little choice in the
matter. I couldn't bear it if my idiocy should lead
to something awful happening to Ada.

With my apologies for my weakness and stupidity,
Guido Liuzzi.

Telegram: 7/4/39

Anna condition serious STOP At John Radcliffe
seeing specialist STOP Your mother with her STOP
Will keep you posted STOP

160

[Various invitations to concerts associated with the Maggio Musicale: Beethoven at the Kunsthistorisches Institut, *Tosca* at the Teatro Verdi (sponsored by Piaggio), Bach at the British Institute, a string quartet hosted by Bernard Berenson at I Tatti.]

He sits in the grand drawing room at Berenson's house, I Tatti, and tries to concentrate on the music. It is Haydn and the string quartet is very good, but he is thinking only of Anna. It was clear she was fighting at Christmas, desperate not to let him see her discomfort, and by the end of his visit was snatching gulps of breath, slinking off for rests in the early afternoon, pausing in the middle of their conversations to collect herself. He wonders if perhaps she might come out to Florence to join him. But war feels so close, so inevitable.

Ada is beside him. She's wearing a dark green dress, long earrings with jade stones. Her pale arms grip the chair beneath her as she sways to the music. She hums so softly that only he can hear. When the movement finishes, she turns to him, clasps her hands to her chest and begins to applaud.

```
Welsh Frankton
Shropshire
26th April

Dear Esmond -
  Anna is back home. It seems as if it was a false
alarm, or that the treatment at the John Radcliffe
worked. Sorry if my telegram alarmed you. She's
rather frail, but she's being a good brave girl.
Rudyard has been wheeling her around the garden in
her bath chair - it's bloody sweet, really.
  Looks like another war is inevitable. I read a
```

historian in <u>The Spectator</u> who has identified only twenty-nine years since the Roman Empire when a war wasn't being fought somewhere in the world. We lurch from crisis to crisis and we learn nothing from history.

You asked in your letter what I could tell you about the last war, the first war, as I suppose we should learn to call it. About Hulme. I'm glad you've stuck on with your novel, sorry that Faber turned it down. (Perhaps we could set up a Fascist Press - not a bad idea!) Hulme was a brute, a gent, a genuine conservative. He was a bloody good friend and I was undone when he died. As for my war, it was a nightmare, but the worst part is that nothing since - not politics, not sex, not hunting, nothing - has lived up to it. The real horror, Esmond, is that I'm not still there, that life will never have the same sheen, quite the purpose it had in those days.

If you ever find yourself fighting, remember this one thing: anger is stronger than fear. It was only years after the war ended, when I stopped being angry, that I began to feel afraid. Remember that and you'll make a fine soldier.

Give my regards to Goad.

Your mother sends her love,

Your father.

```
Tombland,
Norwich.
23rd May '39.

Dear Esmond -
   Sit tight! I'll be back at the end of the week
when we can put our heads together and try to work
out what this all means. In the interim you should
be in loco presbyter, helping the lame dogs over
stiles. Remember: we're not at war yet. Mussolini is
a strong, fine leader and we'll have to trust that
this Pact of Steel he's signed with Hitler is a piece
of political theatre.
   The funeral was as funerals are: dispiriting
to see the reduction of a fine life into so many
platitudes. I read 'This I know: that my avenger
lives' from the Book of Job. Stood a few hairs on
end. Sad to say goodbye to mother, but all flesh,
etc.
   If anything comes up, ask Goad.
   Best of British,
   Bailey.
```

He is lying back in the pool at L'Ombrellino, looking up through
the leaves of the camphor tree. He'd come up to check on the
place for George and Alice Keppel, but the walk up the hill was
so tiring, the abandoned rooms of the villa so stuffy and smoth-
ering, that he'd run past the box hedges of the upper terrace,
down the steps and between the two dodos before he could
think, shedding his clothes along the path as he went.

   If he can just stretch his arm out a little further, he thinks, he'll
be able to grab hold of Gerald's ankle, touch one of Fiamma's

slim limbs. He wonders if the water holds some trace of them: fragments of Fiamma's skin, microscopic, etherised. He takes a mouthful of water and spits it out in a green arc. There is also the present: the water murky with weed, slightly malodorous but still deliciously cool. Cypress cones float about him like miniature wooden roses. They look like love. He is in love. Hopeless, unrequited love. He grins. There's something unseemly in it, with the coming war, with Anna's illness, it feels improper to be lying back here in the water smiling like a child, but he is in love.

She is not beautiful; she is older than him and in his company she is distant and professional. She has given him no sign that she views him as anything other than an employer, a Fascist; certainly not a friend, never a lover. She doesn't know that he's been lying to the increasingly officious Interior Ministry functionaries about her, using his friendship with Pavolini, his letter from Mussolini to make sure she remains unmolested. There are rumours that the Jews will be made to wear yellow stars, to live in a ghetto up above Rifredi. There are camps being built in the south, so the whispers say, trains heading north from stations in the Friuli, rounding up Jews who've fled from Germany, from Austria, sending them back where they came from. He will keep her from all of this.

During the broadcasts, he watches her when she's not looking. – *Ada*, he whispers above the sound of the crickets – *Ada*. He's spent his life turning over stones, looking in rockpools, for someone like her. She has been in front of him for more than a year. There is something upright and idealistic and whole to her that makes him want to lay his hands upon her, to build a shell around her with his arms. He lies back in the water of the swimming pool as the air begins to darken above him and the wind stirs the fingers of the pines. In the hesitant evening he basks in the gorgeous restlessness of his love for her. – *Ada*.

De Koning van Spanje,
Korte Nieuwstraat 12,
Antwerp.
19th June.

Dear Esmond,

We write with bad news. Philip was killed in Spain
on the 23rd of December last year. We have been
moving around a great deal and have only just had the
information ourselves. Amongst his affairs there were
several of your letters and instructions to let you
know in the event of anything happening to him. I'm
aware that you two were terribly close at Cambridge
and I'm sorry to bear news that must come as a shock.

We had a letter from General Walter, the leader
of the XIV International Brigade under which Philip
served for much of his time in Spain. It appears the
death was somewhat heroic. He held a machine-gun
emplacement in Les Borges Blanques for six hours,
single-handed, as the Falangists swarmed over the
area. He was on a small hill in the centre of a grove
of olives and, when he was finally overwhelmed, he
turned his gun upon himself rather than be captured.
A great soldier, General Walter told us, fearless
and loyal.

We blame ourselves for Philip being in Spain. We
had arranged to meet him in Lisbon, but I wanted to
leave Europe as soon as possible. I got us a berth
on a ship bound for Rio de Janeiro that struck rocks
off the Azores. We spent several months attempting
to get safe passage onwards from Ponta Delgada, but
finally we were returned to Lisbon. With almost the

last of the money we carried with us from Austria, we procured a cabin on the MS St Louis, a German ship, to Cuba. We were denied landing in Havana, then in Florida, where we might have swum ashore, so close were we to the beaches. Now we are back in Antwerp, penniless and without hope, to find that our only son is dead. Life can be cruel.

Thank you for the friendship you showed to Philip. We hope that, whatever dark days lie ahead, you continue to flourish.

Martin and Liesl Keller.

Berchtesgadener Hof Hotel
Berchtesgaden
Germany
29th June 1939

Dear Esmond –

I have left your father. I imagine you picked up on the coolness between us while you were there at Christmas, but since then things have deteriorated significantly and I felt I needed to make a Break for Freedom. I married your father for his courage and his conviction; in recent months he is short of both. I have been living too long in the shadow of a man I no longer respect. These must be hard things for you to hear, but I wanted to explain to you why I, too, have left England.

Ever since our first trip to National Socialist Germany, back in the bright days of the spring of

'35, I have felt strongly that the Führer had a vision of the future that would shape the Fate of the World. My visits with Mosley and Diana, and more recently on my own, have only confirmed this. We are moving into a Nazi Future and men like your father who try to resist this will be left behind.

I'm sure it must have seemed cruel to you, the burning of your books, your manuscript. I wanted to explain it to you at the time, but I knew your father would have thought it absurd. There is another Great War coming. Germany has been preparing since 1933, it will draw upon all the resources of Mitteleuropa, it has the kind of Deep Ideological Conviction its opponents lack. By the end of 1940, all Europe will be German, soon after, all of the globe will fly the Glorious Swastika. I burnt your degenerate books, your limp-wristed writing because I knew the risk they'd pose for you in the coming years. (I suggest you burn this letter, too.) We - the British Union, those of us who have remained faithful to the cause - will be at the forefront of Nazi Britain and we can't have bad eggs amongst us. I hope you see that, Esmond.

Diana, Unity and I are in Berchtesgaden. I'm going to dinner at the Kelsteinhaus tonight. I can't tell you how exciting this is. I feel like I'm breathing for the first time in my life, up here in the mountains. Don't worry about your father - he has Anna to look after, his losing battle against the Tides of History to fight. I never really felt I knew my children, but I loved you. I hope you know that.

Heil Hitler!

Your Mother.

Telegram: 13/7/39

Many thanks for your generous wire STOP This has
saved us from a most difficult time STOP We will
repay you once these dark days are over STOP Martin
and Liesl Keller

Royal Shrewsbury Infirmary,
Salop.
24/7/39

Darling E -
Everyone rather glum over mother leaving. Did she
write to you? I can't think she was terribly good
to us, but I do miss her. Every evening now, daddy
goes for mournful gallops across the countryside
with the dogs. Not hunting, but still looking for
something I think, in the copses, along the banks
of the canal. He comes back covered in mud, looking
provoked.
In the hospital, am on a new machine that does
some of my breathing for me. Wonder when it'll be
that machines take over all our vital functions
and we're left sitting out infinity with only our
various looks of unease to distinguish us. Sounds
frightfully dull to me. Put myself in here by going
for a long walk beside the canal two nights ago. It
was damp and I wasn't well-enough wrapped up but O
the joy of it, striding along taking great lungfuls
of air and watching clouds rush across the sky and

168

feeling peppy for the first time in an age. Daddy
doesn't know how to talk to the nurses like mother
did. He's far too polite.

Sorry to hear Faber won't take In Love and War.
Bloody bastards. Don't know a good thing when they
see it. There are other publishers, you know - I do
wish you'd send me a copy. I know you think it's too
filthy for my young eyes, but I promise I'd skip
over the really grubby bits.

Daddy's frightfully keen you should come home
before the war starts. It would be super to have you,
although I've no doubt he'd meet you off the train
and march you straight down to the Knightsbridge
barracks to enlist. Don't go and get killed,
darling. It would be too beastly of you.

Cough oodles cough,

Anna xxx.

Via dei Forbici, 35c
Firenze
12.8.39

Dear Esmond,

I am now going north - to Turin. It is said they
are not implementing their vile laws with the
same rigidity up there. Ettore Ovazza even claims
he can find me work, perhaps. I will not flee to
Switzerland just yet. Ada says she will stay here
and I cannot persuade her otherwise. Look after her,
perhaps bring some dinner over every now and again.

She tends not to eat enough. I will write to her, and to you, often. I wish that she would come with me, but she says she belongs here, that she is a Florentine. It is with great sadness that I leave her, and this city.

With very best wishes and thanks,

Guido Liuzzi.

Welsh Frankton
Shropshire
26th August.

Dear Esmond,

I thought I'd sit down and write while our conversation was still fresh in my mind. It's also an excuse to lock myself away in the library for an hour and not deal with the ghastly necessities of death - funeral invitations and readings and notes from well-wishers. The house is like a florist's - bouquets on every table, pollen staining every carpet. Your mother has come back, of course, but she's flying out again on the 30th. She's frantic not to be trapped in England when the show starts. Odd to have her around the house again - we'd been rather getting used to life without her.

You were very brave on the telephone; I'm sorry I didn't hold up my end quite so well. Anna loved you best of all, you know. You're right that we should feel blessed to have had her in our lives as long as we did. I keep telling myself this in the hope it'll

comfort me. Not yet. So far it's just a terrible
sense that everything dear has reeled away from me.
Your mother, Anna, the Party, the peaceful world I
thought I was serving to build. Must be difficult to
know that your father's a failure, old chap, but the
evidence is there for all to see.

Come home for the funeral, Esmond. Your brother
needs you here. We all do. You don't want to be
scurrying over with every other Tom, Dick and
Harriet when war's declared - push off now, know
that you've made a real contribution over the past
few years and move on. I could get you into the
Guards. Damned fine kit they have - you could do
much worse. You'd be sure to see battle early on and
that's important with a war. Get out early and see
a few bullets - you never know when it might all be
over.

I'm afraid the Party's more or less finished.
Smashed on the rocks of history. I thought the
Molotov-Ribbentrop Pact might turn a few within the
Party my way, might make them see that the Nazis are
the enemy every bit as much as the Reds. Joyce and
Clarke and now, alas, Mosley and your mother have
turned the British Union into Nazis, tout court.
With the stories about what's happening to the
Jews in the work camps, the rounding up of innocent
civilians, the stench of _evil_ settling over Germany,
they've simply hitched their cart to the wrong
horse. Mosley is still making noises about peace,
about the need to avoid another Ypres, another
Somme, but our time is passing.

Wind things up and come back home, Esmond - it's

171

the right thing to do. It's time for you to be the
soldier you were meant to be. If not for me, do it
for Anna.

I send you my love,

Your Father.

He stands with Ada on the Ponte Santa Trinità, his elbows on
the parapet wall, crying into the water below. He feels himself
unravelling with each breath, his spirit unstitching itself, dis-
solving into the yellow Arno. Ada has her hand on his shoulder. She is saying something, but he can't understand her, can
only see her lips move through the blur of his tears. He takes her
in his arms and they stand there, and she feels bone-thin and
so like Anna that he wonders for a moment if he will go mad.
He wonders how much sorrow a mind can take – Anna, Philip,
Fiamma – before it will no longer move through the world and
sleeps in its own dark reaches.

Carità is marching on the north bank of the river. Fifty men
in yellow fezzes, a squad of Fascist Youth, a band playing the
Fascist anthem, 'Giovinezza'. All goose-stepping loyally after
him, this short-trousered messiah, whip in his hand, high voice
reaching even over the music. – *Me ne frego! Vincere e vinceremo!
Viva Il Duce!* Esmond sobs against Ada, watching the marching through his tears. Now that England and Germany are at
war, the MVSN seem louder and more urgent, as do the Fascist politicians who stand on the steps of the Palazzo Vecchio
each afternoon speaking about the coming crisis, the need for a
violent shock to Anglo-American hegemony. There'd been gunshots the night Britain declared war on Germany, fireworks over
the Piazza della Signoria.

Esmond sees that Carità is leading the procession over the
bridge towards them. Like a column of ants they stamp round

172

the corner from the Lungarno and make their way up the curved cobbles. Esmond and Ada press themselves to the wall; he draws a sleeve across his face, swallows a sob. When Carità is level with them, he points his whip, leering. – *Soon*, he says in English. – *Very soon*. They march on, the bridge juddering under their footsteps. The teenage soldiers of the Fascist Youth look scornfully at them as they pass. They can still hear the music, the heartbeat thud of the bass drum, long after the parade has disappeared towards the Palazzo Pitti.

Ada takes him in her arms again and he hugs her back very hard, thinking it so fiercely he's sure she can hear: *I won't lose you*.

≡ Part Four ≡

Recordings. St Mark's English Church

FLORENCE, 1939–1941

(transcribed by Ada Liuzzi)

1. **A-Side:** Harold Goad and Friedrich Kriegbaum discuss the building and authorship of the Ponte Santa Trinità (29 23″)

B-Side: 'This is not a diary. Douglas always said I should keep a diary, record everything. *Everything is interesting,* he used to say. *Get it down.* I don't believe him. I want to forget.

Nor is this an attempt at auto-psycho-analysis, to file my despair with Anna and Philip's letters and Fiamma's snood which, in the days after her death, found its way into my bedroom, I've no idea how.

The only thing to do with unwieldy objects is burn them, the only thing to do with a memory is tug it around like a fusty dog until you're forgiven for tying a brick around its neck and drowning it.

I realised something last night: the discs we record onto, that make up our archive – and what a grandiose word that is for these programmes, which, as I listen to them, strike me as half-baked twaddle. People listen to this because they are charmed by the idea of an outpost of Englishness in Italy, because they visited Florence on some ghastly tour they saw advertised at the back of the *Daily Mail* and they think we're guardians of Anglo-Italian culture.

Where was I? Oh yes, the discs. We've only been recording on one side. So I've begun this little memorandum on the other. It's comforting to think they'll stay here in Florence, in a box in the British Institute, or packed into Ada's attic. And maybe she will, on a whim, very late one night and rather tragic, dig me out, hear my voice and be filled with me. Who would have believed the curved cornet of our direct-to-disc-recorder could be a time-travelling device?

I'll be long gone, in a rum shack by a beach somewhere, or teaching at a frowsty colonial university – Wollongong, perhaps. I'm going to make old bones, you'll see, crawl out of Europe, the dark continent.

Perhaps she'll be with me, Ada. Although there doesn't seem much chance of that now. After practically heaving me over her shoulder after Anna's death, the barricades went straight back up. Every move I make towards her, she bats away. So I'm here, in a funk, mixing metaphors, leading a circumscribed, spinster-ish life, writing postcards into the void.

Three, four, five – that's the bell of Santo Spirito you hear. I'm going to open the shutters a bit. There's the faintest glimmer of dawn out in the square. We're having an Indian summer. It's been like '14 – peace before the nightmare. Although it's beginning to look like it might never start here. We expected Musso to jump straight into bed with Hitler, to invade France, or Greece, or Britain. But it's all gone rather quiet – *Il Duce* is busying himself with Albania, thumbing his nose to Adolf and his war games to the north. Perhaps Italy and Spain really won't join in, perhaps Stalin will realise Hitler is a bigger monster than the one that greets him in the mirror each morning. Good night, whoever you are. I'm shattered.'

2. **A-Side:** Esmond Lowndes and Bernard Berenson discuss symbolism in *Primavera* by Botticelli (27′ 33″)

B-Side: 'I've been trying to isolate the part of my mind where Anna, Philip and Fiamma dwell and close it down, like an aeroplane with an engine on fire. The pilot shuts it off, hoping to glide home safely on the one that remains. Still, my eyes are drawn to the flames on the wing.

I had another letter from my father. The folly of me staying on here, how I've shirked my duty, the essential uselessness of what I'm doing given that the British Union is all but wound up. Circumstances have overtaken them. Pa says he's already spoken to his pal Major-General Fuller about getting me into the Guards. He's tried to sign up himself, but there's not much call for a one-armed fifty-four-year-old. Yet. I haven't answered his letter.

It feels like when I was first in Florence. The warmth has given way to rain. There's no one around. Bloody lonely. Having Ada here every day is too frightful. The way she looks at me as she stands at the door at the end of the evening, her brolly in one hand, already half in the rain. Every time, I dare myself to say *Wait!* but I never do. I think, secretly, I'm rather enjoying the part of tormented lover. It takes my mind off Philip, off Anna, off the more weathered scars left by Fiamma, and all that was lost in '37. Love is a splendid distraction from despair.

I'm recording this on the other side of a discussion Bernard Berenson and I had today. Amazing that he's still here – although he arrived in Florence before the 1919 cut-off, so he's legit. Still, I'd be feeling a bit exposed if I were one of the most famous Jews in the country. I went up to I Tatti for dinner after we'd recorded the show. Strange set-up. I mean, with the wife and secretary and the very obvious tension, but the art makes up for it. Gloriousness on every wall – Pollaiolo, Lorenzetti, Sassetta. Ada came with me, she took my hand as we went through Poggio Gherardo, the city glowing below us. It was astonishing what the mere feel of her hand in mine did – little electrical explosions moving all the way up my arm, across my body. Douglas was right: Fascism is just a refuge from the powerlessness of love.

The talk at the Berensons' was all of the war, of how Italy won't be ready for combat for at least another three years. No automotive industry, an agricultural economy. They'll have to sit it out with the tea and oranges, as pa would say, as the north falls apart. It looks to be a lengthy thing, none of that Panglossian "It'll be over by Christmas" stuff this time.

There was a moment last night, as we came down from the hills into the first streets by lamplight, and a group of working men sat around a wireless on the viale Augusto Righi, when I was suddenly aware of the fact she was Jewish. It's perhaps all this talk of what's going on in Germany, in Poland, the camps holding people to whom – even though she says she doesn't believe in God – she must feel some sort of link. Perhaps it was that we were arm-in-arm in public. I tried talking to her about it, but she's got this way of turning a corner when the conversation is delicate. There's a sad secret in her smile, but I'm buggered if I know what it is.

After I dropped Ada off at her apartment, I cooled my heels on the street and watched her lights go on. I imagined her sitting reading late, preparing material, stretched out on the divan in her father's study. Her sadness reflects my own. I wish we could be sad together, but she doesn't seem to have any need for contact, at least not mine. She's the most island-like person I've ever met. I sat in the church and looked at the triptych tonight when I got back and I kept seeing her face in Mary Magdalene's. Both of them hard, reedy, faraway. I'm so tired. Still a little drunk from dinner. I think I'll go to bed. G'night, whoever-you-are. I may haunt you yet, so speak kindly of me.'

3. A-Side: Harold Goad and Alessandro Pavolini discuss the life and poetry of Gabriele d'Annunzio (27′ 54″)

B-Side: 'Should I be dating these missives from the past? I rather think not. I like to picture you piecing the chronology together from my summation of the war elsewhere, a war which feels so daydreamish and unlikely when I climb up through the stairways, ladders, trap-doors and corridors and then out onto the palazzo's flat roof. I look over the river, towards the dome of the cathedral, and the stories of submarine battles and massacred Poles and bombs dropped on Scottish harbours seem like the work of a very slender imagination indeed, somebody's rejected novel.

It is the 23rd of October. It is a Monday night. A Tuesday morning. The 24th of October. I've grown rather sleepy. Not now, I don't mean, even though it's two and I'm unable to lie still let alone drop off. I'm in the studio in bare feet, recording this in my pyjamas. I've just fallen into a state of lethargy – the more everyone tells me to go, even Bailey now, and Goad, the more my father showers me with letters containing, some of them, ripe old nicknames – the more I feel happy here. I've begun to think a healthy and successful life depends on a kind of accomplished ignorance of good advice. I don't want to be heroic; I want to stay in Florence, look after Ada, read books. I consider the balance between hope and memory that shifts and tilts over the course of a life, giving different reasons for carrying on. At the moment, it feels like I don't have enough of either.

The palazzo is more complex than I'd imagined. I keep finding new passageways, hidden doors, empty rooms that feel just-left – perhaps the ghost of Machiavelli. Stairways cut through the building like rock strata; some end in brick walls, but usually they lead out onto the roof, where I like to sit and watch the tiles of the city crest and fall like a terracotta wave, collecting the last sun before winter. Occasionally, at night, I hear things: mumbling voices, a child crying. The voices of the Florentine dead? It doesn't sound so ridiculous, or at least no more ridiculous than anything else. If God is an artist, we might accept that we are preliminary sketches. Good night.'

4. A-Side: Harold Goad and Esmond Lowndes discuss T. S. Eliot's *The Waste Land* (25' 41")

B-Side: 'Rudyard has signed up! I can hardly believe he's old enough, but we've all been ageing recently. I'm twenty-two now, which means Rudyard's eighteen. That seems impossible, but not unlikely. He took the bus into Shrewsbury on his birthday and signed up then and there. He's a common foot soldier in the 7th Battalion, Cheshire Regiment. Father's awfully proud. I imagine he'll make rather a fine squaddie. He can handle a gun, has the kind of pluck that comes from never being wholly of this world. I always got the impression he lived without an internal narrative, or at least no more than *What a jolly hunt!* and *I* *love shooting!* and *Dogs are faithful friends*. I realised that all the images that come to my mind when I say the name *Rudyard* are outside, distant, bloody. He was always the one on horseback, wheeling a fox's severed brush around his head, galloping off to mete out death to some small, innocent thing. Excluded from the love that Anna and I wrapped around each other, he was thrown together with my father, and into that world of hunting, heroism and intransitive rage. He'll enjoy the war.

Father's letters have gone from angry to ominous. Of course it doesn't help that he's alone now in that mournful house, only Cook for company. His last one said he was thinking of commandeering a Wellington from RAF Shawbury and flying over himself to collect me. He still seems to think it's practicalities that are holding me up. Or he thinks I feel some misplaced loyalty to the Party that I need to keep up Radio Firenze for the sake of the cause. Alas it's just that I'm in love, and a coward. I've stopped answering his letters, although I keep collecting cash from the advertisers, wiring it over when I remember.

Ada's father has been attempting to persuade her to come and join him in Turin, up there where he's near enough to the Swiss border to get out if need be. When I try to talk more generally with her about what was happening to the Jews, how she feels about it, she just casts off again. That distance she has, nothing can get behind it. It's an emotional Maginot Line. She'd make a virtuoso torturer – I wake up exhausted and ashamed, empty of my secrets, and happy. I don't know what I'd do if she left. Throw myself from the Ponte Santa Trinità, I expect.

Bailey has been back to the UK again. Spying, no doubt. In his kitchen, he has a map of the world spread out on the table with different-coloured toy soldiers for the Germans and French and Brits. It has become an evening's fun for us to read the news-papers together and arrange the troops. My Italian's fairly decent now – still a frightful accent, but *posso farmi comprendere, posso leggere i giornale.* I miss Bailey when he's away. Hey! There – did you hear that? More noises in the roof. If it's not ghosts, then it's rats. I should set out traps, or poison. There's certainly some-thing peculiar about this place.

I found a glove on one of the stairs, a lady's glove. It's not Ada's – hers are red, scuffed. This is small and black and exquisite. I can't imagine Bailey had invited in a lady-friend. Uncanny. G'night.'

5. **A-Side:** 'Filippo and Filippino Lippi – A Son in His Father's Shadow', a talk by Esmond Lowndes (27′ 30″)

B-Side: 'Happy Christmas. It's snowing outside the window. There's no heating in the palazzo, but I've lit a fire and I'm wrapped up like a Sherpa: scarf, hat, tweed jacket, two pairs of socks. I'm actually quite warm. It's been a bugger of a Christmas Day.

We lunched at Goad's. We all squeezed into the sad little flat they've let him keep on the ground floor of the Palazzo Arcim-boldi, now the Institute is no more. He greeted us at the door of his burrow, and he seemed so genuinely happy to see us, and so small and tired it was all I could do not to drown him with tears. Gerald is over for a week. He's losing his hair. A bald patch the size of a quail's egg in the centre of his scalp. He looks terribly serious and business-like. He's working at Lloyds Bank. Just like Eliot. After a few drinks, though, he shrugged off the mien of the busy capitalist and was something like his old self. There was still just a shadowiness around him, though. He seems disappointed, shifty somehow.

Ada and Bailey and Reggie Temple joined us for lunch. It was almost merry, to start off with. A rag-tag family pulling Smith's crackers that Gerald brought over. Goose roasted in Goad's little kitchen. A pudding that wouldn't light no matter what we poured on it. I think I drank too much grappa. Became a tad maudlin at the end, raising my glass to the dead ones, singing "Auld Lang Syne", sending Ada long, doleful glances.

We played charades all afternoon until Reggie fell asleep in a chair and Goad and Bailey started arguing about the war. So Gerald and Ada and I went out to walk about the city in our galoshes, looking at the ice floes in the Arno, the bright windows of the shops on the via de' Corsi, snow settling on the cathedral: heavily around the lantern and then thinning out to a dusting as the roof slopes. I have a picture in my mind of the three of us, standing in the empty square looking up at the spiralling snow, the scab-coloured roof glowing beneath it. It felt like being with Fiamma, but now we look older and wounded.

Ada went home and Gerald and I found the bar of the Excelsior open, and we sat on the high stools and drank. The longer we sat there, the easier it was to see Gerald as he had been a year and a half earlier: dashing, rather dangerous. Sexful, as they used to say. We came out of the hotel drunk and it was dark, our footsteps squeaking on the snow. An icy corridor of wind swept down the Lungarno and we burrowed into our overcoats. It reminded me of Philip and the rain storm in Grantchester, and I suppose for that reason I kissed Gerald below the statue of Justice at the end of the via delle Terme. His breath was sour, and there was something too ardent and grateful in the way he kissed me back. I broke off quickly and said goodbye. I stood on the Ponte Santa Trinità until I was frozen sober, thoroughly depressed.

I came back to the church and tried to work on the novel, but it all seemed predictable and tiresome. So now I'm here, earlier than usual, speaking to you. Happy Christmas, whoever-you-are. I'm off to sleep with my hangover.'

6. **A-Side:** 'Dante Today – the Enduring Legacy of the *Divine Comedy*', a lecture by Alessandro Pavolini (31' 51")

B-Side: 'Bailey's obsessed by the Finnish campaign. More by the pluck of the Finns than anything. The way they simply won't give up, even with the aerial bombardments, the tanks, the Russians' vastly superior numbers. We're all cheering them on, but I can't think they'll be able to hold out much longer. I have an image of them: mostly blond, snow-dusted men with blue eyes and unpronounceable names skiing in white fatigues through the endless Arctic night. Rudyard is in France, digging in around the Maginot Line. He wrote me a card – thoroughly censored, of course. He sounds like a man, even in those few words. I wish I'd known him better when we were young. It made me think how alliances form in families, how Anna and I were so close we pushed the others away. I still miss her almost every day. It seems absurd that she should be dead and not there, in her room, waiting for me. That someone so abounding with kindness should act so pitilessly as to die.

Pavolini came to see Goad and me today, ostensibly to record his thoughts on Dante's legacy in contemporary European poetry – actually rather interesting – but in fact to issue instructions about our broadcasts. He's seen the success William Joyce is having in Germany – Lord Haw-Haw of Zeesen they call him there – and he wants us to mirror it. To become a propaganda mouthpiece for Musso. The way he put it to us was that *Il Duce* is certain to get into the war at some point; he's like a hunter waiting for the optimum moment to shoot; and that we need to make up our minds now which side we're on when Italy squares up to Britain. Goad and I sat on for a long time after he left. One of Pavolini's requirements was that we give over a half-hour every day to PNF propaganda that he will script for us. Justifications of the war in Abyssinia, praise for the Italian military machine, hagiographies of *Il Duce*. I've heard the Joyce broadcasts and there's not a chance we'd do something like that, but Pavolini is an intelligent man. Certainly no one who knows Dante like he does, who writes so delicately about poetry and music, can be all bad.

We've agreed we'll see how it goes – there's no gain in shutting things down before we see quite how invasive he'll be. After Goad left, I stood in the studio looking out at the piazza getting rained on. My father wrote me one last letter, cutting me off. As far as he's concerned I'm no longer his son. If I won't be a warrior, I no longer deserve the name Lowndes. It draws a line under things, I suppose.

If only it wasn't so very clear what'll happen to me if I go back. A hair-raising voyage aboard some submarine-stalked ship, a few days at home with the ghost of Anna in every room, then to London with my pa, fitted out at Gieves', on the train at Victoria and pow! a bullet in the brain a week or – worse – a year later. I went down to the church after dinner. I turned on the altar lights and sat looking at the triptych for an hour or so. I feel crumpled, hollowed out, like those three figures in the painting. It's as if Florence has seen me go from a boy who could feel sensuous about *Primavera* and *The Birth of Venus* to a man who can only relate to withered creatures. Don't think I'm not ashamed of my fear: I am. I feel like a bloody hole. But shame, as Marx said, is a revolutionary feeling. Perhaps it will push me into action.

I saw crocuses growing in the Cascine today. Spring is on its way. Good night.'

7. **A-Side:** Shakespeare's *The Merchant of Venice*: a consideration by Harold Goad (28′ 28″)

B-Side: 'The war is utterly confounding. Even Bailey seems to have given up moving his figures around the kitchen table. There's mushroom sauce across Scandinavia, a blob of passata in the waters of the Indian Ocean. I've been learning how to cook – we'd grown bored with eggs on toast. All we had as far as cookbooks were concerned was Douglas's collection of aphrodisiacal recipes, but I'm now able to fashion a passable *pastasciutta*, an encouraging *gnocchi al ragù*, a frankly hopeful *cinghiale salsa agrodolce*. I've converted Bailey to wine. He was teetotal when I turned up and now we get through a bottle of Chianti most evenings. I've started broadcasting Pavolini's propaganda. Generally fairly tame stuff, but today there was something on the Manifesto of Racial Scientists. It wasn't too evil, just the usual guff linking the Jews to the Reds who are disrupting the factories, how there will now be stricter curfews. They wanted us to get Guido Landra, their pet eugenicist on, but Goad drew the line.

All the time I was reading it, I was watching Ada's face. That cold angularity, the way her eyes leave and she follows. I shiver to look at her when she gets like that. It became harder and harder to read the words. I realised how much power there is in those bureaucratic phrases, in the canted, abstract language of the State. I felt, with the suddenness of instinct, that the words I was reading meant something concrete, that translated into actions by Blackshirt thugs on the streets of Turin or Naples, into education or medication denied to Jewish children, into the concentration camp they're building in Campagna. That speech carried a dreadful weight, a weight that would finally fall on Ada's shoulders. I felt my throat closing up, choking off the words as I read them. I barely got through it. When I reached the end, silence like a fog came over us, and I felt as if I'd just carried out some atrocity, some appalling crime as I read. Ada got up from the sound desk and practically ran. I went after her, heard Goad following me. Her footsteps echoed down the stairwell, then the clatter of the wicket gate.

I finally caught up with her at the midpoint of the Ponte Santa Trinità. She was running very quickly. It must have been six – people were walking home from their jobs, standing around in the spring sunlight, watching the fishermen on the Arno. To stop her, I put my arms around her, and she was heaving with sobs, tears streaming down her freckled blue cheeks, onto the soft linen of her shirt where I could see her collarbones pushing through, see her small breasts, and then I was kissing her and I pulled her tightly to me, and the river flowing under us, the rumorous hum of the city, the milky sky overhead, all of them seemed to stop for a moment – we were the still point and the world was rising to a blister on our lips, at the intersection of our bodies as they pressed hopelessly together. I drew back for a moment and stared at her, feeling as if another sun had risen. Then we started kissing again, urgently, both of us. When we pulled back for a second time, I saw Goad at the foot of the bridge, watching. I tore myself away from her, and that was what it felt like: as if our bodies had fused for a moment and now we tore flesh as we parted.

Goad gave me a talking to. About how ill-advised it was for a Brit to be consorting with a Jew. We are under significant scrutiny, and this is just the sort of performance that might tilt it all against us. He apparently assumes it's been going on for some time. He gets terrible itching on his hands when he talks about this kind of thing; he sits there and I can feel the pressure to scratch building up inside him until it's unbearable. Then he gives a rub, runs the back of one hand down the tweed of his thigh. Poor fellow. I can't remember what I said to him. Mumbled apologies, told him it wasn't anything serious, that it was in response to the moment, to her tears.

It's time to turn in. I've found it hard to get Ada out of my head. I tried to telephone her earlier, but there was no answer. Something makes my chest suddenly too small for my heart when I think of her. She's been the anchor tying me to Florence. It's a better excuse than ennui, anyway. I'm reading Benedetto Croce. "Historical judgement is not a variety of knowledge, it is knowledge itself; it is the form which completely fills and exhausts the field of knowing, leaving no room for anything else." Not easy. *Buonanotte.*'

8. **A-Side:** Esmond Lowndes: Milton in Italy, 1638–39 (30′ 21″)

B-Side: 'Hell. Bugger, as Gerald would say. I'd meant to record these things more often, but so much has been happening, and every night Bailey and I sit up planning and plotting, trying to sort our way through the mess that's unfolding across Florence and Europe. So what has happened in the six weeks since my last direct-to-disc? I'll start with the pathetically personal and broaden to the faintly historic. You'll want to know, whoever-you-are, what is going on between me and the admirable-stroke-terrifying Ada Liuzzi.

I join you in your curiosity and only wish I could help. She came in the next day, the day after our kiss on the bridge, and every broadcasting day since, maintaining an air of chilly professionalism, resisting offers of after-work drinks and dinners and dances at the Maggio Musicale and, indeed, that far-off look has barely left her face. Only once, when we ran into each other on the via Porta Rossa, I coming back from dinner with Friedrich Kriegbaum, she from a concert in the Cascine, did I sense a crack in the *froideur*. A heavy rain squall came down over the city, as if the Arno were flowing upwards. Everyone was hurrying with their jackets tented over their heads, and I ran straight into Ada. Her eyes lit up for a moment when she saw me, and I could tell she was a little drunk, very wet. I took her hands and she didn't snatch them away immediately. I kissed her cheek but close enough to the corner of her mouth that she could have turned it into something more had she wanted to. She almost did. I'm stricken, really. It *is* pathetic, to have fallen for someone like this, and to betray myself in so many trite, adolescent ways. I try to manoeuvre opportunities for us to work together, just the two of us; I've been waking from elaborate rescue dreams in the small hours, whisking her out of Europe on the back of a white charger.

I call her when I'm drunk, but she never answers.

My mother's a gaolbird! Mosley was arrested first, then most of the rest of the active British Union. There was even talk of father doing clink, but sense seems to have prevailed there. At least mother's back in Britain. Seems the realities of war broke up the hiking party in Berchtesgaden. It was decided that the squawking posse of English matrons surrounding the Führer were an unnecessary distraction. Hess drove mother and Diana Mosley to the aerodrome himself. They were picked up as soon as they set foot on British soil. They're in Holloway Prison with Mosley, all three of them in a cosy little cabin of their own. Extraordinary that five years ago there was talk of these people running the country.

Mussolini, the hunter in the field, has finally pulled the trigger. Italy is at war with Britain and France. What does this mean? A final exodus of Brits from Florence. A host of women called Gladys have left, although my favourite of them, the indomitable Gladys Hutton, has said she'll stay no matter what. Bailey and I have been frantic, sorting passports for ancient coves living in isolated splendour above Monte Oliveto, persuading Gladyses they can't take their entire wardrobes with them on the train, then hauling suitcases around the station like porters, ordered about by women in pince-nez who colonise their railway carriages like their uncles colonised Poonah.

Goad has moved into the church apartments, a room on the ground floor. He's not well – I suppose you'd call it nerves. He's convinced that, if he'd had more support from his superiors, if he'd been allowed to continue at the Institute for a little longer, he'd have been able to prevent Musso from getting into the war. He writes thick letters to Lloyd George and Churchill and Duff Cooper, but you can't think they'll ever be opened, let alone read. He comes up and joins us some evenings, sits ghostly at the table worrying his food while we plan the latest evacuation. He's been hearing noises in the night, too. A baby crying, rustling footsteps, coughing. He thinks it's part of his illness. Perhaps it is.

As for the Italians declaring war, that's simple – pure opportunism. Mussolini saw which way the tide was turning and jumped. They'll be eating strudel and raising steins on Piccadilly before the end of the year, unless the Americans help us out. Finland, Belgium, Norway have fallen; France has all but gone – there are Germans on the Champs-Elysées, the Brits ferried back from Calais in fishing sloops. If it's all over this year, or early in '41, the Italians will need to show they deserve a seat at the table alongside the Russians and the Germans. That's why they're fighting.

Pavolini called me up last night. With Goad ill, I've been making the broadcasts myself. Apart from the prescribed guff, I've been trying to stay away from matters political, rehashing my notes from F. R. Leavis's lectures, speaking about Shelley and Yeats. Pavolini was awfully pally, described me as *a key asset*. But he pointed out that the *raison d'être* for Radio Firenze was now something of a nonsense. Rapprochement between the Brits and the Italians being, for the moment, off the table. He's given me a plan for the next six weeks of programming. Italian poets, German composers, even more propaganda. Two days devoted to Balbo, the great Italian air hero shot down by his own troops in one of these absurdly antiquated Fiat biplanes that make up the Italian air force.

I imagine I'll eventually find myself heading back to a Britain changed beyond recognition with – who knows – Mosley as

Commander of the British Reich or some such. In the meantime, I'll keep my head down and concentrate on those few small things I can do to help push back that frightful prospect. Good night, whoever-you-are.'

9. A-Side: Esmond Lowndes and Friedrich Kriegbaum discuss Bach's *Goldberg Variations* (33′ 33″)

B-Side: *The Battle of France is over; I expect that the Battle of Britain is about to begin.* That was my Churchill voice. He's bloody good, actually. Much better than Chamberlain, hoisted by the petard of history. Churchill's a bit more like it – feels as if he's up for a fight. I'm no good at accents, really. Just listen to my Italian. I know the words all right, but can't get myself to sound like a local. It's partly why I've become something of a recluse, hiding from the Blackshirt gangs who've grown in number and aggression since war was declared. Mostly bitter older men, veterans from the last war looking for a reason to pull on a uniform and biff people up. Sound familiar?

Some good news, finally. I mean not only that, so far, the British pilots have managed to fight off the Hun. And wasn't this how we always dreamed the wars of the future would be fought, high up in the clouds, sharks of the air ripping chunks off each other? But even better, Goad discovered that Carità has left Florence, joined up and gone to fight in Albania. The town can breathe.

Also, Ada loves me. I waited until we'd worked late recording a show on *The Decameron*. We were still in the studio at nine in the evening. I kept slipping up on the passages in Italian, clanking mistakes in my translation, partly because it was reminding me of first being in Florence and reading the book in the loggia of the Palazzo Arcimboldi with Fiamma. Finally we were done and Ada pulled her scarf around her head, started buttoning her jacket. I asked her to join me for a drink and was surprised when she said yes. I found a three-quarters-full bottle of Chianti in the kitchen and led her up to the roof of the church.

We've been so busy, too busy even to come up and admire the sunsets, and the rooftop has grown over. Weeds spew out between tiles, the little garden where they must once have planted raspberries or tomatoes is now dense with wild fennel, yellow flowers shooting up through chicken-wire. We sat on the roof and drank our wine, and Ada said something about how Florence reflects her hills, how the undulations of the rooftops mirror the rise and fall of the land. It struck me as beautiful and true, and I thought back, again, to sitting on another rooftop with Fiamma and seeing the purple darkness reaching up to cold heights. I told Ada all about Fiamma, or almost all. She listened very carefully and was quiet afterwards. I leant over and kissed her, and she didn't resist, though nor was she anything more than politely encouraging. We spoke for a while longer and then she invited me for dinner the next evening.

I'd imagined a lonely existence for Ada away from the studio. Whenever I telephoned her, after drinking too much and feeling maudlin, I pictured her with some serious book in her lap, reaching out a hand to the telephone and then drawing it back. In fact, her house is something of a salon. It wasn't just me for dinner. I'd made an enormous effort with my clothes, I bathed and perfumed and pomaded. I'd selected a copy of *The Oxford Book of Modern Verse*, edited by Yeats, to give to her. It was a present from Anna, Christmas before last, and it felt like a good sacrifice, to make it Ada's.

I arrived at the via dei Forbici. I could hear conversation echoing in the stairwell as I made my way up. The door to the Liuzzi apartment was open and there were six or seven young people with Ada in the kitchen, more grouped around an older man with thick spectacles and thinning hair who sat on the divan in the drawing room. I'd brought a bouquet of flowers – lilies from the stall in front of the Villa Ventaglio. I stood, holding them stupidly, until Ada swept out of the kitchen and kissed me and took the flowers and cooed over the book, and seemed friendlier and more relaxed than she'd ever been with me before. It wasn't the tête-à-tête I'd been hoping for, but, rather despite myself, I had a smashing time. The party was to celebrate the release of one of Ada's friends – a thin-faced, quiet, good-looking man called Bruno Fanciullacci – from gaol. I saw Ada's eyes slide to him repeatedly, monitoring his position in the room. He carried a matchstick in the corner of his mouth which bobbed gently as he spoke. He was the son of one of the leaders of the local Communist Party and had been arrested on a series of trumped-up charges, given seven years and released after two.

The older man was Piero Calamadrei, a Professor of Law at the university who'd led the legal challenge to Bruno's imprisonment. Whenever he spoke, the rest of the room fell quiet, although his words came in jagged, impressionistic bursts that were hard to follow. We sat on the floor with our bowls in our laps – Ada had made lasagne – and the young people talked as they ate, shouting across each other and filling beakers with wine from unlabelled bottles, looking up reverently at the Professor whenever he held forth on politics, or literature, or law. Ada made sure that I was included in conversations, translated words she thought might be difficult for me, trailed her fingers through my hair as she passed. She introduced me to her friends with a kind of protective warmth I found very touching. It made me realise how, after three and a half years in Florence, I know very few Italians. Shameful, really. This was a strange bunch, though.

The Professor seemed to take against me at first, referring to me as Ada's "pet Fascist" and saying, with a little wrinkle of his nose, that he'd listened to my programme on d'Annunzio. No praise, or comment, just the nose.

In one corner sat a famous cyclist, Gino Bartali, who was a friend of Ada's father and was cheerfully and palpably in love with his new wife, Adrianna. They spoke only to each other, smiling around the room every so often as if allowing us collusion in their bliss. A group of serious young men surrounded Bruno, huddled on one side of the room, watching him move the matchstick around his mouth. They all looked rather tired and ill-fed and trim-moustached. Three young women in Agnes Ayers turbans, smoking Sobranies, stood in the doorway, looking over at the men and letting out little flustered laughs. Finally, sitting with Ada and me, a lady called Maria Luigia Guaita, a plump, friendly sort from the Monte dei Paschi bank where my account is held. I hadn't quite worked out at this point what should perhaps have been rather obvious – that this rag-tag bunch at Ada's house were the Florentine chapter of *Giustizia e Libertà*, that the Professor was their leader, that Ada was testing me somehow by bringing me along.

After dinner, with the French doors open to the square below, the Professor began to talk about books. I lost a little of the subtlety, even with Ada whispering occasional translations in my ear, but he was speaking about the role of literature in politics, the temptation for writers to retreat into symbol and allegory, rather than recording the stony facts of the world. He said it was the writer's duty to speak for those who couldn't speak, who were trapped or overlooked or oppressed. He said, in times like these, novels should be written with broken fingers, and all poets' eyes should be black. He fixed me then and asked me if I wrote at all, and everyone was silent.

I didn't see what else I could do; I told him about *In Love and War*, about Hulme and how writing about him was a way of writing about my father. Their friendship, I thought, had driven my father to Fascism. That staying true to Fascism, Mosley and violence, was all a fidelity to his dead friend. I'd always felt, I told them, that I was out of place, and that my attempt to make Hulme a hero was an attempt to forge someone from my father's world, someone with fierce, Fascist ideas, into a laudable figure. I could show Hulme, a copy of Sorel from the London Library in one hand, a gun in the other, living the philosophy he preached: heroism, duty, standing up for those values that made life worth living. But I'd buggered it up. The novel didn't work. I was writing it with an ugly hand over my eyes. By the end I was exhausted. You must remember I did all of this in Italian, which gave it a kind of clumsy honesty.

Ada raised her glass to me. The Professor swallowed the contents of his own, seemed satisfied, and began to ask me questions about Auden and Spender. He thought Pound a great poet, he said with a sorry smile. Yeats, too. *Now that my ladder's gone*, he quoted in English, *I must lie down where all the ladders start. In the foul rag and bone shop of the heart.* Bloody good. Then everyone began to talk and argue, and a group of university students turned up, and with them a young, pretty girl with white-blonde sparkle, Tosca. Everyone calls her La Toschina. Her boyfriend, a tough-looking fellow named Antonio Ignesti, seemed to take a shine to me – heavy Sicilian accent he had, barely caught a word. He kept urging me to drink from his bottle of grappa and soon it was two in the morning and people were walking out into the night. Finally I was left with Ada on the balcony, looking over the darkened square.

That was last night. No great passion. We kissed, slept in the same bed, but not much more than that. We talked a great deal. She's part of the Resistance, which strikes me as frightfully brave. It's why she stayed in Florence when her parents left, to keep up her work here. Radio Firenze provides her with just enough of a cover story. I was stroking her hair as she told me this, her head in my lap. She's involved in counterfeiting documents. She and the plump cashier, Maria Luigia, create the passports at night with the bank's franking machine, official paper stolen by some-one at the Ministry in Rome. Then Gino Bartali, with the alibi of his gruelling training, cycles out to safe houses. Hiding there are deserters from the Italian Army, Communists threatened with internment, Jews looking to forge authentic Italian identities for themselves before *Il Duce* carries out his threat to round them all up and deliver them to Hitler.

Just before I left, a few hours ago, as the first light broke over the city, she spoke to me in her glowing voice. She said this was why she'd been hesitant about us, why she'd backed off instead of doing what everything in her heart told her to do – to take me in her arms and kiss me. Because I was the enemy. And she needed to know that I was with her, that the decency she sensed in me wasn't just a fabrication of love. I felt like Desdemona, you know: *She loved me for the dangers I had passed, and I loved her that she did pity them.* Ada's bravery undoes me a little.

It's coming up for six. I need a few hours' sleep. Rustling, movement, happy familial sounds from the empty rooms tonight. Not uncanny now – comforting. Good night.'

10. **A-Side:** Gerhard Wolf and Alessandro Pavolini discuss opera from Wagner to Puccini (33′ 54″)

B-Side: 'The picture we receive of the war, through *Radio Londra*, through the Empire Service, through the distorted lens of *La Nazione*, is muddled.

It is easy to think that propaganda only works in one direction, but, as Dr Johnson said, *among the calamities of war may be justly numbered the diminution of the love of truth.* We have no idea how things stand; all we can do is number the facts, the certainties, the casualties. Italy is at war with Greece, using Albania as a springboard into the Peloponnese. Germany and Britain continue to hack each other out of the skies above the Channel; those antediluvian Italian Fiats have joined the Messerschmitts in taking on the Hurricanes and Spitfires. Bombs rain down on the cities in squalls, exploding across Bristol, across Bonn, in strange symmetries which suggest fore-planning, complicity, consent. Liverpool's getting it bad just at the moment. It was Hamburg last month. Under the dark waters of the Atlantic, the U-Boats prowl.

Ada and I spend several nights each week at the via dei Forbici. It feels provisional, unlikely: sometimes I catch sight of us in a shop window, or in the bathroom mirror at her apartment, and I think how odd we look as a couple. She's twenty-six, three years older, but there's something about her, perhaps also about me, that makes that distance seem much greater. She still gets the look occasionally, staring off as if I'm not there. It makes me feel as if any attempt to know her is doomed, but then she'll smile, and never has a face changed so instantly, and she'll place those sparrow-bone wrists around me and pull me in, and I have sudden, primordial charges. We're happy together, or I am.

If it strikes you as strange, after Philip, after Gerald, that I should love Ada, it shouldn't. It is not only that Fiamma, dear dead Fiamma, served as a copula, a springboard, a bridge. I have always loved beauty and the gender of those I love matters to me as little as their shoe size. It seems odd to me that so many humans limit themselves, slavishly. For now, it is Ada.

I realised that, since my last recording, since I spoke about Ada and her Resistance pals, I needed to be more careful with these discs. It didn't strike me until a few days afterwards, walking through the Boboli Gardens on my way up to the Kaffeehaus to meet Ada. Unprompted by any sight or sound, I was gripped by a sudden certainty that someone was listening to the recordings I'd made. I raced back through the Oltrarno, scattering morning shoppers and their baskets, clattered upstairs and found the studio empty, naturally, the discs as I'd left them. But now I've eased up a floorboard, hidden them beneath it, scattered rugs.

One other revelation. I was in my room the other night. Ada won't sleep at the church apartments, even though I'm certain Bailey wouldn't mind, and is away so much anyway, and Goad is so absent-minded and frail he'd barely notice. But she won't and so, two or three nights a week, I'm here alone. I was sitting up writing, going over passages of *In Love and War*, trying to dust some truth off the words. I scratched out whole pages in my notebook, wrote and rewrote, and it was as though I was unbricking a wall behind which bodies had been buried. Fascist blood was burning, burning in the veins of the novel and I would have no truck with it.

A sound brought me from the contemplative fug into which I'd fallen. It was past midnight – the bell of Santo Spirito had stopped and wouldn't be back until five. I crept out into the corridor. It was cold and I had a thick woollen dressing gown wrapped around me, heavy slippers on my feet. Dim light coming up from the stairwell at the end. I felt my way along the passage, down the steps and round towards the entrance of the church. There, a flicker of light. I made my way into the church. Faint incense from Sunday's service. In a pew at the front, looking up at the triptych, sat a young boy. He was humming quietly to himself. A candle in his hand. I walked down the aisle, looking at the soft black hair of his head. A creak of the floorboard and he turned round and there was horror on his face, and his eyes darted first one way, then another, searching for a way out. I got down on my knees, held up my hands, said something minor. He looked at me out of large, dark eyes. I asked him whether he liked the painting. We stared at it together. He didn't answer, but his mouth dropped open a little.

I went to sit beside him. He must have been six, a scrawny scrap of a thing. He was wearing a jumper but his feet were bare. *Sono Dino*, he said, his eyes still fixed on the triptych. I asked him if he wasn't cold. *Un poco*, he said, but he couldn't find his socks in the darkness. I asked him where he lived and now he looked at me. Are you a Fascist? he asked. I shook my head. We're upstairs, he said. I took his feet in my hands and rubbed them warm. We sat, his feet in my lap, for a while longer, staring up at the painting. It is bewitching, that triptych, something in it that shuts out the world. I felt suddenly sleepy, found myself nodding. When I woke, the boy was gone, the candles on the altar burnt down, the air around me still and grave.

Bailey was away on one of his trips and didn't come back until late Saturday night, yesterday. He has lost weight: everyone is leaning on him at the moment – the Gladyses, Goad, certain other eccentric Brits who've decided to stay. He's been enlisted by Cardinal Elia della Costa, the Archbishop of Florence, to advise a group of priests charged with interceding with the regime on behalf of political prisoners. The islands in the south, the blighted villages of exile, now busy with dissidents.

I always half-thought George Keppel's description of Bailey as a spy was far-fetched, but the trips to Milan, to Switzerland, shuttling back and forth to Britain – it makes no sense for a priest. When he walked in that Saturday evening, I poured him a glass of wine and waited for him to sit at the table, where the map of the world has become a record of long dinners and twilit debate. The tanks and miniature soldiers with which he marked out the course of the war are all piled around North Africa, where he'd finally given up, overcome by military complexities, contradictory news. Military fronts, he said, sitting down heavily and unlacing his boots, were as wild and arbitrary as the weather from which they drew their name. I'd kept some *pasta al ragù* on the stove which I heated up and served to him. He ate in silence and I could tell he was waiting for me to speak. I told him about the boy.

He put his fork down, swirled the wine in his glass and sipped at it, not taking his eyes from me. He asked me which side I was on. I thought I could see where this was heading, but feigned innocence. He began a long and rather worn speech about the course of world history, consequentialism, the necessary conditions for evil, et cetera.

I let the silence settle after he'd finished and then told him I was on board. That whatever he was up to, I was with him. It turns out Goad is in, too. Bailey went to call for him and we sat up till late. Goad even drank a glass of Chianti, or half, looking rather sparkier than I'd seen for a while. He's out of love with Fascism, he says. The Corporate State was still the ideal, but not the violence. The Fascists weren't poets – look at Pavolini. Once a thoroughly decent writer, now just another of *Il Duce*'s thugs. Now he smiled, and I realised it was the first smile I'd seen on that pinched, grey face since Fiamma, since Gerald, since everything turned to dust.

After dinner, Bailey led me back into his bedroom, Goad following with his glass of wine – a sight I found oddly funny. It was all so bizarre it was hard *not* to laugh. This vicar and his pale accomplice standing up to the might of Fascism. On the desk in Bailey's room there was a shortwave W/T set. On the floor reams of paper fanned out from manila files; on the wall a map of Tuscany with numerous pins in and around Florence, some as far as Pisa and Lucca.

Bailey says he's working with the Professor – Piero Calamandrei – to mould the rag-tag Resistance into a credible whole. Bailey and Goad are in charge of helping dissidents, refugees and deserters evade the tentacles of the State. The Resistance have a man in Rome, Filippo Caracciolo, who lets them know when new names are added to the list of official enemies. More information comes from local Blackshirts, who are bribed with a few jugs of wine at the Paszkowski Bar, a grappa or two. As soon as they know that a member of *Giustizia e Libertà* is in trouble, they ferry him or, just as often, her, to a safe-house. Bartali, the cyclist, pulls a wooden box behind him in which a man can crouch. When stopped, he claims the box is essential to his fitness for the Giro d'Italia. It is full of stones, he says, and opens the lid. The Blackshirts or *carabinieri* stand back and nod, the fugitive tucked snugly beneath a false bottom.

Recently they've been taking in Jews threatened with internment at the concentration camps in Campagna and Trieste, others who ducked out of sight during the eviction of July '39. Florence's bureaucrats and their henchmen have been more enthusiastic than most in circumscribing the lives of their Jewish residents, but their roll-calls and round-ups are nothing compared to those in the east. Over the past few weeks, Jews have been arriving from Fiume, Friuli, Trieste and all across the Julian March. Some are refugees from Austria and Germany; most fleeing the anti-Semitic officials of Balkan and Adriatic Italy. The boy I'd seen in the church a few nights earlier, Dino, was from a family of fishermen on the Isonzo River.

It was Ada who introduced Bailey to the Professor and his group of *liberalsocialiste*. He is now co-ordinating with *Giustizia e Libertà* cells in Milan and Turin to ferry the refugees under false papers to America, Palestine, Brazil. Sixty have been sent so far; fifty more housed in convents, abbeys, derelict church buildings in the city and Val di Pesa, Cardinal della Costa providing the keys and his blessings. Bailey and Goad told me all this as one bottle of wine, then another, was emptied, me sitting cross-legged on Bailey's bed, Goad perched on the dressing table stool. Goad kept beaming at me, rubbing his hands and saying *Just so* and *Very good*. It grew late.

Bailey told me other things. The presence of the station provides cover for his shortwave communications with Turin and Milan, with the deserters who'd fled the city and were hiding in the wooded hills of Forlì-Cesena. The telephones were tapped – he knew this – and the security police had devices for monitoring radio signals, but the noise generated by the waves of Radio Firenze masked his messages. Was I, he asked, ready to take a more active role in his plans? Could I be relied upon not to give them all up?

I'm recording this early in the morning. I haven't slept, haven't been able to find my way back into *In Love and War*. I remember something my housemaster at Winchester said to me. I'd let down the house in some way – I think it was the time I was out in front in the school run, had stumbled and fallen and had to crawl to the finish. Twenty-fifth place, I recall. That evening, in his study, he'd steepled his fingers. *We only know ourselves,* he'd said, *in crisis. Character is theoretical until we act. I think today, Esmond, you beheld yourself. Not quite the hero your father was, eh?* He'd given me a narrow, nasty smile and dismissed me with a flick of his hand, gone back to pleasanter thoughts. Now I have a chance to do something Ada will admire, something for England, something that, if he ever knew about it, my father would be proud of, I think.

I still feel bloody windy, though. I keep thinking of that brave young man who broke a bottle over Carità's head, grabbed his pudgy wrist in the entrance hall of the British Institute. Perhaps, in the end, those were my crises, my assessments. I didn't do so badly.

Hitler's arriving in Florence today. Musso is already here, encamped in the Palazzo Vecchio, banners fluttering over the ramparts, posters of his granite head on every wall. Blackshirts glower under the carved tabernacles on the street corners, polishing their revolvers. I've not been invited to meet the great men but Pavolini is in town and wants a chat. I intend to be sly, I think. Evasive. Play the part, spy-like. Now dawn is coming up like thunder, and I must go. Good morning, whoever-you-are, good morning.'

11. **A-Side:** Alessandro Pavolini on the March on Rome and the Glorious Patria (35′ 21″)

B-Side: 'It's February, and bitterly cold in the church apartments. There's central heating at the via dei Forbici, and Ada and I have made a nest for ourselves there, piling rugs on the bed and looking out over the branches of the Villa Ventaglio, silhouetted with snow. The Professor comes to see us weekly, bringing other members of the Resistance with him. The persecution of the English, the crackdown on Communists and deserters, even the racial laws appear to have been forgotten as the Italians are buffeted with bad news from all sides: disaster in Greece; ignominy in North Africa; now British warships shell Genoa, RAF bombers hit Livorno. There are sandbags around the foot of Giotto's Campanile, around Ammannati's *Neptune*, which I, for one, wouldn't mourn were it hit. They've constructed a wooden shelter under which David seems smaller, rather ashamed of his city's nerves. The Brancacci Chapel, where Filippino learnt his craft, is cocooned in an asbestos bunker, closed up until peace breaks out.

Ada and I spend our time doing paperwork: small tasks which, when combined with the work of others who take far greater risks than we, will mean a family safely on an *Aliyah Bet* ship bound for Haifa, or a group of young men hidden with friends in the hills. We celebrated Hanukkah with Dino and his family. I gave him a catapult and a book of prints, Lippi's *St Jerome* and Botticelli's *Venus* among them. It's not possible now to see the paintings in person: most of the galleries' important works have been removed to storage. Underground vaults, or in villas in Fiesole, Pontassieve, Impruneta. Dino's father is a quiet, intelligent man; he looks at the book carefully, nodding all the time, then passes it back to his son. His mother is chubby, sweetly smiling, and used her son's catapult briefly to fire peanuts at Bailey and Goad. They have another son with the rebels in the Apennines.

Every day the Resistance grows. We hear of sabotage attacks on railway convoys, bombs planted at factories, ammunition dumps ransacked or destroyed. With so many Italian troops abroad, the security forces are making do with veterans, cripples, recently released prisoners. Carità and his *squadristi* are away in Greece, so the deserters and Communists, the assorted anti-Fascists have the run of the city, putting to use the bomb-making and sabotage skills they learnt during the war in Spain. The Professor is optimistic: he sends Antonio Ignesti, Giuseppe Martini, Giuliano Gattai – names already taking on a lustre of heroism – on daring missions to collect refugees heading over the mountains, to procure boats in Ligurian harbours. They confab with their northern friends, the union leaders in the Fiat and Piaggio factories in the Piedmont. And all the time Bartali pedals that cycle of his, covering hundreds of kilometres each week, passing where others may not pass, returning to the doe-eyed Adrianna with his cheeks flushed, his brow stiff with ice.

I had a letter from my mother, mainly asking what had happened to the advertising revenue. She's beginning to sound like Mosley's puppet. Rudyard, she wrote, has been sent to North Africa, now they're talking about Greece. He's already been promoted, leads a band of sharpshooters, a hero in the making. I haven't answered her. The truth is I've allowed Maria Luigia to use her place at the bank to siphon funds from the broadcasts. It's not much, not enough, but it's a start. I've been on a new round of visits to the major advertisers. I've been trying to persuade them to keep up their contributions despite the pressure of the war. How important it is for them to let the world know it's business as usual in Italy. No luck so far.

Bailey's got a dog – Tatters. Energetic Jack Russell-y little thing with a snowy beard. Turned up at the church one morning in January, half-starved, tail chewed by rats. I chose the name – from *Ulysses*, the whole dog-God thing. I believe in one dog.

The noises in the building have lost their spook since I found out about Dino and the rest. I like wandering through the warren of small rooms and passageways and staircases in the palazzo now. Often I run into Dino chasing mice with his catapult, or come upon his father reading in an empty room, armchair to the window, winter light on a serious-looking novel. There are others, passing through on their way to safe-houses in the hills, stopping for nights between Rome and Turin, or between the coast and the mountains. Young men with devil-may-care moustaches, sallow skin. They sit in close huddles looking at water-stained papers and smoking. I rather want to join in, but they barely seem to notice me. It's almost time to start recording today's programme. I must cut this disc and bury it. Cheerio.'

12. **A-Side:** 'An Address to the People of England' by Benito Mussolini (35′ 42″)

B-Side: 'As you can see, as you may have heard, we broadcast a message from *Il Duce* himself this morning. I'll save you the trouble of listening. The Italians, he says, with their German allies, will drive the Brits out of Africa, batter us for daring to intervene in Greece, and altogether warm our heels to Battersea Bridge. His English isn't terribly good, so it was actually Pavolini reading, doing his best Mussolini-speaking-quite-good-English impression. It's funny, madness in any other job is weeded out and treated. In politics it's classed as fortitude.

Something dreadful happened last week. I was out at a concert of the Maggio Musicale. It was hosted by Gerhard Wolf, the new German Consul. Bailey appeared at the door of Orsanmichele asking someone to come and fish me out. Gently, holding the newspapers but not allowing me to read them, he told me about articles in the *Manchester Guardian* and the *Daily Herald* linking me to William Joyce, calling me a traitor and accusing me of waging "a one-man propaganda war on behalf of Fascism". You can imagine – I was undone. Denounced at home. Furtive abroad. I felt like P. G. Wodehouse. Bailey saw the positive side immediately – how this strengthened my cover, how it would be well received in Rome. He tried to cheer me up. Tatters in my lap all evening – he could tell I was sad, good fellow.

The war follows its coarse, careless path. It feels as if, slowly, the Germans are gaining the upper hand. Rudyard, according to my gaolbird mother, has been evacuated from Greece, pushing out from Piraeus in a fishing boat with a bunch of his wounded comrades. They made it to Crete and there's talk of him getting a King's Commendation at the very least.

Dino and his family have gone to America. I was sad to see it. They made me promise to look out for their son and write when the war's over. Ada and I are now experts at forging passports, visas, emigration forms. Maria Luigia brings photos, paper and card, and for a chilling tale of extradition or escape we can have you a thick wad of documents within the hour, no questions asked. Bailey has been visiting a man named Moses Ricci, Mayor of Casoli, site of the largest concentration camp in the country. He thinks that, with the correct emoluments, Ricci will agree to transfer a number of the foreign Jews in his care to a ship at Pescara. Ada and I may travel down to help arrange it. Life is full and dangerous. I am continuing to make my broadcasts, to act the good Fascist. Just now, I am preparing to have the German Consul speak about Beethoven. He's a kind, clever man, but his delivery is a little dry. I am sipping a glass of Chianti in preparation. *Bis bald, Zukunft.*'

13. **A-Side:** 'Italy in 1950 – A Speculation' by Niccolò Arcimboldi (37' 50")

B-Side: 'I must be quick. I think this'll be the last of these. In fact I've no idea what's going to happen. There was a raid on the church this morning. I have an appointment with the Quaestor – the chief of police – at eleven. He'll grill me about how much

I knew of Bailey's clandestine operations. I'd been at Ada's the night before; when I turned up at the church, the security police were already there, Carità with them. He's back from Greece with a new ugliness about him. He's gained weight, his bare knees are now invisible beneath folds of skin. His hair is longer, the white tuft curling into a question mark above his head. He's a *centurione* now, still in shorts, but with medals on his chest, polished silver eagles on his epaulettes. Tatters wouldn't stop barking – Carità landed a kick at him, but still he yipped and snapped until I shut him in the studio. Bailey was very cool about the whole thing. The police had arrived during the morning mass – only Gladys Hutton in the congregation. Goad was serving, holding a chasuble in the shadows, and managed to sneak out, up and into the apartments. He warned the four young Sicilians living on the fourth floor: they escaped over the rooftops.

Then he went to Bailey's room, picked up the map of Florence, as many papers as he could carry and threw them in the kitchen fire. The W/T radio he brought back down and hid in the sacristy. Bailey forced the thugs to wait in the entrance hall as he filled in the details of the congregation in the service register, and then, underneath it, wrote *Chaplain Rev. F. J. Bailey arrested – sent to concentration camp*. Goad is coming with me to the Quaestor. I don't know what'll happen now. I must bury this disc, find Ada, make sure she's safe. I'm scared, whoever-you-are – pray for me.'

≡Part Five≡

Open City

VILLA DELL'OMBRELLINO, BELLOSGUARDO,
FLORENCE, 1941–1944

1

He wakes with a rising feeling in his chest. An arm draped across him, a gold ring on one finger. The heavy warmth of Tatters on his feet. The dog wakes too and patters around sniffing, looking over eagerly at Esmond. Ada sighs and withdraws the arm, turning over and nesting the sheets between her legs. He stands and crosses to the window, opens a crack in the shutters to see the city, the spires, the dome of the cathedral, all glowing. The sun along the hillsides of Fiesole. Tatters sits behind him, clearing a cone-shaped space in the dust with his tail.

It had been Ada's idea to sleep up here, the eaves which had been Alice Keppel's studio during a brief painting fit in the early '30s. It is large, light, fluttering with doves that roost in soft dun clumps on the roof. This is the sound of their life now: the burble of doves, the wind, the hiss and hum of the radio on the desk by the window. He looks down at her, the hair falling across the pillow, sleep-creases on her face. Against the wall at the end of the bare mattress, stand the three paintings of the triptych. She loves this, she says, almost as much as Anna's collage of photographs, which hangs beside it.

'Today' she says, eyes opening, 'we go to the sea.' He doesn't reply, but stoops to scratch Tatters behind the ear.

'*Vieni qui.*' She rises and draws him and the dog towards her.

'The bonfire was a risk,' he says in her ear.

They'd waited until late twilight, when the air around them was violet and the smoke from their little pyre might drift unnoticed. It had seemed important, somehow, to have a fire, to match his mother's, six years ago, on the icy Shropshire field.

They'd lit it down by the swimming pool, a small pile of sticks on the flagstones, brightening the dodos' patient vigil over the pool. It flared higher as page after page of *In Love and War* was fed into it.

Ada's idea. She'd read the novel in an armchair in the drawing room, hair tied up and a pencil in her teeth, marking the margins, adding a question mark here and there. She'd sipped nettle tea and hummed to herself as she went with Hulme from London to the trenches. When she finished, she sat for a long time, cross-legged in the armchair.

'It's no good,' she said, finally, firmly. 'Don't look at me like that. You write well – I like so many passages, so many individual images and phrases.' She got up to stand beside him at the drawing room window. 'You began to write too early, I think,' she'd said softly. 'You've watched other people living without coming alive yourself. What I read here, it feels— like the difference between *orzo* coffee and the real thing. What do the Germans call it? *Ersatz?*'

He nodded his head and looked glumly out. She took his hands in hers, cold and bony.

'And you're one of us, Esmond,' she said. 'You don't want the world to see you through the lens of a book like this. You'll live a long life, write many great novels, but you'll be followed by this piece of Fascist propaganda—' He bristled and tried to pull his hands away but she'd held onto them. 'However well written. You don't want our children to read this, to know their father ever thought this way. You've outgrown the thing. The truth is, Esmond, you don't need to answer to your family, to Mosley, any more. You're your own man now.'

After the fire, he sat up late with the triptych, candlelight on the faces and then on Ada's sleeping beside him, her eyelids trembling softly under the spell of some dream, her breath quickening and slowing. He let his mind spool into memory before the eerie green of the triptych, Florence concentrated in the layers of paint, the wandering tresses of Mary Magdalene's hair, the sinews and tendons and bones of the Christ.

2

After Bailey's arrest, Esmond and Goad had made their way together to the via Zara for their meeting at the Questura. Count Gaetano, the Podestà, was also there, looking sheepish. Goad gave quiet, precise answers to their questions. Esmond had tried to ask about Bailey, but the Quaestor, alcohol-flushed, held up his hand.

'There is a Red Cross boat to Southampton from Genoa in three days. You must be on it. If not, you will join your friend, the priest, breaking stones in the south.'

That evening, Esmond had packed clothes, his bundle of correspondence and his novel in a morocco travelling case, wrapped Anna's collage in brown paper and closed up the studio. With Tatters at his heels, he walked out of the wicket gate, locking it behind him. He and Goad were booked on a train at eleven the next morning, a change at Pisa and then up the coast to Genoa. As the city's many bells tolled nine, he stood in the middle of the Ponte Santa Trinità, a golden moon rising to the east. To leave all of this behind. He remembered walking across the quad with Blacker after being discovered with Philip. Here, again, he'd found love and was being expelled.

He lit a cigarette, tossing the match into the water. The moon caught the lips of waves in the river and was carried on them downstream before slipping into darkness. He patted the parapet wall and moved off. He turned right along the Lungarno, past where he'd kissed Gerald a year and a half earlier, still a boy, he realised, thinking of his young, unhappy self. Up through the arcade of the Uffizi and into the Piazza della Signoria, *the perfect centre of the human world*. He passed a sandbagged *David*, sheltered under wood, nodded at him and wended his way up past the Bargello into the warren of streets he now knew better than any. He was a Florentine, he realised, more at home here than anywhere.

Ada was waiting at the balcony, looking down at the square. She stood on tiptoes when she saw him, then disappeared and ran out of the front door of the apartment and across the street into his arms. He held her against him, and they couldn't breathe with the force of it, and he felt that, if he could manage not to tell her, not to say that this was their last night together, it might not have to be true.

They sat in the drawing room. She'd understood without words. They talked, sank to the floor and made love very slowly, looking out at the moon-gold trees. He held her head in his hands, covering her pale face with kisses. Tatters trotted from room to room, then found a corner to sleep in and began to snuffle and twitch. Esmond and Ada did not sleep. Only when he handed her Anna's collage did she begin to cry. At eight they walked down to a café on the via della Piazzuola. They fed Tatters pastries under the table, held hands, regretted each sip of coffee, as if by keeping their cups full they might halt time. One last kiss on the corner of the street and then Esmond left, his tears not coming until he'd arrived at the station.

Six Blackshirts, including Carità, were there to see them off. A look of triumph as Goad and Esmond climbed up into their compartment. Carità came right up to the window, rapped on it three times and waved. As the train pulled out, beginning a long arc towards Pisa, Esmond could still see him on the platform, in his shorts, walking with a little bounce and grinning. Goad came and sat next to Esmond and put an arm around his shoulders, but the tears had passed, and he felt something else. The day was hot, the train kept stopping and starting, fishermen lolled by the side of the Arno.

On the outskirts of Pisa, outskirts Esmond recognised with a swell of distress as the same ones he'd driven through the night of Fiamma's death, the train halted again. Almost without thinking, not giving himself time to change his mind, Esmond stood up.

'I'm going back,' he said to Goad.

The older man looked at him through his spectacles, before nodding.

'Will they be looking for us here at Pisa? Or not until Genoa?'

Goad thought for a moment. 'I'd guess Genoa. It will give me time to come up with a convincing – hum – canard.' He rose and took Esmond by the hand. 'Good luck. You'd better get moving.'

The train gave a creak and began to chunter forward. Esmond went into the corridor, reached out of the window, opened the door and leapt down the embankment, tumbling with his case into some thorny bushes, tearing his trousers and opening cuts on his cheeks and hands. He looked up in time to see Goad leaning out of the window, waving discreetly, but furiously.

He walked back along the Arno with his bag over his shoulder, keeping out of the way whenever he saw a cart or bicycle. At Pontedera he bought a ticket for Lucca, but instead boarded for Florence, getting out a stop early at Ginestra Fiorentina. It was dark by the time he reached the Oltrarno.

He waited in the tree-cover of the Villa Ventaglio until past eleven, watching the light in Ada's apartment, her hair, her shadow on the ceiling. Sure that no one was watching, he crossed to ring at the door. She'd taken a while to come down, asked *Chi è?* through the letterbox.

His voice was heavy, choked. 'I couldn't go,' he said, and the door opened, and there she was.

3

Esmond had suggested they move to the villa. There was already talk of the MVSN requisitioning Jewish property, and the apartment was simply too small to hide him for long. Carità's smile at the railway station came to mind. He knew that, if word of his escape reached the Blackshirts, they'd be after his blood. One evening in October, over dinner with the Professor, he mentioned the unoccupied villa that sat on a hilltop to the south, the key to the front door given to Bailey before the Keppels left, now in a drawer in the sacristy. The Professor had nodded.

'It may be the answer to a few other problems we've been having,' he said. 'We need a base out of the city, where people might— disappear.'

Later that night, Bruno Fanciullacci pulled up outside the apartment in a battered and spluttering Bianchi. He'd secured himself a job on the Fiat factory floor in Novoli by day; by night he organised hushed meetings, arranged messages to and from the numerous Communist Party leaders in gaol in Florence. He had shaved and showered since Esmond had seen him in Ada's apartment. His moustache was a slick black line beneath which, ever twirling, the matchstick. He was wearing a new beige suit, a thin navy tie. He looked dashing and capable and Esmond felt a twist of jealousy. Ada sat in front beside Bruno with Tatters on her lap, Esmond in the back. They drove through the deserted town, lights off. The car jerked and squealed around corners, struggled up the smallest incline.

Every plume of mist from the river was a Fascist spy, every shadow hid a Blackshirt with a Beretta. They parked in one of the side streets in front of the Pitti Palace. Ada kept watch outside while Esmond and Bruno went into the church. It was dark inside, cool despite the warm night. Esmond picked up the key to the villa and, under a pile of surplices, Bailey's Army standard W/T radio. Then, just as they were about to leave, he stopped.

'*Aspetta*,' he said, and Bruno shone his torch down the aisle. It found the triptych, which brought Esmond up short. 'D'you think we'll be bombed?' he asked Bruno. 'In Florence, I mean.'

'Maybe. Depends how bad things get. How long it all goes on. They talk about an Open City, but—'

'I want to take the paintings. Keep them with me up at the villa. If they're evacuating art from the Uffizi, the Bargello, all the other churches, we should take care of these.'

Bruno looked at the triptych with a little shake of his head. 'They won't fit in the car.'

'You go ahead, I'll carry them up.'

Bruno shrugged, then smiled, moving the matchstick from one side of his mouth to the other. 'We'll see you up there – if the car makes it. Don't get caught.'

With the paintings balanced on his head – not heavy, but catching every breeze – he set out up the via Romana. The moonlight was broken by clouds, but he kept to the shadows, relieved when he left the main road and began the long climb towards the villa. He heard the sputtering of the Bianchi's engine somewhere ahead.

Bruno and Ada were waiting when he arrived at L'Ombrellino. He carried the paintings up into the house and arranged them by the table in the hall. Bruno had found a bottle of champagne, some glasses in the kitchen. Ada lit the candelabra in the entrance. They stood beside the paintings in the candle-light and toasted the new home. Tatters was already exploring, his footsteps clicking, halting as he caught a new scent, then darting into the upper parts of the house. They were silent in the hallway, listening to the dog's progress. As he left, Bruno embraced them both, the matchstick prodding Esmond's cheek.

'Be careful, you two,' Bruno said. 'It's a risk to love someone these days. They'll use it against you, if they get you.' Esmond drew himself up when Bruno left, the quicker to fill his space. They stood there, in the hall, watching the flames on the gilt of the paintings. Tatters clacked back in with a mouse clamped soft-ly between his jaws. It was still alive, squirming gently. Esmond reached down and eased open the dog's mouth. The mouse dropped, paused for a moment, overcome briefly by this unex-pected redemption, then scurried off into the skirting-board.

4

They have been here at the villa for a year now. They have grown used to the strictures of their new life as eyes grow accustomed to darkness, though Esmond is dreading winter. He can scarcely believe they survived January '42, when snow packed so thickly on the roof they'd heard it groaning like a whale in the night. Ice had patterned the windows, the pool had frozen over and the Arno, flowing heavy with snow-water, was just a black slash across the city below them. He'd had to drop rocks down the well in the garden before he could lower the bucket for water. During the day they'd huddled under eiderdowns bundled in clothes, Tatters a furry, breathy hot-water bottle between them. Later they lit fires in the kitchen, hoping no one would see the smoke.

They barely slept, tucked into the hot fug, feeding vine-wood into the stove, gradually removing clothes and then bathing in a copper tub. They'd pour jugs of near-scalding water over each other, letting out animal bellows and gurgles of pleasure, then sit wrapped in their towels while potatoes baked in the oven, a bowl of carrots boiled on the stove. They read to each other: Ada *Gerusalemme Liberata*, Leopardi's *Zibaldone*, Svevo's *Confessions of Zeno*; Esmond *Eugene Onegin, Mrs Dalloway, The Way We Live Now*. They began to speak Italian as much as English, Ada correcting him on his grammar and pronunciation; now he dreams in both languages.

Once a week – Wednesday afternoons – Bruno would arrive at the wall at the end of the garden with a chicken or a stick of salami or a haunch of ham. He had Communist contacts in the north who could bypass both the government rationing teams and the black marketers, while relatives of Maria Luigia on a pig farm out towards Pistoia happily provided Bruno with supplies. He spoke breathlessly to Esmond of his efforts to unite the various *liberalsocialista* factions and their obdurate Communist cohorts. He was always fizzing with news, the matchstick dancing under his moustache as he talked, his hands sweeping across Florence as he described how they'd hound the Fascists into the Arno, throw them bodily from the Ponte Santa Trinità, and then build a country on the teachings of Gramsci, how Esmond and Ada's children would grow up in a socialist paradise. At this last, Ada would blush and shove him in the chest. As he left, he'd hand them scribbled messages to transmit over the W/T set. They were always in code and made no sense to Esmond, although he began to recognise certain names – Penna, Rossino, Babbo.

Sometimes the Professor came in Bruno's stead, climbing over the wall at the bottom of the garden and rapping on the window

223

of the drawing room until they let him in. He'd brush the snow from his jacket and peer at them: avuncular, anxious. They'd serve him tea, extinguishing the fire as soon as the water boiled. He'd bring news that wasn't on the radio: about the partisans high in the hills waiting for their moment to pounce, strikes at the factories in Milan, about the growing strength of the unions in the big cities and discontent among *contadini* in the south.

Esmond had made several late-night trips to the church that last winter, a hat pushed down over his head, his breath misting in the sharp wild brace of the air. He'd pressed himself into ice-stiff bushes at the slightest sound, leapt garden walls, disappeared into the shadows of buildings where he watched Blackshirts garrulous and greasy after a night in a brothel on the via delle Terme. The curfew was loose, often ignored, but he couldn't afford to be caught by the *carabinieri* and so he waited until the small hours before setting out. He came back loaded with books, jumpers, candles. He found Bailey's service Webley in the priest's bedside drawer, a Sam Browne belt of ammunition under the bed. He sleeps with the gun on the floor beside their mattress.

Finally, April – the trees shrugged of snow, the box-hedge parterre cutting shaggy lines through the whiteness. Only on distant peaks did snow still vein down. The town below woke with difficulty from winter. Petrol was increasingly scarce, food heavily rationed, the young men all away at war. Most of those who stepped out into the serene light of spring wished the snow and cold and darkness would come back. But the sun continued to shine and the city resumed life haltingly, stretching its stiff limbs.

That summer, they lived in the garden. The precise Italianate order at L'Ombrellino unravelled into wild profusion, geometric lines smudged and finally erased by fiercely sprouting fennel, fig, oleander, morning glory. The pool was dark with algae and frog-spawn, knots of weed. Swallows threw themselves down over it to drink from the reflections of their beaks. Esmond imagined them flying up in a great dark wing over the desert where brave sunburnt soldiers stared across a landscape of dunes and mirages of the enemy. When summer ended, they'd swoop – on sudden instinct – southwards to the desert and the dying. The sand would be crossed with bones, dark blood, husks of tanks and troop-carriers. If the swallows knew anything at all, he thought, they'd weep as they passed over, or fly north, back into frozen whiteness.

Ada cut back the weeds on Alice Keppel's vegetable garden. Soon they had tomatoes, zucchini, broad beans and radishes. She asked Bruno to bring her seeds and they planted carrots and celery, beetroot and *cavolo nero*. She worked with her hair in a gypsy bandana, an old shirt of Esmond's hanging over her like a dress. Her hands became hard, the skin of her face dense with freckles. Before dinner they'd swim the dirt and heat of the day from their skinny bodies, lying naked, spreadeagled under the bruising sky.

Bruno and the Professor came more often in summer. Bruno would strip down to his undershorts – placing his matchstick atop his folded shirt – and swim slow lengths. The Professor removed his shoes and dangled his toes, leaning back against the pediment of one of the dodos and speaking with surprise about the destruction of Lübeck: the firestorm that had swept through the medieval city, sucking the oxygen from the air, unleashing tornadoes, turning people to ashes in seconds. He had become obsessed with the bombing raids. He'd started a scrapbook of press clippings, photographs, scholarly articles on the physical and psychological effects of the air war. Two hundred and fifty planes had dropped four hundred tonnes of explosives on the ancient Hanseatic port, he told them, the timbered buildings with their red-tiled roofs passing the flames from one house to the next with a roar. He looked down over Florence and was silent. Bruno's path through the water, the birdsong in the trees below, wind in the pines and bamboo; he sighed and drew his long grey feet from the water.

Some evenings Esmond and Ada would raid the wardrobes of clothes the Keppels had left, opening bottles of *spumante* from the cellar and playing music – just softly – on the gramophone in the drawing room, pushing the divans and canapés and arm-chairs to the side. The discs were marching bands, Christmas carols, Vaughan Williams and Elgar, stolidly English. In one dusty record-case, Ada found three discs of Schubert waltzes. Esmond wore George's white tie and tails, put a monocle in his eye and brilliantined his hair; Ada disappeared into Alice Keppel's ball gowns, gathering up the trains and sweeping them around her *à la* flamenco. They'd jive and foxtrot to the fast-er numbers, working themselves into a sweaty muddle in the warm drawing room as daylight dwindled, then move in dark-ness to the slower music. Some evenings, birdsong in the hills was so loud that it drowned out the gramophone, and they'd find themselves dancing instead to a movement of larks and thrushes, finally falling onto the largest of the divans, panting and happy and lost.

She still has her moments of distance though, when she seems to leave him, to disappear into silence. She has the perfect cheekbones for such distance – high and horizontal, like Anna's. Sometimes he despairs of ever knowing the rills and runnels of her heart. But love without torment, he reasons, is only friend-ship. They lie on their sky-high mattress, kiss, fuck; but it's often as if there's a film between them. One hot night, he'd stood with her in their bedroom and gripped her by the shoulders, shaking her gently. He was a little drunk and half-begged her, finally getting down on his knees.

'Let me in. I want to know you. I can't love you if I don't know you.'

She'd smiled, faltering, then taken her wicker bag from the wardrobe and, looking directly at him, emptied it on the bed.

'This is me,' she said. 'Look at it. This is me.'

Out fell a scallop purse, a diary, several pencils, a bottle of Yardley lavender water, a handkerchief, a blue-bound copy of Mayakovsky's poems and a photograph of Esmond, taken by Goad last Christmas. She held the photograph out as if in triumph, as if to prove that he'd been fixed to the album of her life, and never again should he question her love.

They have talked, now and again, about the death camps. What started out as rumours were now facts: slatted railway carriages heading eastwards, humans herded like cattle, gas chambers. They listen to Radio Vaticana, which had first broken the news, and was now talking about German plans to exterminate the Jews of Europe. The Professor has been in touch with Ada's father, who is in Milan, protected by Ettore Ovazza, safe so far. They can see the eggshell dome of the Great Synagogue from the terrace. Ada stands there some evenings, looking down, a shawl around her, until the light fades and the soft blue dome disappears into darkness.

The leaves are falling in the garden. They will need to be more careful when they step outside, although since the army extended the draft to those aged fifty – sometimes, in the right wind, they can hear the drafted Florentines marching for the war in Russia – they often feel quite alone in the world. L'Ombrellino is like a cloud palace, a vast Zeppelin hanging above an unpeopled city. There are bloodbaths in Greece and Yugoslavia and North Africa, the balance tilts – only slightly – to the Allies, and Esmond and

Ada lie on their bed and listen to the radio, looking at the trip-tych, allowing the tortured figures to stand for what they cannot see, for the suffering that says to them both: it is time to engage.

5

The third of November, 1942: the day after they burnt *In Love and War*. Esmond is standing in uncertain morning light listening to birdsong rising around the villa. Tatters is at his feet, sniffing the air: damp leaves and woodsmoke. After so long spent in old, familiar clothes, he moves with difficulty in the uniform, which is too small for him. He couldn't believe, when Bruno showed him the complicated layers of his disguise, that Italian soldiers still wore puttees, and had spent almost half an hour that morning wrapping and re-wrapping them around his calves. On his head is the red fez of the *Bersagliere*. The right sleeve of his tunic has been pinned behind his back. He thinks of his father.

He hasn't heard from home for over a year now, and he wonders how his parents are getting through the war, if his mother's still locked up. He wonders about Rudyard, whether he's alive, or dry bones in a desert, or heaving a pickaxe in some wind-lashed Silesian prison camp. Now Ada comes out to join him. She is wearing the green and white uniform of an ambulance driver. She hands him a cup of *orzo* which he blows on and sips, pulling a face.

'It's frightful, isn't it?'

'*Parliamo italiano oggi, carino*,' she reminds him, smiling. They've been in the villa so long that Esmond feels panic in his chest at the thought of leaving. He pats the Beretta in the holster on his hip, remembers he isn't meant to use his right arm, and takes another sip. It's the first time since coming to the villa that he has really missed smoking.

'You should put on your cast,' she says, and he has to think for a moment about the word – *ingessatura*. She hands him the white plaster – fashioned by the ever-resourceful Maria Luigia – and a sling which he hooks over his head. His arm feels heavy and strange dangling on his chest. 'We must go,' she says.

They lock Tatters inside the house with a bone that he begins to gnaw, barely noticing them leave. They go down past the swimming pool into the copse, leaves thick and wet underfoot. Esmond helps Ada over the wall at the bottom of the garden – slipping his arm out from the sling and holding her hand with thickly bandaged fingers – and then they are in the via San Carlo where Bruno is leaning against the bonnet of the ancient Bianchi. He smiles at them, cocking his matchstick.

'You're ready?'

Ada nods.

He drives them down through the city and Esmond has to fight an urge not to press his nose to the window. Florence is deserted. A few stray dogs worry bags of rubbish outside the Pitti Palace. Cars sit on their haunches, their wheels removed for the rubber, their owners unable to find or afford petrol. When they come to the via Tornabuoni, Esmond reaches over with his good arm and takes Ada's hand. He can feel his pulse against her cool flesh. She is made for this, he thinks.

'Your British Institute, it's now used for meetings of the Committee of Fascist Youth,' Bruno says. 'They're training the next generation of cannon fodder, teaching range-finding and ordnance in that beautiful library.' He shakes his head and then brings the car to a halt outside Pretini's hair salon. 'I must leave you here,' he says. 'I can't risk anyone seeing me with you. Now, you know what you're required to do?' Ada nods. 'Don't speak too much,' he says, looking at Esmond. 'If you're caught, give them the information we agreed. Nothing about the Professor, nothing about supply lines. Good luck.' They climb out into the cool morning. Esmond finds himself wondering what else he knows that the Fascists could possibly want. Some meaningless code names, a few fuzzily recalled locations in the hills that he's transmitted over the W/T. The Professor is all he has.

He can see his breath in the air as they walk down the via degli Avelli towards the station. Ada is a few steps ahead, carrying a small case with a red cross on it, which she swings jauntily by her side. They wait for a tram to pass and walk out of the shadow of Santa Maria Novella. The railway station stretches in front of them; from under the brow of its porch beetles a line of commuters; travellers trying to keep up with their porters; soldiers embracing their wives and lovers in the gloomy ticket hall, greetings and farewells. Esmond spots another *Bersagliera* with a rifle across his back. The man salutes when he sees the *caporal maggiore* stripes on his shoulders. Esmond nods down at his arm, mutters '*Va bene*,' at the soldier and follows Ada into the station.

Carabinieri stand in their kepis by the ticket gates, asking for documents only from the young girls as they board trains for the coast. Ada, whose hair is up beneath a peaked cap, passes the *carabinieri* and walks forward to the platform where the train to Livorno is beginning to puff. Esmond starts to follow her when one of the policemen holds out an arm.

'*Documenti, per favore*,' the policeman says, scowling at Esmond's bandaged arm. Esmond reaches awkwardly inside his jacket and fumbles for his military identification card and notification of disability. He fights not to look towards Ada on the platform. The policeman stares at the documents and then at Esmond.

'*Dove andate?*'

Esmond clears his throat and hesitates. Now he does see Ada, fumbling in her case, glancing at him. He stares back at the policeman and, in barely more than a whisper, says, '*Vado a una clinica ortopedica a Livorno. Ho un appuntamento con un dottore Hartmann lì.*' He holds his breath as the policeman looks again at his papers, finally handing them back with a '*Grazie*'. Esmond walks through the gates and, without looking at Ada, boards the train for Livorno, his pulse visible in the corners of his eyes.

6

They get off at Empoli. The weather has turned for the worse, thunderclouds rolling across the sky from the west. Esmond makes sure Ada has seen him and crosses the road into the park opposite the station. He waits on a bench beneath a plane tree, where she joins him, at the far end, opening her case on her lap.

'Was it close?' she asks.

'I don't think so. He just wanted to get some sweat out of a soldier. If my Italian isn't good enough by now—'

'Your Italian is fine.'

They leave the park and walk past a group of cafés and down a road of blank-faced houses. After a few hundred yards, they stop in front of a building with a faded sign: 'Hotel Superiore'. There is the sound of singing. Ada rings the bell. They wait for several minutes and finally the bolts are drawn back. A hunched old woman in black opens the door and leads them silently into a courtyard and up a staircase. On the *piano nobile* they make their way into a gloomy apartment. The old lady leaves them, shutting the door behind her. The singing gets louder. Esmond follows Ada into the bedroom where, against the open windows, an enormous man is performing '*E Lucevan le Stelle*' from *Tosca* for the assorted pigeons and sparrows on the rooftops. His back to the room, he quivers at the highest notes, his voice breaking. Finally, after a sudden pause, he turns towards them.

'Welcome,' he says in an accent Esmond cannot place. He kisses Ada and shakes Esmond vigorously by his plaster cast, letting out a burbling laugh. He sits down on the bed, motions to two armchairs opposite and pours them out a glass of wine each from the bottle beside his bed.

'*Bene*,' he says, letting out another laugh and raising his glass. 'I am Oreste Ristori. To your health, young ones – it's never too early for a sip, heh?' His face shines as if recently polished. He's older than Esmond had thought, his vastness hiding wrinkles that only reveal themselves in repose. Above the fireplace on one side of the room are several photographs of a woman who, for a moment, reminds Esmond of Wallis Simpson. In some of the pictures she is in battle fatigues, in another she stands at a waterfall holding a rifle in one hand, her face streaked with mud or blood.

Ristori goes to stand beside the pictures, picking one from the mantel and passing it to Esmond. The silver frame is cold to the touch. She is beautiful. A string of black pearls hangs from her throat.

'My Mercedes,' the man says. 'My star in the dark night. I write to her every day, not knowing even if she receives my letters. She was in gaol in São Paulo. Now she is fighting Vargas's government in the jungle, with the anarchists, the guerrillas. In Brazil. You see how remarkable she is?' He beams at Esmond. 'You see how a man might spend his life for a woman like this?' He knocks back his wine and sits down on the bed, pouring another. He hums a few more bars of *Tosca* as he sips. It is cold in the room and Ada gives a shiver.

'Mr Ristori, we must be on the next train. May we have the documents?'

'Let me get them. I'm sorry.' He kneels down and begins to root beneath the bed. 'It's rare I have visitors now,' he says. 'I attend a literary gathering that is cover for a Marxist discussion group, but still – we are in Empoli, you understand? Revolutions were never made in Empoli. I am back where I began, the Tuscany of my birth. Defeated! Ah, here we go.' He draws out some sheets of paper covered in dense typewritten text. Ada takes them from him and looks at them closely.

'I think this is the sort of thing we were after. Thank you.'

'My pleasure,' he says, smiling broadly again. 'You're sure you won't stay for another drink?'

'We must make our train.'

She stands above Esmond, helps him ease the cast off his wrist, rolls the papers around his arm, and closes it over them. They bid farewell to Ristori, and make their way down the narrow stairs of the hotel, through its silent courtyard. As they walk down the broad street towards the station, the sound of Ristori's singing comes to them again, high and sweet, finally lost in the traffic and the wind.

7

On the train to Pisa, they sit together in an empty compartment. It has begun to rain and the drops are pulled along the window as they gather speed through the Tuscan hills.

'I've no idea if these codes are any good,' she says, looking out.

'But he's dependable. Bruno said so.'

'He's a lunatic.' An inspector comes into the compartment, nods at them both as he checks their tickets and pulls the door shut behind him.

'In some ways he's amazing, obviously, a modern Bakunin.

He fought for the rights of Italian immigrant labourers in South America. They think he's a hero down there. No one knew how badly Italians were being exploited. He wrote long articles about the conditions for workers and kept being put on boats back to Italy, but he'd throw himself overboard and swim back to land.'

'When did he meet—?'

'Mercedes Gomez. She was another anarchist. They created the labour movement in Brazil, unions for plantation workers. When the police started rounding everyone up, Ristori was put on a prison boat back to Genoa. If he ever goes back he'll be shot. He's almost seventy, you know. This isn't the first time he's helped us.'

At Pisa there are gangs of Blackshirts on the platforms, police guarding the exits. He waits for Ada to get off the train and follows some distance behind. He makes his way down into the underpass and boards another train, this time for Genoa. Ada is sitting by herself in a crowded compartment. He stands, holding onto the luggage rack, aware suddenly that his cast is itching, that the papers are dampening against his skin.

They are only on the train for two stops, until Forte dei Marmi. He goes first and, without looking back, crosses the road and boards a bus to the seafront. He walks along the promenade, sheltering from the worst of the rain under the umbrella pines. Then an open stretch past shuttered restaurants and hotels until he comes to the Bagno Dalmazia bathing club; a single waiter stands outside on the sand, down towards the beach. Deckchairs sag under a tattered awning.

'A drink, sir?' he says, as Esmond walks down onto the damp sand.

'I'm waiting for a friend. She's always late,' Esmond says, the carefully remembered code words sounding sham to his ears. He eases himself down into one of the deckchairs. The waiter

234

disappears inside and Esmond can hear him speaking. He sits and watches the sea, a deep and melancholy grey, pocked with rain. Rocks prod up like fins twenty feet out. After fifteen minutes or so, he is aware of a buzzing noise from where the coast curves round for La Spezia. He thinks of Shelley floating in these choppy waters, his skin the grey-green deadness of the sea. Ada arrives and sinks down into the other deckchair.

'You weren't followed?' Esmond asks in English.

'No.'

'I can't think why I asked that. I suppose it sounded like the sort of thing I should say. Of course you weren't.'

'You're a very convincing spy.'

The waiter brings them both a coffee. It is nearing three and they haven't eaten yet.

'They're coming,' Ada says, nodding at two boats moving steadily from the north.

'You're sure it's them?'

'I am.'

They sip their coffee.

'I wonder,' he begins, 'the people who do this kind of thing all the time, the Richard Hannay types, how much they're in it for the thrill? Waiting around for a secret assignations. Being terribly hush-hush. Generally feeling like a Buchan novel.'

She is silent, watching the boats as they approach.

'Because it seems rather a flimsy thing to build your life upon, this kind of frisson, don't you—'

'Shut up, Esmond.'

'Right-o.'

'If you have to speak, speak in Italian. But better, don't speak.'

He looks down the beach, up towards the road, where only the waiter stands, watching them, coolly complicit. A gust of wind showers them with a fine sting of sand.

'Right-o,' he says quietly.

The boats pull up on the shoreline a few hundred yards to the north and one man walks briskly along the beach towards them. He's wearing a dark blue sou'wester and oilskin and puffing on a cigarette, a red glow each time he inhales. When he reaches them he squats down in front of Esmond. He has amused blue eyes, a square jaw peppered with stubble.

'Shoot out your arm and let's have a dekko,' he says, looking swiftly up and down the beach and then peeling apart the plaster cast. He takes out the papers and gives them a brief, frowning glance before slipping them inside his oilskin. 'Think they're kosher?' he asks.

'They look real enough,' Ada says, sitting up as straight as her deck chair will allow. 'Ristori stole them from the Regia Marina headquarters in Livorno. Could be a plant, but I'd bet they were real.'

'Good work,' the man says. 'You know Bailey, don't you?' He looks at Esmond again.

'Yes. Very well.'

'Bloody good egg. We sprung him from a camp in Sicily in August. He's in Spain now, on a job, but he'll be back in the UK before long. Deserves a rest after what he's been through. More or less ran our game in Italy until they picked him up.'

'Your game?'

'Can't stay, I'm afraid. Eyeties I'm with are awfully skittish. Cheerio.'

He pulls his hat down and sets off back up the beach. The rain has eased and there is sunlight on the sea as the two boats pull out and head northwards. They sit for a while longer and then Ada stands and stretches.

'Shall we go for a walk?'

They follow the Englishman's footsteps down to the tide-line.

Ada shucks off her shoes and socks and walks barefoot, stepping over wormcasts and the bubbles of oily seaweed.

'Aren't you cold?' Esmond asks.

'I love it. I love winter. It's worth a little pain to feel like this.'

Esmond takes his own shoes off and they walk together, looking up at the dark windows of holiday houses, hotels, restaurants. They herd wading birds ahead of them along the beach; Esmond spots oystercatchers, sanderlings, dunlin.

'There's nothing so depressing as a holiday resort in winter,' he says.

'But we have it to ourselves.' She takes his hand and he feels the ridge of the ring on her wedding finger. He remembers slipping Bruno an envelope of cash to take to Bernard Berenson at I Tatti in exchange for the small and ancient gold band. Esmond had given it to Ada one evening, as they'd sat out on the terrace with one of the last bottles of wine from the Keppels' cellar, and a rich dusk had fallen over the countryside. He'd told her he loved her, that as soon as the war was over, he'd marry her, that he'd never met anyone so admirable.

Now he takes her in his arms on the beach, aware there must be eyes watching them from the slumbering town, but not wanting to miss this, their toes icy in the surf, his cast heavy on her shoulder. Sun ranges across the sea, now blue and sparking green. He kisses her and she pulls him urgently towards her. A spray of sand and salt water covers them, and he is suddenly aware how far from safety they are, how alone. They break apart, pulling their socks and shoes back onto pale blue feet. Esmond hooks his cast back in the sling, and they make their way up to the train station.

8

It is not until the beginning of December, when, en route to Malta, three *Poeti*-class destroyers are intercepted by Royal Navy corvettes off Lipari and sunk, that they see the fruits of their mission. Bruno, the Professor, Antonio Ignesti and Tosca Bucarelli come to L'Ombrellino to congratulate them. Esmond and Ada are in the kitchen with Tatters when the four appear at the bottom of the terrace, coming up the stone steps by the swimming pool. An unlikely gang – the Professor, slightly stooped, a bottle of wine in each hand, stumbling every so often on the icy gravel, Bruno swinging a whole cured ham, scarf furled around his neck like an undergraduate, Antonio with one arm around Tosca, the other heaving a shopping basket full of pasta and cabbages. He is sturdy and shaven and she blonde and childlike beside him. Tatters gallops down to greet them, speechless with joy at their coming, bouncing up and down until he is tickled and fed a chunk of ham by Bruno.

They sit in the kitchen around another perilous fire, snow falling thickly outside. Corks are pulled from bottles, a pan of water set to boil on the stove, ham and salami sliced on the sideboard. There is an air of quiet satisfaction, of having done something meaningful for Europe, for humanity. The wireless is brought down to the kitchen, and they listen to the news on Radio Vaticana. It is possible, as 1942 runs out of breath, to feel better.

The Allies are on top in most places. Rommel is stuck in Tunisia; the Germans stewing in Stalingrad; the Japanese fading at Guadalcanal. The American war machine is gathering: their bombs fall constantly. Malta – absurdly, it seems to Esmond – stands firm. And here in Italy the Professor tells them of Mussolini's son-in-law, Ciano, uttering rebellious murmurs in Rome

238

as more and more *Alpini* are fed into the maw of the Eastern Front. Slogans have begun to appear on the streets of Florence. *Viva Il Duce* and *Credere, Obbedire, Combattare* are replaced by *Non Mollare!* and *Ricordiamo Matteotti*.

The Professor raises his glass. 'To Esmond and Ada,' he says, grinning. 'And to Oreste Ristori, the madman.'

'And to me,' Tosca says. 'It's my twentieth birthday today.' Esmond hugs her, Bruno uncorks a bottle of *spumante*, the Professor beams soppily as Ada serves out bowls of ravioli. Tatters settles down in Bruno's lap and begins to snore as they talk about the war.

After eating, they go to stand in the drawing room where Esmond lights another fire, burning more of the vine branches that fill the bothies beside the villa. Firelight plays on their faces as they lounge on divans, the Professor sprawled in an armchair, Tosca and Antonio beginning to dance as Ada winds up the gramophone. Bruno is by the window smoking a cigarillo, looking down over Florence.

The Professor swirls the flat wine in his glass. 'All wars are civil wars,' he says woozily, 'because all men are brothers.' Dusk has fallen and the city is a mass of shadows under the hills. Esmond goes to stand beside Bruno.

'You did well,' Bruno says. 'Ada told me.'

'It was a test, I suppose?'

'It was a success. That's all that matters.' Bruno breathes out smoke against the window. 'Those ships might have made the difference for Malta. Malta might make the difference to the war. Everything is connected, especially at a time like this.'

They are silent for a while. Bruno turns towards him and Esmond watches his thin profile in the glass.

'We must all choose sides, you know,' he says.

'I have.'

'You're doing the right thing, certainly. Do you want a cigarillo?'

'Thanks.'

Esmond sees the flame flare in the window. Two heads bend inwards and two red points separate. The Professor leads Ada in a stately waltz beside Antonio and Tosca, the glow of firelight behind them.

'It's important to do the right things for the right reasons. To have ideological certainty to back up your actions.' Bruno's voice is soft. 'Do you see what I mean?'

Esmond swallows the last of his champagne. He feels oddly nervous.

'It's extraordinary,' he says. 'Stalingrad. I mean horrifying, but also terribly moving. Ada and I listen to Radio Moscow in the evenings, when they broadcast in English, and the way the Russians are laying down their lives, that kind of ecstatic self-sacrifice. They have something we don't.'

'Noble, isn't it?' Bruno turns and smiles. A beat. 'You'll want to rescue your fiancée from the Professor. She's beginning to look desperate.'

Esmond and Ada stand at the door a few hours later and watch the four of them stagger down the path towards the swimming pool. They wash up together, then make their way to bed, bundled against the cold. Esmond has found an old tweed jacket of George Keppel's that he wears to sleep. They have talked about bringing the mattress down to the kitchen, but Esmond says there's something medieval about the idea, and they like the cool light of mornings in the studio, the view down over the city, the sense of sleeping away from a sordid day in the city's life.

In bed that night, he waits until she is asleep and crawls along the floor to light the stubby candle in front of the triptych. He thinks of the Italian sailors on the boat, imagines the shock of the torpedo blasts, the way the air would have been sucked out of the cabins, how quickly they went down. He wonders how many of the men on board read poetry, how many had a novel they were working on, or a girl like Ada waiting at home. He wonders how many were locked in each other's arms, in the snug of a hammock below deck, when the torpedoes struck. He'd heard that drowning was an easy way to go once the first lungful of water was drawn in. He looks up at the face of Mary Magdalene and finds himself mouthing something close to a prayer.

'You don't believe in God now, do you?' Ada, wearing a thick jumper over one of Alice Keppel's nightdresses, is raised on her elbow, watching him.

'Of course not,' he says.

'I like having the paintings here, but not if they're making you superstitious. I won't be with a religious man.'

'I was just thinking about the sailors, about how they died.'

'You can't have those thoughts. We're at war. Now blow out the candle.'

He does so and lies beside her, looking up into the darkness until it is almost dawn, then gets up and takes Tatters downstairs. He lets the dog out into the garden and goes back inside. He sees, by the fire, a red leather book. *Il Manifesto del Partito Comunista*. He opens it and begins to read – '*Borghese e Proletari*. The story of every society up to this point is a story of class struggles.' He hears Tatters scratching at the kitchen door. He smiles, closes the book. The dog, with a proud little wag, deposits a baby rabbit on the mat, still weakly twitching, its back broken. Tatters looks up at Esmond with jubilant eyes, then turns tail and rushes back into the garden, barking joyously. By the time they eat breakfast, there are six, soft, motionless pouches of fur curled up on the mat.

'I'll cook them for lunch,' Ada says, smiling.

9

The early months of 1943 bring deep snow and silent, frosty mornings. Esmond had thought that, after the success of their first job, missions for the Resistance would be delivered into their lives in regular, manageable manila envelopes. Instead, apart from frequent visits from Bruno carrying cryptic messages for the W/T, the months of snow and ice pass much as before at L'Ombrellino.

Abroad, though, it is a different matter. Esmond and Ada lying rapt as the good news registers from the Vatican, Moscow, London. The wireless on the table in their bedroom is almost never off. When the German 6th Army surrenders and the Battle of Stalingrad is over, Esmond wakes Ada and they listen together to Radio Moscow playing the *Internationale*. She looks up at him with a sleep-fogged grin. Even the eyes of the three martyrs seem to soften at the news. The music stops and they hear the voice of the Russian announcer, breaking every so often with emotion as he reads a report of the final battle. They understand almost nothing of what he says but the hopeful relief. They make love then, pressing their cold bodies together, and she's crying when she comes. He kisses her mole and tastes salt.

The foul weather, which has cut off the mountain passes, keeps the partisans to their hideouts in the hills. The rag-tag members of the Resistance spend the winter planning, discussing. Esmond makes a night-time foray down into the city to pick up a package from the Professor at the university. He hides it in the bottom of George Keppel's wardrobe until a Chetnik Serb, who grins at him through his thick black beard, comes to collect it.

There are more and more Nazis in Florence; the Professor tells of Bach and Beethoven in the city's churches, Furtwängler and von Karajan flown in to give gala performances. After the concerts, the Germans congregate at the Paszkowski Bar in the Piazza Vittorio Emanuele or at the Braunhaus – a rococo apartment near the German Consulate on the via dei Bardi – where they serve beer from Munich, bratwurst and Wiener schnitzel. Red and black swastika flags hang from the windows and, most evenings, the sound of Hitler's voice giving long, jagged speeches is heard until the cheers of the men inside drown it out. The locals stand with their ration cards in the street below, half-crazed with hunger.

They follow news from the ghetto in Warsaw hopelessly, helplessly. Reports come to them in stuttering bursts, like rifle fire over the radio waves. They hear of the Waffen SS entering on the eve of Passover, the bodies suspended from the clock tower. They hear of members of the Resistance hiding in sewers and culverts, brandishing Molotov cocktails and pilfered weapons. For a moment, just as the first warm sunshine brings buds and birdsong to the garden, there is a window of optimism, as the Nazis retreat. Then silence for a month. In May, when the rebellion is finally crushed, the ghetto torched, the members of the Resistance shot and hanged, Ada stays up in the bedroom, looking at the triptych, her eyes very cold and very clear. Esmond brings her tea and books, sits on the bed and rubs her feet between his hands. She comes downstairs again once she hears that Lampedusa has fallen. A piece of Italy is in Allied hands. Bruno is carrying two bottles of Chianti when he comes to see them that evening and they sit out on the terrace and toast the fall of Fascism.

In July, a Wednesday arrives with no visit from Bruno. Ada is sick and so they spend the day lying in bed listening to the BBC report the British landing on Sicily. The Germans haven't had the time to reinforce the Italian mainland; it is thought that the country will fall in a matter of weeks. Ada leans over the side of the mattress and vomits into a metal bin. Every so often, Esmond goes down to the bottom of the garden to check for Bruno. As night falls, he makes a final trip down to the copse with Tatters and sees the blonde head of Tosca bobbing through the trees towards him.

'Where's Bruno?' he asks.

She is out of breath and sits down on one of the chairs beside the pool. 'Bruno is fine,' she says. 'They have Maria Luigia, though.'

'Who have her?'

'The Blackshirts, Carità,' she says, scowling. 'She was found carrying forged passports. She's been taken to the Murate. Bruno thinks we'll be able to spring her. I think he's crazy.' She circles her finger by her head.

'Is there anything we can do?' he asks.

'Sit tight,' she says. 'I must go now.'

Bruno comes up to see them the next day. Ada is still sick, and so the thin, tired-looking man comes to speak to them in their bedroom.

'You have the paintings up here. Very gothic,' he says when he walks in. 'And a pistol beside the bed. I'm impressed.' He looks down at Ada, who has a sheen of sweat on her forehead. 'Are you all right?' he asks, cocking the matchstick in the corner of his mouth.

'I'm fine,' she says. 'It's just an infection. The water in the well isn't as clean as it was. Is there news of Maria Luigia?'

He stoops to stroke Tatters, who has wandered in at their feet. 'She's being held while they try to extract information from her. She's a strong woman, though. I'd rather it were her than almost anyone else. The bastards will torture her, I'd imagine, but she'll do well.'

Bruno leaves and they sit listening to the radio. Neither of them feels like eating. Night falls and it is hot in the room, even with the windows open. Both of them are sweating and each time Esmond drifts into a shallow sleep, he sees Maria Luigia's plump, friendly face, a shadow looming over it. He wakes with a start, three, four, five times. Finally, Ada turns and puts her arms around him.

'Darling, I'm pregnant,' she says.

10

The first they know is the ringing of the great bell – *La Vacca* – in the Palazzo Vecchio. They are down by the pool, dangling their feet in the water, trying to get cool in the airless evening. Esmond gets a kick of pleasure each time he thinks about the baby. He feels at once braver and more nervous than ever before. Ada is still sick, drained by the heat, irritable. 'The baby is not the most important thing,' she says with a frown, whenever he drapes moony fingers across her belly. Now frogs swim in the pool, pesto-thick with weed and algae. The dodos seem almost alive, so shrouded are they with moss and lichen.

The bell begins to ring just past seven in the evening. It rings for half an hour without stopping and soon there are pistol shots from the town below them. When the bell stops, they catch distant cheers echoing up the hillside. At once, they look at each other and hurry up to the bedroom. Esmond tunes the radio to the BBC. The announcer – it is Alvar Lidell – speaks in a voice of quiet wonder. *The Fascist government of Benito Mussolini has been overthrown in a bloodless coup*, he says. *Marshal Badoglio has announced that Italy will continue to fight alongside its German allies. Former Prime Minister Mussolini has been sent into exile on the island of Maddalena. There will be a further address by King Victor Emmanuel and Prime Minister Badoglio tomorrow at twelve hundred hours Greenwich Mean Time.*

Esmond and Ada stare at each other open-mouthed.

'What does it mean?' she asks. 'Is it over?'

'The war?' he says. 'Not yet. It can't be. The Germans are still here.'

'But Musso, he's gone?'

Esmond nods.

'And Fascism?'

He shrugs. 'Badoglio, he's a soldier, he's not a Fascist.' Ada begins to laugh, her hair bouncing as she laughs, her eyes bright and wide. Esmond runs his hands through her laughing hair as *La Vacca* begins to ring again. They look out of the window and over the city, where puffs of smoke appear and drift in the still evening. Two louder explosions and Esmond cranes his neck around, gazing down over the dusky Boboli Gardens to the Belvedere Fort, which is firing its cannons. Now a crackle of anti-aircraft fire answers from the opposite side of the valley, up towards Fiesole.

'I'm going to go down and see what's going on.'

She takes his hand, fixing her eyes on his. 'I'm coming with you,' she says.

There's an old bicycle in one of the sheds beside the villa. He hunts around for a pump, inflates the tyres and bangs dust from the saddle. Ada perches, nerveless and serene, on the handlebars as they wobble through the darkening lanes. Esmond is aware of the preciousness of his cargo, but is unable to stop himself pedalling when, at one point, they come round a corner and a blast of wind hits them and the searchlights and fireworks and cheering crowds spread out before them.

The bridge is thick with people. They get off the bike and

push it across, murmuring *scusi* every so often. The whole world is smiling, children play, young couples stand arm-in-arm and look over the river. At the dam downstream, a group of boys have gathered to set off fireworks. These rise into the air and burst, shedding bright fragments that scatter their reflection over the Arno and then fall as ashes on the water.

They reach the Piazza della Signoria and chain the bike to the Loggia dei Lanzi. A stage has been set up in front of the Palazzo Vecchio. Michelangelo's *David*, now free of his wooden carapace, looks pointedly in the opposite direction. Esmond can see the Professor and Bruno and a group of other men he recognises from those early days at Ada's apartment. They are arguing, gesturing furiously at each other as a harried-looking engineer rigs up a microphone and tests the Tannoy system – *uno due, uno due* – which once carried Mussolini's speeches to the perfect centre of the human world. Esmond thinks of Florence's future: after throwing off the Fascists, the city will lose itself in petty political squabbles of the sort that is currently, publicly, taking place by the side of the stage. Finally, after glaring threateningly at an older man with a shiny head and round glasses, the Professor makes his way to the microphone.

'In 1922,' he begins, and a sudden hush falls across the piazza. Some are climbing up the monuments to secure a view of the stage. 'In 1922,' he repeats, 'we made Benito Mussolini a freeman of the city of Florence. Today, we celebrate his captivity! Fascism in Italy is dead, the MVSN is dead. Today, black shirts will be hung at the back of cupboards, buried in sacks in the garden, burnt on a thousand bonfires.' A huge cheer goes up, hats are thrown in the air; Esmond thinks of his own British Union uniform, moth-eaten and dusty, abandoned with his room in the church. He takes Ada in his arms and kisses her. 'We have lived a nightmare,' the Professor continues, 'and now we are waking up.

This is not the end, but it is the beginning of the end. Our sons are not yet home, our land is not yet our own, this war is not yet over. But soon, soon! *Viva Firenze!*'

At the heart of the crowd, fist raised, one eye closed by a bruise, is Maria Luigia. She smiles towards them, as if letting them in on the secret of her survival. There are more fireworks, some girls have torn up their ration cards and are throwing them in the air like confetti. Esmond and Ada go to stand beside Maria Luigia's broadness and lift their own fists into the hopeful air. '*Viva Firenze!*'

11

The next day they walk into town together after breakfast. Bad weather came in overnight and a light rain is falling as they wind along the narrow lanes. The city is vague under a canopy of low cloud, the river yellow-grey and fast as they cross the Ponte Santa Trinità. They make their way past *David* into the Palazzo Vecchio. There is a swell of noise as they find the ornate main corridor; they follow the voices up a flight of stone steps and into a long, frescoed hall. People are standing and making speeches around a table, but most of the words are lost under the applause and clinking glasses and conversation. Esmond takes Ada by the hand and they cross the room to stand next to Tosca and Antonio in the bay of a window.

Bruno, stubble-shadowed, matchstick in mouth, sits between the Professor and a young, bespectacled man in a red cravat. Further up the table, Esmond sees the portly Oreste Ristori, a half-empty bottle of wine in front of him. He is leaning back and bellowing with laughter at something someone has said, his wide face rippling with each guffaw. Esmond sees the cyclist

Gino Bartali, sitting next to his wife, grinning broadly and sign-ing the occasional autograph. The Professor stands up and at once there is silence.

'Welcome, all of you.' He smiles, his watery eyes resting for a moment on the man beside Bruno. 'Whatever our divisions – and we are certainly from different worlds, some of us – that which binds us is stronger. A certainty that we are moving into a new and vital age for our nation, for our city; a love of Florence and our fellow Florentines; a hatred of the thugs and monsters who have ruled us for twenty-one years. Today we welcome back some old friends, freed from needless captivity. We welcome Elio Chianesi' – the man next to Bruno, with his studious round glasses, half-rises and waves – 'once a student of mine. He has, for too long, been relying on the books we could smuggle into prison to nourish him. We missed you, Elio. We're delighted to have you back.'

'Thank you, Professor,' he says, his pale cheeks flushing. Another round of applause, which stops suddenly as a young black man in an oyster-white linen suit comes barrelling into the room. He has a wild brush of wiry hair on his head, narrow, oriental eyes. Ada lets out a gasp.

'Alessandro,' she says. Leaving Esmond, she moves swift-ly across the room to where the young man is already being embraced by Bruno, slapped on the back by the Professor, touched and poked by others. One of the ornate chairs is pulled out and he sits down as a glass of wine is poured. He lifts it to Elio and then turns to see Ada standing behind his chair, looking down at him with widening eyes. Esmond doesn't hear what they say to each other, but he thinks he understands what is passing between them. The man's skin is the same colour as the polished mahogany table, his eyes as black as the wine in his glass. Esmond finds himself feeling – not jealousy – but a sleepy melancholy, until he sees Ada, now smiling, gesture towards him and say something to the young man. With a gentle pat on the man's shoulder, Ada makes her way back to his side.

They don't speak until after the meeting is over, and the various *liberalsocialiste* – anarchists, Communists, Christian Democrats and Republicans – stand around drinking up the wine liberated – as Bruno puts it – from the now boarded-up Fascist headquarters at the Piazza Mentana. He and Ada are still at the window, looking out over the elevated cloisters of the Uffizi. The rain is heavier now, the only people moving by the river are hidden by the black domes of their umbrellas.

'An old flame?' he asks, trying to sound light-hearted.

'His name is Alessandro Sinigaglia. His father was a friend of my father's. He's been in Regina Coeli for a long time. I hardly recognise him.'

'Is he Abyssinian? He's extraordinary-looking.'

'His father's Jewish, his mother was the black maid of a family from St Louis who came here just before the first war. She was thrown out when they found out she was pregnant and she made Florence her home.'

He turns to look across the table to where Alessandro, Elio and Bruno are talking. They toast each other, drink, recharge their glasses. They seem bold and worldly, in a way he knows he isn't. He lets out a sigh. Ada takes his hand and gives it a squeeze, speaking softly.

'I love you. I know I don't say it very often – it's not my way. But I always dreamed of this, of you.' She squeezes his hand again, harder this time. 'I told him he could stay with us, just until he finds a place. You don't mind, do you?'

He shrugs and grins, still basking in her words. People begin to leave the hall, moving off into various meeting rooms – as they walk with them, and pass open doors, Esmond hears snatches of welcome to Badoglio's government, admonitions to reform, refuse, tighten with the Church, distance from the State. Bruno sticks his head out of one of the doors and sees them.

'You two should come in here. We're discussing whether to send a delegation to Stalin, declare Florence an independent Soviet republic. Come on.' He disappears back inside. Ada whistles.

'You go,' Esmond says. 'You should be involved in this – you deserve to be.' She smiles and, with a kiss, heads off to join her comrades.

At something of a loss that afternoon, Esmond sits in the condensation-misted window of the Giubbe Rosse, sipping tea. His bicycle is leaning against the window. He has been to the bank, where he was delighted to see Maria Luigia and withdrew a thousand lire from the radio account. He strolled along to the Libreria Gonnelli just off the Piazza del Duomo and bought a copy of Turgenev's *Rudin* in Italian which he now reads, frowning, rubbing a window in the misted glass and looking out over his bicycle into the empty square. He finds himself increasingly drawn to Russian novels, particularly those peopled by what Leavis had referred to in a lecture as the 'superfluous man'. He wonders if fate has marked him as one of these, destined for the footnotes of a great moment, a passenger, an Oblomov.

As evening falls, he sits in the café. His book is finished, the teapot cool, several beer glasses emptied. He is gently drunk and the book lies face-down on his lap. He is beginning to nod as the door opens and Antonio strides in.

'He's here,' he shouts out into the square. 'Esmond!' He's beaming, slaps Esmond on the back and sits down at the table opposite him. Soon Tosca enters, followed by Ada and Bruno, Alessandro and Elio. Oreste Ristori comes in singing the '*Non più andrai, farfallone amoroso*,' from *The Marriage of Figaro*. He smiles as Ristori, still singing, gives a little jig. A waiter brings them over glasses and a bottle of *spumante*, and they sit drinking into the night.

They walk out into the square at around one o'clock and, as they are saying their farewells, there is the sound of aeroplane engines above, a distant rattle of gunfire.

'It's not over yet,' Bruno reminds them. 'We're still with the Germans as far as the Brits are concerned. It's right to celebrate but we should be careful.' Esmond pushes the bike up the hill with Ada walking on one side, Alessandro on the other. When they get to L'Ombrellino, they shake dust from the sheets of the Keppels' bed, where Alessandro is to sleep, and open the windows to the night.

Ada has gone upstairs. Esmond and Alessandro are back in the drawing room having a final brandy. A nightjar creaks somewhere in the garden below them.

'I appreciate you putting me up,' Alessandro says. 'Just until things are clearer in the city and I can find a job, a place to rent. It was fucking mad down there, don't you think?'

'What do you mean?'

'Maybe it's because I've been in gaol. It just seems like they're walking around in a dream. All this shit about declaring a Soviet republic in Florence, or becoming a Papal dependency. This city was the beating heart of Tuscan Fascism. The guys who tortured me are sitting at home right now, picking their toenails, but eventually they'll have to come out, get jobs. What do we do with them?'

'I was wondering—'

'Some fool was walking down the via Guelfa with a Party badge on earlier. A bunch of workers from the Ginori factory almost killed him. But we can't do that, we have to bring them in somehow.'

They sip their drinks a while longer and then go up to bed. On the stairs, just before parting, Alessandro lays a hand on Esmond's arm.

'Ada told me about the baby,' he says. 'Congratulations. She's an astonishing girl, the girl who's meant the most to me. I thought about her a lot when I was in prison and I'm pleased to find her so well. So happy with you.' A throb of sadness in his voice. Esmond can hardly see him in the darkness of the stair-well, but he smiles.

'Thanks,' he says. 'It's good to have you here.'

12

The days are taken up with meetings in the Palazzo Vecchio, speeches in the Piazza della Signoria where the various leaders make – with varying degrees of eloquence – their plays for power. Ada even gives a speech, standing in at the last moment for Bruno, who is caught at a rally in the Fiat factory. She is very straight, very still on the stage in front of the Palazzo, Michelangelo's *David* looking peaceably over her. She speaks – not for long, but with honesty and intelligence – and Esmond feels extraordinarily proud that his child is growing in this fiery, political woman.

Alessandro is rarely at home. When he is, he's an excellent guest, making delicious meals from a mixture of packets and tins and Ada's garden. He goes out with Tatters and Esmond's Webley early in the morning and comes back with woodpigeons, pheasants and partridges which he plucks in the kitchen until the air is thick with feathers and rich fat. The dog loves him. The evenings he's not at a rally or meeting workers at the factories in Rifredi or Sesto Fiorentino, he stands for hours in the garden throwing a ball for Tatters, rolling with him in the long grass, the dog covering his dark skin with bright pink licks.

Ada's thin body doesn't help her hide her expanding belly. Bruno writes a card that he delivers by hand. *Dear Esmond*, it reads, *I surprised myself at the delight with which I greeted Ada's news. There are friendships that are obvious, easily observed. There are others that creep up and surprise you. Ours is the latter kind, but you should know how much I value the contribution you made during the days of Fascism and how much I value now your support to Ada, who will be one of the stars of Italian politics in years to come. I look forward to welcoming your child into the world, and to your help in building a better Italy for that child to live in. I wish you all the best, Bruno.*

They tell Tosca and Antonio together, over dinner at Antonio's apartment on the Lungarno del Pignone. It is a tiny, one-bedroom flat on the top floor of an ancient building, some of whose rooms have been left to fall into ruin, their floors collapsed, plaster caving inwards. Antonio's *salotto* looks out on the river and is deliciously cool even during the muggy August evenings. They sit at the table by the window and eat soup that Antonio has made, dipping into it a precious white ciabatta – far better than the dusty loaves to which they've grown accustomed. When Ada tells them her news, Tosca almost leaps across the table to hold her friend. Antonio rushes off to find a bottle of *spumante* and they sit long into the night, keen and happy.

'It's nothing,' Ada says, shrugging and struggling not to smile. 'It's only biology.'

News of the war comes to them over the W/T, through newspapers and the continually well-informed Professor. The Russians enjoy success after success, driving the Hun back towards the Polish border. Pictures of General Zhukov, looking grim and purposeful, splash across the covers of *La Stampa* and *La Repub-*

blica. The tone of these reports is resolutely neutral, not wishing to alienate the Germans, who remain in Italy in their tens of thousands and are still the ostensible ally. Whenever Esmond sees a German soldier, or the Consul in his black Foreign Office uniform, he is taken by his own astonishment. He would rather forget that the city is still host to these crafty beasts. On the wireless, he hears that Goebbels had announced the departure of the final Jew from Berlin earlier that summer, declaring the city *Judenfrei.* He hears of chambers being built at Auschwitz, the annihilation of ghettoes at Vilna and Minsk, the uprising at the death camp in Bialystok that was brutally crushed, its leaders committing suicide before they could be caught. He looks the Germans in the eye, and thinks of Philip.

Ada speaks briefly to her father in Turin. He is safe, unsure whether to use the moment to escape and join his wife in Switzerland. He thinks he will go to Lake Maggiore with Ettore Ovazza, from where it will be just a brief boat ride to the border. When she tells him that she and Esmond are expecting a baby, he bursts into tears. He is still crying when the pips sound and the call ends. 'I love you,' Ada manages to say, just as the line goes dead. Esmond stands close, his hands folded around her living belly.

Everything changes on the 8th of September. The closeness of August has unravelled into days of low cloud, fierce winds from the hills, sudden and violent showers. Esmond is with Bruno, Elio and Alessandro in the bar of the Excelsior, where they have taken to spending Sunday evenings. Ada is with Tosca and Antonio for dinner, but will join them later. For the first hour, Esmond teaches them English. They are all relatively fluent, but eager to improve their command of the idiom, to perfect their grammar, so that they might – as Alessandro puts it – speak with less shame to the English soldiers when they arrive. Bruno has already met a number of escaped British prisoners-of-war during his trips up into the hills. He reels off military slang – some of which even Esmond doesn't recognise – with enormous and obvious pleasure: he speaks of *ack emmas and emma gees*, *foot-sloggers in mufti*; all soldiers are *Tommies*. When their beers arrive he grins 'Here's how!' and 'Down your sherbets!'

After they eat, the three Italians talk to Esmond about Communism. He has, with some reluctance, read *The Communist Manifesto*. He's now reading *How the Steel Was Tempered*, which Elio had painstakingly, and very badly it seems to Esmond, translated into Italian during his time in prison. He finds its men the opposite of superfluous, and, for the first time, is bored by a Russian novel. The hero, Pavel, is all action, a Communist superman, almost entirely lacking an internal life. If this is the literature of the socialist utopia, he'd rather have the dissolute despotism of the nineteenth century.

Despite this, Esmond is drawn to the grandness of the socialist dream. There is such pure-souled hopefulness in the way that Alessandro, Elio and Bruno speak about politics, Bruno's matchstick quivering as he talks, Elio's cheeks flushing beneath his round spectacles, Alessandro's hands twitching like nervous birds in the air as he describes his vision of an Italy where no one is judged on the basis of race, religion or gender. They look out into the dusk over the river, where waves are whipped up by the wind coming down from the hills. They feel like serious young men, at the centre of things.

'You must be engaged,' Alessandro says, nodding his spring-curled hair. 'To act in good faith you must feel the cause deep in your bones, the justness of our mission must beat with your heart.' He quotes a letter of Marx several times, conducting the air with a finger as he speaks. 'If we work for all mankind,' he says, 'our happiness will belong to millions, our deeds will live on quietly but perpetually at work, and over our ashes will be shed the hot tears of noble people.'

While he is speaking, there is a commotion behind the reception desk, loud shouts from the kitchens. Alessandro stops, midstream, and beckons to a waiter.

'Comrade,' he says, eliciting a look that mixes scorn and confusion, 'will you find out what gives?'

After a few minutes, the waiter comes back with a bottle of grappa and four glasses. 'May I sit with you?' he asks and pulls up a chair beside Esmond. He fills the four glasses and raises his own. 'Badoglio has just signed an Armistice with the Allies. An American radio station announced it earlier. The war is officially over for Italy. *Saluti*.' They knock back their drinks.

'But what about the Germans?' Esmond asks. 'They're still here, in Italy I mean, so many of them.'

A communal shrug. 'Have a gargle of this,' Bruno says, filling his glass. 'And stop worrying.'

When Esmond and Ada get back to L'Ombrellino, it is raining so hard that they can't sleep, and so lie in each other's arms watching lightning like suddenly recalled memories illuminating the sky. Just before dawn the storm passes, and the air around them is washed silent and clean. A feeling of extraordinary peace in the house. He doesn't even think about winter. The Allies would be there before the end of the month, bringing with them oil and butter and real life. He realises he should be worrying instead about what he'll do to earn his living, how to feed his family – what an idea! – now the war is drawing to a close, but he can't muster any more than a brief flutter of anxiety. Time would catch up with him eventually; until then, everything is arrested and provisional, as if preserved in amber. He drifts to sleep thinking of Rudyard being welcomed by grinning Italian

soldiers as he steps off the boat at Reggio Calabria, of seeing his
brother for the first time in five years.

Sleep manages somehow to conflate Rudyard and Anna and
the joy in his dream celebrates both his brother's unlikely passage through Italy and his sister's return from her longer, darker
journey. He wakes just after nine with a shriven, bare feeling,
longing to return to the unearthly brightness of his dream.

13

He hears them several minutes before he sees them. He is having
lunch at the Giubbe Rosse. The bar has taken delivery of a crate
of tomatoes from a group of friendly *contadini* who, in payment,
are getting riotously drunk in a room at the back. Because of the
noise inside, he is sitting at a round, glass-topped table in the
piazza and eating the tomatoes on bread made with chestnut
flour. It is not good, but with a glass of Chianti it is edible. It has
turned cold and he is wearing George Keppel's double-breasted
ulster buttoned to his throat.

He is reading Lermontov's *A Hero of Our Time*, which, barely
a third of the way through, is having a powerful effect upon
him. He realises the superfluous man is a Slavic counterpart
to the Italian notion of *sprezzatura,* a kind of studied careless-
ness affected by all the young men who surround the Professor.
Philip had it, and Mosley; Bruno, Elio and Alessandro have it in
spades. Ada, too, he thinks with a wistful smile. He decides he
needs to affect a little more *sprezzatura* himself. Played right it is
almost indistinguishable from heroism.

He looks up from his book with bother. His knife is rattling
on the glass surface of the table. He picks it up, puts it on his
plate and continues to read. Now the plate begins to move on

the table, taking little hops and jumps until it smashes on the ground. A low rumbling that grows gradually louder until he feels the cobbles tremble beneath his feet.

'Gianni, quickly,' he shouts. The waiter comes to stand beside Esmond, who has risen breathlessly from his seat. The rumbling grows louder until all of the *contadini* are out in the square, throwing their caps in the air and cheering.

'*Gli Americani!*'

'*Gli Inglesi!*'

It takes a moment for Esmond to adjust once the first tank pulls through the triumphal arch and into the square. The smile stays on his face, the happiness flips in his stomach. The *contadini* stand in idiotic silence, their caps like shot birds at their feet.

'*Porca Madonna*,' Gianni whispers. Esmond's smile finally gives way. There are now two tanks in the square, now three: a procession of them making their way over the cobbles and into the via Calimala. They come in a grey stream, thundering past the café. Some of the tables fall over at the vibration, their glass tops shattering. Each of the tanks bears on its side an unmistakable Iron Cross. White flags flutter from the Panzers' cannons, but their turrets swivel, taking in the square until one points at the group standing amidst the tables and broken glass. A *contadino* with ruddy cheeks and the wounded blue eyes of a husky flinches. The tanks – Esmond counts sixteen – are followed by armoured personnel carriers, two enormous Hummel guns, and finally a fleet of ten covered Kübelwagens in which sit officers in the grey uniforms of the SD. Their jackets match the sky, Esmond thinks, as one of the cars stops in front of the group.

A young lieutenant leaps out and begins to speak in heavy Italian, looking past them as he passes out handbills on yellow paper. 'We inform you that this city has been declared a site of specific strategic importance and will be occupied by the forces of the *Großdeutsches Reich* indefinitely. All men between the ages of eighteen and forty-five should be ready to present themselves to the *Stadtskommandatur* within a day's notice. Any resistance will be treated with the greatest severity. Please' – a smile, thin – 'enjoy your lunch.'

An hour later, Esmond is standing on the terrace at L'Ombrellino with Alessandro, who is looking at the town through George Keppel's binoculars. The tanks have been arranged in formal lines in the Piazza della Signoria, the two Hummel guns on the Lungarno beside the Ponte Vecchio.

'It looks like they're basing themselves towards the station,' Alessandro says. 'All of the personnel carriers are heading that way. It's only the tanks and artillery that are going to the centre of town. A show of force. Fuck!'

Elio is the first to arrive, his face flushed. He stands beside them on the terrace. An icy wind funnels down from the mountains. Ada comes to join them.

'How many do you think are there?'

Alessandro puts down the binoculars and shakes his head. 'Probably not that many, but they're trying to make it look like a full-scale invasion. Twenty tanks, perhaps a thousand men.'

'We can call on more than that, surely.' She looks from Alessandro to Elio.

'You forget', Elio says, 'the Fascists who'll come crawling out of their holes. People like Carità, Koch – this is what they've been praying for.'

By early afternoon, they are all seated in the drawing room at L'Ombrellino. Esmond makes tea on the stove in the kitchen and brings it through to them. It is raining heavily, the city hidden under a grey wash. The Professor sits in a wing-back chair in front of the empty fireplace and blows on his tea, a standard lamp lit behind him.

'Badoglio and the King have fled,' he says. 'They're in Brindisi, well within Allied-held territory. But this alters everything. This is war, and on our doorstep.'

There is a murmur amongst the group. Esmond knows most of the men and women sitting around the dusty room. Bruno and Alessandro are there, of course, as are Antonio and Tosca. Bruno had gone from house to house on his bicycle, telling the news, ordering them up to L'Ombrellino. Maria Luigia sits on the divan next to Elio, chiding him for not eating enough. Gino Bartali is there in his cycling kit, peaked cap on his head. There is only one stranger in the room, in a shadowy corner, a wave of sculpted hair and bronzed skin and white teeth that flash whenever particular ironies are expressed. Esmond realises with surprise that this is Pretini, owner of the hair salon on the via Tornabuoni.

'The Germans', the Professor says, 'have established head-quarters in the Piazza San Marco, and taken over the university buildings towards Sanitissima Annunziata. There aren't an enormous number yet, but enough to hurt us. And they're well armed.'

'What about the Allies?' Alessandro asks. 'Aren't they supposed to be landing at Livorno? Weren't they due to parachute into the countryside around Rome? Surely this is just a matter of a few days holing up here with Esmond and Ada until the Brits and Americans come and boot these fuckers out.'

The Professor shakes his head. 'I spoke to the head of the *Giustizia e Libertà* cell in Milan, Ferruccio Parri. The Allies have been surprised at how quickly the Germans reinforced. They were expecting to sign the Armistice quickly, to be in Rome by early August, but Badoglio and the King dithered. The Allies are going to come up from the south, and it's going to take time. We are in this for the long haul.'

'So what now?' It is Pretini who speaks, steepling his fingers and sitting back. He is wearing an expensive-looking worsted suit, well-polished ostrich loafers, a red bow-tie.

The Professor clears his throat. 'The Germans have offered Italian soldiers a choice – they can either continue to fight along-side the Nazis or be sent to the camps. They'll call up Florentine men in the next few days and offer them the same choice. So it's a matter of hiding, fighting or – in all probability – dying.'

Bruno cuts in. 'This villa is too close to the town. We can use it as a temporary base until we establish a permanent headquar-ters. Gino and I cycled up towards Monte Morello a few weeks ago. It's wooded and there are caves, shepherds' huts, plenty of routes into the mountains.'

The group continues to talk and plot well into the night. By the time Pretini drives off down the narrow lane after mid-night, the plans are set. Antonio and Tosca are to go at once to Monte Morello. Bruno, Elio and Alessandro will take charge of rounding up fellow partisans in the city and driving them out to the new headquarters of the Resistance. Esmond and Ada will remain at L'Ombrellino until further notice, using the W/T to convey news from the city to the group in the hills.

The house feels empty when everyone has left. Esmond real-ises he'd grown used to having Alessandro there, a tough, con-fident presence on the floor below. Ada lies with her back to him and tugs his arms around her. 'What are we going to do?' he says.

'What do you mean?'

'With you two?'

'I'm pregnant, I'm not disabled,' she says, drawing herself out of his arms and turning to look at him in the dim light. 'I want to – how do you say it? – rock the boat, not a cradle. I'm going to work for the Resistance until I go into labour. If the Germans are still here after I have the baby, I'll give it to the nuns and carry on fighting.'

'But what if something happens to you?'

She pauses, takes his hand, her voice gentler. 'There's too much *what if?* with you, darling. Who knows what's going to happen? I trust my friends, I trust you, I trust that things are going to work themselves out. Now let's sleep. There are big days ahead.'

14

Over the next weeks, they hardly leave the bedroom. They take turns at the W/T, sitting under the triptych, reading and repeating the instructions that come through before speaking them into the small silver microphone on the desk or tapping out endless streams of Morse. At first only Ada can do this, but eventually Esmond, although slow and checking his crib with every word, manages brief messages. Pretini, whose code name is *Penna* – the Feather – has another small radio in the back room of his salon. The partisan camp at Monte Morello has a more sophisticated transmitter that the Professor pilfered from the university's physics department.

The Professor, who comes up to L'Ombrellino as often as he can, tells them of the Germans flooding into the city by road and rail. They have taken over the Excelsior, the Grand, the Savoy. They stand in khaki uniforms in the Piazza della Signoria armed with Mauser submachine-guns, Berettas and MAB 38s requisitioned from surrendered Italian troops. The Gestapo and SD have set up in the cells of the monastery attached to San Marco. The Professor says, with a dry chuckle, that SS Captain Alberti, head of the SD in Florence, has taken Savonarola's cell for himself and sits beneath Fra Angelico's gorgeous frescoes as he spins his web across the city.

Mussolini, shipped from one secret location to another by his Italian captors, is finally located by the Germans at Campo Imperatore high in the Abruzzo Apennines. It would – as the Professor tells Esmond and Ada over dinner – have been easy for them to walk through the gates and seize him, so poorly guarded was the old ski resort. Instead the Germans launched a paratrooper raid, with the dashing Otto Skorzeny crashing his glider into the mountainside above the hotel and overpowering the guards. Now Mussolini has been flown to Vienna, where he is photographed with Hitler. A week later, the Germans declare northern Italy the Italian Social Republic, led by Mussolini from its *de facto* capital at Salò on Lake Garda.

In Florence, SS Captain Alberti prefers to keep a certain distance from the ugly necessities of occupation. He is an aesthete and is using his time in the city to further his knowledge of the *quattrocento*. What he likes, he takes. Göring and Hitler have both sent 'art buyers' to Florence to snap up the city's treasures at joke prices. The masterpieces of the Uffizi and the Bargello stay hidden in the cellars and laundry houses and guest wings of grand Renaissance palazzi.

The Professor tells them that Alberti has dismissed Count Gaetano and replaced him with the hunchbacked Raffaele Mangianello, who cruises around town on his Aprilia motorcycle, waving a gun. The new Podestà's first act in office – as much from personal interest as to curry favour with the Germans – is to open the Ufficio Affari Ebraici. His aim, boasted on ten thousand paper flyers, is to make Florence the first *Judenfrei* city in Italy. The day after his appointment, a group of *squadristi* raid the Great Synagogue, hauling out copies of the Torah, scrolls and sacred writings onto the steps and burning them in the street. Then artworks, silver menorahs and golden lanterns are taken out, piled in the back of a van, and sent with Mangianello's compliments to Alfred Rosenberg's Library for the Jewish Question in Frankfurt-on-Main.

Carità and Mangianello are old friends, the Professor recalls sadly, and through the intercession of the new Podestà the former electrician swiftly becomes one of the most powerful men in the city. He is named head of the Ufficio Politico Investigativo, a branch of the Republican Guard styled on the Gestapo. Declaring himself the 'Biting Axe of Florence', he leads a group of a hundred thugs and hangers-on – the *Banda Carità*. He requisitions a grey stone apartment block in the via Bolognese which becomes his Villa Triste: the site of brutal interrogations, a storehouse for his enormous weapons cache and a place to feast and frolic with his mistress, Milly. The Professor tells them everything now with an apologetic air, taking off his spectacles and wiping them with a handkerchief, looking towards them with old, watery eyes.

Despite the Professor's visits and the constant companionship of the wireless, Esmond and Ada feel increasingly cut off in the house on the hill. Vegetables are still plentiful in the garden, but they have run out of meat and milk, butter and eggs. Ada is growing thinner as her belly fattens, the melonish bump sticking out from beneath accordion ribs. Esmond tries to hunt partridges with Tatters as Alessandro had, but he's unwilling to use bullets unnecessarily and so only fires when he has a clear shot. Even then he often misses. After his fifth morning hunting, when he has used sixteen of the thirty bullets he has left and has nothing more to show for it than one small pigeon, he gives up. The bread ration in the city has been reduced to two hundred grams per person; even so, the Professor brings them several grey chestnut-flour loaves when he comes. Esmond makes Ada eat spinach with every meal, for the sake of the baby.

The cold and rain that marked the first weeks of the German

occupation have given way to brilliant skies, cool nights of fresh, mountain-like air. Esmond feels gloriously healthy, rising early to go running with Tatters in the hills above Bellosguardo, feeling an extraordinary physical lightness, which he knows to be youth. He is always careful, keeping to the mule-tracks, ducking into bushes at the sound of an engine, but he wouldn't give up those runs in the morning light for anything. The dog bounces alongside him, pink tongue flapping wild and wet as they gallop along the pale rises.

15

One eleven o'clock in the middle of that sunny October, Bruno and Alessandro pull up in front of the villa in the old Bianchi. Esmond and Ada run out, calling to their friends, who have brought them twelve slices of cured ham, some pecorino, a bottle of home-brewed grappa. They sit in the garden's lush abundance eating figs and persimmons, medlars and grapes – the last fruits of the year.

'It's not all bad news,' Alessandro says. His skin is very dark after weeks outside; his hair is even longer and wilder, a wiry zigzag on top of his head. 'The *carabinieri* have been refusing to serve the Germans. Decent fuckers after all! They're in love with the King – they used to be his personal bodyguards, of course. So they're laying down their weapons and joining us in the hills.'

'And we had our first run-in with Carità and his thugs.'

Alessandro interrupts. 'From which I think we emerged pretty fucking well for a bunch of intellectuals.'

Bruno lobs a fig at him. 'Bastard. I want to tell it.' Esmond feels happy merely being in the presence of these carefree young men. Bruno has filled out in the chest. He looks cool and clever

266

and able in his blue serge suit, a beret pulled down on his close-cropped head. 'You've heard about the *Banda Carità*, I guess?'

'Yes,' Ada nods. 'The Professor told us he's been arresting anyone with links to the monarchy.'

'It's true,' Alessandro says. 'He's after the aristocrats of Florence. He was an orphan and was brought up by some wealthy family in Milan who treated him like shit. You must always look for the psychological explanation.'

'He decided,' says Bruno, rolling his eyes, 'to try to find our hideout in the hills. They came up late yesterday afternoon, eighteen of them armed to the teeth. Our sentries spotted them miles away and we'd rehearsed what to do. We expected it to be the Germans of course, but it's all the same. We pulled branches in front of the caves, dropped away into the gullies and ravines, shimmied up trees, led the bastards into the high mountain passes.'

'We know them even in the dark,' coughed Alessandro. 'Dusk had fallen and they didn't have dogs, so we lost them easily. They were so badly organised, the idiots just ran at anyone, blasting their guns like crazy. I was up a tree and saw Carità's fat head with its queer tuft of white pass right below me. He was with Piero Koch, the fucker who gave me a going over in Regina Coeli. I almost dropped down and went for them.'

'In the end,' Bruno says, 'we got two of them.'

'Got them?' Esmond asks.

'Killed them.'

'Jesus.'

'We're not playing games, my friend.'

'You should have seen Elio,' Alessandro laughs. 'He was amazing. He led these goons down a sheep track and hid behind a rock. When they'd passed he jumped out, with a Red Indian yell, made sure they had time to reach for their guns and then bang!

bang! he shot the fuckers in the head, right between the eyes. It was like a film, honestly.'

'He's a maniac,' Bruno says. 'He had to lie down for three hours afterwards and recover.'

'He's a hero,' Alessandro insists.

'Do we know who they were?'

'Luigi di Giovanni and Erno Rossilini,' Bruno says. 'Both members of Carità's assassin squad. Killed by a man with a doctorate in Latin law who speaks five languages.'

'And wears spectacles so thick I'm surprised he could see them at all,' Alessandro adds.

'We've achieved a lot over the past few weeks,' Bruno tells them. 'There are cells springing up all over the country, mostly out of *Giustizia e Libertà*. This is no local unrest. This is revolution.'

The Bianchi is looking even more careworn than usual, its front bumper hanging by one loose bracket, its rear window cracked, waves of dust and mud rising up its once-white chassis. Bruno tells them the Germans have set up roadblocks on all the routes leading into Florence, and they'd had to drive here over mule tracks, along the bed of a dried-up river. The two young men have dust in their hair, mud streaks on their cheeks. After a cup of *orzo*, Bruno and Alessandro strip off and go swimming in the pool, laughing at the icy water, splashing each other and then standing, clapping themselves, by the stone dodos as they dry. The October sun finds their skin, finds the glittering green water, the brightly flickering leaves in the copse below, the canted roofs of the city. Esmond and Ada have pulled their chairs into the shade of the vine-hung umbrella sculpture.

As they are walking back to the house, Bruno drapes an arm around Esmond's shoulder. 'You should come over to the base at some point, see the set-up. If nothing else, it'd do you two good to get out of here for a while.' He pauses. 'Before the baby comes.'

Esmond gives a weak smile. 'Do you think we'll be all right?' he asks.

Bruno squeezes his shoulder. 'Of course you will. We'll all pull around when the time comes.'

When their friends have left, Ada and Esmond potter helplessly around the house until dusk. A sense of dejection comes with night. They sleep restlessly and, in the small hours, Esmond wakes to hear the dying cry that haunted his sleep at the Institute. He pulls Ada closely against him, folding his hands around her belly.

16

Pretini calls them on the radio just after eight, his voice low and distant.

'You two should come down to the town,' he says. 'Maria Luigia has put together some new documents for you. And we need to talk.'

They walk arm-in-arm, heads down and hurrying past the guards who now stand sentry at either end of the Ponte Santa Trinità. Esmond realises he held his breath the whole length of the bridge. As they come onto the via Tornabuoni, a Kübelwagen with a grey-suited SD officer inside drives slowly past them. He feels Ada's grip tighten on his arm. They pass the Palazzo Strozzi and hurry through the wood-framed glass door into Pretini's hot, bright salon.

The master hairdresser is standing behind the cash desk at the back of the room making notes in a small ledger while one of his assistants, a good-looking chap a few years younger than Esmond, sweeps an immaculate floor.

'Come,' Pretini beckons, without looking up. Esmond and Ada move forward, stepping out of the way of the broom. Now Pretini puts his pen down. 'Shall we go through to the back room? It's quieter there. You can talk in front of Giacomo, though. He's on-side.' The boy stops his sweeping and smiles shyly at them for a moment, then continues. 'I have the Marchesa Origo at eleven, but she won't mind waiting a few minutes.'

He leads them into a windowless room at the end of a small passageway where there is a desk, a small sofa and an armchair. On the desk is Pretini's wireless, which is smaller than the W/T up at L'Ombrellino, and older. Pretini sees him looking at it.

'From the Great War. I was an Alpino, you know. I won the Silver Medal for Military Valour after the Battle of Caporetto, too.' He shows them his teeth, absurdly white. 'Now sit, both of you.' He sighs into the armchair and Ada and Esmond perch on the sofa. 'Here we go. These documents have you both as key personnel at the psychiatric hospital in via San Salvi. You'll be in trouble if the Blackshirts get hold of you, but these should at least see you past the Germans.' He passes Esmond a manila folder. Esmond takes out the documents, inspects them briefly and hands Ada hers.

She looks at them with a smile. 'Nella Ferrari,' she says. 'I like it. Very *sportif*.'

Now Pretini settles back. 'How are you holding up?' he asks.

'We're fine,' she says quickly, returning Esmond's glance. 'We're ready to do whatever it takes.'

'Good,' Pretini smiles at her, tapping his fingers on the arm of his chair. 'Good.' A silence. 'You know it's a matter of time. The Allies will get here eventually, we just have to hold out, make sure that as few of us get hurt as possible, help those we can—' He trails off. 'They picked up Oreste Ristori in Empoli.'

'No—' Ada says.

'He's completely crazy. He was singing anti-German songs in the square in front of the station, saying he was going to walk to Salò and rip Mussolini's head from his neck. He's lucky they took him for a drunk and not a partisan. He's in the Murate now, probably driving his fellow prisoners mad with his singing. He'll be out in a month at the latest. At least he doesn't know the location of the camp at Monte Morello. He won't give us away—' He smiles but with a terrible sadness.

'What else?' Esmond asks, watching closely.

The hairdresser sighs and folds his hands in his lap. 'What else. Other news and I'm afraid it isn't good.' Esmond's mind cycles through the likely disasters. So many of those he's loved are dead already, he thinks, what could hurt him now?

'Go on,' he says.

'It's my father,' Ada says coldly.

Pretini nods. 'He almost made it. He and Ovazza joined up with a group of Croatian refugees in the Val d'Aosta and tried to bluff their way over the border. They were arrested by Swiss police and put on a train back to Turin. At the first station they reached they were picked up by the SS. I'm so sorry.'

'Did they send him to a camp?'

Pretini is silent.

'What happened to him?'

'They were taken to Verbania. We have a man there who helps get people across the border. It's typical of Ovazza that he wouldn't think to contact us. We could have made it so much easier for them both. They were locked up in the girls' school which is now the SS headquarters. They didn't come out.'

'He's dead?'

Pretini nods. 'I'm sorry.'

Esmond reaches out for Ada's hand.

'I'm sorry,' Pretini repeats.

Back up at L'Ombrellino, Ada sits silently in the drawing room while Esmond mans the radio. During a brief break that he allows himself, he comes down to see her. It is growing dark, but she hasn't turned the lights on. She is very still in the shadowy room.

'Do you want anything?' he asks. 'A cup of tea?'

'No. Thank you.' Elio's voice comes over the radio upstairs. As he turns to leave the room, Ada says something he doesn't catch.

'What was that, darling?'

'I keep wondering if he heard me, that last time we spoke. I told him that I loved him as the line went dead. I just hope he heard me.'

He goes to kneel in front of her and takes her hands, breathes on them to warm them. 'Darling,' he says, kissing her hands, her wrists, 'I'm sure he did. And he knew it, anyway. You didn't have to say it.'

'I always thought him such a fool, pathetic for cosying up to the Fascists. He knew I looked down on him. But he was a good father, he was such a good father.' He thinks she is going to cry, but instead she stands and makes her way to the door. 'I'll take a turn on the radio,' she says. 'You must be tired.'

'But—'

'Please. It'll help.' He listens to the sound of her footsteps disappear up the stairs, then Elio's voice, her reply. He walks to the window, draws the curtains and turns on the standard lamp. He reads for an hour and then falls asleep on the divan. Tatters wakes him later, a rough pink tongue on his cheeks and neck. He lies, propped on an elbow, and listens to Ada's voice, reciting a long list of coded co-ordinates onto the airborne waves.

17

They are at the window, looking down on the city, whose roof-tops are just now being touched by morning. It is the first Saturday of November. Esmond is standing behind Ada with his arms around her. Her hair is twisted in a knot on her head and she is wearing one of Alice Keppel's caftans. He kisses the white hollow of her neck and she shivers.

She has been quiet since the news of her father's death, working long hours at the radio. There is a map of Tuscany spread out on the floor of their bedroom on which she has ringed certain hills where partisans are gathering, has marked up German roadblocks, potential routes between the various Resistance encampments. She speaks to Pretini four or five times each day. The Professor came up to offer his condolences the night after they'd heard. Alessandro and Bruno sent their love over the wireless. When she isn't working, she sits on the bed and stares at the triptych.

Now, shrugging out of his embrace, she lifts the caftan over her head and stands naked in front of the painting.

'Like so?' She poses in front of the portrait of Mary Magdalene, crosses her arms over her breasts and affects an anguished expression. They both begin to laugh. Her hands slip down to rest on the bulge in her stomach.

'Exactly,' Esmond says. 'You'd do for a wonderful martyr.'

'Not just yet.'

They make love then, slipping beneath the covers of the bed for warmth, burrowing down until their heads are under and they feel themselves lost in a darkness of skin and hot breath. When they are done he throws the covers back and they emerge, gasping, as if they have been saved from drowning. Looking down at her hair flared out on the pillow, he imagines rushing her westwards, to safety, to Spain and then – who knows – Brazil, America, even back to Britain. He sees them in Shropshire together, the presence of the child flitting around the picture like a firefly, illuminating Welsh Frankton, bringing joy to his father's withered heart.

He is downstairs brewing their *orzo* when Pretini's voice comes over the radio. Ada calls down, although Esmond can't hear what she says above the crackle of logs in the fire. He carries the mugs upstairs, his bare feet cold on the polished wood. As he enters the room, he sees that Ada is getting dressed, pulling on a pair of slacks, leaning back against the cupboard as she wriggles in.

'They're raiding the synagogue,' she says. 'The Gestapo and the *Banda Carità*. We need to get down there.' She takes the mug of coffee and gulps at it. 'Fuck!' She winces. 'Hot.' Esmond pulls on a shirt and his blue twill suit. He's about to leave the room when he stops and bends to pick up Bailey's revolver, which he tucks into the waistband at the back of his trousers. It feels awkward, almost indecent against his tailbone as he comes down.

Ada is already out on the gravel in front of the house, scratching Tatters behind the ear. 'I said we'd meet Pretini at the Salon at eleven thirty,' she says. They walk briskly down into the city, which is still for a Saturday morning. The guards on the Ponte Santa Trinità eye them warily, but let them pass.

'They moved in just after the start of the Shabbat service,' Pretini says as they enter. 'They've got two hundred of them in holding camps in Santa Croce. They'll be taken up to the train station tomorrow morning, then to Germany.' The Professor and Elio are in the salon, bent over a railway map on the floor. Pretini is cutting the Marchesa Corsini's hair. 'She's one of us,' he says to Esmond, noting his face.

'And I have a very important party this evening,' the Marchesa says frostily. 'I was booked for an appointment last Saturday, but the bastard Carità had me in his Villa Triste.'

Ada stands over the Professor, looking at the map. 'They're taking them to the trains?' The Professor nods. 'Then we need to act now.'

'Yes,' Pretini says, snipping carefully at the Marchesa's softly waved hair. 'We stop the trains as they head north.'

'If we can.' Elio indicates a point near Pistoia where the railway line curves around the swell of a hill. 'Alessandro and Bruno are going to drive a truck onto the tracks here. They'll overpower the guards and stage a rescue. We've enlisted help from a group of Czechs who're hiding out by the Lago di Suviana. A much greater chance of success than if we try to do anything in town. Agreed?'

'Agreed,' says Pretini. The Professor nods. Even the Marchesa, with a subtle incline of the head, is in.

'What can *we* do?' Ada asks.

Pretini, standing back to admire the Marchesa's hair, gives one final snip of his scissors. He removes the gown that protects her Ferragamo suit and bows for a moment, like a man saying grace. Only then does he turn towards Ada. 'One of Carità's hit squads has gone to the Ashkenazi prayer house by the Porta Romana. Rabbi Cassuto moved all of the records down there at the beginning of the war. It'll mean they have the address of every Jew in Florence.'

'So you need to warn them,' the Professor says. 'Those who can should leave. The rest you must take up to L'Ombrellino until we can work out how to make them safe.'

'Where do we start?' Esmond asks.

'We had a call from Professor Rossi at the Bargello,' the Professor says. 'He's been hiding Rudolf Levy, the painter. The Nazis want escaped German Jews more than anything and they know he's here. Levy and Rossi have been seen together, it won't be long until they go looking there. He lives at Apartment 18c, via del Proconsolo, by the cathedral.'

'And when we have him?' Esmond asks.

'Get him up to L'Ombrellino and wait for instructions. He might have to stay with you for a few days, until things calm down.'

Esmond's heart is thumping as they walk out onto the via Tornabuoni. German soldiers march up past the Palazzo Arcimboldi, their feet echoing on the cobbles. Esmond checks the gun in his waistband and hurries to keep up with Ada. She has on the beige tunic she wore the first time he met her, a green cardigan over it. Her hair is still knotted on her head, a nest of dark red snakes.

There are tanks in the Piazza del Duomo. At the sandbagged foot of the Campanile, three Germans are arguing with a Blackshirt. A monk hurries up the steps of the cathedral. Otherwise the square is deserted. Esmond remembers going into the Duomo that drunken night with Douglas and Orioli. Five years, he realises. He barely recognises the boy he sees in his mind, standing in front of Uccello's portrait of Sir John Hawkwood, swaying with drink, half-hard with lust for Gerald and Fiamma. Ada reaches out for his hand as they come onto the via del Proconsolo and he can feel his pulse against hers. They walk in time to the thud of their hearts.

Professor Rossi's apartment is on the third floor of a wide building in the shadow of the cathedral. The front door is open and they make their way into the hallway and up stone stairs. Ada rings the bell, Rossi's name beneath. They wait, breathless. The door opens.

'You came,' he says. He's a short man, bald at the crown. He looks exhausted, unshaven. He loosens his tie with a nervous movement as they enter a gloomy drawing room. The bulk of the cathedral blocks out light in the flat. Everything is bathed in a dim terracotta glow from the tiles on the roof of the Duomo. In an armchair in one corner sits an elderly man, breathing audibly. Behind him, one hand on his shoulder, is a slender woman.

'Some coffee?' Rossi asks. 'It's the real thing.'

'We should move,' Ada says.

The elderly man gets slowly to his feet. He picks up a stick that is leaning against the arm of the chair and walks towards them.

'I am Rudolf Levy.' A deep, musical voice. 'Very pleased to make your acquaintance.'

'We need to leave now,' Ada says, crossing to the window and looking down onto the square.

Rossi clears his throat. 'My wife,' he says. The slim woman steps forward from the shadows. Esmond sees that despite being quite young – she must be forty or so, he reckons – her hair is ice-white. 'My wife,' Rossi repeats, 'is on Rabbi Nathan's list.'

Ada nods. 'We'll have to take her too.'

'It's ridiculous,' the woman says, slightly shrill. 'I've never been to the synagogue. I subscribed to a charity drive Nathan Cassuto was holding for Jews in Russia ten years ago. We got talking and I told him that my parents were Jewish. I'm an Italian, though. I go to church, for Christ's sake.'

'It's better that you go,' her husband says.

'Can I take a suitcase?'

'A small bag,' Ada says. 'something you'd take shopping. You can't draw attention to yourself.'

Rossi and Levy embrace. 'Good luck, old friend,' Rossi says. He then takes his wife in his arms and places a long kiss on her lips. They pull apart, and it is painful to observe, and Esmond averts his eyes. He can see Rossi standing watching them as they make their way slowly down the stairs, Levy leaning on Esmond's shoulder. At the bottom of the steps, the old man apologises.

'It's my asthma. I was gassed in the war.'

It is bright in the square when they step outside. Esmond feels exposed, singled out by the light. The four of them hurry past the tanks. The Germans have gone but Esmond can make out a group of Blackshirts on the other side of the square. Ada stops to look in a shop window, taking Levy by the arm.

'Be natural,' she says. 'We're going for a walk with our aunt and uncle. Assume you're being watched at all times.'

Esmond holds out his arm to Signora Rossi. He can feel dampness spreading under his shirt, sweat gathering on his face. He is gripped by a sudden fear that, if they are stopped, he'll forget all of his Italian. That he'll stand there mouthing uselessly, his brain an empty phrasebook. Rossi's wife gives his arm a little squeeze. 'She's pregnant, your wife,' she says. 'It's very brave. Of both of you I mean.'

There are guards on all of the bridges. The Ponte alle Grazie is manned by Blackshirts; on the others, a pair of Germans stand at either end in khaki, regular soldiers for whom this is just another day. They smoke when they think they aren't being watched, chat, look at the flowing river.

'We'll take the Santa Trinità,' Ada says. She and Levy are walking a few yards behind Esmond and Signora Rossi. 'There are more guards on the Ponte Vecchio and anything else takes us too far out. Have you got the key to the church on you, Esmond?'

He feels in his pocket. He still has the key to his digs at Emmanuel, a heavy iron one that opens the front gates at L'Ombrellino, some dimly remembered doors and cupboards in Shropshire. Now he holds up a brass Yale attached to a tasselled fob. 'Here it is.'

'Levy's going to need to rest before we go up to the villa. Perhaps we should wait there until night,' she says. They are on the via degli Strozzi. At the corner of the via Tornabuoni, Esmond sees Pretini leaning against a wall, reading a copy of *La Nazione*. The hairdresser gives an almost imperceptible nod as they pass. Ada and Levy drop further back as they approach the bridge.

His heart hammering in his head, Esmond leads Signora Rossi past the first pair of German guards, who are talking in broken Italian to a Blackshirt smoking on the parapet wall. Two nuns are walking over the bridge ahead of them; a group of *contadini* drive a mule in the opposite direction. It is loaded with corn and moving irritably over the cobbles. Esmond is holding his breath. Signora Rossi swings her shopping bag casually. He looks back once and sees that Ada is having to help Levy, who leans heavily on his stick, pausing every so often. They, too, have passed the first set of guards.

Now Esmond and Signora Rossi reach the first of the buttresses that jut out V-shaped into the water. He can see the second pair of guards over the gentle arc of the bridge. One of them has his helmet off. His hair is the same colour as Esmond's; he can't be far out of his teens. The other guard is older, darker, obscured by the shadow of his helmet. Now they are at the second buttress and the bridge is sloping downwards. Esmond's heart is beating so hard it seems to shudder the air around him. He dare not look back at Ada. He is hurrying without realising it. They are level with the guards. The younger one suddenly smiles, raising his arm in the Fascist salute towards Esmond. Signora Rossi hesitates for a moment and then moves on. Esmond returns the salute.

'*Sie sind Deutsch?*' the guard asks. Esmond thinks quickly.
'*Mi dispiace, sono italiano.*'

279

The guard points to his own head. '*I capelli*,' he says, laughing. Esmond forces himself to laugh back.

'*Auf Wiedersehen*,' he says, and then walks on, hurrying to Signora Rossi. It is only when they are outside the gate of the church that Esmond bends down and pretends to tie his shoelace. Looking back along the via Maggio, he sees that Ada and Levy have also been stopped by the guards. Ada is speaking to the older German, who hasn't taken off his helmet. She is smiling, shaking her head. Esmond opens the wicket gate and motions Signora Rossi inside.

'Hide yourself,' he says. 'I'll be back as soon as I can.' She steps into the dark entrance porch and Esmond shuts the door quietly. He walks back up towards the bridge.

The younger soldier has disappeared and the other has his rifle pointed at Levy and Ada. Esmond feels the gun in his waistband. He thinks of the easy shots he'd missed while out with Tatters, then catches sight of the swell under Ada's tunic and draws the revolver out, hidden under the lapel of his jacket, walking towards the bridge. Ada has seen him; her eyes brighten. He takes a deep breath. At that moment, horn blaring, a Kübelwagen screeches around the corner from the Borgo San Jacopo and comes to a halt between Esmond and the bridge. In the passenger seat is the young blond soldier, excitement on his face. In the back is an SS officer. Esmond steps into the shadow of a building. The guards from the other end of the bridge now hurry to join the group. Ada holds out her documents to the SS officer, who inspects them coldly. He then says something to Levy, who shrugs.

For a moment, he thinks they're going to let Ada go. She says something which makes the SS officer smile; the young soldier lets out a laugh. The officer goes to the car and speaks into the radio there, waiting. He comes back out and rejoins the group, still in apparent good humour. Then he barks out an order and Levy is bundled into the car. Apologetically, the SS man takes Ada by the elbow and helps her in. He goes around to sit in the front seat. Esmond stands on the Lungarno watching as the Kübelwagen pulls away. He sees Ada's face at the rear window, looking urgently outwards, one hand pressed to the glass. He watches the car pull over the Ponte Vecchio and out of sight.

Dazed, he walks back to the church and lets himself in through the wicket gate. He is still gripping the revolver in his pocket, he realises, as he goes into the dark church and sits at a pew. He places the gun on the wooden seat beside him and slumps forward, his head in his hands. 'Signora Rossi,' he calls out. 'Signora Rossi, they got them. You can come out, but they got them.'

18

They wait in the church until darkness has fallen and the street outside is empty before they make their way up to L'Ombrellino. A German patrol car comes past at one point, its searchlight shining into the surrounding gardens. Esmond forces Signora Rossi over a fence and down behind a laurel bush. They crouch against one another as the rumbling car with its sweeping beam stops. The sound of German voices, footsteps, a match being lit. The car begins to move again, its searchlight flickering against house-fronts further down. They wait for a few minutes, breathing the same air, then rise and continue the climb up the hill to Bellosguardo.

When they're inside, Esmond rushes straight to the bedroom and the W/T.

'Penna, come in Penna.' It is several minutes before a reply.

'Esmond, I'm so sorry, Esmond.'

'You know?'

'We know.'

'What's going to happen to them?'

'Levy will be on the train with the rest of the Jews for Germany tomorrow. We'll do our best to fish him out.'

'But Ada?'

There is the crackle of static. Then, in a graveyard voice, 'They've handed her over to Carità.' Esmond staggers into his chair. 'It's not as bad as it might be,' Pretini says. 'If they knew she was Jewish, they'd have taken her to the camp by the station with Levy. It means her identity is holding up. Carità will interrogate her, knock her about a bit, no more.'

'Where is she?'

'At the Villa Triste. You sit tight and I imagine she'll be out this time tomorrow. She's a tough one, your Ada.'

He cannot sleep. He paces up and down the floor of the drawing room. Signora Rossi sits upright on a divan, watching him. He imagines going down to the Villa Triste with his gun and shooting his way in. He wonders if Alessandro would come with him. But the other members of the Resistance are planning their raid on the German train the following afternoon. If he does it, he'll have to do it alone. Several times he shouts out, kicks at the furniture, sobs. He feels madness stammering at the edge of his mind, and all his mind can hold is the memory of Ada's green eyes, stretched impossibly wide. Finally he slumps down in an armchair.

Signora Rossi makes him a cup of tea, pulls up a footstool beside him and sits. She takes his hand in hers and strokes it, not speaking. He can't choke down the image of Carità's pudgy face, his wide nostrils, his schoolboy's shorts with their fat, hairless knees. Tatters comes into the room and curls up in his lap, begins to snore. They are sitting like that, Signora Rossi holding his hand, Tatters grumbling quietly, Esmond hunched and hopeless, when the sun comes up.

He waits by the radio all day. He knows he mustn't call Pretini or the partisans at Monte Morello. All efforts will be centred on the rescue attempt. There's nothing he can do for Ada. Signora Rossi sits reading Chekhov in the drawing room. She makes a lunch of pasta and beans, but he can't eat. As darkness falls, he's standing in front of the triptych. He has tuned the wireless to Radio Moscow. The news in English at 7 p.m. speaks of the Anglo-American bombing raids on Berlin, thousands of tonnes dropped on the already blazing city, lines of refugees spidering out into the countryside. The Allies now hold most of Southern Italy. They have broken through the first of Kesselring's defensive positions above Naples and are at Monte Cassino, approaching the Gustav Line, beyond which, Rome. They will not arrive, he reasons, in time for Ada.

It is very late when he finally hears Pretini's voice over the W/T. He'd been dozing on the bed wrapped in George Keppel's tweed jacket, not wanting to sleep but eventually sinking into a series of rapid nightmares. 'This is Penna, come in Esmond.'

'Esmond here.' He waits, as if the world has stopped. Then he hears Pretini sigh and his heart sinks.

'It was a catastrophe. A fucking catastrophe from start to finish. They'd been warned of our plans. The train was preceded by a Krupp K5. It blasted the truck from the tracks then started shelling the hills. There were snipers, several heavy machine guns, at least a hundred soldiers with the carriages. We had no chance. We lost two Serbians. Elio took a bullet in the shoulder.'

'And the train, it's gone?'

'Gone. I've had Rabbi Cassuto here all afternoon. Two hundred young men taken today. He fears another round-up later in the month.'

'And Ada?'

'No word, I'm afraid.'

19

On Tuesday morning Bruno arrives at the villa. He's riding a red Moto Guzzi, goggles down around his neck when he comes to the door. He holds onto Esmond's hand for a long time when he sees him. 'We'll go in and get her,' he says. 'I promise you, if she isn't out by Friday, we'll blast our way in there.' Esmond nods. 'She'll be all right,' Bruno says.

Signora Rossi hugs Esmond on the steps of the villa and then climbs up behind Bruno with her shopping bag on her lap. She puts her arms around him and he pulls up his goggles. Bruno waves as he drives through the gates and out into the road. Esmond stands on the gravel in front of the villa listening until he can no longer pick out the engine from the other sounds in the air. The house is silent and cold.

He can't face waiting alone by the radio for another day and so goes out for a run. He and Tatters pound along the cypress-lined hillsides, past the Arcetri Observatory and the Torre del Gallo, along towards San Miniato. He feels if he can keep running, can keep up hammering his feet and heart and breath, then he might never have to face losing Ada. He realises, as he stands, exhausted, on a hilltop beside an abandoned shepherd's hut and looks down into a valley where the first mist is gathering beneath the trees, that he was tested on the bridge and that he came up short. He should have saved Ada, should have held a gun to the SS officer's head until he let her go. He reaches down and flings a handful of shingle into the valley.

When he gets back to the villa it is almost three. He is drenched in sweat, already cooling on his brow. Tatters is panting at his feet and goes immediately to his bowl of water which he laps in rapid strokes. Esmond hears Pretini's voice on the radio. He takes the stairs two at a time.

'Hello.'

'We have Ada.'

He looks up, up to the bright sky. 'Where is she?'

'At the Careggi Hospital, by the university. She's officially still under arrest, but we have people near her. We'll get her out.'

'How is she?'

'She'll live. She's conscious.'

'When can I see her?'

'That wouldn't be wise, for you to be down there. My friend, the doctor, wants to keep her overnight. In the morning they'll tell the guards that they're taking her for surgery and bring her up to L'Ombrellino in an ambulance.'

'Tomorrow, then.'

'Yes, tomorrow.'

He clumps back downstairs, searches the shelves in the drawing room until he comes upon a book of Hopkins's poems and sits reading all afternoon and well into the night. He hears nothing more on the radio but finds some consolation in the poems. 'Not, I'll not, carrion comfort, / Despair, not feast on thee,' he repeats the lines to himself, remembering how Leavis's voice would rise into the mad eaves as he read. He takes the book with him to bed and by the time he turns out he has all of the 'Terrible Sonnets', each hopeful-hopeless line, by heart (a phrase which gains sudden new truth). He drifts off to the echo of: 'I can; / Can something, hope, wish day come, not choose not to be.'

20

The ambulance arrives just after eight next morning. Esmond has been up since before dawn. He realises he has been allowing plates to pile up in the sink, dirty clothes to fall across the room. He sweeps the floor of the drawing room, scrubs the sideboard in the kitchen, changes the sheets on their bed. He even dusts the triptych. By the time the doctor comes up the steps and rings the bell, the inside of the villa is gleaming.

'I am Morandi,' he says. 'I have your friend.' Esmond looks out towards the ambulance parked on the gravel. 'She will need some care. Normally I would not have wanted her to leave so early, but these are special circumstances, no? She is still losing blood. Rather a lot of blood. Will you help me get her inside?'

Ada is trying to step from the back of the ambulance, her face lifting towards the light. Her cheeks are heavily bruised and one ear is bandaged. Her left hand is wrapped in plaster. Esmond rushes towards her. 'Ada!'

'You shouldn't be walking,' Dr Morandi says.

They sling her between them and carry her up to the bedroom, where she lies down in obstinate obedience, burrows beneath blankets, and pulls the sheet up over her head. They go back downstairs and stand by the ambulance.

'She needs to stay in bed indefinitely. Plenty of water to drink and change the dressings every day. Here's a bag with bandages, some pills to help with the pain. You mustn't be surprised by the amount of blood. It's normal. She's given birth, you know. In all but name.'

'But— the baby?'

'I'm sorry. At twenty weeks, there was no chance. We didn't even try.'

The doctor gets back into the ambulance and pulls away. Esmond stands in the driveway for a few moments, overcome by a heaviness so complete it almost crushes him. He goes up and sits beside the bed, watching the slight rise and fall of the covers, sending all his love and pity towards the hidden, sleeping figure, so as not to think of himself.

When he pulls back her clothes that first night, he cannot believe that a body that looks like this can live on. There is barely a patch of skin that is not broken or bruised. The bruises are like clouds at sunset: billowing purple, magenta and yellow. One on the inside of her thigh is exactly the colour of the water in the pool – spring-green. The fingernails of her left hand are missing and the wrist is broken. When he changes the dressing on her ear, he sees that the lobe has been ripped away from the skin. He bathes it in iodine and she winces. Her stomach is soft, the skin there like a balloon as it begins to deflate. They look down at her body together, and there is fascination alongside the horror.

She first speaks to him on the second day, when he and Tatters come up the stairs with a bowl of soup. The dog lies looking up at her as Esmond spoons it between burst lips. When it is finished, she says 'Thank you,' very softly. He is amazed that she hasn't cried. While she is sleeping, he sits at the table in the kitchen with his head on his arms, or throws himself on the divan in the drawing room and sobs and howls, Tatters pressing a rough tongue against his cheeks.

On the third day, she sits up and fixes him with her green eyes. Her voice when it comes, is unchanged, surprising him. 'After they got rid of the baby—'

'Was it—? Did you—?' He looks at her and is silent.

'After they got rid of the baby, they had to clear other stuff out of me, a hurried operation before they got me out of the hospital. I remember Morandi saying, *This is going to hurt*. But it didn't, not at all, and I'd be surprised if anything does again.'

'Because of what Carità had done to you.'

'That? Nothing. Do you understand nothing?' She burrows beneath the covers again and he resumes his helpless bedside vigil.

The days pass and the bruises lose their brilliance. The blood which had flowed so thick and red between her legs that he'd quickly used up the bandages and had resorted to tearing up George Keppel's Turnbull & Asser shirts for dressings, slowly abates. He brings the gramophone up to the room and they sit in darkness, her head in his lap, listening to Rachmaninoff's Vespers, the Goldberg Variations, Liszt's Hungarian Rhapsodies. Still, she doesn't cry. After dinner, which he carries up from the kitchen, his powers of culinary invention increasingly tested as the garden turns in on itself for winter, they sit on the bed and stare at the triptych.

With a choir singing Rachmaninoff's Alleluias in the background, he tells her the story of the triptych, of Filippino Lippi's life, of the painter's dissipated father. With the covers pulled up, her head in his lap, he speaks for hours, thinking back to his father's gallery in the chapel at Aston and the stories Sir Lionel had told him about Filippino. He calls to mind lines from Browning's 'Fra Lippo Lippi', from Vasari and Cellini. That which he cannot remember, he invents, hoping that a story, even one as melancholy as this, might reach her in a way he cannot.

He tells her of the vagabond priest, Fra Lippo, the greatest painter of his day, a rogue, a libertine. He'd made a teenaged nun pose as the Madonna, had locked the doors of the cathedral. Nine months later our hero, Filippino, was born.

The atmosphere of his youth was rich with the scent of gesso and tempera, with the sound of apprentices grinding pigments, stretching *cartone*, hammering gold leaf. Sandro Botticelli, Lippo's most gifted pupil, was often there, helping the older Lippi, schooling the younger. When Fra Lippo was poisoned by his brother-in-law, dying on the floor of Spoleto cathedral, Filippino went to live with Botticelli in Florence.

Botticelli introduced Filippino to Lorenzo de Medici and very soon the young man with the famous name was commissioned by Florentine bankers to decorate family chapels, wedding chests, tondo portraits of wives and mistresses. As he turned eighteen, he was able to call upon the city's greatest artists, Verrocchio, Perugino, Ghirlandaio.

Filippino was certain he'd eclipse even his father, whose name trailed like a ghost behind him. He was, after all, Filippino – Little Filippo. In 1483 he completed the frescoing of the Brancacci Chapel that had been halted sixty years earlier, when his father's master, Masaccio, was struck down by the plague. At twenty-five he was painting himself into history, onto the walls of all of the city's most magnificent churches.

But life was chaotic. He'd inherited his father's love of wine and women. The days began to darken. Botticelli's great love, Simonetta Vespucci, died of tuberculosis and he fled to Rome. Filippino was passed over for a number of major commissions, left others unfinished, drowning himself in the city's fleshpits. There were love affairs that ended in rows. His closest friend, Betto Pialla, was arrested for sodomy and hung on the *strappado* at the Murate prison. Filippino spent a night in debtor's gaol before Verrocchio bailed him out. His work became obvious, slapdash, cynical. There were new painters appearing whose work made Filippino's seem stale and outmoded – Michelangelo and Leonardo in Florence, Bosch and Dürer abroad.

Botticelli returned to Florence, Esmond continues, and

painted three masterpieces: *Primavera*, *The Birth of Venus* and *Diana and Actaeon*. Each of them used as the principal character the face and body of Simonetta, whom Botticelli said he saw in his mind clearer than any living person. Filippino's old master was a mournful, bitter figure now, caught up in his memories of his dead lover, his increasing religiosity, his professional rivalries.

He reaches out for Ada and takes her hand. The world grew darker still, he says. The priest Savonarola came to the city, preaching from the Book of Revelation about the horrors to come. He was followed by keening, dead-eyed acolytes, the Weepers. Black-coated Officials of the Night rounded up prostitutes, cutting their noses off to mark them; homosexuals were beaten and dragged through the streets. Women were no longer encouraged out; when they did leave their homes, the new city frowned upon colour, decoration. The world of twill and lawn and damask and brocade became dull overnight, all prompted by this flat-faced monk in his Fra Angelico-frescoed cell in San Marco. *I'm not an artist, just a humble craftsman*, Filippino would say when people asked him what he did.

Then King Charles VIII of France crossed the Alps and, picking up Swiss mercenaries along the way, pitched siege outside the walls of Florence. There was an outbreak of the plague, some of the city's walls were burning. Penitents whipped themselves on the steps of the Duomo. Food ran out and people starved. The flames of hell seemed close to them then. A pyre was built in the centre of the Piazza della Signoria. The city brought its armfuls of pagan texts, graven images which formerly, encouraged by Poliziano, by Pico della Mirandola, they'd hoped to smuggle into their Christian faith. The Bonfire of the Vanities.

Picture, Esmond says, Filippino arguing with Botticelli, desperate to stop him carrying out all three of his Simonettainspired masterpieces. Finally his old master leaves with *Diana and Actaeon*, sobbing, saying that he must make his peace with God. That only in the kind cruelty of Savonarola's words can he escape from the despair that has hunkered over him since Simonetta, coughing blood, left the world. Filippino watches from the window as the painting burns. That evening, he begins the triptych. He doesn't sleep until the three paintings are finished.

Now we see him, ten years later, dying in the airy bedroom of a house overlooking the Piazza della Signoria. Only forty-eight. The triptych is at the end of the bed – Esmond points towards it – hanging there, watching over him just as it watches over us. Out of his window he can see the massive form of *David* moving by. One of the last things he did was to vote on where Florence should house its new masterpiece, sculpted by the man who would go on to be the true inheritor of Lippo's title, the greatest painter in Florence – Michelangelo. The triptych is his own monument, a relic of those sinister days when it seemed as though Florence would fall.

As he dies, he feels himself being soaked into the triptych. These paintings, he realises, are enough. They may not have the surface beauty of *Primavera* or the grace of his father's work, but they tell the truth, and that is what matters. To an echo of applause as *David* is set down outside the Palazzo Vecchio, Filippino drifts deeper into the paintings, feeling the tendons and sinews of his own body coil around those of St John. He begins to disappear. Now his wife is here, mopping his brow with a damp cloth, his son, another Filippo, mouthing words he cannot hear, grasping his hand. As if lifted on a cloud he looks down on himself, on his family. He dies with the triptych before him and tendrils of love pouring out from his beatless heart into the still, soft world.

*

He tells the story of Filippino over and over, becoming more inventive with each iteration, knowing that the brighter the images he offers Ada, the more she is able to leave her own suffering. It's not a happy story, but it begins to gather a life, and helps to heal her mind, just as his careful ministrations heal her body. After a fortnight, she rises from the bed. The scar on her ear has become infected, an indignant red; her wrist remains in its cast, the nails do not grow back; otherwise she is as recovered as she'll ever be. In silence, Esmond helps her to dress, pulling the old tunic with its scent of lavender over her head, lacing her shoes. When they are finished, they stand facing each other, and she takes his hands and leans forward to kiss him.

Esmond puts in a call to Pretini on the W/T that afternoon. It is the twenty-third of November. 'Ada is up and about,' he says. 'We're ready to help again. To do whatever we can.'

A little after nine that evening, there is a ring at the front door. Pretini is with them, and the Professor and Elio, his arm in a sling. As Esmond and Ada are greeting their guests, a motorbike pulls into the driveway with its front light off. Bruno and Alessandro skip up the steps to the door and soon they are all in the drawing room, a fire roaring in the grate. The Professor has brought brandy and a lasagne made by his wife, which they heat in the kitchen. Ada is distant but composed. The men are careful with her, take care to let her know that she is included in their plans but not unthinkingly. After they have eaten, Bruno passes around a box of Toscanos. Pretini looks first at Esmond, then at Ada.

'A second wave of round-ups this weekend. They're trying to grab every Jew in the city, this *Judenfrei* dream of Mangianello's. We've been attempting to get as many as possible out, but the Germans are breathing down our necks. The convent at Prato was raided last night. Six nuns arrested for harbouring Jews, although Cardinal della Costa marched down to the *Stadtskommandatur* immediately in full sacerdotal dress and had them released. We're going to send two families from the Oltrarno up to you tomorrow. They're holed up at the back of the salon at the moment, but there simply isn't room for them.'

'There are too many who need our help, too few of us to give it,' the Professor says. 'The best we can do is warn them and hope they get away. I have spoken to Rabbi Cassuto. He's aware of the dangers. He's tough, for such a young man.'

Esmond nods. The fire has died down and he adds another vine branch to it.

'We need to take the fight to the enemy,' Bruno says, slapping his hand on his thigh and making Ada start. 'It's not enough to simply react. As the Allies approach – and they will, soon, Monte Cassino is only a temporary hold-up – we need to make the Fascists feel like they're under attack from within and without.' He throws his cigarillo into the fire and puts a matchstick in his mouth, which he moves from side to side as he thinks.

'So what do we do?' Esmond asks.

'We attack. Our first target is Gino Gobbi. A Colonel in the MVSN. He's in charge of the Blackshirt squads rounding up conscription shirkers in the hills. We have information that he's planning to lead a more serious attempt on Monte Morello just before Christmas.' He knocks back his glass of brandy. 'We're going to get him before he does.'

'Why not go for Carità?' Esmond says. 'Or Alberti? Why go for this Gobbi? I've never even heard of him.'

'Because he's easy and he's official,' Bruno says. 'He lives on his own in an apartment on the Lungarno Soderini, just upriver from Antonio's. He's regular, leaves his place on the dot of seven-thirty every night and strolls up to a restaurant near the

Ponte alla Carraia. We'll hit him on the evening of the first of December.'

'We want to get Carità as much as you do,' Alessandro says. 'But he's heavily guarded. He's a paranoid fucker and we'll need to plan carefully. But we'll get him, never fear.'

'Fine,' Esmond says, looking across at Ada, who is sitting still, listening. 'At least we're doing something.'

21

The next day, they hear nothing from Pretini. They had been expecting the Jewish families to arrive, but when evening comes and there is still no news, Esmond calls down to the salon. There is no response, just the dull buzz of static. It is dark outside. They have not yet had dinner. He radios through to the partisans at Monte Morello and Maria Luigia answers.

'They're all down in the city,' she says. 'Carità has Penna. We shouldn't speak any more. The Germans will be listening in. Goodbye.'

A little after midnight, the doorbell rings. Esmond and Ada are both in bed, neither asleep. They go downstairs together, Esmond looking through the shuttered window beside the door before opening it. Antonio and Tosca are standing on the doorstep. He is shaggy-headed, exhausted-looking; she is as neat as usual, but agitated.

'Carità raided the salon this morning. Pretini had no chance,' she says as they follow Esmond into the kitchen. 'They found the two families in the rooms at the back, handed them over to the Gestapo, hauled Pretini and his assistant, Giacomo, off to the Villa Triste. At least we found out where the leaks have been coming from. There was a priest with Carità, a Father Idelfonso.

294

He's been hanging around the monasteries and convents, picking up news from the monks. Unworldly bastards don't know any better and reveal everything. One of them must have told him about Pretini. Now we just have to hope that Pretini's able to keep his mouth shut about the location of the camp.'

Esmond places a bottle of grappa on the table and Tosca pours herself a drink. 'He's tough. There's nothing to worry about there. And we're still going to take Gobbi down,' she says, gulping and pouring another. 'We need to prove they can't scare us.'

On Saturday morning, the twenty-seventh, Ada and Esmond stand in the garden with their binoculars trained down on the streets around the synagogue. They see nothing, they hear nothing, and they feel useless and cut off now that Pretini is no longer on hand to keep them up to date with news from the streets. It is only on the Sunday evening, when Gino Bartali pulls up on his bicycle, his peaked cap and racing colours bright even in winter, that they learn.

Bartali tells them that SS Captain Alberti brought specially trained commandos over from Trieste to manage the round-up. Jews were hunted down in all corners of the city: in the convents, in the hospitals, in the empty galleries of the Bargello where several had been hidden by Professor Rossi. Eight Jews in their seventies were taken from a care home in Novoli and rolled in their wheelchairs to the slatted train at Santa Maria Novella station.

Carità had led gangs through the streets of the Jewish quarter breaking windows, entering houses and looting. What they didn't steal, they destroyed. They found six grubby-faced children hiding in a cellar and Carità led them up to the station himself, waving the train off as it chugged slowly out of Santa Maria Novella station. That train would eventually, after agonising stops on windswept mountain passes, long waits at empty platforms whose lamps swung yellow light into blackness – all of this seen through slats no wider than a finger – end up at Auschwitz-Birkenau. The last man who stepped onto the train at Santa Maria Novella that Sunday morning, holding himself very tall despite the weight he must have felt, was Nathan Cassuto, the city's youthful Chief Rabbi.

Bartali also gives them a message from Bruno. They are to meet at the side of Santo Spirito at six-thirty the next evening. Esmond should bring his revolver.

22

It is cold as they make their way down into the city. The trees have dropped their leaves on the lanes and there is damp squelching beneath their feet. It had rained earlier in the day and now there is a fine mist. The lights of the town look smudged. Esmond is wearing George Keppel's ulster, the revolver snug in one pocket.

As they reach the first houses, he hears the drone of aeroplanes overhead. They look up as searchlights slash across the sky. The anti-aircraft guns crackle over Fiesole but the planes surge on, through the air and mist.

The red coal of a solitary Toscano burns in the shadows behind the facade of Santo Spirito. Esmond and Ada walk along to the right of the church where they find Bruno attached to the glowing cigarillo, Elio and Alessandro beside him. 'We're waiting for Antonio and Tosca,' Bruno says. Esmond stands back and looks up at the darkened windows of St Mark's. He picks out the French windows of his old studio, the rooftop terrace where he'd spent his sweltering days three summers ago. This is his seventh December in Florence, he realises. He asks Bruno for a smoke and lights it, brightening them all for a moment with the flare of his match. Five earnest, eager faces.

A few minutes later, Antonio and Tosca arrive. They gather around Bruno.

'Elio's going to make the hit,' Bruno says. Esmond has noticed before that, when they discuss death, they speak like characters in a trashy American novel. He gives a little smile in the darkness. 'We'll get him in front of San Frediano, at the Piazza di Castello. I'll be waiting around the corner. If Elio misses, I'll go after Gobbi.'

'I won't miss,' Elio says. He looks very young in the dim light, Esmond thinks. His round glasses reflect the Toscano.

'There are guards on both bridges – the Vittoria and the Carraia. We need to have them covered. Make sure that Elio can escape. If they come near, we shoot them, is that understood? Antonio and Tosca, you take the guards on the Ponte della Vittoria; Esmond and Ada, you'll be on the Ponte alla Carraia. Alessandro will have the Moto Guzzi to get Elio away afterwards. Listen, Ada, here's a gun for you.' He hands her a small Beretta that she places quickly in the pocket of her jacket.

The seven friends look at each other for a moment and then, without speaking, make their way in separate groups up towards the river. Esmond hears the engine of the motorbike start and then fade into the distance. He and Ada wend their way through the streets directly behind the Lungarno until they come to a small passageway leading to the riverfront. They lose themselves in shadows and look over towards the bridge. The two German soldiers are smoking in the mist, waterproof jackets over their uniforms. There is no traffic on the Lungarno. They can hear the river slapping against its banks every now and again, the sound of the Germans talking. Esmond looks at his watch. It is twenty past seven. The revolver is heavy in his pocket.

They hear the bells of Santo Spirito chime seven-thirty, those of San Frediano answering a few moments later. Ada places a swift kiss on his cheek. 'It'll be fine,' she says. They wait. The breeze over the river swirls the mist like a brush through grey paint. They wait for the sound of Elio's gun. Five minutes pass, now ten. When the bells toll quarter to eight, first Santo Spirito, then San Frediano, Esmond gives Ada's hand a squeeze.

'You stay here,' he says. 'I'm going to wander along and see if I can see anything.'

'Be careful.'

He walks in the darkness thrown by the buildings, his hand in his pocket, his fingers wrapped around the cold metal of the gun. He stops for a while at the midpoint of the Lungarno, where he can see both sets of guards. The two on the Ponte della Vittoria are sitting down on the stone wall playing whist, holding their cards inside their jackets to shield them from the rain. He stands there, watching, for another ten minutes. He wonders how long Bruno will wait before giving up. He decides to make his way along to the piazza in front of San Frediano. He keeps himself hidden against the dark bulk of the buildings, stepping out into the street to avoid the cone of light beneath a streetlamp. As he's there, in the middle of the road, he hears a door slam shut ahead of him.

He scurries further along, pressing against the damp stone of the next building. He sees a man walking towards him, hands in the pockets of an overcoat, stopping for a moment to light a cigarette and then walking on. The bells of Santo Spirito begin to strike eight. Suddenly, appearing through the mist behind the man, a figure, running, a gun glinting in the streetlight. The assailant lets out a high cry, audible over the bells, holds the pistol out straight-armed, and then nothing. Esmond watches with horror as the man turns around to face his pursuer. Elio looks down at his gun, pulls at it and slaps it against his knee in frustration as the man turns again and begins to run lumber-ingly down the Lungarno away from Elio, towards Esmond.

In the seconds it takes for San Frediano to ring out – a single peal and then eight deep notes – Esmond has drawn the revolver from his pocket and stepped from the shadows. The sprinting Colonel Gobbi doesn't see him until it's too late. He stumbles into Esmond's arms, the cigarette falling from his mouth. Esmond holds him up with his left arm and relief passes across the man's face.

'*Aiuto*,' he says, '*c'è un pazzo qui—*'

There have been five strikes of San Frediano's bell above them. On the sixth, Esmond pushes the revolver up into Gobbi's ribs and flicks off the safety catch. The Colonel's eyes open very wide. On the seventh strike Esmond pulls the trigger, again on the eighth. Gobbi slumps forward, giving a tight spasm. Esmond lays him down carefully in the shadowy lee of the building, looking towards first one bridge, then the other. The guards have heard nothing over the sound of the bells. Elio is still standing in the road, watching. He walks slowly towards Esmond. Together they look down at the slumped figure. Then Elio shakes his head, as if awakening from a dream.

'You need to go,' he says. 'Run to the piazza, Alessandro will look after you.'

'No,' says Esmond. 'I'm not leaving Ada again.' He starts back along the Lungarno towards the Ponte alla Carraia. Elio runs to keep up with him. 'You need to get rid of the gun,' he hisses.

Esmond shakes his head. 'I'm fucked if I'm caught either way. I'll keep the gun.' They have almost reached the passageway when, ahead of them, the light of a German Kübelwagen appears, sweeping from side to side along the Lungarno.

'Quick,' Elio says, trying to drag Esmond back the way they have come.

'No,' he says again.

Ada is standing in the shadows of the passageway, her skin

299

dimly glowing. 'Quick,' Esmond says. The three of them move down the passageway in single file, coming out on the Borgo San Frediano. Esmond tries to lead them back towards Santo Spirito, but Elio hesitates.

'Wait,' he says. Esmond feels an urge to wipe Elio's glasses, misted with rain. 'They'll find the body any minute. There'll be Germans crawling all over the place. We'll never make it all the way up to the villa.'

'What about Antonio's place?' Ada says.

They walk swiftly along the road, again in the shadows. The rain is starting to drum the street, casting a misty scrim before them. Just as they turn up towards the Ponte della Vittoria, there is the sound of a police siren. Soon, a second joins it. 'They've found the body,' Elio says. They begin to run. When they reach the river, they look along to see half a dozen searchlights illuminating the Lungarno. Soldiers are spewing across the bridge from the north, their feet rhythmic on the cobblestones.

Outside Antonio's apartment, they pull the bell and wait. Nothing. One of the German Kübelwagens is moving up the Lungarno towards them. 'Fuck,' Elio says. Esmond looks along the river and sees two figures moving quickly, keeping just out of reach of the searchlight that is oscillating first one way, then the other, on top of the car. The figures run across the traffic circle at the bottom of the Ponte della Vittoria and come stumbling up to the front door of the building. Antonio fumbles with his keyring, gets the key in the latch and the five of them spill inside. Esmond slams the door shut with his foot. They hear the slow rumble of the car pass by, and then they are all laughing, breathless, staggering up the stairs.

'I need a drink,' Elio says.

'What a blast. Wowee!' Tosca spreads happily back on the wall on the first landing.

Esmond takes Ada's hand and they come up last of all. She kisses him at the doorway and they go inside.

'It was horrifying, but distant,' he's saying, much later, as they sit by the window, a bottle of limoncello on the table in front of them. 'As if it wasn't me pulling the trigger, but me in a novel, a film. Do you see what I'm getting at?' Tosca is curled asleep in an armchair in the corner. Antonio is cooking at the small stove in his kitchen. Elio is staring out into the night, watching the lights move along the Lungarno.

'We did it, that's what matters,' Elio says. 'The bastards will take us seriously from now on.'

An hour later, they are all drunk and dead tired. Elio is slumped across the table, sleeping. Antonio insists that Esmond and Ada take his bed and stretches out on the floor by Tosca's feet. Their faces together on the pillow, Esmond tries to recite 'God's Grandeur' to Ada, but falls asleep somewhere in the first line. They are woken every so often by police sirens. In the night, winds blow away the clouds and they wake to a dawn that is bright and still.

23

Bruno arrives at the apartment just after seven. Elio, rubbing his eyes, answers the door. Antonio is curled in the chair with Tosca in his lap. Esmond and Ada get up slowly and take turns washing in the sink. Bruno is sitting at the table with a cup of coffee. His face bears none of the triumph that Esmond had expected.

'Well done last night,' he says grimly. 'We did what we had to do.'

'But—' Esmond sits down opposite his friend.

'But Alberti and Mangianello convened a special court in the

301

night, after they found out about Gobbi, I mean. It was decided they should send a strong message to the Resistance. Five prisoners are being executed over in the Cascine this morning.'

'Not Pretini—' Ada says. Esmond's eyes dart to the window and the park.

'No, not yet. It would seem they think they can get more from him. But Oreste Ristori is one of them.'

At ten o'clock sharp, the soldiers begin to arrive in the park across the river. The shooting range is swept of fallen leaves and then a Black Maria pulls up. Five men are dragged out, their hands cuffed. There is no crowd, just a group of Blackshirts and a single man in a dark suit who begins to scream and swear at the prisoners. Antonio comes back with a pair of binoculars. 'That's Gobbi's brother,' he says, touching the focus ring. 'I've seen him around.' The five men are tied to posts in front of the shooting range. 'Alberti is there,' Antonio continues, 'and Mangianello.' Now an ambulance with a lightning flash on the side pulls up.

'That's—' Ada begins.

'Carità. Yes.' Antonio says.

Gobbi's brother continues to shout at the five prisoners, the harsh notes of his voice coming across the still waters of the river. 'Can you make out any of the others?' Bruno asks. 'Let me look for a moment.' He takes the binoculars. 'There's Luigi Pugi, Gino Manetti. I don't know the other two. They're not even partisans apart from Oreste. Just anarchists rounded up because the Germans don't want troublemakers on the street. This is appalling, it's criminal.'

As the men are tied to their posts, Carità steps from the ambulance and embraces Alberti and Mangianello. Bruno points out Piero Koch, once as infamous in Rome as Carità in Florence. He is hunched and long-limbed, like a spider. Esmond watches the Blackshirts struggle to tie their ropes around Ristori's enormous belly. Gobbi's brother's voice rises higher as Carità, Koch and three other Blackshirts take their positions facing the men. Over the harsh cries, though, another sound drifts out. Ristori is singing. As the *Banda Carità* raise their rifles to their shoulders, Ristori leads the five prisoners in the *Internationale*, although only Ristori's voice can be heard over Gobbi's brother's screams. Esmond reaches his hand out in the air towards the man, towards the voice. '*C'est la lutte finale / Groupons-nous et demain / L'Internationale / Sera le genre humain.*' Five shots. Five bodies slump forward, Ristori's heavily enough that his ropes break and he tumbles into the sand. Esmond thinks of Mercedes Gomez, mud-streaked in a jungle clearing, the pictures on Ristori's mantel, the things for which we live.

Tosca is crying and Ada sits with her. Bruno shakes his head, lowering the binoculars. Elio's face is set hard. Esmond, still looking down over the five bodies, their five murderers, sees Shelley sitting in the same park a hundred and twenty years ago, writing 'Ode to the West Wind'. Very quietly, to himself, he mouths: 'O Wind, if Winter comes, can Spring be far behind?'

24

They spend Christmas at L'Ombrellino. The Professor comes up in the Bianchi with Bruno, the back loaded down with bottles of wine and food. Maria Luigia's cousins have given them three chickens, there are carrots and potatoes from the garden. Alessandro has been brewing grappa in the caves at Monte Morello. He and Elio arrive on the Moto Guzzi with a rucksack full of alcohol. Maria Luigia turns up on a bicycle, her plump cheeks flushed from the cold, an enormous salami hanging around her neck, the chickens dangling from the handlebars. Gino Bartali and his wife also cycle up, while Antonio and Tosca, in evening dress, come late, as the chickens are being carved. Antonio's hair has been carefully cut. He is cleanly shaven and smells of rose water.

'I wouldn't let him up here until he looked half-decent,' Tosca says. She is wearing a long red dress and a red carnation in her hair.

Esmond sits next to Alessandro at lunch, immaculate in his oyster-white suit. After they have eaten, they sip *orzo* coffee, leaning back in their chairs, and Esmond drapes a fraternal arm around his friend's shoulder. 'That was smashing,' he says.

'I've eaten too much.' Alessandro opens the button at his waist. 'I wish Pretini were here. It's the only thing that spoils it, you know?'

'I've been thinking about him, too. What's the chance he gives us away? Tells Carità the location of the camp, I mean.'

'Pretini? Never. He may look like a playboy, but he's a tough fucker.'

'It's pretty strange, this foppish hairdresser now a rebel leader. Only in Italy, I guess.'

Alessandro offers Esmond a cigarette. He takes it and bends his head to the flame of his friend's lighter. Alessandro lets out a stream of smoke with a sigh. 'Guys like Pretini, they're exceptional. It's obvious why I'm fighting.' He holds his hand up to his face, smiling. 'If they don't go after me because I'm half-Jewish, they'll go after me because I'm half-black. I'm like a Christmas present to those fuckers, tick all the boxes.' He laughs. 'But Pretini, it's all about idealism, honour. He says the Fascists, the Nazis, they offend his sense of decency. And he's willing to die for that. I think that's remarkable.'

After lunch, they sit in front of the fire in the drawing room. The Professor raises a glass to Pretini. They have heard from

Morandi, the doctor, who has been brought in to treat him at the Villa Triste, the apartment block in the via Bolognese whose upper floors are now the administrative headquarters of the SD. The Germans have been complaining about the screams coming from the basement rooms, so rumour has it. Pretini has refused to give Carità any information. His bright teeth have been ripped out, he has been thrown down a flight of stone stairs, fourteen bones broken in all, but still he will not speak. The Professor has taken Pretini's wife and daughter – whose existence was kept from all but a handful of friends, bad for business with the assorted Marchesas and Contessas – up to the Marchese Serlupi's villa.

'This may be the last time we are all together,' the Professor says, peering around the room through thick spectacles. 'The Allies are on the move again. Things will only get closer to the edge from now on. Elio and Alessandro have what you might call a functioning bomb factory in Monte Morello. In January, we will begin a full-scale campaign of terrorism. The Germans will wish they had never set foot in Florence.'

There is a moan of approval, the clinking of glasses. Antonio, who has taken off his tie and untucked his shirt, kisses Tosca.

'Maria Luigia is taking charge of CoRa, our radio network. Ferruccio Parri has sent us a high-powered portable transmitter from Milan which we will use to co-ordinate the various cells gathering in the hills. The set here at L'Ombrellino isn't strong enough to reach the mountain passes. Its presence also poses a threat to Esmond and Ada. With the new machinery we will be able to transmit detailed information to the British SOE. They've already sent ammunition and supplies. You will all—' – his voice catches a little here – 'be remembered in years to come for your bravery, for your dedication to the people of Florence, the cause of freedom.'

The partisans stand, applauding, and their applause grows louder until it hurts the ears. The noise grows and grows until it gives over to the sound of screaming, the sound of gunfire, the sound of the bombs that explode throughout January. It is the sound of the briefcase bomb left by Alessandro in the lobby of the Fascist Federation on the via dei Servi and the childlike shrieks of the Blackshirt guard whose legs are ripped off by the blast. It is the sound of the bomb that Bruno places in the brothel on the via delle Terme, patting the madam on the bottom and whispering a warning as he leaves. Two SS *Sturmbannführers* are killed in their underwear, waiting for their girls to arrive. It is the sound of bullets tearing through the greatcoats and shirts and underclothes of the two guards on the Ponte della Vittoria, bullets which come from guns fired out of Antonio's window. He can never go back to the flat, and he and Tosca join the partisans in the caves at Monte Morello. It is the sound of bombs destroying railway lines, Esmond and Ada's particular speciality: charges placed at strategic positions on the Florence to Rome line, on the tracks at Campo di Marte, just outside Santa Maria Novella station.

One wintry afternoon, they are strapping sticks of dynamite to the Florence–Bologna line, a line which Mussolini calls the masterpiece of his railway network (although even here, contrary to boasts, the trains don't always run on time). Ada snaps at Esmond as he fumbles with a fuse. She takes the IMCO lighter from his fingers and lights it. They retreat to the cover of rail-side brush and wait. A rush and a suck of air as the bomb detonates, sending a train carrying six hundred Mauser semi-automatic rifles, sixteen hundred rounds of ammunition, eighty Model 24 *Stielhandgranate*, twenty-four barrels of Bavarian beer, two refrigerated containers of wurst and schnitzel, a dozen rats and a terrified driver careening into the Arno.

They don't know it until later, but at the very moment that the train sank beneath the river's roiled waters, Carità was pressing the cold muzzle of his revolver into the warm nape of Alessandro's neck. Alessandro, a priest who was watching from the steps of the church tells the Professor that evening, dropped to his knees with a dreamy look on his dark face, his oyster-white suit immaculate and angel-like as he keeled over into the dust.

25

The next day, around eight, Esmond wakes. Tatters is standing up at the end of their bed, ears pricked. Esmond remembers Alessandro, the news of whose death had been given to them by Maria Luigia over the radio the night before, and he feels grief settle over him. Tatters begins to growl and Esmond kicks out at the dog, then regrets it. Tatters steps off the bed, sulking, and patters downstairs. Esmond hears the sound of the front door opening. He reaches over and nudges Ada just as Tatters begins to bark.

'There's someone downstairs,' he says. Ada's eyes open and she sits up as Esmond leans out over the bannisters. The sound of boots on the wooden floor, voices. Tatters barking.

'*Stai zitto!*' someone yells. The front door is opened, a whimper and then a single gunshot. No more barking. Esmond runs back into the room to pick up his pistol, ready to go down and confront the men, but Ada places her hand on his shoulder.

'Not now.' The boots clump up the stairs to the first floor. Ada quickly pulls the covers up over the bed. She then unplugs the W/T and puts it in the cupboard. Esmond takes his gun and the book of poetry from his bedside. They jam themselves in beside the Italian soldier's uniform, relic of their first mission, still hanging there with Esmond's suits, Ada's dresses. They make themselves as comfortable as they can and wait. They can hear men moving through the rooms of the floor below them, looking in the bedroom where first Alessandro, then Signora Rossi slept. There is a tightening of the air as someone enters the room and then, through a crack between the cupboard doors, Esmond sees a squat figure in shorts, a flash of white hair.

'They haven't been gone long,' Carità says.

'We'll have the place thoroughly cleaned before the *Reichsmarschall* gets here,' another voice says. Esmond sees Alberti, whom he recognises from the shootings in the Cascine. 'He's very particular. Ah, what do we have here?' Esmond can see Alberti standing in front of the triptych. 'These are rather good. Our rebel friends have taste.'

'Hmm,' Carità has taken Anna's collage off the wall and is scrutinising it. Esmond can feel Ada's breath on his cheek. He thinks of Tatters with a stab of sadness. 'I know the little bastard holing up here. He's a pathetic little faggot, nothing to worry about.'

Alberti is still standing in front of the triptych. 'I will make a gift of these paintings to the *Reichsmarschall* when he arrives,' he says. 'To welcome him to Florence.'

'Fine,' Carità replies. 'I'll have my men bring them down to San Marco today. I'll take this one for myself now, though,' he says, tucking the collage beneath his arm.

They stomp back down the stairs. Esmond listens for the sound of the door slamming and then looks out of the window as a motorcycle and sidecar pulls through the front gate. 'Shit,' says Ada behind him. Esmond runs down and out to where Tatters is lying, a red patch spreading slowly across his wiry white fur. Esmond kneels down beside the dog's body, which is still warm, and cradles it in his lap. He begins to cry. For the dog, certainly, but for Alessandro, too. For Oreste Ristori. For his baby. He's still crying when Ada comes down and takes his head against her and speaks soothingly. He feels the flatness of her stomach, the bony undulations of the ribs above them and lets out another sob.

'We need to get out of here,' she says. 'I radioed down to Maria Luigia at CoRa. Bruno's coming to take us to Monte Morello. We should go up and pack.'

'I need to do this, first,' he says.

Esmond takes the dog's body down into the garden and lays it beneath the umbrella sculpture, from which the dead fingers of last summer's vines hang down. He brings up stones from the terrace by the swimming pool and soon he has constructed a small cairn over the body. He walks back up to the house, his eyes now dry, his mouth set in a firm, bloodless line.

He fills his morocco bag with clothes, runs down to the drawing room to grab an armful of books, then back up to the bedroom, where he places the books with his revolver and a bundle of letters in the top of the bag. He and Ada stand staring at the triptych together.

'I suppose it's goodbye,' she says.

He looks at the painting of Christ, the two smaller panels either side. 'Don't be so sure,' he says.

'But the centrepiece is too big to—?'

'He can stay,' he says. 'Cast his judgement on the Germans. Maybe one of them will catch a glimpse of something that keeps him from the worst.'

When Bruno pulls up half an hour later, they are standing on the gravel driveway with two small bags beside them. In Ada's arms, she holds the painting of Mary Magdalene. John the Baptist leans back against Esmond.

'You realise how conspicuous they'll make us?' Bruno says from the window of the car.

'We're conspicuous already,' Ada says. She and Esmond sit in the back seat while the paintings jolt and bounce in the front beside Bruno, as they make their way over mule tracks and through vineyards to the hills.

After forty minutes of driving, they begin to climb steeply. Pine trees clamber up the hillside, then gorse bushes and heather. The road takes them under the lip of rocky bluffs, winding along ridges looking down on deep valleys. Finally, after driving through a pine forest so thick it's like night has been called back, they pull into a clearing, where Elio is standing, waiting for them. The university bus is parked to one side, branches teepeed over it. Nets covered in camouflage material hang over the mouths of three caves inside which Esmond can see figures, the glow of cigarettes.

'You heard about Alessandro?' Elio asks as they get out of the car. Esmond nods grimly. 'What are those?' Elio points to the paintings which, despite the journey, look sublime as ever. Ada embraces him and soon Antonio and Tosca are out with other assorted deserters and partisans, some of whom Esmond dimly recognises from those first meetings at the Palazzo Vecchio. He reads Alessandro's death in each face.

They are led into the wide mouth of a cave, where sleeping bags are arranged, each within a neatly marked-out area, most with boots and guns and small personal items beside them. They go deeper inside and Elio gestures to a small alcove formed by a group of glittering stalactites that drip down from the roof.

'We thought you might like this spot. It's darker, of course, but there's a little more privacy. Your bed-rolls and sleeping bags are there, candles. I hope it's all to your liking. I know it's not L'Ombrellino, but we try.'

'It's fine,' Ada says, putting down her bag on the rock floor of the cave. They bring the paintings inside, leaning them against a wall which still finds some daylight from the mouth. The two figures seem lost without their Lord. Esmond takes Ada in his arms and they look at the saints.

'They're alone now.'

'They have each other.'

'I loved being with you,' Esmond says. 'Up there at the villa.'

'I loved it too.' She pauses. 'But this feels real. We can get things done here. After Alessandro, we need to.' He can feel the hardness of the Beretta, which Bruno had given her the night they'd killed Gobbi and which she's kept in her pocket ever since, digging into his thigh. That night, Esmond is woken by the skinny howling of mountain wolves. He reaches out for Ada's hand in the damp darkness, squeezing it tightly.

26

They go after Carità in the middle of March. The spring of '44 is a warm one and the partisans in the hills are buoyed by the mild weather, by the news coming out of Monte Cassino, where the third battle has just ended and the Allies at last scent victory. In the north, there is a wave of crippling strikes in the factories, further rumours of a deterioration in Mussolini's mental state after, under pressure from Pavolini, he is forced to execute his son-in-law Ciano.

Elio and Bruno have drawn it all up in great detail. There have been rehearsals in the clearing in front of the cave. There are fallback plans taking in any number of contingencies, a broad range of less and less likely outcomes. Each of them is given a card with typed instructions as to where they must be, what they must do as the assassination unfolds.

It is eleven in the morning. Esmond, his blond hair under a beret, is sitting at the Caffè Gilli beside a round-topped laurel bush. He sips at his second *orzo* espresso of the morning and tries to remember not the taste but the buzz, the lift he used to feel when drinking real coffee. He can see Tosca's blonde head in the shadows of the triumphal arch. She is standing back from the road, her bag at her feet, looking young and carefree and entirely uninterested in the workers hurrying past, the German soldiers who glance at her, the Blackshirts who wolf-whistle. In the other direction, down towards the via Calimala, Antonio leans back against a wall with a copy of the *Corriere della Sera* held up to his face.

There are businessmen at the tables around Esmond, mostly Italian, their conversations carried out in low, confidential voices. He sips, looking at his watch and then along to the Paszkowski next door, where German soldiers eat pastries with their coffee, the golden flakes lifted skywards by the breeze that drifts up from the Arno. An SS *Hauptsturmführer* leafs through a copy of *Der Schwarze Korps*, licking his finger to turn the page. Waiters come and go, nodding their heads and muttering a half-insolent *Danke* when one of the Germans settles his bill.

Ada comes to sit at Esmond's table, her hair tucked up under a cloche hat. 'Hello,' she smiles thinly at him, her voice cool and businesslike. She puts her purse on the table and from it draws out a make-up compact, dabbing a thin layer of powder under her eyes. 'He's coming,' she says, without looking up.

Esmond waits until Tosca catches his eye and then nods. She, a small, blonde figure, walks up from underneath the arch swinging her bag, large and black. Esmond watches her take a seat at the Paszkowski and attach the bag to the hook beneath the table. She smiles at the waiter when he comes to take her order. Now Antonio lowers his newspaper and begins to move up towards the cafés on the north side of the piazza. He reaches Tosca just as Carità's ambulance pulls into the square.

The tall figure of Piero Koch, in a long coat of black leather, is the first to step from the ambulance, then two guards, one of whom Esmond recognises from the shootings in the Cascine. The guards carry MAB 38s on straps around their shoulders. Finally, Carità and his mistress, the giggling, underdressed Milly. They sit down in their usual place at the front of the Paszkowski, two tables away from where Antonio and Tosca are locked in conversation, their heads leaning in towards one another. Koch and the guards stand at the entrance of the bar, scanning the piazza warily. The waiter brings two glasses of brandy to the table and Esmond can hear Carità's high, yelping laugh.

He takes a sip of his coffee and glances at his watch again. Just on time, the Bianchi pulls up the via Calimala. Bruno is at the wheel, his elbow resting on the open window, the matchstick dancing in his mouth the only sign of his nerves. The car is moving very slowly, comes to a stop in front of the Savoy, and waits. Somewhere, a bell tolls the quarter-hour. In the stillness after, Esmond hears a dull clunk and Ada draws in a breath, almost a sob. He looks across to the Paszkowski and sees Tosca, hand to her mouth, staring down at the floor where Antonio is desperately scrabbling on his hands and knees. Esmond feels his lungs empty, his eyes fixed on Tosca's horrified face.

'*Eine bombe!*' The SS officer is on his feet, pointing at Antonio, who gives up on whatever he's looking for and rises, pulling a revolver from his waistband. The two guards bring their guns to their shoulders, but there are too many Germans and they can't get a clear shot at him. Now Carità is up, hands raised, an unctuous grin on his face. Tosca goes to stand beside her lover, pressing herself against him as, with his jaw set, he points his revolver straight at Carità. Stillness.

'A Mexican standoff? I don't like your odds.' Carità's voice rises into a cackle. 'Time is also not on your side.' He gestures towards the German soldiers who are standing at the south side of the square and now, alerted by the SS officer's shout, heading up towards the Paszkowski. 'I'd surrender now if I were you. Less chance of your girlfriend getting killed.'

'Go fuck yourself,' Antonio says, his Sicilian accent punching out.

'Go fuck yourself,' Tosca repeats.

There is a longer silence. Esmond watches Koch's hunched, angular frame shuffling slowly round to stand behind Antonio, a long hand reaching into the pocket of his coat. He thinks about shouting out, tries to stir himself into action, but feels jammed. A chair scrapes beside him as Ada gets to her feet. He looks up at her, helplessly, as she draws the Beretta from her pocket. Koch has pulled out his own gun and is aiming at Antonio's head as Ada fires, twice, at the hunched back, and the gangly frame rears up, gives a little shudder, and then bends over on itself, two scorched holes in the black leather. There are shouts from the guards, Milly lets out a cry, one of the waiters begins a prayer. Koch collapses forward onto a table and draws plates and glasses clattering to the floor beside him.

Ada shoots again, this time over the heads of the Germans standing motionless on the terrace of the Paszkowski. She takes off her cloche hat and shakes her hair down over her shoulders. The soldiers run, perhaps thirty of them, their boots crackling on the stones of the square. Antonio is firing at Carità, who is crouching with Milly behind an upturned table, but the bullets ping off the metal. Ada looks down at Esmond.

'Come on!' he says, rising. 'We can get to the car if we go now.'

She shakes her head, eyes wide and bright, her wet lips open. 'I love you,' she says, and turns. Firing at the guards, at Carità,

Ada crosses at a crouching run to where Antonio and Tosca are standing. Then the three of them back slowly away from the terrace and onto the via Brunelleschi. Antonio is empty; soon Ada too. Just before they move out of sight, Esmond sees Ada looking over towards him, a grin, her pale face softening. He rises, moves to follow, everything in him rushing towards her, love minting courage in his heart. Again, a little shake of her head. Then she turns, takes Tosca by the hand, and they run.

The terraces of the two cafés erupt. The SS officer is shouting into the café's telephone, which has been brought to his table. The businessmen around Esmond rise, dusting their clothes. Everyone is talking, a few relieved chuckles. The soldiers have arrived and Carità is yelling at them, gesturing up the road. Milly is standing over Koch's body, her hand pressed to her mouth. Esmond pulls the beret down on his head, aware of the approaching soldiers. As the patrons of the two cafés begin to scuttle away in nervous clusters, he hurries to the Bianchi, his heart an animal flutter in his chest. Opening the passenger door, he slips into the seat.

'Quickly, after them,' he says.

Bruno is mouthing *Cazzo, cazzo, cazzo*, slamming his hand down on the steering wheel.

'She shot Koch. Is he—?'

'I think so.'

'Fuck.'

'Let's go after them.' Esmond says.

Bruno looks over at Esmond and shakes his head. 'Too risky. They'll have more chance on foot. They're together, they know what they're doing.'

'But—'

Bruno holds up a hand. 'We have a rendezvous at the Corsini Gardens at one. We need to stick to the plan.'

Esmond sees the soldiers in the café glance over towards the car. Bruno starts the engine and they speed up the via Roma and through the city. They're half an hour early when they arrive at the gates of the Palazzo Corsini. The Marchesa seats them in the lemon house, overlooking the gardens where birds sing spring and fountains babble. Esmond taps his foot, looks at his watch every few seconds, gets up and paces from one end of the glass house to the other, the image of Koch's death-shudder in every direction. Bruno sits very still, breathing slowly. Finally they see a figure making its way towards them through the parterre.

'What happened?' Bruno says.

'I don't know.' It's Antonio. 'They were right behind me and then—'

'I mean with the bomb, *stronzo*! What happened with the fucking bomb?'

'I dropped the fuse. I was trying to attach it under the table, but it was more fiddly than the one we practised on. I dropped the fuse and then, when I was looking for it, the bomb fell out of the bag. I'm sorry.'

'And the girls?'

'Like I said, they were behind me—'

They wait at the Palazzo until two o'clock. The Marchesa has a dinner party that evening, drinks in the garden beforehand. White-jacketed waiters are laying out trestle tables on the lawns. She escorts them to the gates, the battered Bianchi outside, wringing her hands in sympathy. They travel back up to Monte Morello in silence.

They are sitting in the cave that evening, Esmond staring at the paintings, Bruno upright at the radio desk, Antonio slumped on his bed, arm crooked over his face and sighing. Finally there is the sound of Maria Luigia's voice over the wireless.

'I have news,' she says. 'They were taken by the Germans.

Carità couldn't get to them first. They've been taken to Santa Verdiana, to the women's prison. It could be worse. I know the prison governor, she's a good woman, she'll try to make sure they aren't hurt. And Koch is dead, by the way. They took him to Santa Maria Nuova, but they couldn't save him.' Esmond remembers the jolt of his body just before he collapsed, the scorched holes in the leather. When Bruno has finished speaking to Maria Luigia, he makes another call on the wireless. Esmond hears a British accent.

'Please come down as soon as possible,' Bruno says. 'We need help.'

An hour later, a man pulls into the clearing in front of the cave on his motorbike. Esmond recognises the British agent they'd met with on the beach at Forte di Marmi. The man nods in Esmond's direction.

'Wotcha,' he says, grinning. 'Wondered if I'd see you about.'

27

The next morning, Esmond, Bruno, Elio and the British man, Creighton, set off towards the city in the bus. Bruno lets the heavy vehicle coast down the slope. There are now regular aerial drops of fuel from the Allies, but Bruno seems to enjoy sending the bus whistling down the mountainside with its engine off, spraying gravel over cliff-edges, dodging pot-holes and fallen rocks. The four of them are dressed in sand-coloured Wehrmacht *Feldbluse* and peaked caps. Esmond has a rifle slung across his midriff. Bruno sports two holsters, each holding a Walther PPK. Creighton is sitting beside Esmond at the back of the bus, polishing his revolver.

'I'll do the talking,' he says.

'My German's pretty good,' Esmond says.

'You look fifteen. And the German doesn't need to be good, it just needs to be authoritative.'

They continue in silence for a while. Esmond notices it feels strange to be speaking English.

'So you're SOE – what is that? Army? Secret Service?'

'The less you know, young man,' Creighton says, smiling softly, blue eyes darting out over the countryside. 'We'll have a good chinwag when the war's over. We should get together with old Bailey in London. Have a sherbet or two.'

They take a circuitous route through the north of the city and into Le Cure until they come to the via dell'Agnolo. They park in front of the gates of Santa Verdiana, the former convent, now with a chain on the gate, glass shards cemented to the top of the walls, guards leaning on their guns in the courtyard.

'Are we ready?' Creighton says. The four men walk out of the bus and up to the gates. Bruno is carrying a silver-topped stick and raps on the wood. Elio, like Esmond, has a rifle cradled in his arms. A black door at the side opens and a white-bearded guard peers out at them.

'*Dov è la Direttore?*' Bruno barks. The guard ushers them through. They wait in the courtyard, listening to the sound of crockery in a kitchen somewhere, a woman singing on one of the prison's upper floors. After a few minutes, a kindly-looking woman in a grey suit comes to meet them.

'Can I help you?' she says, taking in their uniforms.

'*Sprechen sie Deutsch?*' Creighton asks, giving a small and patronising smile.

The governor shakes her head doubtfully. '*Ein bißchen,*' she offers up.

Creighton switches into Bavarian-tinted Italian. 'We're here for the political prisoners.'

'Which ones?'

'All of them,' he says, flatly. 'They're being transferred to the SD holding cells at San Marco. We have a new female interrogator.'

The governor looks hesitantly from Creighton to Elio. Elio nods briskly. '*Auf einmal!*' he shouts, shaking his rifle in the woman's direction.

'My colleague is lacking patience,' Creighton says. 'Do excuse him. We can of course bring our new interrogator here. We might see what she got from your other prisoners, make a day or two of it.'

'That won't be necessary. We have five politicals at the moment. Please wait here.'

A few minutes pass and then two women wander blinking into the yard, accompanied by a female guard with a truncheon. Soon after, Tosca walks out. She is limping and doesn't meet Esmond's eye when he looks towards her. Finally a pair of older women appear, accompanied by the governor.

'These last two are Royalists. I'm not sure you're interested in them.'

'Oh, we're interested in everyone,' Creighton says, smiling. 'But you should have one more.' He reaches into his pocket and pulls out a piece of paper. 'A certain Nella Ferrari. Ring any bells?'

She nods. 'Oh yes, but she's already gone. All of the Jews went last night. The Ferrari girl tried to protest and I must say her documents looked in order, but the men were very insistent.'

'Were they Germans?'

'No. Italian. *Centurione* Carità – perhaps you know him?'

Creighton smiles at her again. 'We must improve our communication with our Italian comrades,' he says, bowing. 'You have been most helpful, *direttora.*'

They load the prisoners into the bus, first asking the guards to remove the handcuffs.

'They won't try anything with us,' Creighton says, winking.

Only when they're sure that they aren't being followed does Bruno turn northwards towards the mountains. Esmond sits stunned as they make their way through the suburbs and out into the wide fields of the plain. Everyone is silent apart from the two Royalist ladies who chatter busily in the back. Tosca reaches over and puts a small hand on Esmond's shoulder. When they reach the clearing, they get out and stand disconsolately on the grass. Creighton comes and puts his arm around Esmond.

'I'm awfully sorry, old chap,' he says. 'Let me get on the blower and see if I can find out what happened.'

Ten minutes later and Esmond is sitting, sobbing silently. He holds his revolver in his hand, flicking the safety catch on and off, breathing unsteadily. Tosca is leaning against Antonio, her eyes bright with tears. Elio and Bruno are awkwardly silent. Creighton shakes his head.

'There's simply nothing we can do. The train is already in the Salò Republic. It's out of our reach. Listen, mate,' he says, putting his arm around Esmond's shoulder again, 'she's got a sporting chance, she really does. There's six months of this war left, if that. She's in good health. The Germans are losing heart. I'd back her, you know.'

28

Now that Ada is gone, she is everywhere, her name hymning in his mind. He yokes the thud of his heart to those two syllables: *A-da, A-da, A-da*. He sleeps in her sleeping bag, deep dreamful sleeps, the painting of Mary Magdalene beside him. He lives like a pilgrim, barely listens to the news, doesn't want to know what is happening at Monte Cassino, in the Pacific, in Britain, is scarcely aware of preparations for the invasion of Europe. Ada is all the points of the compass for him, all the map of the world, all the war. In saying her name, he draws up a hard and secret energy, and he fights as if she were there, at his shoulder, urging him on. He plants bombs on the railway lines alone now, riding down on the Moto Guzzi and coming back with a steady expression. Every explosion is like an offering. He and Bruno kill two German guards they find lying smoking in a field not far from the turning up towards Monte Morello. It is easier than killing Gobbi, he realises. This time he pities the men, but his mind is too full to dwell on them.

He is silhouetted against a pale dawn sky, cresting a hill on the motorbike. The saddlebags are plump with explosives, a Sten gun stiffens his back. He's wearing a long leather jacket and silver goggles. He passes before a dark row of cypresses, through an olive grove, is obscured by a crumbling Roman wall and then emerges, a wind-whipped cigarillo in his teeth. He knows the goat-tracks of these hills as he once knew the streets of Cambridge, of Shrewsbury, of Florence. At night, before sleeping, he rehearses his route, laying the tracks over the swell of hills like a lattice, then growling the Moto Guzzi towards its destination: an arms silo; an aerodrome; a railway line.

Dawn still hasn't broken over the mountains when he comes into the village of Sant'Ellero. Pine trees line the road as he free-wheels the motorbike down the hill and parks in a lay-by. The station crouches below him, further down is the Arno, which is narrower, faster-flowing here by its source. The Florence–Rome railway line meanders like the river, unexpected tributaries shooting off. He lifts the saddlebags from the bike and scrambles down to the tracks.

Creighton has supplied him with blocks of plastic explosives, small and wrapped in brown paper. He looks up the tracks towards the station, where an elderly woman is sweeping dust into desultory clouds. The hillsides around are thickly wooded. Even though the sun is now rising above the high mountains in the east, he is still in shadow. He darts to the rails, presses the packages of explosives like nougat into hollows he digs out of the stones beneath and around the tracks. He checks the connections and plays out the fuse, concealing himself in the dark shade of a pine tree a little further up the hill.

He looks at his watch. The train is late. He lights a cigarette and stares up through the branches to the blue air above. Sometimes, in the moments of calm, he is seized by a lightness of spirit that feels almost crude without Ada beside him. He can hear birdsong, the plash and spatter of the rocky Arno, and now, in the distance, the whispering rattle of the approaching train. He carefully stubs out his cigarette and gives a last glance up to the sky.

The information is never certain. He relies on messages from mouth to mouth, passed behind menus in noisy restaurants, or in snatched conversations in the lanes of Milan or Turin, through the bars of a gaol at night. The messages are written on slips of paper and sewn into the lining of jackets, or swallowed and fastidiously retrieved, or dropped from moving cars. In the fading echoes of these whispers it is suggested that a certain person, or group of persons, will be in a particular place at a particular time. And he must go and kill them there.

Thus in theory, Creighton had told him, in the second and third carriages of the train now coming towards him are eighteen members of the SS *Einsatzgruppen* – the death brigade that would be responsible for rounding up the remaining pockets of resistance in Florence, shepherding the last Jews, gypsies and Communists into the slatted wagons at Santa Maria Novella, executing any who stood in their way. A decent target, Esmond thinks.

He can see the train coming around the bend towards the station. His view of the carriages telescopes as the track uncurves and he is left with only a front-on picture of the locomotive, the driver dimly visible in the cab. The woman has stopped sweeping and is leaning on her broom, exchanging a few words with the driver through the steam. The train lets out a whistle and begins to pull away from the station and towards him. Esmond flicks open his IMCO and lights the fuse, which hisses its snaking path down towards the tracks. He scurries further up and raises a pair of field glasses to his eyes. The high wheeze of the engine as it gathers speed. A sudden, incongruous burst of birdsong as the sun breaks over the nearest hills and illuminates the valley. Almost, almost, the train is there.

The locomotive passes over the nest of explosives. The first carriage, in the windows of which he sees two young men in fedoras, smoking, a woman at her knitting. The second carriage, which is empty. The third. Not eighteen, but five slate-suited German officers. Their carriage passes over the explosives. He's misjudged the length of the fuse, or the damp air has snuffed out the flame. He pulls out his revolver and takes aim. Now the fourth and penultimate carriage, also empty, rolls over the brown packages of nitroglycerine. Nothing. He raises his revolver, closes one eye, aims at the brown packages. A crack, a split-second of vacuumed air and everything stops, then with a roar like a living beast the tracks rear up from the earth.

A wave passes along the train's long steel spine and the carriages buck from the rails, forming a jagged W before the locomotive plunges down the hill and into the Arno. It comes to rest in the roiled water, steam still rising from the engine. The woman on the station platform has dropped her broom, raising her hands to her mouth. The birds have stopped singing. He doesn't wait to see who – if anyone – crawls from the capsized

323

train. He doesn't think of the driver, or the woman, or the young men in the first carriage. Or passengers who may or may not have been in the last. He gets back on his motorbike and lights a cigarillo, pulls the goggles down over his eyes and takes off up the hill, a hard knot of satisfaction in his chest.

29

Esmond feels his energy grow until he can barely sleep, and sits all night in the cool moistness of the cave thinking of Ada, recalling their moments of love. He pictures her in the studio, frowning over a desk of knobs and dials; he sees her in their bed at L'Ombrellino, Tatters tummy-up beside her, afternoon light slanting into her hair; then he sees her broken, sees her fighting, calls to his mind that last look between them, the little shake of the head. These memories tie a wire around his heart. Tosca and Antonio look at him as if he were a stranger now, Bruno and Elio struggle to keep up.

Maria Luigia is captured in a building on the Piazza Vittorio Emanuele on the 13th of May. The radio is discovered and destroyed. Less than a month later she is murdered by a firing squad in the yard of the Murate prison. Her body is returned to her cousins in the country and Esmond goes with Elio, who is undone, to stand in one corner of the graveyard of Porte Sante, in the shadow of a row of cypresses, and look across as her coffin is lowered into the earth. Her family wring and crumple on the cusp of the grave; the priest a magpie, hopping nervously, aware of the shadowy figures watching, some friendly, some not. Esmond and Elio leave quickly, before the end, by scrambling over the cemetery wall, down the steps in front of San Miniato al Monte, and into the waiting Bianchi. When they get back to the cave, Elio goes to sit in front of the paintings. For all of them now, this has become a place of retreat. They can sense the end of things – disaster, victory, resolution – and they contemplate the two saints, together into the night, a sense of shared purpose stringing between them.

News of the fall of Rome reaches them in early June. The front is so close that Esmond fancies, lying in the cave at night, that he can feel the breath of English soldiers on his skin, the rumble of their marching feet in the rocks beneath. Soon afterwards, Pretini is released by Carità. The Professor brings him up the mountain to see them. The hairdresser's face is unrecognisable, his mouth a twisted empty snarl without its teeth. He has lost an eye and the socket weeps yellowish fluid. His nose is flattened against his face. He tells them, calmly and clearly, about his time in the anonymous-looking building on the via Bolognese, of walls lined in spikes, the carefully reconstructed version of the *strappado* – a medieval torture device – the cat's paws and crocodile shears and whips and thumbscrews. He tells them of Carità applying electric shocks to his gums, to his ears, to his genitals, while Father Idelfonso played Schubert's Unfinished Symphony on the piano to drown out his screams. He tells them of the mock executions where a gun was placed against his temple and the trigger pulled, and how each time he was sure it was loaded, and the peace that came with that. Two Serbians that were captured by Carità have also been returned alive; blind, castrated, their tongues cut out, but alive. Bruno drives them to the nuns at Prato where Morandi, his doctor friend, does his best to make them human again.

The mention of Morandi brings Ada closer. He remembers the doctor's words – *She gave birth, you know*. He thinks of the child that never was, the life that might have been. How much would he have loved that baby, knowing that half of it was her? That evening, alone, he sits in front of the paintings, very

325

close, so that he can see their ancient crazing, and rearranges the bright, broken pieces of memory, the chaos of vague possibilities that was their child. Someone said – St Augustine, he thinks – that memory is a place of palaces and caverns. His is only caverns now.

One night he sits in the dirt at the mouth of the cave with Creighton. They no longer light fires. Only the glow of his cigarillo, Creighton's pipe which breathes tender red threads in its bowl. There are regular patrols – German and Fascist – whose searchlights sweep across the hillsides. The sound of dogs, shouts in the still air, engines toiling up rocky inclines. Esmond can tell that they're getting closer.

'Destroy yourself,' Creighton says, tapping his pipe and relighting it, 'that's how you become a better soldier. It's unnatural, I'm sure. Young chap like you, you feel like you're the centre of the bloody world. But the story of your life isn't about you any more – it's about us. The Resistance, the GAP, the Allies. In war, individuals disappear – it's a group experience. It's why the Russians are so bloody good at it. Submit yourself to the collective will. Learn to think of yourself as a pawn, you see?'

Esmond lets a smoky breath out into the night. Somewhere, high above, a wolf. 'I see it differently,' he says, directing a cool glance at the Englishman. 'We're all individuals now. Now more than ever. My story – me and Ada, everything that happened – it's simple enough, really. The war is a million such stories stacked on top of each other, entwining, competing. You find the right story, you find the truth, the war's secret centre.'

The drone of aircraft. Creighton looks up. 'Brits,' he says. 'We bomb at night.'

They smoke in silence until the planes have gone. With a nod, Creighton stands, taps out his pipe and disappears into the cave.

Esmond sits for a while longer, listening to the wolves and, further off, gunfire, explosions. Finally he goes into the dark interior, lies down next to Mary Magdalene and sleeps.

Time gathers to a bright point. Everything is in flux. Esmond, Bruno and Elio now barely pause for breath; they come back to the hills only to pick up supplies, reload their guns. Esmond feels a kind of joy each time they head down into the city, calm in the knowledge that each journey may be the last, and bring him closer to her.

30

Elio is the next to be caught. He sets out to plant a bomb in the Piazza San Marco and doesn't return. A day later, they hear that Carità has him in the Villa Triste. There is a meeting in the clearing at which the Professor lays out various plans of attack. But even as he speaks, it is clear that only one course is now possible. Everyone looks at Esmond and Bruno. Carità thinks of himself as a vengeful angel, invulnerable. It is up to them to prove him mortal.

The two young men arm themselves with MAB 38s, Berettas, grenades, and drive down into the city. Esmond fastens his Old Wykehamist tie around his head to keep his hair from his eyes. The rebels come out to watch them as they go. Tosca gives a small wave, Creighton salutes. It is evening, the 15th of June. They drive in silence and pull up a block away from the Villa Triste. They step out into the warm air, both of them breathing hard. At the entrance to the high, grey apartment block, they stop and embrace.

'For Ada,' Esmond whispers, gripping Bruno.

'For all of them,' Bruno says. '*In bocca al lupo.*'

'*Crepi il lupo.*'

They move swift and silently into the courtyard. The lower levels of the building are dark, but there is a light up on the third floor, the sound of someone playing the piano. Two guards stand beside Carità's ambulance, smoking. They close in until they are breathing the Blackshirts' smoke and then two bright flashes from two guns, the explosions ricocheting up the steep walls of the building, and the guards slump forward. The piano stops. They are inside and climbing up a darkened stairwell.

Esmond moves easily, his legs taking the steps two, three at a time, his heart pumping fiercely in his chest, his revolver out in front. They reach the second landing and pause, panting. The sound of many feet coming down from above, guns being loaded, shouts that become whispers as the Blackshirts approach. The damp, nostalgic air of the old building. Bruno takes out a grenade, pulls the pin, waits for a moment and then, leaning out into the empty space in the stairwell, hurls it upwards. They press themselves against the wall and listen to the falling plaster, a man screaming, and then Carità's voice.

'It's over now. I've got men outside. Alberti is on his way with stormtroopers. You're trapped rats. If you throw down your guns, come up here with your hands raised, I'll make sure it's quick. You'll get to keep your bollocks, unlike your friend Elio.'

Bruno looks across at Esmond and gives a little nod. Esmond shrugs and smiles, pushes the tie further up his forehead. They run up the stairs, firing all the time, but now there are doors opening on the landings, smoke grenades being dropped, the flash of guns from all sides. Two Blackshirts fling themselves out of the fumes. Bruno steps around them, but Esmond is caught in the face by a fist and stumbles. He pulls the trigger of his revolver, but it jams, or he's out of bullets, and then it all seems to slow down as he reaches round to pull the MAB-38 from his shoulder. A volley of gunfire which he has time to stand back and watch as it comes towards him. He's hit in the collarbone and the thigh and falls, groaning. He realises that he hasn't even seen his enemy yet, and a sudden surge of energy lifts him to his feet. He makes it up another flight of steps before there, above him, grinning, is Carità, Bruno lying crumpled at his feet. Esmond sees the pudgy knees, the quiff of white hair, before a rifle butt thuds down onto his skull, bringing blackness.

31

Esmond wakes to the sound of music. Schubert's Unfinished Symphony. He's in a long hall, balconied French windows open to the courtyard several floors below. A man in a monk's habit, dark hair swept over a balding crown, is playing a grand piano. The bass notes throb in time with the pain in Esmond's shoulders. He realises his arms have been tied behind his back. He is standing on a high stool beneath a wooden frame. Carità sits at a table beside the frame, eating slices of beef which he spears and presses between fleshy lips. There is a bottle of wine on the table and he pours himself a glass, stands, and kicks the stool from under Esmond's feet. Esmond's arms, tied at the wrists, swing up behind him as he drops. His muscles spasm, fight for a moment, then a splintering sound as his shoulder-balls leave their sockets. The dreadful parting of bone and with it a pain that brings darkness.

He is in a small, windowless room, blue-lit. He is naked, tied to a chair that is raised on a platform, almost a stage. Carità stands beside a car battery, holding two wires in gloved hands. The ends of these wires are taped to the end of Esmond's cock, to his lips, to his earlobes. They are pressed into the weeping bullet wounds in his thigh and his collarbone. He is astonished at the noises that come from him, not language, not human. He is losing his words, forgetting books, people, names, giving himself entirely to the endless moment of pain. He feels as if he is drowning in black milk. He lives strung up between the brief respites, a kind of torture in themselves, when Carità goes out for a piss, or when he lights a cigarette and blows the smoke in Esmond's face, mouthing again, 'Tell us where your friends are hiding. Don't be an idiot. This can stop, just tell us where they are.' He feels the secret inside him, wrapped like a gift, and sees how natural is Carità's belief that he can burn, hack, bleed it out of him.

An early morning, when Carità has gone out for breakfast, and he is there, alone on the blue-lit stage, he remembers how in *The Magic Mountain* Settembrini has to give up his attempt to record the literature of suffering because *all* literature is suffering. Esmond understands, there in the eye of his pain, how wrong Mann was. Heartache, loss, loneliness: these are literature; but suffering like this, of the body, it is beyond the reach of language. Every so often, he hears, very close, a mechanical wail that gradually opens out into the screaming of a human voice.

Esmond, bound to the chair, wakes to find Carità standing under the swaying blue bulb. He is staggering drunk, his face flushed and glistening, his lips moistly fleering. Resting against his schoolboy's legs is Anna's collage. He reaches down and begins to peel the photographs from the backing board to which, a lifetime ago, his sister had glued them.

'Tell me where your friends are, Esmond.' The picture of Anna on the carousel is peeled off. 'Where are they hiding?' Carità flicks open a silver cigarette lighter and the photograph curls and then burns. Carità drops it to the ground and Esmond remembers his mother, burning letters in a Shropshire field. Esmond and Rudyard, cricket and Cambridge, Anna and Aston Magna. Carità, with long, grubby grey nails, picks at the edges, tears them up from their moorings, holds them to the greedy tongue of flame. Esmond realises that he has no photograph of Ada, and it feels like a victory, for to see her burnt would be too much, would take away the one thing holding him together.

'Tell me where your friends are hiding, Esmond. We'll find them anyway. Do it for your father, for Goad. Imagine what they'd say if they knew you were protecting a gang of Communists. Tell us and we can walk out of here together.' Now the picture of Esmond and his father at the Albert Hall rally. The old man's hopeful smile, one strong arm and an empty sleeve. Esmond feels a rush of love for his father that meets a wave of certainty that he'll never see him again. The picture flickers and burns.

Finally, the collage is scraps of charred paper, a glue-marked board. Carità leaves and Esmond, husked out, slumps in his chair and weeps.

Carità. Pliers.

'Tell me where they are.' The little finger of his left hand breaks. A brief moment between the snap and the detonation of pain.

'Tell me where.' Now the nail is pulled out of the broken finger, and it is as if his hand is on fire.

'We know they're in the mountains. Where?' His ring finger. The sound is like biting on a stick of grissini.

'Are they in the east? With the Serbians?' Both of his thumbs, now. They take more work and Carità grunts as he breaks them.

'In Monte Morello? Monte Oliveto? Where are they, you pig, where?'

Esmond remembers his father's words – *anger is stronger than fear*. He lifts his head and spits, first on his own chin, then in Carità's face.

He and Elio in the blue-lit room. Elio is owlish and astonished without his glasses, his nose flattened to his face.

'You know, whatever happens to us—'

'Yes?'

'History—' Elio's voice is cracked and fading.

'Yes?'

'Brecht. You know? Burn me. Do not fear death—'

'But rather the inadequate life.'

'Good.'

Silence. Esmond looks down at Elio who is silent, sleeping, and smiles.

He is standing next to Bruno in the hall with the wooden frame which had dislocated his shoulders. It is hot and the French windows, with their birdcage-like Juliet balconies, are wide open. A fan turns in the corner where Father Idelfonso is still playing Schubert. Esmond cannot move his arms and presumes they are bound, but looking down he realises that it is just that they are broken, hanging at his sides. When Carità comes to punch him, to cut obscure symbols on the skin of his chest with a stiletto knife, he can do nothing. Milly enters the room wearing only stockings and suspenders, her breasts threatening to overbalance her. Bruno starts to laugh. Esmond looks across at his friend, who is covered in bruises, one of his eyes closed, his mouth empty of teeth, then back at the overweight, absurd figure of Carità's mistress. He begins to laugh as well. Milly has crossed her arms over her chest, her mouth open in a scandalised O. Carità is irate, storming back and forth in front of them.

'Why are you laughing? Don't you realise that you're going to die?'

They stop laughing when Elio's body is dragged into the room. Father Idelfonso interrupts Schubert to play Chopin's Funeral March. Carità goes over to the body and lifts the head back to show, beneath a face, toothless and eyeless, the opened neck darkly smiling. A whisper of breeze through the French windows. Esmond can hear Bruno's breath coming fast and ragged. Carità lets Elio's head drop back down and comes towards them.

'It's time to end this, don't you think?' he says, drawing out his long, ivory-handled knife. He presses the blade against Esmond's Adam's apple. Esmond winces and feels blood running warmly down his chest. Carità draws the blade away.

'I'll give you one last chance. For form's sake.' He smiles and walks to the end of the room, unlocking the door and opening it. 'You may be a little unsteady on your feet, but no one will stop you. Just tell me where the camp is and you can go. Think of the taste of the air, the freedom.'

Esmond is holding his throat, blood rising between his fingers. Carità crosses to stand by the window, his hands, black with gore, twining over the balcony. 'This is your last chance, boys.' He looks down into the shadowy courtyard, his pudgy face caught in the evening's dying light and nods with a sudden, serious goodwill. A glance between Esmond and Bruno – a swift decision. On legs that can hardly bear his weight, Esmond plunges forward. He stumbles, then seizes upon an image of Ada in the high room at L'Ombrellino, her arms crossed over her bare chest, the triptych behind her. From her, he draws a final burst of energy, as if love alone might staunch blood, knit bones. Now beside him, Bruno, staggering and certain. They grab Carità by his black shirt with their broken fingers, lift him up with their

333

broken arms, and with the very last of their strength they pull
him out into the void, shrieking.

32

As he falls, Esmond doesn't think of Bruno, or Carità, falling
with him. He doesn't think of Elio, or what remains of him. He
doesn't think of Alessandro in the graveyard beside the Great
Synagogue or Maria Luigia buried in the cemetery at San Miniato. He doesn't think of Tatters running at his heels along the
cypress-lined mule-tracks of Bellosguardo, or the doggy cairn by
the swimming pool. He doesn't think of Philip lying in a grave
in the blushing heights above Barcelona. He doesn't think about
Anna. He doesn't think about Rudyard, who is not more than
a hundred miles away, marching towards Florence. He doesn't
think of Gerald or Fiamma. He doesn't even think of Ada, who
is, however, thinking of him. Under a sky of fast-moving sulphurous clouds, she sits and pictures him, and it makes her
smile, the shape of his face in her mind.

Instead, as he falls, he remembers, aged seven or eight, when
a dog had died at Aston Magna. It was a stable dog, not one of
the hounds, and his father had refused to call the vet. She didn't
even have a name. She'd given birth to three healthy pups who
were now with Cook in the kitchen, sucking milk from plump
fingers. One of the pups was still inside her, though, and after
dragging herself around the yard on her hunkers for an hour,
straining every so often, groaning after the stable lads had tired
of their attempts to fish the dead, sack-wrapped pup out of her,
she'd crawled up to Esmond's room to die.

He'd sat with her all night, the shuddering weight of her in
his arms, her head on his shoulder, sour breath in his ear until

finally she'd stopped breathing. He sat with her a while longer and then carried her out into the pale morning and buried her in his mother's rose garden, beneath a Crown Princess Margareta. He was astonished by the lightness of her body, as if life were substantial. Back in the warmth of the house, he went into the kitchen where Cook was still sitting in a deep armchair, the silky knot of puppies in her lap, cooing a gentle song to them. He'd said nothing, but sat on the arm of the chair and watched, wonderstruck, as the new lives writhed and shivered.

He even has time, on his journey to the hard earth, to marvel at the workings of the mind, where this forgotten image from his youth has arrived, unbidden, and filled his heart with sorrow and joy. And now, as if the dog, whose mottled fur and wet nose he can see with extraordinary clarity, there beside him, has unblocked some obstruction, a flood of love comes. Anna speaking gentle words in his ear; Philip in the foliage at Cambridge, the sound of rain on leaves; Fiamma and Gerald in the island-studded river. He pictures Douglas and Orioli, Mosley and his father swinging him between them as a child, his mother burning books in a field, and he loves them all. Now the parade of figures wisps across the cyclorama of his mind, the Unfinished Symphony loud around them, the city's angels peeling themselves from the bridges and loggias. St John and Mary Magdalene dance, wild-eyed, sweeping their tattered robes about them, Mary's hair like a russet river. And Ada – and he swells at the thought of her, and the last thing he does, before the ground rushes up, is to send arrowing towards her everything that is left of his strength.

As he dies, he realises that the last few months of his life have been spent chasing after the wrong thing. His father's idea of pluck. But he knows he has done enough, and that it doesn't matter. Carità hits the ground first, a wet thud. Esmond feels himself turn inside himself and can now see the largeness of the palpitating earth, the depth of human love, the stars in the firmament, Ada singing gently into the sulphurous sky. As he draws his last breath, he realises that this is the thing: this is joy and courage and hope. Ada. A feeling of extraordinary peace washes over him, a feeling of bliss. Ada. Blackness.

EPILOGUE

Excerpt from *In Love and War*, the Autobiography of Rudyard Lowndes (Faber & Faber, London, 1956)

The morning after we arrived in Florence, I was up early, keen to be out in the city. It had been a wheeze the night before – the bells of the great church ringing, gunshots echoing in the hills, German stragglers to be mopped up, toasts drunk with jubilant partisans. From midnight to 2 a.m. I oversaw a team of sappers clearing mines from the road leading up from the Ponte Vecchio towards the Piazza della Signoria. I recognised the names from Esmond's letters, from the broadcasts we used to listen to, all of us clustered around the wireless in the library at Welsh Frankton.

It was a very luminous morning as I walked out of the villa where we'd stationed ourselves, a good-looking place called L'Ombrellino that sits on the hillside overlooking the town. There were already younger coves splashing in the murky pool in the garden, others smoking on the terrace. I enjoyed the walk down towards the river, swinging my arms with a tra-la-la. In the city proper I slowed down, picking carefully through the rubble of the via de Guicciardini. British squaddies are the best there are, but I'd seen too many chaps with misplaced limbs in military hospitals, with the hangdog expression of blighters who'd made a frightful hash of something quite simple. I'd got this far by being a trifle slower and a trifle more careful than other fellows. I wasn't going to stop now.

I sat down halfway along the Ponte Vecchio, where there's a break between the jewellers and leather shops, all boarded up, empty and windowless, of course. I eased myself onto the little stone bench there and pulled out a cigarette. There's nothing quite like the first fag of the day. Soldiers thrive on routine, and one of mine was to clear a moment of peace for a smoke, even if it meant getting up earlier than other chaps. Taking a dekko downriver, I could see the blasted ruins of the next bridge – the Ponte Santa Trinità – lying just below the surface. Here and there a jagged piece of stone would break through, causing a flurry of white water. Further away, past the remains of another blown-up bridge, lay the pontoon we'd constructed to get our men and their tanks onto the north side of the river.

When I'd finished my cigarette, giving a nod of thanks to Herr Hitler for ordering that this bridge, at least, be preserved by his retreating troops, I set out into the city proper. It was astonishingly intact given that I was standing where, less than twenty-four hours earlier, the enemy had been. Walls riddled with bullet holes, a burnt-out Kübelwagen in front of that famous statue of David, a dead paratrooper – one of the Green Devils – lying quite serene in the middle of the great, empty square in front of the town hall. But it seemed as if the Germans had more or less respected the unofficial Open City. Apart from the bridges, of course. I wandered haphazardly until I found the rebel headquarters in the Piazza San Marco, where members of the Resistance had taken over rooms in a convent formerly used by the SD. A filly, blonde hair, was brought to me in the cloisters of the church. Name was Tosca Buccarelli. She offered to escort me back over the river to the Allori Cemetery, to Esmond's grave.

As we walked through the city, she told me about my brother's war, or as much as she knew of it. About the assassination of a Fascist colonel, attacks on train lines, scores of refugees saved from the hands of first the Blackshirts, and the Nazis. She told me about a girl, Ada Liuzzi, a Jew who'd been taken north to a camp by the Germans, with whom my brother had lived, to whom he'd been engaged. She told me about the two other members of the Resistance who'd been, with my brother, a trio of unlikely heroes – two Communist students and a foppish Englishman. She told me about a capture, a rescue attempt that went wrong, a tragic ending.

I must say I didn't recognise the fellow she was talking about, but then I dare say he wouldn't recognise me if he was looking down as I made my way between the cluttered rows of the cemetery, where the graves jostle and slant amid the cypresses. His body, it seems, was badly broken by the fall and the chopping and slicing he'd suffered at the hands of this Carità and so he'd been cremated, his ashes scattered on the Arno. There is a modest gravestone.

ESMOND LIONEL LOWNDES
21ST MAY 1917–25TH JULY 1944

I stood, thinking of all the life, all the love, contained in that single engraved hyphen, and I placed down a nosegay of flowers I'd picked as we strolled through the cemetery. Tosca was crying beside me, this brassy, voluptuous girl, crying over dear old Esmond. I hardly knew him, or at least the person he'd become – Tosca knew him better – but I, too, loved him. And I thought of all the lives he'd touched, the web of affection he'd weaved that stretched from Shropshire to Cambridge to Italy to who knows elsewhere, and deep under the earth to all those who'd died before. I thought of the girl, Ada, in Auschwitz, perhaps not yet aware that my brother, her lover, was dead. I said a prayer for her there on the consecrated ground, that she might make it through alive.

Then I walked out of the gatehouse and up towards the river, Tosca at my side, and we spoke of Esmond, and of the days of freedom ahead, and the great bells of the Duomo began to chime, and then the bell of the Palazzo Vecchio, which they call *La Vacca*, and I could see the bevelled red roofs in the bright August light, the churches clamouring skywards, the sculptures and tabernacles and all the ravishing splendour of the place and I carried my love for my brother in my heart like a flame into the streets of the city he called home. Florence.

Acknowledgements

Thanks to the following, without whom this book would have been longer, less accurate or never written at all: my editor, Walter Donohue, and my agent, Anna Power. To Matt Shoard. To all at Faber & Faber, particularly Hannah Griffiths, Lee Brackstone and Kate McQuaid. To Silvia Crompton, who held it all together (in exchange for wine). To all at Johnson & Alcock, particularly Ed Wilson. To Glenn Haybittle and Penny Mittler, two *inglesi italianati*, who were there at the beginning and at the end. To Enrico Giachetti, for priceless first-hand recollections of *Firenze Fascistissima*. To Michael Brod and the Palazzo Tornabuoni, for their hospitality. To all at St Mark's Anglican Church in Florence, where all of this started. To James Holland, for making sure that my errors in military history were chosen rather than accidental. To Mark Miller and de Havilland Support Ltd for a wonderful day with the Dragon Rapide. To Gerald Wells and the British Vintage Wireless and Television Museum, for their endless patience. To Neil Gower, for the stunning illustrations. To Emma Smith, for strong women. To Hannah Miller, for Cambridge. To Bill Davies, for corrections. To Damian Barr, Emer Gillespie, Tom Edmunds, Helen Benckendorff, Florence Ballard and Ele Simpson, for their early, insightful and encouraging readings. To my grandfather and my parents, for inspiration past and present. Finally, as ever, to Al, Ray and Ary, with endless love.

Author's Note

There was no Author's Note in the hardback publication of this book. I didn't feel it needed one, that the story should exist on its own terms. Now I'm not so sure. At the launch of *In Love and War* in Florence, I was approached by an expat septuagenarian who might have stepped straight from the pages of the novel. 'Why didn't you tell us that it was all true?' she said, as if summoning the events of *In Love and War* from my imagination would have been somehow easier, less impressive. But I realise that the thing that makes this novel different, that makes it more ambitious and difficult than anything I've written before, is my fidelity to the historical facts of the war, to the historical figures who lived and died in Florence in the years 1937–1945.

In Love and War almost wasn't a novel. I found so many extraordinary stories during my time in Florence, so many untold tales of bravery and selfless sacrifice, of real evil and the resistance to that evil, that I wanted to set them down in a cool, clear work of non-fiction. I started writing the book, but felt distanced from the heroic figures I was writing about, as if viewing them on a far-off stage. It was only when I discovered Esmond, my (fictional) hero, that I was able to insert myself into the heat of the action, into the heart of the story. Esmond is my concession to fiction; the rest of the novel is as true as I could make it. I drew on interviews with those who lived through the war in Florence, four years of research in libraries in Italy and the UK, extensive reading of primary sources in English and Italian, on endless novels and films and documentaries.

So Mario Carità and his Villa Triste were real. Norman

Douglas and his peripatetic pederasty were real. Gino Bartoli's courageous bicycle trips really happened. Ferdinando Pretini, coiffeur to Florence's contessas, was also a member of the Resistance. The assassination attempts, the car chases, the acts of sabotage – all of these draw as closely as possible on real historical events. I tried, as much as possible, to put words in the mouths of my characters that they actually said (or might have done). Whenever the urge to fictionalise, to invent, to move away from the facts of history seized me, I resisted. Whenever I could edit the novel to make it truer, more faithful to historical truth, I did. Even Esmond isn't as fictional as he might seem; his voice came to me through a journal I found in the archive of the British Institute, left by a young Englishman who'd come to Florence on his Grand Tour, suffered several amorous setbacks, and departed, heartbroken.

I was lucky enough to meet Laurent Binet, author of *HHhH*, in Paris just as I was beginning *In Love and War*. His ethical entreaties as to the duty of the historical novelist to his subject(s) rang loud for me as I moved through the world of my novel. Similarly, I was much influenced by Francis Spufford's marvellous *Red Plenty*, which begins with a warning: 'This is not a novel. It has too much to explain, to be one of those. But it is not a history either, for it does its explaining in the form of a story. . .' The critic Roman Jakobson tells us that as a preamble to their performances, traditional storytellers in Majorca would say, 'It was and it was not so.' Perhaps I would begin *In Love and War* with, 'It was so (as much as I could make it so).'

So this Author's Note is in effect the reverse of the habitual (and largely pointless) *All characters appearing in this work are fictitious. Any resemblance to real persons, living or dead, is purely coincidental.* Evelyn Waugh felt moved to distance himself from those who read *Decline and Fall* as a *roman-à-clef*. 'I apologise to anyone who sees himself in this tarnished little mirror,' he wrote. 'Everything is drawn, without malice, from the vaguest imaginations.' Instead, in *In Love and War*, I ask you to look for real characters, to believe as much as you dare, to find in what you have just read not only a novel about a young Englishman learning the paths of his heart. I hope *In Love and War* can stand as a monument to the extraordinary bravery of the young men and women who wrested control of the story of modern Italy from the Fascists and the Nazis, to the lives they led, the deaths they suffered, to the history they forged through their actions.

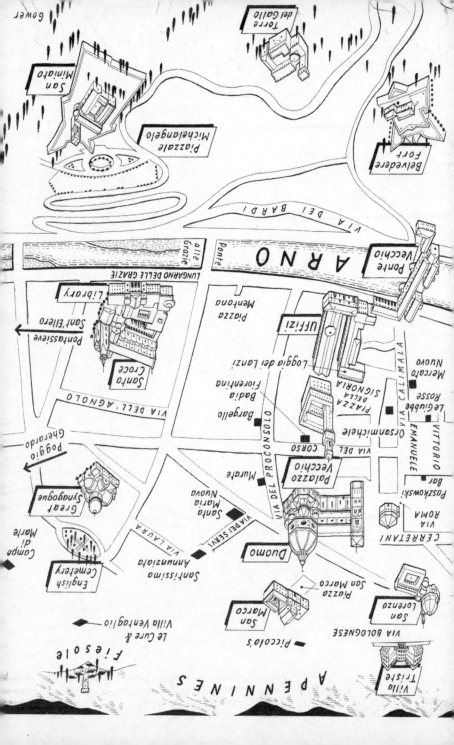

LIST OF PRINCIPAL CHARACTERS

The Lowndes Family

Esmond Lowndes – our hero

Sir Lionel Lowndes – Esmond's father, Chairman of the British
Union of Fascists

Lady Ursula Lowndes – Esmond's mother, failed novelist

Anna and Rudyard Lowndes – Esmond's brother and sister

The British Institute

Harold Goad – Director of the British Institute in Florence

Gerald Goad – Harold's son

Gesuina Ricci – Housekeeper at the British Institute

Fiamma Ricci – Gesuina's daughter, a student

The Blackshirts

Mario Carità – Head of Fascist Secret Police in Florence, electrician

Piero Koch – Carità's accomplice

Alessandro Pavolini – Mussolini's Minister for Popular Culture

The Expats

Father Frederick Bailey – Chaplain of St Mark's English Church, spy

George and Alice Keppel – owners of the Villa dell'Ombrellino

Norman Douglas – author of *South Wind* and other novels

Pino Orioli – Norman's companion, publisher

The Partisans

Bruno Fanciullacci, Antonio Agnesti, Elio Chianesi and Alessandro
Sinigaglia – Communists

Tosca Buccarelli – Antonio's girlfriend

Maria Luigia Guaita – a bank clerk

Piero Calamadrei – Professor at the University of Florence

Ferdinando Pretini – a hairdresser

Oreste Ristoro – a South American adventurer

Assorted Others

Philip Keller – Esmond's (former) lover

Ada Liuzzi – a student and translator

Filippino Lippi – a Renaissance painter

Tatters – a dog

First published in 2014
by Faber & Faber Ltd
Bloomsbury House
74–77 Great Russell Street
London WC1B 3DA

This paperback edition first published in 2015

Typeset by Faber & Faber Ltd
Printed in the UK by CPI Group Ltd, Croydon, CR0 4YY

Extract from *The Master of Petersburg* by J. M. Coetzee (Martin Secker and Warburg)
reprinted by permission of The Random House Group Ltd

Extract from *HHhH* by Laurent Binet (Harvill Secker) reprinted by permission of
the author

The right of Alex Preston to be identified as author
of this work has been asserted in accordance with Section 77
of the Copyright, Designs and Patents Act 1988

This is a work of fiction. While many of the people, places and events are
based on historical sources, the final responsibility is to the story.

A CIP record for this book
is available from the British Library

ISBN 978–0–571–27946–3

2 4 6 8 10 9 7 5 3 1

In Love and War

ALEX PRESTON

FABER & FABER

and compelling novel leaves behind.' LoveReading Book of the Month

'Preston is a real talent, who can combine history and the personal, big ideas and intimate plots. Impressive.' James Kidd, *South China Post*

'This is one of those novels that captivates the reader immediately then ramps up the tension until you literally can't put it down.' Sally Hughes, *We Love This Book*

'Fact and fiction are masterfully woven to create an intimate portrait of a remarkable man . . . With a dramatic finale, it is an enthralling and visually spectacular epic narrative.' Lily Cox, *The Lady*

'A moving account of one man's journey towards commitment to a cause ... Preston writes, in unaffected but affecting prose, of Lowndes's realisation of what the times demand of him.' Nick Rennison, *Sunday Times*

'Rich and evocative ... Powerfully affecting, ambitious in its scope, precise in its attention to detail and infused with a love for Florence and its motley eccentrics – their courage and their suffering.' Stephanie Merritt, *Observer*

'*In Love and War* prompts the reflection that evil triumphs because good men have not so much done nothing as done the wrong thing with the best of intentions ... A fresh and captivating novel.' Jake Kerridge, *Literary Review*

'An evocative portrait of passion and fascism. There is much to admire in Alex Preston's third book ... a living, breathing Forsterian idyll, complete with eccentric and glamorous expats, bohemian writers, and passionate love affairs, all played out against the backdrop of scorching heat and iced Negronis.' Lucy Scholes, *Independent*

'The deeply moving and thrilling tale of the resistance fighters who battled Mussolini's thugs in pre-war and wartime Florence. There are brilliant and funny cameos of Ezra Pound, Norman Douglas and Diana Mosley; but Preston gradually takes you into places of darkness and evil.' *Tablet*, Books of the Year

'A remarkably captivating book that starts as a slow-burner then sparks into an absolute firecracker of a read ... Prepare to sit on the edge of the precipice, prepare for the heartrending plummet of shock and upset, prepare for the impact that a powerful

IN LOVE AND WAR

Alex Preston was born in 1979. He is an award-winning novelist and journalist who appears regularly on BBC television and radio. He teaches Creative Writing at the University of Kent. *In Love and War* is his third novel.

Further praise for *In Love and War*:

'Deeply moving.' Nick Rennison, *BBC History Magazine* Best Historical Fiction Books of 2014

'Exhilarating . . . Preston's flair for recreating atmosphere and contemporary speech is immaculate . . . may remind some of *The English Patient.*' Suzy Feay, *Financial Times*

'Preston conjures up a picture of 1930s Florence that is rich in historical detail and utterly compelling – look out for brilliant guest appearances of real-life figures, such as Alice Keppel, once mistress of Edward VII.' Kate Saunders, *The Times*

'It's a title befitting an epic, and Preston emphatically delivers in this, his third novel but his first foray into historical fiction. That he's a natural at it is clear . . . Vividly imagined and richly atmospheric, Preston's dramatic tale propels the reader towards a tense and tragic final showdown.' Stephanie Cross, *Daily Mail*